MW01129091

WORTH THE RISK

Richard Gustafson

For the real Kelli, Danny, and Maria

www.RichardGustafson.com

Chapter 1

The hotel phone rang shortly after Nick Wallace's wife left for the airport.

The telephone was old, cracked, lime green, with a dirt-caked cord running from the base to the handset. His grandmother used to have one just like it, back in 1970s North Dakota. But he doubted hers ever spoke Russian.

This one did. The girl on the other end sounded young, nervous. Nick's Russian was lousy, basically just hello, goodbye, and a few phrases dealing with adoption. All he caught crackling out of the handset was "fax message."

"Excuse me?" he said.

There was a pause, then the girl spoke slowly, in halting English. "I have a fax message for you."

Nick immediately thought of Kelli. She was probably at the Rostov airport by now, heading home while Nick stayed in Russia, but her flight to Moscow was not scheduled to leave for another two hours. His stomach tightened. Something had happened, either to his wife or to the adoption process.

"Who's the fax message from?" he asked.

There was another pause, longer this time. Finally she said, "May I come to your room?"

"Yes, of course, please bring it up," Nick said. "I'm in room 402."

"Twenty dollars."

Twenty bucks for a fax? But he couldn't turn it down because it might be important. If Kelli was in trouble and Nick didn't help her because of a few dollars, he'd have some serious explaining to do, both to himself and to her. Besides, the price apparently included delivery. So Nick agreed, hung up, and waited for the fax.

It took longer to arrive than it should have for twenty dollars. At least ten minutes went by before he heard a quiet knock. He turned down the TV, which he couldn't understand anyway, and opened the door.

The girl in front of Nick was definitely not from the desk downstairs, unless they had very recently taken to wearing lingerie. A coat, once white, lay over her arm and she smiled shyly. She was short, with light brown hair down to her shoulders. Her eyes were also brown, and she wore a tired look that matched the faded black lingerie. He quickly noticed bruises on her neck. Bruises she had half-heartedly tried to cover up with makeup a few shades too dark.

The girl flinched involuntarily as Nick's six-foot-two, muscular frame filled the doorway. He smiled uncertainly at her, teeth white against a tan face and short black hair. She looked in his brown eyes and relaxed, slightly.

Nick instinctively glanced behind her, looking for cameras or old military buddies pulling a prank.

She was alone. "May I come in?" she asked. Her smiled slipped a bit when she saw the confused expression on his face.

Nick hesitated, then held the door open without a word. She eased in past him. He took one more look around and closed the door quietly.

"Um, may I help you?" he asked.

Now it was her turn to look confused. "I'm here for sex massage. We talked on phone," she said.

"*Sex* massage?" Nick said. He laughed. "I thought you said fax message!" When she showed no comprehension, he pantomimed a piece of paper. "Do you know fax?"

She shook her head.

"Oh, well, never mind, not important. I'm sorry, no sex massage. I was mistaken."

"You said to come!"

"I know I did," Nick said. "And I'll pay you. But no sex."

She narrowed her eyes and pursed her lips together in the universal sign of a woman spurned. "Don't you like me?" she finally asked.

"It's not that," he said. He held up his left hand and showed her the wedding band. "I'm married. And I'm here to adopt a baby."

"So?"

"So, that's important to me."

3

She stared at Nick as if he was some kind of freak, then sighed. Her shoulders slumped and she said, "OK. You pay me and I leave."

Nick handed her twenty dollars in rubles. She eyed the colorful paper doubtfully. "Do you have American dollars?" she asked. He took back the Russian money and handed her a crisp twenty dollar bill.

"I'm sorry," he said as she shrugged into her coat. Her lingerie peeked out from under the short hem, now sad instead of inviting. She adjusted herself once she was bundled up and gave him a fleeting smile.

"What's your baby's name?" she asked.

"Nonna."

The girl nodded. "That's a pretty name. She's very lucky to go to America."

"Thank you."

He glimpsed the tears in her eyes before she turned away and walked quickly out the door.

Nick stood for a long moment inside the doorway. He hadn't realized staying faithful could make a person feel so lousy.

Ten minutes, two blocks, and a world away, the woman paused outside a door. She fingered the twenty dollar bill in her hand. At least it was American. It would be worse with rubles.

If she had some money of her own, she could have added it to the twenty. See, she'd say, the American liked me. He may even want me to come back to his room later. Perhaps she'd get a smile or a hug instead of a fist.

But of course she had no money of her own. She knew she deserved what was coming.

She squared her shoulders and willed her mind away from the present. She thought about what it might be like in America. Ice cream. They have ice cream every day in America. That would be lovely. Chocolate. She'd never eaten chocolate ice cream. If she was in America, she'd have it for breakfast. Maybe on pancakes.

The thought made her smile slightly.

Finally she sighed, squared her shoulders, and opened the door.

4

"So, how are things without Kelli?" Michelle Donohue, one of three American women in their original group of six, asked between bites of chicken. She was tall, with broad shoulders and short-cropped brown hair. She wore a yellow tank top, and her shoulders were slightly burned from a day in the sun. Her eyes glinted as she tore into the chicken.

"A hooker stopped by my room after she left," Nick said.

Silence descended on the table. A piece of chicken may have fallen from Michelle's mouth, but Nick was too busy not looking at her to know for certain.

They were in the middle of dinner, outside at the Chicken Shack, enjoying the warm Rostov summer evening air. The restaurant wasn't really called the Chicken Shack, but they only served rotisserie chicken and the place was a shack, so the name stuck. It was tiny, cheap, and the food was excellent. The wooden structure, originally painted white but now with smoke stains lending an elaborate swirl to the walls, sat across the parking lot from the Hotel Rostov. American parents-to-be gathered at the Shack most evenings for beer, chicken, and war stories about their adoptions.

Michelle and Katie Pearson, the other adopting mother, were disgusted. Their husbands, on the other hand, looked envious.

"Was she cute?" Tom, Michelle's husband, asked with a wink.

Michelle slugged him on the arm. Not much larger than his wife, Tom flinched from the playful hit and rubbed his arm in mock pain.

Nick grinned and explained the situation. He left nothing out, including paying the girl twenty dollars not to have sex with her.

"Heck," Tom said, "I'd only charge you fifteen bucks not to have sex with me."

"And I'm sure it'd be money well spent, Tom," Nick replied. The girls laughed as Tom rolled his eyes and gave Nick the finger. "But I do feel terrible, making her walk all the way over to the hotel for nothing."

"Well, she didn't come that far, you know," Katie said. They passed the brothel every day when they walked the thirty minutes to Baby Home Number Four, where Nonna and their son, Valiera, waited to be rescued. There were no signs announcing the brothel, but the continuous presence of painted women in robes on the sidewalk, smoking cigarettes and looking fed up with life, was sign enough.

"Don't listen to him," Michelle said. "You only have nine days left, right? Be a good boy and don't get into trouble."

Nick held up his hands, palms out. "I don't plan to. Once the grace period's up, I'm out of here with Nonna."

"That's a stupid rule, anyway," Katie said. "The kids have been in the orphanage for months, and we have to wait ten more days in case their parents show up and want them after all? What a crock. Has that ever happened, anyway?"

"Our driver says it hasn't," Tom said. "He said no kid's been claimed by family once they get on the international database."

"It's just a rule to keep us here and get more of our money," Nick said.

"Like they're not getting most of it, anyway," Michelle grumbled. Nick hardly knew her, except that she and Tom were cops in upstate New York, but could already tell she didn't like being taken advantage of. She had a hard time dealing with what they had to go through to get their kids.

"How about you guys?" Nick asked her. "Any news on Alexei?"

"We go to court tomorrow," Michelle said. "Assuming it all goes well, our ten days start tomorrow."

"It'll go fine," Nick said. "You meet with the judge before court, and she tells you exactly what to say. Piece of cake."

"So they say. I'm still nervous, though. At least we're both staying." She looked at Nick quickly. "Sorry."

"Don't be." Kelli was heading home early to care for their son, Danny. Danny was at home with Kelli's parents now, but his stress would grow every day they were gone. The Russians were OK with only one parent staying, as long as they filled out the thirty-eight forms that went along with it.

Nick glanced at Scott. The tall Texan was uncharacteristically quiet, staring vacantly at his dark bottle of Baltica beer. One hand was meshed in his brown hair while he twirled the bottle between two fingers of his other hand. He abruptly raised it to his lips and killed it.

He stood up. "I'm getting a refill. Anybody else want one?" The two women nodded and Tom raised an index finger. Nick rose and said, "I'll go with you."

The bartender, Sergei, saw them coming and reached into the beer cooler. Sergei wasn't a big guy but had a competent air about him. Nick thought he may have been Russian military in a past life, but something about the man struck Nick as off, so their conversations were typically limited to the disbursement of alcohol in one direction and rubles in the other. They had swapped names and a handshake the first day and that was about it.

Scott held up his thumb and four fingers and nodded when Sergei hoisted a Baltica. He got out his wallet and pushed Nick's bills away. "I've got it," he said.

"Thanks," Nick said, and put his money back in his pocket. They leaned against the wooden bar as the bartender opened the bottles. The bar was unfinished wood, comfortable in a shack, with furrows and initials carved in by previous patrons. Scott ran his finger along one of the grooves absently, mind clearly elsewhere.

"So, was it the blonde or a different girl?" Nick asked casually.

Scott's head snapped up. "Who?"

"The woman who came to your room."

Scott started to protest, then sighed. "That obvious?"

Nick nodded. "I doubt Katie noticed anything, but you didn't ask about the girl. In fact, you looked like somebody sucker-punched you."

Scott gazed down at the bar for a long moment. Finally he said, "Katie went shopping with Michelle for the afternoon a few days ago. When they were gone I got a call." He shrugged. "It sounded fun, harmless. And a lot cheaper than in the states." He smirked at the bar. "Now I know why."

"Herpes?" Nick asked, only half joking.

"Nah, nothing like that. The next day I got another phone call. This time from some punk who said he knew what I'd done. If I didn't pay them off, he'd tell Katie."

Nick whistled. He felt better about turning the girl down. "Did you pay them?"

"Yeah, I left a hundy at the hotel desk."

7

Nick was silent, non-judgmental, as Sergei put the bottles down next to the Americans. Scott looked up. The man's face was shiny with sweat and his eyes were slightly glazed. Nick wondered how many beers Scott had already put away.

"The bastard called again this morning. Now they want two hundred."

Nick groaned and rubbed his forehead. "Oh, boy, Scott, you're in it now. When do they want it?"

Before Scott could answer, Sergei leaned in close, elbows on the table, breath sour in their faces. "Da, Scott," he said in heavily accented English, his voice a low rumble. "When you pay us the damn money?"

Chapter 2

Scott recoiled, eyes wide in shock. Nick just stared at the bartender.

"What the hell…" Scott said thickly, as if he had a wad of peat moss in his mouth. "Sergei?"

Sergei smiled, all teeth, all predator. "So we're friends, da, Scott? Tovarich?" He slapped the bar hard enough that Scott jumped. "Then pay your friend Sergei, like we ask."

Scott looked at Nick, then back at Sergei, then back at Nick, then back to Sergei. He was an animal trapped in a cage.

"I don't have two hundred dollars," he finally said in a rush. "All of our money is for the adoption and if I take any more Katie will find out—"

Sergei slapped the bar again and Scott stopped cold. Nick glanced back at their table. Tom watched them, concern on his face, but the women were talking, oblivious. Tom started to stand but Nick waved him off.

"You had enough money to play with Marina," Sergei said. "Did you use adoption money for that?"

Scott just looked at the Russian. His mouth moved but no sound came out. Then all of the fight went out of him. His shoulders slumped and he cupped his head in both hands.

"Back off, Sergei," Nick said. "He told you he can't get the money. You have a hundred, be happy with that."

Sergei slowly turned to look at Nick. "Shut up, American. This isn't your concern."

"I'm making it my concern."

"That's a bad idea," Sergei said. "You're weak, like all Americans. Be careful we don't become your enemy."

The Russian turned back to Scott. "I work until ten o'clock. I want the money then. Do you remember what happens if you do not pay?"

Scott mumbled something into his hands. Nick couldn't make out what he said. Sergei leaned in close to Scott and said, "What?"

Scott spread his hands but did not look up. "I visit my son tomorrow with only one eye."

"Da, that is correct. Do you want that?"

Scott put his head back in his hands. Nick stood up abruptly. "Jesus, Sergei! We're done with this conversation." He put his hand on Scott's shoulder and spoke softly to his friend. "We have our beer. Let's go back."

Scott nodded numbly and stood up. He didn't look at Sergei as he picked up three brown bottles. He turned and walked slowly back to the table.

Sergei grabbed Nick's arm as Nick reached for the last two bottles. "If your friend doesn't pay, you will. One way or the other."

Nick sat quietly with the others, biding his time, only half-listening as Katie and Michelle droned on about kids, their homes, work. Nick's mind kept wandering back to the conversation with Sergei. From time to time he glanced over at Scott, who sat stone-faced, brooding, also obviously not listening to the conversation.

Eventually, as he knew they would, the ladies announced a trip to the restroom. Since the Chicken Shack had no bathrooms, the closest points of relief were their hotel rooms. Nick knew he had time to talk while the wives were gone.

As soon as they disappeared out the door, Tom turned to Nick and Scott. "So, what the hell happened over there?" he asked.

Nick looked at Scott, but the man barely moved. He appeared to be in shock, so Nick answered. "Well, it looks like a girl also went to Scott's room."

"Uh, oh."

"Yeah. After Scott was, um, with her, her bosses decided a little blackmailing was in order."

Scott snorted and Tom whistled. "Sergei?" Tom asked.

"Yep," Nick said. "I'm not sure if Sergei's the only one, but he wants Scott to give him two hundred bucks. And that's after one hundred yesterday."

"Are you going to pay it?" Tom asked.

"Hell, no," Scott replied, looking up. "I don't have that kind of money, and if I did I wouldn't give it to that bastard."

"Tell him what Sergei said he'd do if you didn't pay," Nick said.

"He said he'd carve my eye out," Scott said through clenched teeth. His shock seemed to be receding, replaced by anger. "He said I'd visit Valiera with one eye."

Tom glared at Sergei, who had his back turned, helping a customer. "Sonofabitch," he said. "We should call the cops."

"That was my first thought, too," Nick said. "But I wonder if that'd complicate things."

Scott nodded. "I'd prefer not to get the cops involved. I don't need that kind of hassle."

"Besides," Tom said, "Katie doesn't know."

Scott shrugged.

"You gotta tell her, man," Tom said. "She's going to find out anyway, and better it come from you."

"No way," Scott said as he shook his head. "She'd probably take *both* my eyes out."

Nick sighed. "So, what are you going to do?" he asked.

"I'm not sure," Scott said. "I guess I'm hoping to stay away from Sergei until we get Valiera, then we're out of here."

"Gonna be tough, with him working at the Chicken Shack and all," Nick said.

"I know," Scott said. "But let's take it one day at a time. He's going to be here until ten. Let's go somewhere else."

Tom shrugged. "Fine by me. Where should we go?"

"How about that club we passed the other day?" Scott said. "You know, the one with the dolphins in front. We can have a drink and listen to music." They had noticed a club on their way to a recommended restaurant a few days ago. The restaurant wasn't anything to get excited about, but the club had looked interesting.

The women walked up as Scott was talking. Katie put her hand on her husband's shoulder and rubbed it. She hadn't said anything, but Nick was sure she'd noticed Scott's moodiness. Wives were good that way. At least his was.

"Do you want to go to the Dolphin Club?" Scott asked her.

She giggled. "Is that what it's called?"

"It is now," Nick said.

The women exchanged glances. "Sounds good," Michelle said. "Just give me some time to freshen up. Should we meet back here?"

Scott looked uncomfortable.

11

"Let's meet in the hotel lobby," Nick said. He saw Scott relax slightly, then turn rigid again. Nick followed his friend's gaze back to the bar.

Sergei was staring at them, a malevolent look on his face. He was cleaning something with a cloth. As the two Americans watched, he finished rubbing and put the item down on the bar.

It was a knife.

The lobby of the Hotel Rostov was large and brightly lit, with a wide stairway curving up the back. Dark red runners graced the traffic areas, and it would have been classy except for the newsstand in the middle of the room. Magazines gave way to cigarettes which in turn gave way to essentials like toothbrushes and Band-Aids, the latter behind dirty glass for some reason. An older man with a gaunt face and a brown jacket a few sizes too large stood like a sentry behind the counter, waiting for customers. He stared impassively at the five Americans as they walked past him and up the stairs. Cigarette smoke drifted up lazily from the dirty ashtray on the counter.

Their rooms were clustered together on the fourth floor. When they reached the top of the stairs, slightly out of breath, they found another sentry waiting.

The fourth floor key lady sat sternly at her desk, almost daring them to pass without proper authorization.

There was a peculiar constant in Russian hotels, at least the ones Nick had been in. Each floor contained what the parents called a key lady. Typically grumpy and older than employees should be, key ladies were tasked with knowing who was in their room at any given moment. They did this by storing all of the room keys in little cubby holes at their desks in the main hallway. When a guest arrived from outside, they gave the key lady a piece of paper with their room number printed on it. The woman exchanged it for the key to their room. Conversely, when somebody left they would deposit the key with the woman and get their slip of paper back.

Perhaps it was a holdover from the Stalin era, when They wanted to know where everybody was at all times. Perhaps it was a Communist standard, so They could say They had full employment. Whatever the case, Nick didn't mind it because it meant he just had to carry a piece of paper in his pocket when he was out, rather than a large Russian key.

On the other hand, he didn't appreciate it when they dialed up the local brothel after his wife left, in hopes of getting a kickback from a trick.

Three people fumbled in their clothes for their papers, and three hands turned over the green slips for three rooms with some trepidation. Nick had forgotten to give his key to the key lady one morning, and she had landed on him without mercy. He didn't need to know Russian to realize he had committed a cardinal sin.

Unsmiling, she took all three papers and handed back their keys.

"Spasiva," Nick said. She looked at him for a long moment, face impassive. Finally she turned away and sat down at her desk, where she clasped her hands together and waited for the next troublemaker.

The crowd of people outside the club looked happier than the key lady, although that wasn't saying much. The sun had disappeared, and with that their inhibitions. Couples made out in the shadows, oblivious to the patrons coming and going within feet of them. Nick smelled the unmistakable odor of marijuana as he passed a group of guys. He wondered if they had as much trouble getting arrested for it here as they did in Oregon.

They paid a few rubles to a large man in a sport coat at the door, and walked in to the crowded club. It felt much like a dance club anywhere in the world: loud music pounding up through the floorboards and into Nick's legs; a variety of smells, from perfume to beer to sweat to who-knew-what-else; people in various stages of drunkenness, dancing or sitting limp at tables splayed around the outside of the large dance floor. It was a not-unpleasant assault on the senses that brought Nick back several years. He grinned.

Two women passed the group at that moment, a blond and a brunette, both in skimpy sequined dresses with their hair pulled up and drinks in their hands. The brunette in the back saw his grin and smiled back, eyes lingering appreciatively over his broad chest. They passed and Nick turned, watching them slink away.

Katie grabbed his arm. "A good boy, remember?" she said.

13

Nick sighed. "Yes, dear," he said.

He turned back and almost bumped into a woman walking unsteadily past him. He caught a glimpse of brown hair. A green dress. When he saw her last she had been wearing lingerie and a white coat.

Instinctively he reached out to steady her. She turned to him and

made eye contact for a moment before she turned away. But it was too late.

Even in the dim light he could see that her lip was cut and crusted over. Her right eye was black and blue, and she had a bruise the size of an apple on her cheek.

Somebody had worked her over.

Chapter 3

The roaring began in his left ear, as it always did, and quickly spread to the right. Nick closed his eyes to compose himself.

He opened them and shook his arm loose from Katie. "Please go find a table," he said. His voice was low and hard, and Katie shrunk back from it. "I'll catch up." She saw the expression in his face and immediately left.

Nick found an open chair at the bar and led the shaken girl to it. She sat down, hard, and he stood over her. A dark-haired woman in a dress stood, angry eyes on Nick. They looked silver in the light. The girl saw her and tiredly waved her away. Nick assumed she was another prostitute.

"Zdrastvoitya," he said. Hello.

She nodded. Nick was sure she recognized him, but she didn't say anything. Her one good eye was red from crying.

He leaned towards her so he could keep his voice low in the din of the bar. "What happened?" he asked.

She shook her head.

"Somebody hit you. Was it a customer?" Nick wasn't sure why he grilled her. He knew he should keep walking. No way was that going to happen, though.

She turned so she could see Nick out of her undamaged eye. "No. I was hurt because I came back with twenty dollars."

Nick sighed and swore softly. Much of the anger drained from him. "I'm sorry," he told her. She shrugged.

"It happens," she replied. Her nonchalance made him feel worse.

"What's your name?" Nick asked after a moment.

"Why?"

"Because I'd like to know. My name is Nick. Minya savoot Nick."

She smiled, a tiny one, but the first he'd seen from her, at his feeble attempt at Russian.

"You know Russian," she said.

"You just heard almost all of it."

She smiled again, a little wider this time, and said, "Minya savoot Lauren."

15

"Nice to meet you, Lauren," he said. An interesting name for a Russian, he thought.

She ducked her head shyly, and they remained like that for several seconds, Nick feeling awkward because of questions he knew he shouldn't ask her.

She finally looked at him. "I came from baby home, too, you know."

Nick nodded. It made sense. He had read that unwanted kids were thrown out of the orphanages in their mid-teens, with nothing to sell except their bodies. "Where are you from?" he asked.

"Not here. In Taganrog, by the sea. Nice orphanage. Not so nice after that." She shrugged again. She seemed to shrug a lot. "Now you know me, so now you leave."

"I want to know who did this to you."

"Why?"

That stopped him. Why, indeed? It was none of his business.

But in a way it was.

"Because I need to tell him that you don't hit women."

She shook her head sadly. "He will not listen."

"I'll make him listen."

"No," she said. "Please. No. Then he will hit harder."

Nick paused, thought about it, and nodded. "OK, Lauren. You're right. I should leave."

She touched his arm. "You're a nice man. Be good for your daughter."

Nick stared to reply but then saw fear touch her eye as he felt a presence behind him. Lauren pulled her hand back from his arm as Nick turned. A young man, skinny to the point of emaciation, with black tattoos on his forearms and crew cut blonde hair, stared at Nick.

"I'm Maxsim. You want girl?" he motioned brusquely towards Lauren, as if she wasn't there. "Fifty dollars." He spoke English. Perhaps he had heard them talk, or perhaps Nick had "Made in America" stamped on his forehead. Nick tried to dress like a local, in ripped jeans and a faded dark blue t-shirt, but people seemed to know.

Nick glared at the Russian for several seconds without speaking. Just the chance that he may have been the one who beat up Lauren made him hate the man on the spot.

"Twenty, then," the punk said, misunderstanding Nick's anger.

Nick shook his head. What he really wanted to do was shake Maxsim's.

The Russian seemed confused, then angry. "You don't talk to my whores, you talk to me! You pay, you stay. Otherwise you go!" His eyes were bloodshot and he kept blinking. Alcohol, perhaps, but more likely drugs. Nick had seen that look before.

Nick flexed his fingers, ready to go at it, but a thought made him pull back. Lauren looked at the two men towering over her, jerking her head from one to the other, fear in her eyes. Nick knew who would get the worst of it if he attacked Maxsim. Maybe not immediately, but soon. And she didn't deserve another beating. She didn't deserve the first one.

He relaxed, lifting his hands up, palms out. "I have no money," he told Maxsim. "I'm sure she'd be worth it, but I cannot pay."

Maxsim smirked. This put him on a level above the westerner. "If you cannot pay, then you cannot talk to my girls. Leave now."

Nick backed off, palms still out. "I'm sorry," he said. His eyes were on Maxsim, but his words were directed to Lauren. She looked at him sadly as he walked away.

Nick saw Scott waiting for him, several feet away, holding two beers. Nick took one gratefully and downed half of it on the spot. Katie must have asked Scott to go check on the crazy American.

"Is that her?" Scott asked, motioning with his head towards the bar.

"Lauren, yes," Nick answered.

"Was she hurt?"

Nick turned to look back. Maxsim had grabbed Lauren's arm and was leading her away roughly. Another man, larger than Maxsim and probably a bodyguard, glanced at Nick before turning to follow them out.

"Yep," Nick replied, glaring at Maxsim's back. "She got beat up."

"Who's the punk?"

"Maxsim, her pimp," Nick said. "He's the one who did the beating."

"Asshole."

"Got that right."

They were silent for a second, then Scott said, "If he's her pimp, he probably knows Sergei."

Nick nodded. "I'm sure of it. My guess is they're part of the Russian mafia."

Scott didn't look happy. "You think so? Maybe they just work for themselves."

"I doubt it. I read that the mafia controls most of the brothels in the cities. Sergei and Maxsim are probably just the, how did they put it, the enforcers."

"You read too damn much, Nick."

Nick sighed. "Don't I know it. Let's get back to the others. Not much we can do now."

The Americans had found an empty table on the far side of the dance floor and settled in. Nick and Scott plopped heavily into seats on either side of Katie.

"I'm glad you came here with us, Nick," Katie said. She leaned in to him and raised her voice to be heard over the beat of some anonymous song. "It's good to get out." She still looked concerned, but was obviously relieved that Nick was back with them.

"Plus, Kelli asked you to keep an eye on me, right?" Nick asked. He was still in a sour mood.

Katie looked sheepish. "Well, she did mention that we should stick together."

Tom leaned in and said, with a grin, "Sounds like somebody doesn't trust her hubby," he said.

"And I should?" Michelle shot back playfully. "No way am I leaving you here alone."

"It's not that she doesn't trust Nick," Katie said. "I'm sure it's scary to leave your husband in a foreign country by himself. I'd hate to do it."

"I've been in a few foreign countries by myself," Nick said. And here we aren't shooting at each other.

"Not with a kid," Tom pointed out.

Nick shrugged. "They won't hand over Nonna until I leave, so she's safe from my corrupting influence, at least for another week or so."

The others grinned and sat quietly for a few minutes, people-watching and sipping beer. Nick stewed about what just happened, but knew there wasn't much he could do about it at that point. He knew he should just move on, but it was hard to get Lauren's ravaged face out of his mind. He had the feeling it would be hard to move on from that.

Eventually Katie, whom Nick had noticed abhorred silence, leaned over again and said, "I like Kelli. Where did you two meet?"

Nick took a long pull on his beer and thought about how to answer. He didn't really want to talk but it might be a good distraction. Besides, if he didn't she'd likely just ask again. "After I got out of the military," he said, "I moved to Bend, a small town in Oregon." He left out that it took him several years to land in Bend. He had eventually picked the town because it was close to Portland, where his step-brother lived. Gary was Nick's only family within 2,000 miles. He had never really known Gary, but he was willing to give it a shot. Unfortunately, he quickly discovered they had almost nothing in common. He found Gary living in a dirty, cramped house with his third wife, sponging off her job at the local Fred Meyer and indulging in his love of Budweiser. They saw each other a few times, but eventually their relationship fell apart from mutual apathy.

He also picked Bend because it was far from most everybody else in America. After several years in the Marines, where he had seen fanatics repeatedly do nasty things to each other in hot climates, he decided to move where there were few people. It just seemed easier that way. He lived off his military pension and sporadic payments from odd and mostly unsavory jobs.

He stayed away from people through a long, dark winter. Then, in the spring, he met Kelli. She was bright and colorful and full of life, all of the things he had been missing for several years. She ran her own business ferreting out computer crimes. Apparently she was quite good at it if she could make a living at it from Bend. As she told Nick, it didn't really matter where you were, as long as

19

you had a good internet connection and were willing to work long hours to make your clients forget your office was in the boonies.

Nick shook his head slightly to clear it, and realized Katie was looking at him intently, a look of amusement on her face.

"Sorry about that," he said. He realized he had stopped talking.

Katie laughed. "It's OK, Nick. Thinking about Kelli?"

"Yep."

"Well, you'll see her soon, with your daughter! And you have a son, too, right?"

Nick smiled. "Yeah, Danny. We're buddies. I think it's because we're at the same level intellectually." Katie smiled back. She knew Danny, Kelli's son from a previous marriage, was Autistic.

Nick's bond with Danny was one of the things that had cemented his relationship with Kelli. Nick had never been around Autistic kids before, especially severely affected ones like Danny, but they clicked immediately. Nick figured it was because they both loved cars, trains, anything with wheels, and going fast. Kelli wouldn't let her son ride on Nick's Harley, but the boys spent many hours cruising around eastern Oregon in her Honda Accord with the windows open, yelling "yeeeeee-ha!" and laughing.

Nick always felt better after spending time with Danny. It was all so simple, so happy. The kid never stopped laughing. Sometimes he thought Autistic kids were the lucky ones.

Nick smiled. Thinking of his family always made him feel better.

Then Scott murmured, "Oh, shit."

Chapter 4

Nick glanced at Scott. His friend was staring at a point behind Nick, a stunned look on his face.

Nick turned in his chair and looked over his left shoulder. Sergei stood a few feet behind him, arms crossed over his chest, a scowl on his face. Nick started to stand and saw Sergei's eyes flick to his right, behind Nick. Almost immediately a strong pair of hands pushed him back into his seat. Nick struggled briefly but had no leverage, so he gave it up and sunk back in the chair. The hands stayed on his shoulders.

"Hey, asshole," Sergei said to Scott. His voice was loud even in the din of the club. It was rough, too. "Where's my money?"

Scott sat still in his chair, wide eyes on Sergei. His mouth opened, closed, opened again, and closed. At that point Nick hoped Scott wouldn't say anything.

Nick glanced at Tom. The man's face was tense. He looked ready to jump the Russian. He noticed Nick's stare and glanced at him. Nick shook his head slightly. Tom pursed his lips but didn't move.

"You don't think I know when five Americans leave my hotel?" Sergei said. He moved to his right, around whoever restrained Nick, to be closer to Scott. His attention was completely on his prey now.

Nick's hands were in his lap. He shifted slightly, moving each hand to a thigh. The man towering over him didn't respond except to reflexively push down a bit harder. Nick figured the man was watching Scott struggle.

And Scott was struggling. He looked as if he was going to throw up all over the table. Katie looked at Sergei, then back at her husband. "What's this all about, Scott?" she asked. Her voice was high-pitched, her eyes wide, confused. Nick knew she was on the verge of losing it. He glanced at Michelle. The woman was silent, taking it all in. A professional.

"Yeah, asshole," Sergei said. "What's this all about? Tell her."

Scott was silent, miserable, his gaze on the table in front of him.

Sergei took a step forward, between Nick and Katie. Nick was now out of his sight, forgotten, as Sergei glared over Katie's shocked face at Scott.

"No?" he said. "OK, I'll tell her." He shifted his gaze to Katie. "Your husband slept with one of my whores." The corner of his mouth curled up slightly at the look of horror that spread over Katie's face. "Now he won't pay what he owes me."

Katie turned to Scott in a grotesque slow motion, her chair sliding backwards as she shifted her weight. "Is this true?" she said. Her face was now rigid, the emotions refusing to come to the surface. Nick knew she didn't care about the money. It was Scott's betrayal that mattered.

Scott stared down at the table in front of him. He was completely defeated. Sergei laughed.

Katie slapped Scott. Hard. His head snapped to the right, then came back to a neutral position, still looking down. He didn't fight it, which increased Katie's fury. Sergei laughed again.

Nick felt his rising anger quickly flow away. The Calm came over him, and knew it was time. The Calm had only surfaced a handful of times in his life, but more often than not, somebody soon was dead because of it. He figured The Calm was his body's way of getting focused, ready to fight. He didn't like when it showed up, but knew it prepared him for what came next.

He flexed his right hand, making a fist, relaxing it, making it again, relaxing, getting a feel for the power.

Katie stood up. Nick knew she was seconds from disintegration. He made a tight fist and glanced down at the legs behind him. Not yet.

The man holding Nick down then made his mistake. He laughed along with Sergei, made a short comment in Russian that made them both laugh again, and moved to his right. Later Nick figured he meant to give Sergei a high-five. It never landed.

The man shifted his weight and stepped forward, giving Nick a clear path to his knee. Nick took a breath, allowed The Calm to take over. He smashed his right elbow viciously into the man's knee.

Nick knew he didn't have enough leverage to break the man's kneecap, but he didn't have to. He knew there would be one of two results: if the blow wasn't hard enough, the man would haul off and hit Nick upside the head. Or worse, move his hands slightly and choke him into unconsciousness. If the blow was hard enough, he would double over instinctively and grab his knee.

The blow was hard enough.

The man gasped and the hands left Nick's shoulders. Nick sensed him bending over to clutch his knee. Nick reached up with both hands, grasped where he figured the man's collar would be. He felt cloth and pulled down hard. The man's face slammed into the table, the sounds of the club drowning out both his shocked yell and the pop as his nose exploded on the wood.

Nick jumped up and faced Sergei. The Russian's laughter died in his throat as he saw his bodyguard crumple to the ground, groggy, blood pouring out of his face. The bartender recovered quickly. He pulled a knife out of his suit coat pocket and flicked it open in one quick move as Nick descended on him.

Nick grabbed Sergei's knife hand in both of his own before the Russian had a chance to think, and thrust upwards. Sergei didn't expect the speed of the attack, and almost immediately his knife was at his own throat. He brought up his other hand to defend himself, and found both hands in Nick's grasp.

Nick stepped in closer, his face only inches from Sergei's shocked expression. He hissed at the Russian, "Think about what you're doing, Sergei." Sergei struggled, not willing to accept defeat. Nick pushed the knife up, the tip entered the flesh behind Sergei's chin. A thin line of blood oozed down the blade, and Sergei abruptly stopped moving.

"Is a small amount of money from one American worth it, Sergei?" Nick said in a low voice, so only the Russian could hear. "You told his wife, so you don't have that leverage anymore. Just let it drop." He spoke slowly, carefully, so the Russian would understand every word. Sergei glared back at Nick, silent.

"Just let it drop, Sergei," Nick said again. The Russian eyed him, and his mouth turned up slightly in a sneer. Nick took that as a "no" and pushed harder on the knife. More blood dripped down the knife and onto their hands, but Sergei didn't flinch.

"Don't fuck with us," Sergei finally said. "You don't know what you're getting into."

They were at an impasse. Nick knew it. He knew he wasn't going to stab a Russian enforcer in a Moscow club and get away with it. But he wasn't about to let Sergei get away with threatening his friends. He and the Russian glared into each other's eyes for a long moment.

Then Nick felt a touch on his arm. He had been so focused on Sergei that he didn't notice Katie approach them.

"How much does he owe you?" she asked Sergei softly, hand still on Nick's arm.

Surprise flickered in the Russian's eyes for a moment, replaced quickly by a glint of triumph. "Two hundred dollars," he said.

She started to open her purse.

"But the price has gone up," Sergei said. He motioned to the bodyguard, still dazed on the floor. "Since I now have to bring my friend to the doctor."

"How much?" she asked again.

Sergei thought quickly. "Double. Four hundred dollars."

Nick felt a surge of anger and nudged the blade deeper. Sergei turned slowly to Nick. "I trust you don't want the price to go higher," he said softly.

Gritting his teeth, Nick let off on the pressure.

"I don't have that kind of money now," Katie said. She was obviously in shock. Her words were slow, measured. "Can I give it to you tomorrow?"

Sergei paused for a moment before speaking. "By noon tomorrow. Bring it to me at the restaurant."

"Then you'll leave us alone."

"I never said that. But if you don't pay, I won't leave you alone."

"I'll pay," she said, and without another word turned away. She stumbled back to the table and sat down. Scott didn't look at her.

"Now give me that damn knife," Sergei growled to Nick. Nick reluctantly lowered the knife and handed it to Sergei, who grabbed it with a grunt and wiped it on a napkin from the table before closing it.

A man walked up behind Sergei. He was large and looked familiar. It took Nick a moment to remember where he had seen him. Then it came to him: the bodyguard who had been with Maxsim. So Maxsim and Sergei were connected. Nick wasn't surprised.

Up close, Nick noticed the man had a long scar that ran from the corner of his mouth down below his jawbone. He had a hardened look to him. Apparently Sergei wasn't the only ex-military in the mob.

The man looked from Sergei to Nick. He murmured something to Sergei, who shook his head. "No, it's over," he said as he motioned towards Katie. "The woman saved him." Sergei spoke in English for Nick's benefit. He saw Nick's furious expression and smiled. The larger man just looked at Nick with a curious expression for several seconds, until Sergei said, "Let's go."

He and Sergei helped their friend to his feet, which he gained with difficulty, and they disappeared into the washroom to clean up. The small group of club-goers who had witnessed the altercation dispersed, likely disappointed there wasn't more bloodshed.

Nick turned to the others. Michelle was the only one who didn't look like she had been maced. She put her arm around Katie, who had her face buried in her hands, and whispered something to her. Katie nodded slightly, or perhaps it was her head shaking from the sobs.

Michelle looked up at Nick. "I'm going to take her back to the hotel," she said. Her voice was even, collected. Nick nodded. Tom said, "Do you want me to go with you?"

Michelle nodded. "Yeah, but walk behind us. I doubt Katie will even know you're there." She glanced at Scott and there was disgust in her voice as she said, "And get Scott home, too. They have some talking to do."

The women left, one supporting the other, while the men walked behind them. Scott was in shock, his feet moving mechanically. Tom murmured to Nick, "What did she say?"

Nick replied in a low voice, although he was pretty sure Scott wasn't hearing anything at the moment. "She bought him off. Hopefully we're done with them now."

"Do you think so?" Tom sounded skeptical.

Nick didn't reply. He suspected all her four hundred dollars had bought was time.

The man knelt gently by Lauren, who sat stiffly in a chair on the other side of the club. He kept his face turned, so the scar by his mouth did not intimidate her.

"Do you know the man who talked to you earlier, the American?" he asked Lauren.

Lauren shook her head, but the man kept his gaze on her until she nodded, once, timidly. "I don't know his name but he's staying at the Hotel Rostov."

"Room?" They both knew she'd have his room number.

She sighed. "402."

He stood up. "Thank you. Give me a moment, then I'll take you home."

Maxsim had disappeared. Probably doing blow in the bathroom, the man thought with disgust. No time to waste. The bodyguard pulled out his cell phone. It contained several speed dial numbers, but he ignored them. He dialed a different number from memory.

A moment later the connection was established and a tinny voice answered. He said, "I may have something. Can you meet tonight?" A pause. "Good."

He terminated the call, then opened up the call history for the phone and deleted the last number. By the time Maxsim returned, rubbing his nose furiously, the man had put the phone away and stood against a post, impassive.

Chapter 5

The fallout began immediately.

Nick locked himself in his room, breathed a big sigh of relief and leaned against the door for several moments. When he finally started to get ready for bed, it was nearing midnight and he was exhausted.

There was a quiet knock on the door as he crawled into bed. He turned and looked at the heavy wooden door, hoping the sound had come from another room.

It hadn't. The knock repeated, louder this time.

Nick sighed, pulled on sweatpants, and opened the door. Michelle stood outside, ready to pound again. She lowered her arm and asked, "Can I come in for a second?"

Nick swung the door open and motioned inside. "What's up?" he asked.

"Katie won't let Scott sleep in their room."

Nick groaned. He knew what was coming. "He's not sleeping in my bed. It's barely big enough for one."

Katie nodded. "You have a couch."

Nick closed his eyes. "Fine. But those two need to talk."

"I know, I know. But Katie's in shock right now. They can talk tomorrow. Maybe the day after."

"OK," Nick said. He sighed. "Do you want me to go get him?"

"If you wouldn't mind. He's with Tom in our room."

"How's he doing?"

She shrugged. "About the same. Not saying anything. Just stares. Maybe you can talk to him."

Nick grabbed his key so they wouldn't be locked out. He was in no mood for a key lady's anger tonight. "I'll talk to him in the morning. He needs some sleep, and so do I."

But they didn't talk in the morning. Nick woke late, curled up on the side of the bed, arm asleep as usual. He turned over and reached for Kelli, then sat up when he realized she wasn't there. He listened for sounds from the bathroom for a few seconds before remembering she was gone, and most likely thousands of miles away at that point. He remembered last night. As it came back to him, he felt very lonely

Groaning loudly, Nick sank back into the bed, wishing Kelli was there with him. She was a great listener, giving advice when she knew the speaker wanted some, or just sitting quietly when the other person just needed to vent.

And Nick needed to vent. He looked over at the couch. Scott was curled up in as close to a fetal position as he could get, face pressed against the back of the couch, away from reality. He wasn't moving and Nick had no interest in waking him.

Nick rolled into a sitting position on the edge of the bed and stayed there for several minutes, thinking, before he got up to grab some breakfast. Bread and Lucky Charms, which was the only cereal he could find at the small grocery store near the baby home. He poured bottled water over the cereal and gulped it down. They were told to stay away from the unpasteurized milk, but marshmallow bits in lukewarm water didn't do much for him, so he once again considered giving milk a shot later that day. The bread, baked yesterday, tasted much better.

He opened the curtains and was happy to see another cloudless day. In July, they had learned the hard way, the hotel turned off the hot water to save money. He and Kelli got around it by filling several two-liter soda bottles with water in the morning and letting them heat in the sun in front of pulled curtains all day. By late afternoon they had enough mildly warm water to at least take a quick shower or shave. With his dark hair and seemingly permanent stubble, shaving every day was important to Nick.

Nick filled the bottles, tidied up a bit, and put his book and MP3 player in a backpack. He looked over at Scott. Still no movement. Nick stared at Scott's back for a moment, not feeling much sympathy.

It was 9:15 am. He could see Nonna every day, provided he was there by 10:00 am sharp and didn't pitch a fit when they threw him out of the orphanage ninety minutes later. He had no idea why they could only see their child between 10:00 and 11:30; it was just one of those lame rules they came up with to keep parents in their place. As with the other lame rules, parents took it because eventually you do what you have to do to get your baby.

But Nick would have ninety minutes with Nonna. It would be a good day.

The bodyguard stood, absently rubbing his scar, as his boss maneuvered through an easily-penetrated US armed forces web site. He knew better than to talk; his job was simply to bring the information to his boss, who would then know what to do with it.

"Nick Wallace," the man repeated several times, slowly, subconsciously, as he trolled the database. "So you thought he was older?" He spoke Russian.

"Yes," the bodyguard replied. "Late thirties, early forties. Big, dark. Definitely military, probably retired."

"But still dangerous?"

"He took down Vladimir easily enough and would've cut Sergei's head off if the woman hadn't intervened," the bodyguard replied.

The second man nodded, the beginnings of a smile on his face. Dangerous. He continued to troll.

Even at the early hour, Crazy Boris's was running at full volume. Crazy Boris owned an electronics shop a block from the hotel, where loud rock music blasted from speakers placed outside. Nick assumed Rostov didn't have noise ordinances. Like the Chicken Shack, Crazy Boris's was not the name of the place, and the owner probably was not named Boris, but it fit. Nick could easily see one of their commercials, complete with loud music and a frantic guy in a tacky suit running around, yelling, "My name may be Crazy Boris, but these prices are insaaaaaaane!"

His favorite part of the shop was the music section. Copyright laws were as non-existent as noise ordinances, and Boris had rack upon rack of CDs at about a dollar US each. New releases, rarities, even the complete Beatles collection, which Nick already had but bought anyway because it was such a deal. He wasn't sure how he'd get all the music past customs, but he'd figure out a way. Maybe slide them between diapers, or pinch Nonna so she'd cry and they'd let them through quickly, without checking closely. He grinned to himself. He knew that wasn't going to happen. Kelli had taken the Beatles home with her yesterday so he knew they were safe, at least.

Nick looked through the CDs for the third time in as many days, and decided on a few from The Who. Crazy Boris seemed to have a better selection of the oldies than current artists.

He walked his CDs up to the counter and was slightly surprised to see Boris himself behind the old-fashioned cash register. Usually he had a kid on the register while he chatted with customers. Boris was probably fifty, with a salt-and-pepper goatee and thinning hair pulled back into a ponytail.

He took the CDs and gave Nick a big smile. "Ahh, The Who!" he said in a booming voice. "The kids are alright! Are you American?"

Nick nodded.

Crazy Boris thrust his hand over the counter so quickly that Nick flinched, and shook Nick's hand with vigor.

"Hello, American! Someday I go America, Miami Beach. Miami Vice, great show!" He pronounced "Vice" with a "W," and made a machine gun sound with his lips as he simulated spraying bullets around the store. "Don Johnson, good actor."

"If you say so," Nick said with a smile.

"And California. I must to see California! Hollywood. Maybe see Harry Ford at a café!"

Nick paid and accepted his change and CDs with a few words of encouragement. He decided to let Crazy Boris find out the bad news himself about how far apart the two states were. At least he'd be happy until then.

Nick walked out, feeling good. He liked Boris. Maybe the man wasn't crazy, perhaps just a bit eccentric.

"She's been good girl this morning," the orphanage nurse, Olga, said with a smile as she handed Nonna to Nick. Olga was short and overweight, hair tied up inside her nurse's cap. Stains decorated her white uniform and several different baby-related odors floated around her. "She sleep well. Drink bottle. Soon another bottle."

"Spasiva," he replied. Thank you.

Olga hesitated, then made a motion with her hand, circling her face. "Nonna like you. Dark. Dark eyes. Her mother Georgian."

30

Nick nodded and smiled. He had heard from the orphanage director about Nonna's parents. The mother from the republic of Georgia, the father from Russia. According to norms and history, they weren't supposed to like each other. But those two did, quite passionately, and when Nonna came she was quickly shuttled to an orphanage before word got out.

"Perhaps you Georgian, too." Olga said. Nick smiled, nodded and said "perhaps," to keep her happy. If she felt better about a fellow Georgian adopting Nonna, then it would be better for Nonna, too.

Nonna looked at Nick doubtfully. She was eight months old and, like most orphans who didn't get enough to eat, was quite small for her age. Black hair peeked out from under a white knit cap, and she had at least four layers of clothes on, culminating in a pink jumper. The poor thing was sweating in the heat, but they were told never to remove layers of clothes. The orphanage workers erred on the side of being too warm when they dressed the kids. Way too warm.

Nick put his hand on her cheek. She had a heat rash on her nose and forehead, but there wasn't much he could do about that yet. Nine days from now, yes, but not now. Prospective parents weren't the only ones who just had to take it.

He hoisted her on one hip, arm around her waist, and took a bottle from Olga. Nonna clasped her hands together in front of her. Olga had said the kids frequently did this, since nobody else was there to hold their hands. It was their way of coping. The first time Nick heard that, he vowed she would never want for hand-holding once he got her home.

They walked out into the courtyard for some air. It was hot, but fresh relative to the orphanage. There were many tall, leafy trees, but little else, in the courtyard. No play sets or tricycles. Just several benches, paint peeling, scattered around. A sturdy metal fence ringed the courtyard, with the only entrance being the one they had just walked through.

A few other families sat on benches with their kids, playing, talking, or just enjoying each other. Nick sat off to the side with Nonna. He wanted to be with her alone, as this was the first time he had visited the orphanage by himself. Over the few days since they met, Nick had noticed Nonna displayed a distinct preference for women. Olga said this was common, due to the fact that the kids typically only see women in the orphanage. Nick stayed diligent with the razor, but still got the impression Nonna didn't know what to do with him.

He sat her on his knee and brought out a few toys he had jammed in his backpack. A stuffed giraffe and plastic rings were first out, with the rings immediately going into her mouth. She chewed quietly, without expression, like a tiny cow with heat rash.

He pulled a red hat out of his backpack and handed it to her. "Here you go, honey," he said. "Mommy knitted it herself, because she loves you." Nonna looked at it for a moment, then put it in her mouth. Nick watched with amusement as she tasted it. Apparently not finding it appetizing, she took it out of her mouth and abruptly threw it on the ground.

Nick laughed, leaned over, and picked it up. He brushed a few twigs and some dirt off of it, then replaced the old and faded hat she wore with the new one. By that time Nonna was back to playing with the plastic rings.

Nick spent the next hour on the bench with her, in their own little world, just getting to know each other. He bounced her on his knee, played with the toys, fed her thick gruel from a bottle. He noticed the hole in the nozzle had been opened quite a bit to allow the oatmeal stuff to come squirting out when she sucked it, which was vaguely disconcerting to him. They also went inside to change her into a diaper, which was also disconcerting since Kelli had handled diaper duty before. For some reason they couldn't provide diapers to the orphanage, but they could put one on Nonna when they were with her. Nick suspected she wore it most of the day.

Nonna never made a sound. No smiles, either, but she did spend a lot of time exploring Nick's face with her fingers, when she wasn't chewing on toys. At one point she stuck a finger in his mouth. He rewarded it with a Bronx cheer. He thought for a moment she would giggle, but nothing.

He vowed to keep trying.

Too soon, Nick told his daughter he'd be back tomorrow and reluctantly gave her to Olga. He hoped she'd cry when he handed her over, or at least stretch out her arms towards him, but she was pretty stoic about the whole thing. If anything, she seemed relieved to be rid of that odd American man. Nick kissed the top of her head and left her in good hands.

Typically he and Kelli would head back to their hotel room after seeing Nonna, to eat lunch in the air conditioned room during the hottest part of the day. Today, though, Nick decided to walk along the Don River. Kelli had been nervous about going so far from the hotel, so they didn't get around much.

Now it was time to do some exploring.

He knew the river was east, so he hoisted his backpack and found the first busy street going his way. He passed several jewelry shops. He thought it odd that a town with so much poverty also had multiple jewelry shops. Perhaps they were for the New Russians.

Their driver had initially brought up the New Russians when he first drove them to Baby Home Number Four. They passed several SUV's on the way. He pointed to one.

"The New Russians," he told them. "After Gorbachev, a lot changed here. Now the mob owns many things."

"So the mafia drives the SUV's?" Nick asked.

"Yes. They drive the nice cars, eat good beef at the nice restaurants, dress the best, have the most beautiful girlfriends." He stopped, and they didn't get much more out of him on the subject. He didn't sound jealous. He sounded as if he were afraid to be jealous. Nick let it drop.

He passed the jewelry stores without entering.

Chapter 6

Across town, the short man sat behind a desk. He leaned back and steepled his fingers in a way which made him look contemplative, thoughtful. The truth was that he had made up his mind hours ago how this meeting would progress. And so far it had gone completely to plan. But he knew it would, because he was Dmitri and they weren't.

Dmitri Kopolov sat because the pressure on his back was less when he sat, and therefore his left leg, or what remained of his left leg, pained him less. The large wooden desk also hid his leg from anybody who came too close to him, which in his opinion was several feet. He wore long pants, high-quality merchandise from one of the best tailors in Rostov, but he knew people would be looking at his leg, trying to figure out exactly where flesh ended and prosthetic began.

Very few people outside his inner circle knew for sure, but Dmitri's left leg concluded above his knee. The knee was steel, covered by hard molded plastic. The ankle and foot were wood but everything between was plastic. It was the result of three bullets placed there by a Rostov police officer several years before, during a run-in after a drug deal gone bad. The man cornered Dmitri in a warehouse and shot when Dmitri charged him. For some inexplicable reason the man had aimed low. Dmitri was in the hospital for several weeks and never walked normally again.

It had taken nearly a year, but Dmitri finally caught up with the cop late one night. The man was bound by rope in the basement of Dmitri's estate, then systematically shot in both arms and both legs. After the third shot the man begged Dmitri to kill him, but Dmitri wasn't finished. He pumped three bullets into the man's left leg, above the knee, and left him hanging for two hours. It would've been longer but by then the man had lost consciousness and Dmitri had grown weary of revenge. He put one final bullet in the man's skull, cut him down, and delivered his body, along with flowers, to his widow.

Two years later, a rival called Dmitri a gimp. It wasn't to his face or the man wouldn't have survived the day. It was to a colleague, and word quickly got back to Dmitri. The next day the rival was delivered, unconscious, to a local hospital. There a team of doctors quickly and professionally severed his left leg above the knee. He spent months learning how to walk again.

Dmitri paid for the prosthetic and sent a get well card to the man's home after he left the hospital.

Nobody ever mentioned the leg again.

The man across the desk from Dmitri was understandably nervous. He sat as still as possible in the metal chair, and kept his eyes as high as he could without raising Dmitri's ire. He looked carefully at Dmitri's thick black hair, or at his shoulders or arms, now strong from compensating for weakened legs, and didn't say anything.

Dmitri kept the man waiting, on edge, for several moments. Finally he opened his fingers and leaned forward, looking the man in the eyes.

"So what would you have me do, Anton?" he asked. His voice was soft, but there was no mistaking the menace. "We have a deal for your protection."

Anton gulped. "Yes, Mr. Kopolov, we have a deal, but business hasn't been good. With this economy, people don't come in to buy furniture so much…" he trailed off, realizing how weak he sounded.

"I don't care how your business is," Dmitri said. He kept his voice low. "What I know is that you told my men you didn't have my July payment. Now what kind of businessman would I be if I let that go?"

Anton gulped again, and visibly paled. "I can get you the money, Dmitri."

"How? You said business is off."

"Well, umm…" Anton stammered, then the words poured out in a rush. "Perhaps you can loan me the money. I'd pay you back, but it will just take a little more time."

Dmitri relaxed a bit. He was Dmitri and they weren't. "I think we could work something out. But I require collateral now, since you have proven not to be such an astute businessman, and I must protect my interests."

"What collateral?"

Dmitri spread his hands out. "Nothing too much, I'm a fair man. Inventory equal to twice your July payment will suffice. And

35

your monthly payment will be twenty percent higher now, to compensate me for my troubles."

"But…but…" Anton fell silent. As they always do.

"Would you like to see what will happen if you don't make your next payment?" Dmitri asked.

Anton looked like he definitely did not want to see what would happen if he didn't make his next payment, but he nodded anyway.

Dmitri glanced at the large guard standing near the doorway and inclined his head slightly. The man opened the door and a second man, even larger than the first, walked in, pushing a woman ahead of him. One meaty paw was fastened on her arm, and she struggled against his grip.

She spied her husband sitting with Dmitri and let out a small gasp. "Anton…" she said.

Anton whirled around in his chair and groaned at the sight of his wife. Forgetting where he was for a moment, he started to get out of his chair.

"Sit down!" Dmitri yelled. Anton collapsed back into the chair but did not take his eyes off his wife. His body tensed and his hands gripped the sides of his chair tightly as his wife was dragged around to Dmitri's side of the desk. She cringed away from Dmitri as he snaked an arm around her waist. The bodyguard blocked her path, standing over her with his arms crossed.

Dmitri pulled her toward him. She stumbled and sat down hard on his lap, then tried to back off by putting her hands on his shoulders and pushing. Dmitri grinned and pulled her closer until she stopped struggling.

Dmitri gave Anton a look of triumph. "You see, little man," he said to Anton, who appeared to be trying very hard not to launch himself across the desk. "It's not just you who suffers when you fail. I'll find your family and make them pay."

"I'll pay you!" Anton shouted, rising from his seat. The bodyguard behind him put a restraining hand on his shoulder, but the shopkeeper shrugged him off, and Dmitri waved the bodyguard back. He wanted to hear what Anton had to say.

"I'll pay you, dammit," Anton said through clenched teeth. "There's no need to do anything to my family. You'll get your money on your terms." Twin tears rolled down his cheeks as he looked at his terrified wife.

Dmitri ignored him and turned to the woman on his lap. "Your name is Larissa, is it not?"

She paused. Nodded. She didn't look at him.

"You are a beautiful woman."

She struggled a bit in his lap at that, not comfortable with where his thoughts might be heading.

His right arm tightened around her as he reached into his desk with his left hand. It came out holding a small object. Larissa struggled harder as she realized it was a knife.

"Your husband tried to cheat me," Dmitri said as he held the knife up to inspect it. The blade was small, only a few inches, the type used to trim nails, but it gave Larissa no comfort. "He's unable to pay me what he owes me."

"No," Anton moaned, beginning to panic. "I'll pay you!"

"He tells me this," Dmitri said to Larissa, clucking his tongue and trying his best to look sad. "I'm concerned he's not being truthful."

"I am!" Anton protested. Dmitri ignored him. He pressed the blade to Larissa's left cheek. She flinched and a small drop of blood appeared at the point of the blade. She closed her eyes, tears squeezing out from the sides.

"Your husband needs to learn to pay his debts," Dmitri said. "He needs to learn to be a businessman. Perhaps all he needs is proper motivation."

He pressed the point into her skin. Larissa let out a moan and began to struggle in his grip. The bodyguard next to her stepped sideways and grabbed the top of her head, holding it in place as Dmitri dragged the knife down her cheek, three inches, four. Blood poured out over the blade and ran down Dmitri's hand as he carved a straight line to her chin. She squeezed her eyes shut from the pain. Tears flowed out and mingled with the blood.

Anton finally had had enough. He let out a roar and lunged at Dmitri. He was stopped short by the second bodyguard, who reached forward, grabbed Anton's shoulders from behind, and pulled him backwards into his chair. Anton landed roughly and struggled against the harsh pressure on his shoulders.

Dmitri finally stopped cutting. He pulled out a white handkerchief from his pocket and handed it to Larissa, who immediately thrust it onto the cut. Dmitri pulled out a second handkerchief and wiped his knife and hand on it, turning it red. He tossed the handkerchief into a wastebasket under the desk, and turned to Anton.

"Now perhaps you'll take me more seriously," he told the crying shopkeeper. "You'll not want to see what happens to your lovely Larissa if you miss another payment."

He let go of Larissa, who immediately got up and rushed around the desk to Anton. She stopped short of her husband, however, and glared at him.

Dmitri laughed. "You think it's bad now," he told the shaken shopkeeper. "Just wait until it heals and she sees the scar every morning. She'll blame you for destroying her beauty, you know."

He waved an arm. "Now leave. I'll send a man to you tomorrow to discuss our new arrangements."

After the door closed Dmitri leaned back and lit a cigarette. It was good to be Dmitri.

"Here, Mikhail," the boss said. "Marines. Left eight years ago. Iraq, mainly." He paused, and his heartbeat sped up slightly. "Recon Marines," he said, almost proudly.

"Special Forces?" Mikhail asked, leaning forward.

"Yes," the second man said as he read. "Definitely Force Recon, although they don't say as much here."

"Can you find details?" the bodyguard asked.

"Eventually," the second man replied. "But the details are not important. His being a Recon Marine is what's important." He turned around in his leather chair to look at the bodyguard. "And you say he attacked Sergei and Vlad only after they went after his friend?"

"Yes."

"And it was triggered by…"

"The prostitute. The one Maxsim beat up. Vlad thinks this Nick was angry because she had been hurt. He thought the man wanted to tear Maxsim apart even before Sergei got there."

The second man thought hard. "Hmmm, Recon Marine. Chivalrous."

Mikhail subconsciously rubbed his scar. "He could be very dangerous."

The other man nodded. "He could be very dangerous, indeed."

He smiled.

Chapter 7

The Don River flowed through the southern edge of Rostov, separating the city from the fields beyond. Connecting Rostov to the Caususes, Turkey, and beyond, it played a major part in making the city one of the main ports in southern Russia and a major hub of commerce.

At least, that was what the guide book said. Nick put it down and stared at the river. Vital or not, the water was brown and uninviting, and he had no plan to jump in it any time soon. He was sure there was a lot of history there, but he was more interested in the truck parked on grass near the river. The truck was large and had a picture of a very happy hot dog dancing with a very happy hamburger, big grins on their meaty faces. It was an eerie picture, Nick decided, but it made him hungry.

He sighed, got up, and walked across the street to the truck. It was hot, and he was thirsty. An ecstatic bottle of soda on the side of the truck, spindly arms waving wildly, beckoned him.

He lined up behind several teens who boisterously ordered food and drink. He stood back a few feet and watched what they were doing, since he hadn't ordered before from somebody who didn't speak English. The large Russian man in an extremely dirty, formerly white t-shirt behind the counter most likely didn't speak a word of it.

The kids took their food and moved to concrete tables set permanently on the grass by the river, several feet from the truck. Nick stepped up and pointed to a rack of hot dogs slowly spinning behind the man. He held up one finger and somewhat self-consciously said, "One hot dog, please."

The man narrowed his eyes and held up his hands in the universal sign of confusion. Nick tried again, pointing more strongly. Nothing.

He heard shuffling and knew the people behind him were witnessing the scene. He pantomimed the shape of a hot dog with his hands and heard a giggle over his shoulder.

Face burning, he thought about the happy hot dog on the truck, just a few feet to his right. He slapped the painted metal hog dog and raised his finger again, but the cook just glared at him.

Laughter floated up from the kids at the tables. He glanced over and saw them looking at him. He waved to a tall, lanky kid with most of his dog left to come over, but the kid just grinned and shook his head. Nick motioned again. The kid turned away and the teens laughed again.

Frustrated, Nick marched over to the group and grabbed the hot dog out of the startled teen's hand. Seconds later he was back in front of the cook. He shook the tube of questionable meat in the man's face and said "Adin," which he knew was Russian for one.

The man sighed, turned, and started to put a hot dog together for Nick. Nick turned, walked back to the group of kids, and tossed the hot dog to the teen. The boy caught it awkwardly and stared at Nick, who said "Spasiva" with a glare.

He paid and grabbed the dog and drink silently. He was disgusted, but also relieved he had food and drink in hand. He considered it a victory, even though the trophy might shorten his life.

He turned and came face-to-face with a grinning, dark-haired woman. She was next in line but her attention was on him, not the man behind the counter.

"You handled that well," she said. "I wasn't sure if you were going to end up with a hot dog or not."

Nick was still disgusted. "He's an idiot," he said.

"No, he's not," she replied. "Boris just doesn't like people who can't speak Russian."

"You know him?"

"Oh, sure. I come here often. Hold on." She turned to Boris, flashed him a bright smile, and ordered lunch in fluent Russian. The cook's demeanor changed instantly. Without a glance at Nick, he laughed and said something to her in a loud, booming voice. She laughed in return and glanced at Nick, who groaned.

"What did he say?" Nick asked.

She grabbed her lunch, cheeseburger in a paper basket in one hand and bottle of cola in the other, and walked towards a table with him. She giggled again as she told him, "Boris just said he thought you were going to eat that poor kid's hot dog."

Nick grunted. "I would have, too, if Boris hadn't given that dog up!" She laughed again.

He found himself warming to her. She was younger, probably late 20s, with black hair cut in bangs that ended just above

41

her eyes, giving her a punkish appearance. Like most Russians, she wore long pants even in the middle of summer. Their habit annoyed Nick because it meant he had to wear jeans, too, or risk sticking out as an American, but he had to admit jeans looked pretty good on her.

"Mind if I join you?" she asked.

Nick motioned to a table. "Sure, have a seat. Minya savoot Nick." It felt good to be able to air out one of the few Russian phrases he knew.

Her eyes lit up. "Ahhh, so you do know a bit of Russian! I'm impressed. You should've said that to Boris. Maybe he would've given you your lunch sooner."

Nick glanced over at the food truck. "Sour old man," he muttered at he glared at the dancing meat on the side of the vehicle. "He shouldn't have such a happy looking truck if he's going to be so grumpy."

She laughed again. Nick decided he liked her laugh. "Oh, he's harmless. My name's Anya, by the way." She wiped her hand on a napkin and stuck it out. "Nice to meet you."

"Nice to meet you, too, Anya," he said as they shook. "So you're Russian?"

"Da."

"Your English is excellent. Where did you learn it?"

"Thank you," she said around a mouthful of burger. "My father made sure I learned English when I was a kid, and I've been to England several times with him, once for several months."

"Did you like it?"

"I did! Although, well, we had to leave rather quickly the last time, and I'm not sure we'll go back."

Nick raised his eyebrows. "That sounds like an interesting story!"

She sighed. "It is, but you'll probably never hear it. Papa'd kill me if I ever told anyone."

They ate their meal in a comfortable silence for a few minutes, watching the barges make their way along the Don. The sun was high but it was just starting to get hot. It would be another glorious day in Rostov.

"So, what brings you to Russia?" Anya asked as she took a sip of coke. She wiped the bottle on her cheeks to cool them.

Nick remembered Lauren's advice. "I'm here on business."

She looked at him a long time, then said, "Liar."

"Excuse me?"

Anya smiled. "Yes, you could be here on business. But I think you're here to adopt a baby."

Nick sighed. "Why do you say that?"

"You're trying to blend in," she answered. "Trying to dress like a Russian, being here on your own. Businessmen seem to like to, how do you say, flaunt their watches and nice clothes. You look normal."

"Thank you, I guess."

"Where's your wife? With your child?"

Nick took another bite of hot dog before answering. The tube steak was actually pretty good, although he assumed a large part of that had to do with how hungry he was. It was spicier than a normal dog. He didn't plan on having too many more, but this one wasn't bad.

"No," he answered. "She went back to the states."

Anya's eyes widened. "Why would she do that? Doesn't she like Russia?"

"She likes Russia fine," he said. He explained the whole ten-day rule and how she would spend time with their son while he waited to retrieve their daughter. When he talked to Americans he used the word "rescue," but he refrained from phrasing it that way to Anya.

Anya was astonished. "So you have to wait for ten days to get your daughter, even though the paperwork is complete?"

Nick shrugged. "I don't know if it's completed or not but yes, I'm here for another week. But you know, I'm looking forward to exploring your town and Nonna's heritage."

Anya's eyes flashed and she slapped one hand on the table. "Well, you must let me show you around then! I'll play your tour guide."

Nick wasn't so sure that was a good idea, with her looking so cute in her jeans. On the other hand, there were many things she could tell him about Rostov that he could pass on to Kelli and Nonna when he returned. A week with Anya would most likely pay dividends to his baby girl as she grew up. Maybe they'd even correspond later in life so she had a connection back to her homeland.

43

He knew he was just talking himself into it so he could spend time with Anya, but decided to go with it anyway. He had no interest in dallying and was sure he could handle himself if she got the wrong idea.

They finished their meal and walked around by the river for over an hour, Anya giving him a history lesson on Russia in general and Rostov in particular.

"The Nazis first came in 1941," she said as she swung an arm out over the Don. "But it was in the winter and they were only here a week. Our army attacked and pushed them back, and this is as far as they got." She sounded proud.

"Was your family here then?" Nick asked.

She nodded. "My grandmother was, yes. My grandfather had been forced into the army, so she hid in a house with her sister until the fascists left. When the Hitlerites came back later, she went east with her sister until we threw them out for good."

"That must've been tough," Nick said.

"Yes, it was. She used to tell lots of stories about it. We're a tough family, though, especially the women. It takes more than the German army to push us around!"

Nick laughed. He liked her already.

Nick had long since lost his bearings when Anya brought them back to a familiar road. She pointed to the west. "Your hotel is that way," she said. "It's several kilometers, I hope your feet are not worn out."

"Nah, I'll be fine," Nick said. "I'm just getting started."

She glanced at him coyly. "Then perhaps you are strong enough to come back tonight and see me. I work at a very nice restaurant."

"Which one is that?"

"The Café Olymp, down the block. Have you ever seen it?"

Nick shrugged. "I wouldn't know, to tell you the truth."

"Two stories, white columns in the front. It's a fun place. I've worked there for years. We have some of the best steaks in the city. Corn fed beef from the Ukraine."

He licked his lips. After the hot dog, steak sounded great.

She noticed and laughed. "You must come. I'll personally serve you one of our best steaks from the back room."

Nick nodded. A good steak, conversation with Anya, and half a town away from Sergei. It sounded like just what he needed.

Chapter 8

Lately Dmitri felt as if he were in the middle of a video game, one of those violent ones his enforcers played. Things kept coming at him from all directions, demanding his attention. Nothing was trivial, and if he didn't deal with an issue in a timely manner, it would grow until it swallowed him up.

And his damn stump hurt. Late afternoon was typically the worst for him. He had to move around all day, dealing with crisis upon crisis that needed his attention, so that by dinnertime the lotion he applied liberally to where the stump met his prosthesis had worn down. On a slow day he would take fifteen minutes to remove the leg and give his body a break, but lately the days hadn't been slow.

It seemed everybody wanted a piece of his pie.

He'd spent nearly twenty years marking his territory. He started out selling videotapes on a street corner, but his interests quickly led him to a profitable career dealing drugs. He never took them himself, of course, because drugs dimmed your instincts and your desire, and Dmitri was nothing without his instincts and desire. But he had no problem helping others overcome their desires. Or at least change what they desired.

Dmitri had grown up in a poor family, with three brothers and a sister in a small flat that usually contained his father, drunk in a chair by the window. His mother supported the family as best she could by constantly cleaning up other peoples' messes, but her pay barely provided the basics.

Unlike his siblings, who made do with what they had and didn't think much about it, Dmitri knew he was poor. In those days, prior to Gorbachev, the rich people were generally out of sight. But Dmitri saw families who had enough to eat, who had clothes to wear, and toys to play with. He pledged to himself that one day he'd be rich. And his family, especially his drunken father, would get none of it. When he made enough money to survive on his own from his videotape sales, he moved out of the flat and severed ties with his family. None of his family members came after him, begging, which annoyed him even more.

It was a natural progression from drugs to prostitution. As people used more and more of his heroin and cocaine, they came to him in crisis, broke, willing to barter anything. The poor ones came first, since they had fewer assets to draw against. Initially Dmitri traded his drugs for gold watches, rings, or bracelets at an obscene exchange rate. After that came family heirlooms. Gradually his wealthier clients began approaching him on their knees, willing to give up more gold, cameras, even cars in exchange for drugs.

Many of those trophies now adorned a wall in Dmitri's office. Dmitri liked to stand in front of the wall and just stare at them. Gold, diamonds, jewelery. It reminded Dmitri where he came from. And it was worth a fortune. Probably the most expensive wall in Rostov, Dmitri thought.

Dmitri's wealth grew dramatically during those years, making him richer than even he thought he would ever be. But he kept pushing, looking for new revenue streams. He knew he'd never be satisfied.

Eventually his clients began to run out of material goods to barter. They came to him more desperate, more pathetic than ever. He reminded them they still had one thing left to give, especially his female users or the wives or sisters of his male clients. And so prostitution provided another avenue to the riches Dmitri coveted.

The growth of his prostitution business led Dmitri to hire several large, discreet men to function as his pimps. As his empire grew, Dmitri moved some of the larger and more menacing men into a new job: protection.

His phone rang. Dmitri sighed and glanced at the caller ID. He pressed a button and said, "Yes, Boris."

"I'm having trouble with Anton," Boris, one of the enforcers, said. His voice was low and hurried. He was a man afraid to give bad news.

"What kind of trouble?"

"I'm, uh, requisitioning the furniture you requested. He's not cooperating."

"Put him on."

A pause, a brief muffled conversation, then Anton's voice on the other end of the connection. "Yes?" he said.

"Anton, have you forgotten our agreement yesterday?" Dmitri said. He kept his voice quiet. He knew it got more results than yelling.

"No, of course not, Dmitri. But your man wants to take my best pieces! I can pay you back easier if I can sell my furniture."

Now Dmitri's voice rose. "Anton, I don't give a fuck how you get the money, but you'll pay me what you owe me! And you'll forfeit what I say you'll forfeit. Do you understand?"

A pause, then "Yes, Dmitri."

"You love your wife, correct?"

Another pause.

"Yes, Dmitri."

"And you want her to be safe."

"Yes."

"Well, if you fuck me over, you'll lose her! And not just her beauty!"

Another pause while Dmitri looked over his notes. "You have a daughter as well," he said. It was a statement, not a question.

Silence on the line.

"She's thirteen, if I remember right. You must be very careful, Anton. Some of my men like young girls. Right now I can control them, but if you don't honor your agreement…" his voice trailed off, leaving the threat unspoken.

Anton replied, voice soft and defeated. "Of course I'll honor my agreement, Dmitri. Your man can take what he pleases."

"You are a wise man, Anton," Dmitri replied. "I give my clients one do-over. You've had yours. From now on I expect you to keep your word."

Anton sighed, the sound loud on the line. Dmitri was not elated. He knew submission was inevitable. He disconnected the call and turned to the men sitting across from him.

Maxsim and Scrgci had heard everything, which was precisely the point. But the threats didn't affect the two men as much as they would have affected most others, which was why Dmitri had plucked them off the street years ago.

Sergei sat still, composed, staring at something over Dmitri's head. Maxsim, however, fidgeted in his chair. He pounded his right fist into his thigh. Perhaps it was nerves, perhaps he was coming down. Whatever it was, Dmitri planned to ignore it for now. He ignored many things about Max because the man delivered. Whatever gene drove fear in men was absent from Max, key when dealing with drug runners and other lowlifes who used his girls at the brothel.

But it had its downside as well. Dmitri had to send men to clean up after Max killed somebody who offended him, who offended one of his men, or who was just in the wrong place. On the other hand, the number of offenders had gone down in recent years.

"So, what happened at the club last night?" Dmitri asked.

"Nothing we can't handle," Sergei said. He eyed his boss calmly. Despite having known him for several years, many things about Sergei were still hidden from Dmitri. Oh, he knew where the man lived, who he lived with, and whom to threaten if the man ever got out of line. He knew Sergei had gained a reputation for ruthlessness against rebels, which helped him gain a spot in Dmitri's operation.

What he didn't understand was why the man was so damn calm. In periods of honesty to himself, Dmitri wondered if he really had as much control over the man as he thought. But so far it worked, and he could always shoot him and dump the body in the Don if he caused issues. It had happened before to similar types. So Dmitri wasn't too worried. He was, after all, Dmitri.

"I didn't ask if you could handle it, Sergei," Dmitri said. "I asked what happened. One of my men is in the hospital this morning, and that isn't good for business."

"We're shaking down a tourist who slept with one of Max's whores," Sergei replied. Max nodded vigorously, proud to be a part of it. "One of his friends wanted to get involved. He sucker-punched Vlad and then pulled a knife on me. We took care of it."

Maxsim's right fist continued to pound on his thigh rhythmically. Dmitri assumed the man had used before coming to see him, which was annoying but not worth bringing up unless Max got out of hand.

Dmitri knew it hadn't happened quite like Sergei said. He knew the second American had put Vlad on the ground and then turned Sergei's own weapon on him. This couldn't be tolerated. It showed weakness.

"Word around the club was that you were saved by a woman," Dmitri said.

Sergei stiffened.

"This man got the drop on you, and the only reason your head is still attached to the rest of your body is that the woman made a deal with you."

Sergei relaxed and smiled. "Perhaps it appeared that way. But I had already won. She saved *him*. For now. But we know where he's staying. We'll take care of him."

Dmitri nodded. Sergei had not backed down. Not last night, and more importantly not now, to him. He had picked the right man. As usual.

"You need to make it right, Sergei," Dmitri said. "Who is this man?"

"Just some American."

"An *American* put you down?" Dmitri asked with derision. He rubbed his forehead in mock disgust. He knew all along it had been an American. "Americans are weak, Sergei, soft. My men shouldn't be bested by a westerner."

Maxsim looked ready to explode. His face reddened and the pounding on his leg grew harder. "This man was *not* weak. He was big, and violent." His head still hurt from the night before. The coke helped a bit, but Maxsim still wished he could lie down in a dark room.

But when Dmitri calls, you obey.

Dmitri leaned back in his chair and turned his attention to Maxsim. "My people don't get sent to the hospital by westerners. Perhaps you've become soft from the whores and coke I supply you with."

Maxsim went still.

"Show me what you are made of, both of you," Dmitri said. "Find this man and take him down. And do it so people *see*. I cannot have people questioning our power."

Maxsim and Sergei stood up. They knew when meetings with the boss were done. "We will, Dmitri," Sergei said. "We know where to start."

After they left, Mikhail entered through a side door. Dmitri leaned back and sighed, rubbing his stump. Mikhail was one of the few people who saw Dmitri in a time of weakness.

"You heard?" Dmitri asked.

"Da," Mikhail replied. "Sergei and Max have declared war on the Americans."

Dmitri laughed. "I wouldn't want to be American right now."

Mikhail smiled, scar crinkling in the light. "No, certainly not."

"Do you know anything about this American, the one who put Vlad in the hospital?"

Mikhail shook his head. "Nothing. Except that we won't have to worry about him tomorrow."

Dmitri laughed again. It was good to be Dmitri.

Chapter 9

Nick stood outside Anya's restaurant. It was six o'clock in the evening and he was back near the river. He hadn't seen the other Americans during the afternoon, which suited him just fine. He figured they were off visiting their kids. He knew Alexei, Tom and Michelle's son, was in Taganrog, a small town on the Black Sea ninety minutes away from Rostov. He felt bad for Tom and Michelle. Not only did they have to drive three hours round-trip to see their son every day, but their driver charged them one hundred dollars to be on call. After paying the price of a BMW SUV to get this far, a hundred dollars did not seem like much, but it was much easier to just walk to Baby Home Number Four.

He spied the white building across the street from the river. It read "Olymp" in huge red Cyrillic letters across the top. Two impressive-looking staircases led from the ground level to a balcony, one on each side of large double doors. It was very well cared for, which set it apart from other buildings nearby. He could see red-and-white umbrellas on the balcony. Sure looked like a restaurant to him.

Nick crossed the street and walked up to the double doors. They were frosted glass, and the one on the right had a menu with Cyrillic letters pasted to it. He was able to recognize words for chicken and beef. Prices were a bit high, but in this case he took it to mean quality, especially after what Anya had said. He went in.

The entryway was dim and air-conditioned, a welcome contrast to the heat outside. Classical music played softly through hidden speakers, loud enough to provide ambiance but soft enough for patrons to converse. Nick heard a few voices from deeper in the building, but couldn't see any customers; the seating area was through a small door on the other side of the room.

The walls were dark wood paneling, and expensive-looking vases adorned recesses every several feet. Nick felt underdressed in his jeans and polo shirt, one of the fanciest shirts he had brought, but a delicious smell coming from that small door kept him waiting.

He didn't have to wait long. The room was empty when he entered but within seconds a young woman in a low-cut red shirt and black skirt came out to greet him. Her dark hair was up and she wore glasses, which gave her a slightly haughty appearance. But she gave Nick a nice smile and asked in Russian if she could help him. At least, that's what he thought she asked.

Nick held up one finger, pointed to a stack of menus, and asked, "English?" She smiled again, grabbed one from behind the podium, and held it out to him. He read "Café Olymp" and a list of entrees in English. He grinned back and nodded.

She led Nick through the doorway. The seating area was as ornate as the entryway, but only a few tables were in use at the early hour. A few older couples looked up as they passed. Nick noticed he brought the median age of the customers down significantly.

"In or out?" the hostess asked, pointing up toward the balcony. Nick replied, "Where is Anya?" The hostess, with a gleam in her eye, said, "Ahh, you are Nick?"

Nick smiled and was pretty sure he blushed a bit. "Da," he replied.

"I bring you to her," the hostess said with a wink.

They walked up an inside staircase and emerged onto a large patio. Several round, white tables were dispersed around, each with one of the red and white umbrellas Nick had seen from the street.

The patio was empty except for three twenty-somethings sitting around a table in the corner, chatting and laughing. A man and two women. One of the women was dressed in the red shirt and black skirt of the Olymp. Anya. The guy wore a black shirt and gray sportcoat, while the other woman had on a yellow sun dress. Nick saw a sandaled foot peeking out from under the table, bright red on the toes.

Nick raised his hand in greeting to Anya, who returned it with a big smile.

The hostess waved her arm around the tables, indicating Nick had his pick of spots. He chose one near the edge, so he could look out and see the river. She pulled out a chair and placed the menu on the table while he sat.

The music on the patio was more upbeat. Nick listened to Mick Jagger sing about how he wanted to paint it black while he looked through the menu. Nick's mouth watered for the steak but he wanted to see what else they had. Pretty much everything, he found.

Anya stood up, stretched languidly, and glided over to Nick. She looked taller and thinner in her red and black Von outfit. He had to admit the uniform accentuated her curves nicely.

"Zdrastvoytye, Mr. Nick," she said to him formally, and grinned.

He ordered a Baltica on tap, and she disappeared for a few minutes. When she returned she also carried a bowl of unshelled peanuts in a small wicker basket.

"I heard Americans love to eat peanuts with their beer," she said.

Nick cracked a peanut open and tossed the nuts into his mouth. He pointed to the chair next to him. "Want some?"

She looked around briefly, then slid into the chair.

Nick looked at her, eyes wide. "Seriously?"

She shrugged and smiled. "Well, we're not busy yet."

They chatted for several minutes about nothing in particular. Eventually she said, "Can I ask you a personal question?"

An alarm bell began to ring in Nick's head. "Perhaps," he said.

"Why do you come to Russia to adopt? Are you not able to make your own babies?" She said it with a worried look on her face. "You can tell me to go away if you want."

"No, no, that's OK," Nick said. "You're not the first person to ask that. We tried to…make babies, but it didn't work out so well. We were going to try something new when our doctor died in a car accident. We took that as a sign to adopt."

"But why Russia? Aren't there American babies for you to adopt?"

"There are, but it takes a long time because there are so many couples who want to adopt. Plus, the birth parents can change their mind and take their baby back. I'm not sure I could handle that." He took a deep breath; just thinking about it made him queasy. "So we decided to go international. Adopting from Russia is much faster than adopting from other countries, like China or Korea. It's more expensive, but quicker." He shrugged. "We had more money than time, I guess."

She looked sad. "It's a pity you had to make that choice."

"It is what it is. You should see Nonna, though. She's awesome!"

54

Anya smiled. "I'd love to meet her some day!"

A young couple emerged onto the patio. Anya saw them, sighed, and stood up. "Here it comes, time to get back to work."

Nick was sorry to see her go. "Stop back if you get a chance," he said.

She smiled. "OK, I will."

He hoisted his beer at her. "I'm sure I'll need a refill."

She gave Nick a glare, then turned away and walked to the couple. She popped him the finger behind her back, and Nick laughed. It had been a long time since he had flirted.

For the next few hours he watched the patrons as they arrived and began enjoying themselves. He watched Anya. He watched the two she had left at the table. He was good at watching. Anya would stop by periodically with a new Baltica, so by the end of the time Nick was not quite as observant as earlier in the evening. However, he did notice how homogenous the clientele was. Young, beautiful, well dressed, obviously with money. He suspected he knew where the money came from.

Anya stopped by with her two friends later in the evening. "This is my cousin, Andrei," she said. "And his girlfriend, Svetlana."

Andrei was dark like his cousin, and had a sideways grin that made Nick like him immediately. He sat next to Nick and said, "So, I hear you're American!"

"Yes," Nick replied. "And I hear you're Russian!"

Andrei slammed his fist on the table and laughed heartily. Nick was sure part of it was his nature and part of it was the beer. "Yes, a member of the Evil Empire, as your President Reagan used to say."

Nick tipped his mug towards him. "Here's to the end of that nonsense," he said. Andrei and Svetlana joined in the toast, and they were on their way.

Several more toasts followed. Anya came back frequently, and as the evening wore on she rested her hand on Nick's shoulder as she stood next to him.

Several people stopped by to say hello, and Nick got the impression Andrei was pretty much a permanent fixture on the patio. Svetlana was quieter, preferring to talk to people one-on-one. She also drank a lot less than Andrei.

At one point, after the Balticas started to take their toll, Nick asked Andrei what exactly he did for a living.

The beer obviously was taking its toll on Andrei as well, because he leaned in close and said, "I'm an enforcer. You don't want me showing up at your door."

Nick sat back, saying nothing.

Darkness fell and tiki lanterns were lit. They reminded Nick that he still had a long walk home in the dark, so he got up to say his goodbyes.

"You must let me drive you home!" Andrei insisted. Nick told him, quite honestly, that he would feel safer walking home alone than having Andrei drive in his condition.

He pooh-poohed Nick. "Russians know how to drink!" he boomed. Of that Nick had no doubt, but he insisted that Andrei stay at the restaurant and have more fun. Reluctantly, Andrei gave in. Nick said goodbye to everybody, and Anya walked him to the door.

"It's safe out there, right?" Nick asked her.

She nodded. "As long as you stay on this main street, you'll be OK." Her eyes suddenly twinkled. "But you know, my flat is not far from here. If you want, we could go back there for the night."

"I'd love to," Nick said, "but I have to get up early in the morning, to see my daughter." He emphasized the last word, to make sure she caught the meaning. He put his hand on her shoulder. "But if I was single, I'd definitely take you up on your offer."

Anya sighed and forced a smile. "I understand. I thought you might say that, but I wanted to ask."

"Thank you."

"And your baby is a good reason for not wanting to sleep with me, no?" she asked.

Nick had to agree, although it was getting more difficult. He kissed her forehead and said, "Good night, Anya."

"Good night, Nick. Will I see you again?"

He grinned. "Promise! Maybe even tomorrow. Your food is excellent." He winked. "And so's the company."

Anya put a hand on Nick's arm and said, "Wait." She dashed off to the kitchen and came back with a small flashlight. "Here, take this. You can bring it back tomorrow."

He thanked her, walked out the door, and took a left onto the sidewalk. The road to the hotel was lit, but not as bright as he would have liked. He flicked on the flashlight and trudged up the slight incline, whistling a David Bowie tune and feeling good.

He didn't even think to look behind him.

Chapter 10

In hindsight, Nick knew he should have noticed the two men tailing him, but drowsiness and beer kept him from being very observant on the way home. He walked along behind the beam of the flashlight for several blocks, then turned it off when the road became brighter.

He thought about Anya and the restaurant. He hoped he hadn't offended her, but he wasn't at all interested in dallying. Although if he was, Nick had to admit she'd be a great person to dally around with. She seemed to take it well, and the fact that she didn't cry or hit him impressed Nick even more.

He sighed and crossed a road. There were few streetlights around, and those in operation cast a sickly yellow glow over the mostly deserted streets. It was before midnight, but people turned in early around here, he guessed. The lights on the other side of the avenue were out, so he flicked the flashlight back on.

After going half a block in the darkness, Nick heard a sound behind him. He glanced back and saw two men coming up fast, so he stepped out of their way, holding the flashlight so it illuminated the ground in front of him.

They slowed. Nick couldn't get a good look at them in the darkness, except to see they were big, and he didn't want to shine his flashlight on them.

They wore coats on the warm evening, but that oddity didn't come to Nick until it was too late. He saw both of them reach into their pockets, which was about the time the bells started ringing in his head.

"Hello, dead man," one of them said. In English.

One thing Nick always valued about military training was, if you did it long enough and took it seriously enough, your body knew what it had to do without getting your mind involved. Time slows and you don't think, you just react.

So, he didn't really remember the eight seconds that followed. Yet, looking back, he knew exactly what happened.

One: he flipped the flashlight up to highlight the men so he could see what he was dealing with. Their hands came out of the coats and he was relieved to see one with a knife and the other with a metal bar. No guns. Big mistake on their part. Guns are ideal for attack because you don't have to get in close. With knives and blunt instruments you need to wade into the fight. Heavy metal bars ranked way down Nick's list of weapons of choice. They throw off your balance when you swing them, and you end up with uncontrolled momentum if you miss.

Two: Nick continued the arc of the flashlight so it flew in the air, the light spinning wildly. He could sense both men following it with their eyes. They would have been less than human not to. They held their weapons in front of them, momentarily forgotten.

Three: Nick went for the man with the knife first, the one on his left. He was holding it in his right hand, blade out. Mistake number two: he should have held it in his fist next to his body, with the blade pointing down and towards him to protect from exactly what Nick did next. The American kicked out with his right foot, connecting with the wrist that held the knife, and the blade spun away into the darkness. The man's arm extended in the same direction, leaving his ribs exposed.

Four: Nick ducked in close and pounded his attacker's rib cage with three staccato jabs, right, left, right. The man folded in pain and Nick finished him off with an uppercut. Not enough to break ribs or jaw, but the guy was unconscious before he hit the ground. Nick swung on the second man, the first one instantly disregarded.

Five: the remaining attacker began to swing the bar. Unfortunately for him, he did what he had to do to get any velocity on the bar: he swung it *away* from Nick in a backhanded motion with his right hand. In his defense, he really had no option after placing the bar in his right hand, the one nearest Nick. Before he could complete the motion, Nick was on him.

Six: Nick saw the man's elbow thrust out towards him as the bar hit the apex of the backswing. Nick smashed into it hard with the heel of his hand, the force of his blow causing the ball of the elbow to move one way, the weight of the swinging bar pulling it the other way. Nick felt rather than heard the elbow joint crack.

Seven: the attacker's wrist, now overextended and with no muscle control, opened and the bar began to drop. His eyes widened and Nick knew the next sound out of his mouth would be a howl of pain. Nick head-butted him savagely, bone on bone, before any sound came out. The bones in the head, especially at the top of the forehead, are among the hardest in the human body, and Nick's head was harder than most. When Nick connected with the man's lower forehead, between and just above the eyes, the attacker went down on his back. Hard. He beat the bar to the concrete slab and Nick swore he bounced higher.

Eight: Nick stood over the men, waiting to see if they would move. They didn't.

Eight seconds, two men down. He'd done worse, Nick thought.

Nick swung the heavy hotel room door shut and clicked the deadbolt. Then he checked it to make sure it was secure. He took a deep breath as reaction started to hit. It had been years since he had put men on the ground.

"So what the hell happened?" Nick heard behind him. He turned to face Tom. He had run into his friend in the hotel foyer, and he was sure Tom immediately knew something was up. Nick didn't have a scratch on him, but he was breathing hard and had a wild look in his eyes. They had walked silently up the wide, carpeted stairs to their rooms and retrieved their room keys from the Key Lady. Nick appreciated that Tom hadn't asked anything until they got to his room.

"I was mugged," Nick said.

"Holy crap!" Tom said. "Did they take your wallet?"

Nick shook his head. "No, I managed to get away. It was pretty scary, though."

"No doubt. Wow, I've never heard of that happening around here." "Well," Nick replied, "It was closer to the river. I was on my way back from dinner."

"Yeah, we missed you at the Chicken Shack."

Nick told him about the restaurant, Anya, and the others. He didn't leave much out but didn't elaborate, either.

Tom grinned. "Sounds like you had some fun," he said, with a touch of envy.

"Until I was mugged."

His grin faltered. "Oh, yeah. Sorry."

"There's something else," Nick said.

Tom looked at him.

"One of them spoke to me," Nick said.

"So?"

"In English"

"What'd he say?"

"He said, 'Hello, dead man.'"

Tom stared at Nick for a second, then said, "That's kind of a messed-up thing to say, even in a mugging, isn't it?"

Nick nodded. "It's almost as if he knew who I was."

"Do you think he did?"

Nick nodded again.

"Sergei?"

"Yep. Or Maxsim, that punk pimp."

Tom got up, went to the fridge, and pulled out two Balticas. He handed one to Nick. "So, you think those guys followed you?" he asked.

"That's about all I can come up with," Nick said after draining most of the bottle, "unless it was a very coincidental robbery attempt. And I don't believe in coincidences."

Tom stared into his beer bottle for a long time, as if trying to find the answer in the brew. He finally looked at Nick. "You'd better be careful, big fellah."

"Thanks for the tip, Sherlock," Nick said.

"Maybe one of us should go with you from now on."

"No," Nick replied. "I'll just be careful. Maybe they're satisfied now, knowing they put a scare into me." Nick knew it wasn't true, but he had to keep Tom and Michelle out of the mess. He didn't think putting two of his goons in the hospital would make his enemies feel any kinder towards him, but it was his fight and not theirs.

"Are you going to tell Kelli?" Tom asked.

Nick had thought about that on the way back to the hotel. "Yes, I will," he said. "As soon as I get home with Nonna."

He stopped and looked around. It had suddenly occurred to him that they were alone. "Hey, where's Scott?" he asked.

Tom looked uneasy. "I was hoping you knew. I haven't seen him all day. I figured he was in here."

They checked on Scott's whereabouts with Michelle, but she hadn't kept track of him. She was too busy making sure Katie didn't

61

slit her wrists, she said. She made it sound as if she didn't care what happened to Scott.

Nick wasn't too concerned about the man, either, so he unlocked his door and went to bed.

He slept better than he thought he would, and in the morning took a long shower in the cold water. It helped clear his head. He thought hard for a moment, then came to the conclusion it was Saturday. The days seemed to blur together. Eight days left. Or maybe it was seven. He shrugged as the water coursed over him. Nick knew they'd tell him when it was time to leave.

Scott had come in early in the morning, being none too quiet about it. Nick was glad he didn't waste time worrying about the idiot the night before. Scott was still asleep when Nick stepped out of the cool, air-conditioned hotel room and into the steamy hallway. It was only mid-morning but he knew it would be another hot and sunny day. Wherever they made clouds, it was nowhere near Rostov. He grinned and told himself he'd have to mention that to Nonna when she was older.

If Nonna was happy to see him she didn't show it, but she did let him hold her for the entire time and they had fun playing in the courtyard. After talking with Lauren, Nick was anxious to get Nonna out of the orphanage and bring her home, where she'd have a chance to make something of herself. For the first time, he found himself looking at the other babies, wondering who was going to rescue them. He wished he could take them all home with him.

He saw her leaning against a tree near his hotel, and had to look twice to make sure it was Lauren. She motioned him over. She still had her bruises, but they were beginning to fade.

"You're in danger," she said without preamble. She showed little emotion. She could have been saying "It's going to be warm today," or "We need potatoes for dinner." She was simply stating a fact. "Sergei?" Nick asked.

She nodded. "And Maxsim."

"So they work together."

Lauren nodded. "They are, how you say, partners."

"Two of their goons attacked me last night," Nick said. He'd been pretty sure it was Sergei. Now he was certain, and Maxsim was thrown in as well. Nick felt popular.

"It seems you did attacking."

Nick shook his head. "I just got the jump on them. They weren't very observant."

"You shouldn't break their knees."

"What?" Nick asked. "I didn't break any knees. I knocked them out and probably broke an elbow, but that was it."

"Max said you broke knees, they go to hospital."

"That's a lie," Nick said. That bastard.

She shrugged. "Perhaps. But they are very angry. They want…" She pounded one fist into her open palm a few times.

"Revenge."

"Yes, that's it. Revenge."

"What are they planning to do?"

"I don't know. I heard Max yell, through wall. But not good. He's killed men for less."

Nick sighed. Being told somebody was planning to kill you was bad enough, but he had something else on his mind.

"Do they know about the adoption?" he asked.

"No," Lauren replied. "Sergei asked me why you here. I said business."

Nick felt relief flow through him, and touched her hand. "Thank you," he said.

She smiled briefly, and now Nick saw tears in her eyes. "You should not have angered him. Not for me."

He felt the frustration come on again as he remembered the scene in the club. "Somebody had to. He beat you up!"

Now the tears flowed down her cheeks. She made no motion to wipe them away. "He does that. You shouldn't be in danger for me."

"I can handle myself," Nick said.

"No, no," she said, and her lower lip trembled. "Maxsim is bad man, very angry. Sergei is…not so angry, but a bad man, too."

"So what should I do?" he asked.

"Can you get your baby now, and leave?"

"No, I can't," Nick replied. "I have to wait another week."

She wiped away the tear on her right cheek. "That's a pity," she said.

Nick had to agree. "So they definitely don't know about— about my baby?"

She shook her head. "They never say it."

"I wonder how they found me?"

"I think Sergei's man saw you at restaurant."

"At the Olymp?" He wondered who it was. He really hoped it wasn't Anya or her cousin. They didn't seem like people who would associate with Sergei, though.

When he looked back at Lauren, her eyes were wide. "You went to Café Olymp? How did you know to go there?"

"I didn't know to go there, I just found it as I walked." He immediately felt bad about the lie, but didn't want to mention Anya.

"Really," she said. She looked doubtful.

"Yes. Why?"

She started to tell him, then stopped herself. "Nothing, no reason. It's far away. I'm surprised you knew of it."

"I walked a long way. I had a lot to think about."

She pulled herself away from the tree. He could tell she was getting ready to leave. "You still have things to think about. You must be careful. You must get your baby home!" The tears welled in her eyes again.

"Your English is very good," he said, trying to change the subject and to make her feel better.

She rubbed an eye and managed a smile. "Thank you. I studied from book with a friend in orphanage. And now I like to practice with my American clients."

He gave her a hug. She started to pull away, but relaxed and laid her head against his shoulder, briefly. She then straightened up and stepped back.

"I must go, Maxsim might see me here."

He looked around quickly. "Damn, I didn't think of that. If they're on to me, they're going to see you talking to me."

"Yes," she replied, more calmly than he felt. "But they aren't here yet. Max doesn't move fast, and Sergei is away this morning. I must leave now and we cannot talk again. You must leave as well. Perhaps find another hotel."

"Perhaps," Nick replied. He didn't like the sound of that. The adoption people wouldn't have the new hotel name, and when they found out he had moved they'd ask all sorts of questions that he'd prefer not to answer. And Kelli would immediately suspect the worst.

Lauren hesitated, then stepped up on her toes and gave him a quick kiss on the cheek. Before he could react, she was gone.

Somehow he knew he'd never see her again.

Chapter 11

Nick decided to stay in his room the rest of the day. Originally it was only going to be for a few hours. Take a nap, read, reflect on how to avoid being killed. But his thinking rapidly led him to a conclusion: he was here to start a family, not a war, and he had to do what he had to do to get Nonna and get out of Russia. Alive.

He didn't like it, though. Lauren's situation bothered him. Forced into prostitution, beat up by her pimp. Nick had grown up around the U.S. and wasn't naïve. He knew what was going on. But to have it thrust in his face like that was disconcerting. Lauren seemed like an intelligent woman. More likely, she would have been intelligent if she had had a chance to develop herself. But now she was doomed to a life slaving away for bastards like Maxsim, chastising people for daring to help her. She was a good person. Could still be a good person. It took guts for her to warn him about Maxsim and his goons. She didn't have to do that.

But she did. And that meant something to him.

Deep inside, Nick knew part of the reason he had started to back down was to protect her. Because of what happened yesterday, she was linked with him in Maxsim's mind. Best if Nick just disappeared.

But he had to eat, so he joined Tom and Michelle at the Chicken Shack. He walked along the side of the parking lot, keeping the rest of the shack between him and the bar. When he got to the wooden structure he peered around the side and was relieved to see another bartender behind the counter.

"We missed you last night," Michelle said as they sat down. "Where did you go?"

"Oh, I was out walking and found a nice place down by the river," Nick said. Tom looked up, but said nothing.

"How's Katie doing?" Nick asked.

Michelle shook her head and pursed her lips. "I talked to her this morning, she's taking it pretty hard. A lot of crying. She wouldn't come to the door tonight, but the key lady said she's still in her room. I'll check again before bed. Poor kid."

Nick expected her to ask about Scott, but she didn't.

The chicken came and went, the beer came and went, and more beer came. The entire time Nick kept glancing around the periphery, wondering if there were goons out there, waiting for him to venture out on his own. And if he didn't, would they try something in the Chicken Shack? He doubted it, but his back tingled every so often at the thought of a bullet hitting him out of nowhere.

At eight o'clock, as Nick was getting ready to creep back up to his room, the mood at the table suddenly tensed up. Nick, who had been talking to Michelle, turned and saw Sergei standing in the entrance to the shack. The man saw Nick, stopped as if he couldn't believe his eyes, smiled widely, and went behind the bar. A few moments later the other bartender left.

Michelle gamely tried to move on, asking Tom if he had heard how the Yankees were doing. Nick tried to listen, but his eyes kept returning to the bar. Most of the time Sergei was watching him, a sneer on his face. Sergei knew he was stressing Nick and the others out.

Finally Nick had enough. He stood up. "I'm going to go over and piss in Sergei's sandbox," he said. He brushed off his shirt and the front of his pants and turned towards the bar.

"Why would you want to do that?" Michelle asked. "He's pissed off enough at you."

"I need to see what he's up to," Nick said. "If he wants a piece of me, I'm going to give him the chance instead of skulking around in the dark."

He walked to the bar, knowing Tom and Michelle were watching him. He walked as confidently as he could, a confidence he wasn't feeling.

Sergei saw him approach and leaned on the bar, hands clasped in front of him. Nick walked up and leaned against the bar in a similar pose, two feet away. He didn't look at Sergei as he said. "How's your chin?"

Sergei smirked. "I'm fine. I don't think your friends can say the same." He made a show of looking around the room. "I don't see them here."

"They have a few things to talk over. But they'll be fine."

Sergei grunted. "I wouldn't be so sure about that."

Now Nick did look at the bartender. "Sergei," he said, "I don't know if Katie's paid you, and to be honest, I don't care. But if you keep hassling her, it's going to be my pleasure to knock your teeth down your throat."

"Oh, she's paid us," the Russian replied with a grin that didn't touch his eyes. "She's much more cooperative than you. You could learn something from her."

Nick leaned in until his face was a foot from Sergei's. "I'm serious, Sergei. You have your money. It's time to move on."

"You're next, American," Sergei replied, his breath sour in Nick's face. "You should be more worried about yourself than about your friends."

Nick smiled. "Your goons tried it last night, big fellah. I hope they had good insurance. You know, maybe you'd better make sure your medical and dental insurance is paid up, because I don't see you winning any fights any time soon." He leaned back. "Unless, of course, some woman walks by and bails your ass out."

Sergei's grinned slipped, and the two men stared at each other a long moment. Finally Nick said, "Now get me a Baltica. I need to wash my mouth out after being this close to you."

Sergei breathed hard several times, and Nick knew the man wanted to launch himself over the bar. But the Russian visibly calmed himself, turned, and grabbed a brown bottle out of the cooler. Nick watched carefully as Sergei flipped the cap off with his opener and carefully placed the bottle on the bar. Nick slid several bills across the counter to Sergei. "Here's a little extra for you. You'll probably want to save it to tip the nurses."

Sergei watched Nick walk away, a dark expression on his face.

Tom looked over Nick's shoulder as Nick approached the table. "He looks mad as hell, dude. What did you say to him?"

"Nothing much. I just wanted to feel him out, see what's on his mind."

"And what's on his mind?"

Nick tipped his bottle in the direction of the couple. "Me. Which is a hell of a lot better than Katie or Scott. Cheers."

Sunday morning was as bright as Saturday's had been. Scott had not returned during the night, which surprised Nick. He hoped

Scott was in his own room with Katie. He told himself he'd check on it later in the day.

Nick refilled his bottles and nestled them back in the window. He double-checked the lock on the window. It was rusty and not thick. If anybody wanted to get in they wouldn't be slowed down much. But there wasn't much he could do about that. He didn't expect a full frontal assault at the hotel, anyway. And if he was careful, they might not know where he went in the morning, either.

Nick had thought about not seeing Nonna, but couldn't bring himself to do it. He'd sacrifice a lot, but not the chance to see his daughter. He'd just take a different route and keep an eye out behind him. And in front of him. And to the sides. He'd manage. He'd been in worse.

He left by the side door and walked two blocks west before heading south towards the orphanage. The road was narrower than the busy one he usually took, with plenty of places for an ambush, and Nick began to doubt the wisdom of his choice, but he made it to within a block of the orphanage without incident.

He edged up to a block apartment building across the street from the orphanage. Scraggly bushes lined the walkway to the gray building, and Nick smelled urine as he crept past the doorway. A dark cat stared at him from a first floor window, but nothing moved around him. He heard the faint rattle of cars a few blocks away.

Nick peered around the corner, trying to spot anybody lurking outside the orphanage. He couldn't see well enough, and decided to just chance it. He didn't want somebody calling the police because he was sneaking around their building.

He walked back out the walkway to the street, turned left, then left again so he was heading directly to the orphanage, a short block away. He put his hands in his pockets and walked fast, to avoid suspicion. Lauren said they didn't know about Nonna, but arriving from a different direction than expected might give Nick a few seconds of surprise in case she was wrong.

Three green-and-white police cars were parked at odd angles in front of the orphanage gate, lights flashing. A dozen people in drab clothing milled around, watching. Nick saw two cops leaning against one of the cars, arms folded.

Heart thumping, Nick slowed and crossed the street, keeping the three squads between him and the two visible cops. He pushed through a group of teenage boys standing on the sidewalk under the branches of a tree. They looked at Nick and grudgingly shifted out of his way.

A body lay on the pavement outside the gate. Two cops were kneeling next to it, talking to each other and staring down at the girl. Light brown hair, faded dress, bare feet.

Nick had seen plenty of dead bodies in Iraq and Afghanistan, and the sight of shapeless indignity didn't move him as much as it used to. He had seen men killed in front of him as they saved his life. But Nick had never seen a powerless, caring woman executed for helping him.

Lauren looked at Nick with reproach from the ground. No, that wasn't quite right, because her lower jaw was blown off and one of the cops had closed her eyes.

"Where were you, Nick?" she didn't have to ask. "I needed you, and you weren't there to protect me." Nick's eyes blurred with tears, for which he was thankful because then he didn't have to look at the sadness in what remained of her face.

He turned away, collected himself, and turned back with what he hoped was a more clinical eye.

She had not died there. One, her shoes were gone. Two, she had obviously been shot from behind, execution style, and victims shot from behind typically do not end up on their backs.

No, she had been killed elsewhere and her body dumped here, as a warning.

And he damn well knew who had executed her.

He felt the roaring start in his ears. He was wrong to hide in his hotel room, he knew now, leaving her out there with *them*. He should've been there, protecting her. She tried to protect him and when she needed him, he hid in his hotel room.

Deep inside he knew how irrational his thoughts were, but he didn't care. She had tried to warn him, to help him, and now she was dead. Left like a sack of garbage on a dirty sidewalk.

And she had started out like Nonna, in an orphanage. Would Nonna end up like this if he didn't bring her home? What about the other kids sharing a room in Baby Home Number Four with her?

He watched as one of the officers bent over the body and began to draw a chalk line on the asphalt. As he got to her right hand he made a wide circle around it. Nick realized she was clutching something.

He moved forward, almost on top of the policeman. The cop looked up and frowned at him, but something in Nick's expression made him back off and continue the chalk line.

In her right hand Nick saw, as clear as a brilliant beacon on a dark night, a message.

Nonna's red hat was in Lauren's hand, almost hidden beneath her fingers. Nick knew it had been placed there after she had been killed and her body dumped. It had been placed there as a sign to him.

They knew about his daughter.

The rush of emotions almost knocked him to his knees. He staggered back, then leaned against a tree trunk next to the street. He had the presence of mind to move to the far side of the tree, so the cops wouldn't notice his panic.

He regulated his breath, which always calmed him in time of stress. Four seconds in, four seconds holding, four seconds out, four seconds holding. Gradually his pulse slowed to merely frenetic and he could think again.

They knew about Nonna. What was their next step? Would they harm her? Maxsim was a psychopath and Sergei wasn't much better, but they wouldn't gain much by harming Nonna. No, they would use her as a bargaining chip against Nick. They would block the adoption, and do what they could do to ensure Nick left without her. At least, Nick hoped that was what they'd do. He knew the dangers of applying logic to those who didn't operate on logic.

Nick felt overwhelmed. But he knew what he needed. He needed a gun.

And he knew just where to get one.

It didn't take him long to pick up the tail. The man really didn't know how to stay hidden. Or perhaps he didn't care, thinking he had Nick on the run. Either way, Nick made him within minutes of leaving the orphanage.

Nick had decided not to visit Nonna after all. It wasn't much of a decision. He wasn't going to make her more of a target than she already was. He walked towards the hotel, making sure he stayed visible. He assumed they would pick him up at the orphanage, but to be safe he kept on the path he had taken the previous several days. He veered over a block when he got close to the brothel. No sense in overdoing it.

It was when he cut across the street that he noticed the man following him. Only one this time. Bulky guy. Not tall but broad, like a wrestler. Dark hair in a crew cut. Looked cut and formidable.

The man casually crossed the road in almost the exact same spot as Nick had, about ten seconds behind Nick. If he had been smart he would have trailed from the other side of the street and crossed at the corner. But he followed in Nick's footsteps and lit up like a beacon.

Nick stopped in front of a few storefronts, pretending to window shop but keeping an eye on the reflection of the man behind him. Nick didn't see a weapon but he was sure one was there, waiting to come out when the man made his move.

Nick turned down a side street. Trees overhung the street and alleys sprouted out every twenty feet or so, disappearing between tall buildings. An older woman carrying a basket of oranges tottered past Nick without a glance. Behind her the street was empty.

Nick stuck his hands in his pockets and moved fast down the street. He could feel his pursuer getting closer. He knew this would be a perfect place for the man to make his move.

The roaring was back. Nick now welcomed it. It signaled a lethal decision was imminent. Somebody was about to get severely hurt. Or maybe dead.

And at this point, it was time for a lethal decision. It was time to send a message back.

About five feet past the entrance to an alley Nick stopped and quickly turned on his pursuer. The man was about ten feet behind him, coming up fast. He slowed in surprise and the knife in his right hand swung up.

The Russian was as stocky as Nick had thought, with no neck and solid all the way down. Young, younger than he had appeared from a distance. He couldn't have been more than twenty. That meant no military service. He was obviously trained in something, though, to get that physique. Didn't matter. Not now. Not with

Lauren lying shattered on the road. The man could've been Hercules and he was going down.

Nick closed the gap quickly. He easily ducked under the thrust the man telegraphed from a mile away, and let loose with a savage donkey kick against the side of his left knee, the one currently bearing most of his weight.

Nick's heel slammed the Russian's knee sideways, bone meeting and then slicing painfully through cartilage, and the man went down with a scream. He grabbed his knee with both hands and immediately forgot about Nick. Nick finished him off quickly with a hard fist to the temple, and the Russian folded onto his side.

The roaring in his ears began to subside.

Nick dragged the heavy, inert body into the alley slowly, perspiring heavily and grunting as quietly as he could. He then went back to the street, found the knife, flicked it open to make sure it was worth taking, and shut it again. A ceramic knife. Black handle, collapsible. Not too large, but quality made. It could come in handy. He stuck it in his pocket.

Back to the alley and a quick exam through the man's pockets only came up with a smaller blade taped to his calf. Damn. Nick was hoping for more.

Nick needed a better weapon. Back to Plan A.

Nick spent the better part of two hours waiting outside the Café Olymp before he saw Anya. He could have figured out where she lived, but he didn't want to hand her over to anybody following him, even though he was pretty sure he had eluded them for the moment.

He stepped out from behind a tree when he saw her approach. Anya looked surprised and pleased to see him. At least until he opened his mouth.

"I need a gun," he told her. "Where's Andrei?"

Chapter 12

The shop took up a small storefront in a three story brick building near the Olymp. It was in the center of the building and Nick would have missed it if it hadn't been adorned with gaudy painted swirls, neon circles, and a large barber's pole planted out front. "Wonka's" was painted in huge letters over a large glass window, each letter in a different color. Underneath, in smaller but only slightly less vibrant colors, was, "Real American Candy." At least there wasn't dancing, happy candy in the window.

Nick stepped through the door and heard a bell ring somewhere in the back. The small, long room was empty of people but filled with chocolate bars, bags of hard candy, popcorn, and another barber's pole. Three small tables, each one with a round aluminum top and barely big enough to hold two people, sat ready but empty in the middle of the room. Nick walked in and saw more candy bars displayed under the glass counters.

A small door in the back opened and Andrei walked out, wiping his hands. "Nick!" he called out, a happy look coming over his face. He draped the towel on one of the chairs and extended his hand. "Nice to see you again so soon," he said. He was once again dressed in a dark sport coat and obviously didn't care that he looked woefully out of place.

"Seriously, a candy store?" Nick said. "Nice touch."

Andrei spread his arms wide. "Of course! Everybody's happy in a candy store. I've never once had a firefight here!"

He held up a finger and went behind the counter. "The one video I had as a child was 'Willy Wonka and the Chocolate Factory.' You know, that old one with the guy with crazy hair."

"Gene Wilder."

"Yes. I watched it every week. I told myself that one day I'd own a candy store."

Nick smiled. "And here you are."

"And here I am. Svetlana and I live above the store, too, so it's easy to get here," Andrei said as he rummaged around under the counter. He came out with a small colorful package. "Kazoozle?"

"What the heck's a Kazoozle?"

Andrei turned the package on end. "A filled licorice. Good but sweet. I can only eat one or two before my teeth hurt."

He tossed the candy to Nick, who caught it with one hand. "Thanks," Nick said as he glanced at the wrapper. Bright red lettering on a blue wrapper. Definitely made to be noticed.

Andrei motioned Nick to sit down. He grabbed two water bottles from a cooler and brought them over. "Anything sweeter than water with a Kazoozle is just crazy," he said.

Nick looked around the empty store. "Do you get many customers?" he asked.

Andrei shrugged. "Kids come in after school, but no, not so many customers. Sometimes that's best."

Nick nodded. It might be tough to deal with his other line of work while selling Nerds to kids.

"So, I heard you had difficulty last night," the Russian said.

Nick glanced sharply at Andrei. "You heard about that? How?" He hadn't told Anya yet.

"I sent two men after you, to make sure you made it home safely."

A piece of the puzzle clicked into place. "Ahh," Nick said. "And your friends have something against knees, I assume?"

Andrei leaned back and for the first time looked uncomfortable. "That part was regrettable," he replied. "I wouldn't have chosen that course of action. But my men knew your attackers and...took advantage of the situation. Not to worry, though, I had a talk with them and they won't do that again."

Nick wondered if any talk had ever taken place, but remained silent.

Andrei looked closely at Nick. "You didn't have much trouble with them, though. I don't think we needed to send any protection for you."

"Perhaps," Nick answered. "But I could use some protection now."

Andrei leaned forward in his chair. "Oh? How?"

"I need a gun."

The Russian's eyes widened. "A gun? You're an American adopting a little girl in my country. Why would you need a gun? Because somebody tried to mug you?"

75

Nick paused. How much to tell Andrei? He could play coy and just say he was nervous after the attack last night, but then Andrei may insist on providing a bodyguard and Nick didn't need that hassle. Or the Russian could just pooh-pooh Nick's fears and refuse to help.

So he decided to tell the truth, albeit abbreviated. When he got to his theory that his key lady had spilled the beans about him being alone, Andrei pursed his lips and nodded.

"Yes," he said. "They make much more by arranging for girls and drugs than they do from keys."

Nick continued, going through the events at the club last night and ending with finding Lauren dead on the sidewalk, half of her head blown off. He didn't mention the part about Nonna's hat.

"That's a terrible thing," Andrei said, shaking his head. His voice was low, all joviality gone. "So you think they're sending you a message?"

"Yes."

"And you want a gun to send a message back."

Nick shook his head emphatically. "No. No attacking. I just want to be able to protect myself." And my daughter, he thought.

Andrei pondered a moment, hand on his chin, stroking the stubble there as he thought. Eventually he got up and walked into the back room. Long moments passed before he reappeared again, this time holding a black handgun.

"A third generation Glock 19," he said, handing it to Nick. "There are 15 rounds in the magazine, which should be plenty for you to, uh, protect yourself."

He handed the gun to Nick, who looked it over appreciatively.

"You're familiar with Glocks?" Andrei asked with a wry smile.

Nick deftly removed the magazine, checked to see it was fully loaded, and clicked it back in. "I've been around a few," he answered.

Andrei sat back down in his chair while Nick continued to inspect the Glock. Eventually Nick looked up, noticed the Russian staring intently at him, and slowly put the gun down.

"This isn't a gift, is it?"

Andrei shook his head. "I don't want your money, but there is a certain…opportunity…for you to help us."

Nick stared back at the Russian, eyes flashing. "You want me to make a hit for you."

A pause, then, "Yes."

Nick stood up. "No. No way. I'm not getting involved in anything illegal." Not unless I had to, he told himself. The thought of risking his daughter and ending up in a Russian jail made him shudder.

"You're already involved in something illegal."

"You know what I mean, Andrei. I can't do this! I'm here for a little over another week, then I go home with my daughter. I can't risk that."

Andrei also stood up. Nick had a few inches on him but the Russian was bulkier. Nick certainly did not want to meet him in a dark alley. "That's what makes this perfect, Nick! You make the hit late in the week and then leave. They'll never connect you."

Nick shook his head. The whole thing made him faintly ill and he wished he hadn't come. He put the gun on the table. "I'm sorry for wasting your time, Andrei. Thank you for the hospitality." He turned to go.

"Wait," Andrei called after him. When Nick turned back, the Russian looked embarrassed. "I'm sorry. I shouldn't put you in this dilemma. Of course I'll help you. I have another gun that is more suited for…protection." He disappeared again and came out with a small, silver gun with a black handle. "Here's an old Czech VZ," he said, almost apologetically. "Not powerful, but it gets the job done. You can have it until you leave. When you are done, throw it in the river."

Nick knew the old, small pistol wouldn't stop much, but it might at least make somebody pause long enough for Nick to get the hell out of wherever he was.

He took the gun warily. "No strings?"

Andrei smiled. "No strings. Anya would kick my ass if I didn't help you," he said.

"Thank you, Andrei," Nick said. He looked the gun over. It was scuffed up pretty bad, and there were only a few rounds, but it would do.

"Untraceable?" he asked Andrei.

"Even better," the candy store owner said. "My men got it off one of your friends last night."

Nick grimaced. Not until this morning had it occurred to him that he should have checked his attackers for weapons. At the time he was stunned from the assault and just wanted to get out before the police showed up. Besides, if they had a gun wouldn't they have used it? Not if they wanted to remain silent. He sighed.

"That works, then, Andrei. Thank you very much."

Andrei reached into his pocket. "I have another gift for you," he said. He pulled out a cell phone and handed it to Nick. It was small, silver, beat up. But it worked, or at least it lit up when Nick flipped it open.

"Call me if you get into trouble," Andrei said. "Just hold down the number one."

"Thank you, Andrei," Nick said, and he meant it. "I appreciate the help."

The Russian smiled and clapped Nick on the back. "You are a good man, Nick, and Anya likes you. If she likes you, I like you." He walked Nick to the door. "Good luck to you, my friend. I hope you won't have to use your new gift."

Nick left with a wave. Andrei stood inside the door for a long while, thinking. Small smiles occasionally flitted across his face. He didn't move. Finally he locked the door and walked into the back room, still deep in thought.

Anya reclined against a tree, arms folded, a block away from the candy store. When she saw Nick approach she pushed herself out from the trunk and smoothed her skirt. She fell into step beside him.

"So, did he give it to you?" She asked.

Nick looked sideways at her. He was slightly surprised but not unhappy she had stuck around. The gun made him feel he was getting deeper into...something...and it felt good to have someone to talk to about it. Someone unrelated. True, Andrei was not after Nick, but the man was not exactly an innocent. Of course, Anya was his cousin so she was not exactly an innocent, either, but she seemed to not want to get too close to Andrei's line of work.

"Yeah, he gave me a gun," Nick answered after looking around to make sure they were alone. "Not a great one, but it'll do."

She didn't reply, just stared ahead. After several steps she said, without looking at him, "What job are you going to do?"

"None," Nick replied. "I turned him down and he took the nice gun back." Anya snorted and nodded. "But Maxsim and his goons are after me, and I need protection, so he took pity on me. He gave me a phone, too."

Anya held out her hand. "Good, I was hoping he would. Here, I'll put my number in." He passed the phone over and she typed in her contact info.

"For a good time, call…" Nick said and smiled as she handed the phone back.

They passed an ice cream cart on the side of the road. Painted on the side was a Russian version of an ice cream bar with a huge grin.

Nick pointed to it. "My god, is all of your food happy in this town?"

Anya laughed, and nodded when he asked if she wanted one. He bought two ice cream bars and they found a nearby bench to sit on.

"You know what I don't get," Nick said as he and Anya dug into the treats. "Why are Sergei and Maxsim so intent on bringing me down? I mean, things got out of hand at the club, and again after I left the restaurant, but it certainly wasn't worth killing Lauren over." He felt a twinge at the mention of her name.

"Apparently it was," Anya said. She finished off the bar and wiped her mouth with a napkin. "You don't know these people, Nick. They don't care who gets hurt. You embarrassed Sergei in front of many people, including his bodyguards and his girls. Then you beat up one his bodyguards."

Nick sighed. "I know. It just happened so fast..." his voice trailed off as he thought about what had happened. "We all should've just kept to ourselves."

"Yes, you should have," Anya said with force that surprised Nick. He glanced at her as she continued. "These are bad men, Nick, and you shouldn't be involved with them."

"I'm trying not to be involved with them, Anya," Nick protested.

"By buying a gun?"

"I didn't buy it, Andrei gave it to me to protect myself," Nick said, knowing how lame it sounded as he said it.

Anya turned to face him fully and laid her hand on his arm. Her hand was hot, and her eyes shimmered with unshed tears. "Andrei doesn't just give something to someone," she said. "He expects something in return."

"Like me killing one of his enemies?"

"Yes. But you don't have to do it! Just stay away from Sergei. And stay away from Andrei, too. You don't want to get too close to either of them. You're here for your baby! Don't forget that."

"But can't you see, Anya, that's why I'm doing this. Me getting killed and dumped on the side of a road isn't going to help Nonna get out of the orphanage. I need to stay alive for her."

Now the tears did fall from Anya's eyes. "Just promise me you'll stay away from the bad guys."

"Of course I will," Nick said. "But will they stay away from me?"

Nick was preoccupied when he got back to his room, so it took him several minutes to realize Scott was still not there. The plaid blanket Scott had used was folded up and placed on one end of the sofa. In the bathroom, Scott's toothbrush sat at an angle on the edge of the sink, but the rest of his toiletries were gone.

Nick smiled to himself. Scott and Katie must have made up, or at least come to an understanding. He was a bit surprised it only took a few days, but nobody wants to be alone so far from home, and for such an important process. Perhaps they decided to put their differences on hold until they returned to the states.

He grabbed the toothbrush and made a quick run down the hall to Scott and Katie's room. He intended to return it but they weren't in, so he brought it back. Nick wrote a quick note to Scott saying he still had his toothbrush, and slid it halfway under their door.

He went back to his room and locked the door behind him. He peeled off his clothes, which clung to his skin limply after hours in the heat and humidity, and took a quick shower. After that he crawled into bed with a big sigh and was asleep within minutes.

He woke up hours later to a pounding on his door. He lifted his head a bit, not sure if he had really heard the pounding. It repeated, this time louder.

He groaned and swung his legs out of bed. He pulled his shorts on quickly and padded lightly over to the door. On the way he glanced at a clock Kelli had propped on top of the TV. Seven o'clock in the morning.

"Who is it?" he whispered through the door.

"Michelle."

Heart suddenly thumping, Nick unlocked the door and swung it open. Michelle stood in front of him, holding his note.

She looked terrified.

Chapter 13

"Two days!" Michelle yelled. She threw the note at Nick, and neither one noticed as it fluttered limply to the floor between them. "He's been gone for two days and you're just getting around to writing a note?" She was dressed in a black tank top and white running shorts, nothing on her feet. Her short hair stuck up on one side and she looked like someone who had just gotten up. Nick assumed she went to Katie's room as soon as she woke.

"I figured he was back with Katie," Nick answered, feeling the heat of embarrassment rise in his face. The truth was, he had other things to worry about than Scott, but he didn't want to go there with Michelle.

She swore and muttered something that sounded like "dumbass." Nick wasn't sure which guy she was talking about, but figured it was both, and she was probably right. She took two steps away, then whirled back at him. "So now he's had two days to get himself into trouble, and we have no idea where the hell he is!" She rubbed her eyes. "So, no notes or calls or anything from him?"

Nick shook his head.

"And you last saw him Saturday morning."

Nick nodded. "On my way out to the orphanage. I didn't get home until late that night, and he was gone." He hoped she didn't grill him on where he had been or who he had beaten up. He didn't feel like launching another round of lies.

"I haven't seen Katie, either," Michelle said. She plopped heavily into the sofa and leaned back. "I heard her crying in her room on Saturday, I guess it would be. Late in the day. It was quiet yesterday, though, and she wouldn't answer my knock."

"Is she still in her room?" Nick asked.

Michelle closed her eyes, let out a big sigh, then opened them again. "The key lady says she is. She says Katie hasn't left since Friday."

"And you believe her?"

"Why would she lie?" Michelle asked.

Why indeed, Nick wondered. "Maybe we should check her room," he said.

"I tried that," Michelle answered, "but the old bitch wouldn't let me in. She said something in Russian and glared at me."

"We need to check on Katie," Nick said. "She's been alone long enough." He walked to the door and heard Michelle stand up.

"You ask her this time," she said from behind him.

The key lady heard them coming, because she had swiveled in her chair and was facing them as they rounded the corner. One arm on the desk, one elbow on the top of her chair, one sullen expression on her face. There were several old women who rotated the position, but Nick always seemed to run into the one who yelled at him on his first day, when he left with his key.

"Room 406," Nick said, holding up four fingers and then six fingers.

She shook her head and said something negative in Russian, then made a show of turning back to her desk, her business with him complete.

The keys were in cubby holes on the right side of the desk, each one in a labeled box. Nick scanned the boxes behind her back and saw the empty one for 406. On the top row of cubbies he saw a keychain with several keys. Odds were good they were master keys for the fourth floor rooms. He reached over the startled woman, grabbed the keys, and started back to Katie and Scott's room.

The woman stood up, her chair scraping a few feet across the floor with a screech, and reached for the keys in Nick's hand, but he easily sidestepped her. She yelled something at him.

"Nyah zhnyoo!" he told her sharply. She stopped and looked at him strangely. He took the opportunity to quickly walk down the hall to Katie's room.

"What did you say?" Michelle asked, almost running to keep up.

"I told her I didn't give a damn," Nick replied.

"No, you didn't," Michelle said.

Nick turned to look at her, not slowing. He didn't see the key lady following them, which he wasn't sure was a good thing or a bad thing. "What are you talking about?" he asked.

"You said you didn't know."

"Huh?"

In spite of the circumstances, Michelle giggled. "Our driver told us that 'Nyah zhnyoo' means 'I don't know.' Or maybe it was 'leave me alone.' I don't remember which."

"Really?"

"Yes."

"Well, it stopped her, so get off my case."

The fourth key opened the door. Nick and Michelle stepped inside, leaving the door open. Michelle yelled out, "Katie, it's us!" while Nick quickly checked out the room.

It was empty.

Michelle stood in the middle of the room, looking like she got hit by a truck, while Nick checked the closet, the tub, the floor between the double bed and the wall. Nothing.

"Her clothes are still here," Nick called out.

"Not all of them," Michelle answered. She quickly recovered, her police training taking over. "She had a red day bag. Do you see it?"

Nick looked around. "No."

"Then where the hell is she?"

Nick dropped the keys back in their cubby hole with a clang. The key lady, who Nick decided to call Olga because there was no way he was going to ask her for her name, avoided his gaze.

She knew what happened to Katie. And he feared the worst.

"Nick, I have to visit my son," Michelle said. She sounded guilty.

"I know you do," Nick answered. "Go play with him, give him some love. We'll figure this out when you get back."

She left with Tom, both of them feeling they should stay and help out. They had a ninety minute trip to Taganrog, so they would likely be gone all day. It was Nick's turn to feel guilty for being relieved they were out of the way.

As soon as the cab left the curb, Nick grabbed his new cell phone and dialed Anya's number. It was slightly past eight o'clock but he didn't think she'd mind if he woke her.

She didn't. Her only comment after he explained his morning was, "What can I do?"

"I could really use your help in tracking Scott and Katie down," Nick said. "I don't think I'll be able to talk to most of the shop owners, and I think the best way to start is to walk the streets, asking if anybody's seen them."

"Of course I'll come with you," Anya said without hesitation. "That poor woman. I can't imagine what she's going through."

"Thank you, Anya," Nick said.

"But what makes you think they'll tell us anything?"

"Because you're going to ask them nicely," Nick said.

She arrived thirty minutes later, out of breath and slightly flushed.

Nick looked at her and said, "You didn't have to run."

She waved him off. "I could've taken my car, but I wanted a walk. It's good for me. I was thinking on the way over that we should talk to the key lady first. She might have an idea where they were going."

Nick wasn't so sure about that idea, but didn't say anything. Perhaps if Anya did the talking they might learn something.

They went up the stairs and approached the key lady on Nick's floor. She watched them less impassively than usual. As Nick walked up she glared at him, and the corner of her wrinkled mouth curled up.

"Friend of yours?" Anya murmured.

"She's the one who sent Lauren to my room," Nick replied under his breath, even though he knew she didn't speak English. "Oh, and I just stole her room keys."

Anya looked at Nick sideways. "Unfortunate," she said. "That means she works for your new friends. And she probably hates you anyway for stealing her keys. I doubt we'll get anything out of her."

They stopped in front of the desk. Anya smiled and said hello. When the woman didn't reply, Anya cleared her throat and started to talk in Russian. The woman listened to her words but kept her eyes on Nick. When Anya was done talking, she replied in staccato Russian. Nick got the impression she didn't like being interrupted. Or didn't like Americans. Or maybe she just didn't like people.

Anya turned to Nick and shook her head. "She doesn't remember seeing either of them leave."

"Well, they didn't climb out the damn window," Nick shot back. He was reaching his limit with old ladies. "Ask her if she remembers either of them at all."

Anya repeated the question to the old woman, who nodded slightly and said, "da." She rattled off a string of words that caused Anya to wince.

"What did she say?" Nick asked.

But Anya just shook her head. "Nothing that would help us. She remembers Scott but didn't seem to like him."

The woman paused, then said something else. Anya translated to Nick. "She said he was quite angry when she last saw him. He went from one room to another. Maybe from yours to his wife's."

"Did she say that?"

Anya blushed slightly. "No, that was my comment."

Nick let it pass. "But she never saw him leave."

"That's what she said."

"Do you believe her?"

Anya shrugged. "I never know when to believe these crazy babushkas."

Nick pulled out a hundred Ruble note and handed it to the woman. She looked at it briefly and put it down the front of her shirt. Nick winced.

But she started talking.

Anya gave a running commentary. "OK, she's suddenly starting to remember now. He did leave two days ago. Twice. He left after you, came back quite angry, then left again late in the day. She said he carried a package with him when he left the second time."

"A large package."

"No," Anya replied after asking the old woman. "Small. He carried it in one hand."

"Hmm, OK. Anything else?"

She asked the woman, who shook her head. "No, that's all she remembers. You could give her more money, but usually one bribe opens them up. I think that's all she knows. Or at least all she'll tell us."

"What about Katie?"

She asked. Nick didn't need any help translating the shake of the old woman's head. But he wasn't sure if she really didn't know, or was afraid to tell them.

Anya thanked the key lady and they walked back down to the lobby and out the door. "Let's try the stores," she said.

Five shops and five negative answers later, they trudged slowly along the sidewalk together, their energy waning.

"Are you asking them nicely?" Nick said.

Anya forced a smile. "I'm trying, Nick," she said.

"Because I feel like we're getting the brush off."

"What do you mean, brush off?"

Nick pantomimed brushing something off his shoulder. "It means nobody wants to tell us anything."

She nodded, lips pursed. "In that case, we're definitely being brushed off."

He stopped suddenly. Anya took another step and then turned back to him. "What?"

"Hold on a moment," Nick said. He walked back to the coffee shop and looked in the window, nose pressed against the glass, hands cupped around his eyes to shield the glare. He stood there for a moment, then slowly walked back to Anya, eyes on the pavement, deep in thought.

"What?" Anya asked again.

He looked up at her, still thinking. "So," he said slowly. "In the protection biz, if some of the shops get protection from somebody, do the other ones fall in line with the same guy?"

"You're better off asking Andrei that," Anya replied, averting his eyes.

"I'm asking you."

She shrugged. "Well, from what I know, usually they all fall in line, as you say. Declining protection when everybody else has it would make you a target."

Nick nodded. "Yeah, that's kind of what I'm thinking, too. This last guy was on the phone just now. He saw me and looked like he just ate a worm. I think he was calling the bad guys."

She nodded. "Probably, yes. They're keeping tabs on you. On us."

"So let's give them something."

"What kind of something?"

He motioned to the record shop in front of them. "Let's talk to Boris. And this time it's my turn to ask nicely."

Chapter 14

Boris didn't meet Nick's gaze. So Nick knew.

"Where are they?" he asked.

"Who?" the Russian said, running a finger along the counter.

Nick leaned forward, knuckles on the counter on either side of the finger. "You know who," he said. "And I need to know. They're in trouble. You're a good man. So tell me where they took them."

Boris shook his head. Long gone was the flippant nature from yesterday. He was one scared man. "I don't say," he said. "They kill me if I say."

Nick knew it wasn't an idle threat. He was sure the mob provided protection for at least a few stores along this street, and probably all of them. Maxsim or Sergei could easily kill the man, or at least bring enough pressure down on a simple store owner to close him down quickly.

Nick was at a loss. There was nothing he could do to apply more pressure to Boris, except perhaps shoot him in a knee with a Czech pop gun, and Nick wasn't about to do that.

But then Boris came to the rescue.

"They tell me to call them if you here," he mumbled, still looking down.

Bingo, Nick thought. "Then you'd better call."

Boris looked up, his eyes wide. "You want me call them?"

"Yes," Nick replied. "Do it now."

Boris looked at Nick as if he was crazy, then took out his cell phone and dialed a number. Nick told Anya to leave the store and keep an eye out from across the street. When she reluctantly left, he leaned against a wall. He crossed his arms and faced the front door, a look of relaxation on his face. Relaxation that didn't touch the rest of his body.

Maxsim was a happy man.

He hadn't been so happy yesterday. Yesterday he was one mean sonofabitch, even by his own standards. The attack on Sergei and Vlad by the American had caused him to lose face in front of the entire club. And he knew the news didn't stay in the club. As early as the next morning he had noticed smirks where there had once been fear. And that wasn't acceptable.

So he'd taken steps, not unenjoyable steps, to flush the Americans out, and it worked better than he could have hoped. First the noisy obnoxious one showed up at the music store with a gun. And now, now he received word that the quiet American, the one who hit very hard, was at the store looking for the first two Americans. Could it really be that easy to bring the three Americans in? Easy for a man of his intelligence, anyway. Smarter than a few Americans, obviously.

The call had come in to one of his lieutenants, who immediately called Maxsim. Maxsim just as fast dispatched the man and his partner to the store to bring the last American in.

He walked in to the room next to his office and looked at the man hanging from the wall. The American didn't handle pain well, which wasn't surprising because the noisy ones usually screamed first. He had given up their hotel and room numbers fast enough, but Maxsim hadn't moved on it yet. And now he didn't need to because the last American, whom Maxsim suspected wouldn't scream nearly as much, had come to him.

Scott had cigarette burns on his chest and arms, and his other wrist was broken above where the chains gripped his flesh. He writhed in agony against the wall, eyes screwed shut, not noticing Maxsim had returned.

But the real prize wasn't the two men. It was the woman upstairs. For years Maxsim's colleagues had put up with the arrogance of the Americans. More than once they had said to Maxsim, "Screw America."

And now they would get their chance, one at a time. Maxsim smiled to himself. He took her first, since she was his. Nobody else knew where these two—soon to be three—were, and she would keep his colleagues pleased for a long time, before eventually being found in the Don.

Yes, it was definitely a good day.

Two men barged through the front door of Crazy Boris's. They weren't as big as the bodyguards from the club, but they had the wiry, confident look of well-trained fighters. Nick didn't move. His left leg was bent at the knee, foot flat against the wall, arms

90

crossed in front of him. He waited patiently as the men sought him out. They seemed surprised to find him waiting for them.

They stopped in front of him, one on each side, just outside of his reach.

"Come with us," the one on the left said in a low guttural voice.

"No," Nick replied.

They looked even more surprised.

"You come with us now," the man said, a bit dramatically, Nick thought.

Nick shook his head. "I don't think so," he said.

Surprise was rapidly replaced by frustration in the men. They closed in on Nick. The man on the left flicked his hand in a follow-me gesture.

Nick looked at him steadily, ignoring the man on the right. "Maxsim only sent two of you? He must overestimate your abilities. Maybe next time he'll send more."

The Russians only understood part of what Nick said, but what they understood made it clear that Nick was mocking them. Two hands went into their suit pockets and two hands came out with black guns. High-powered Glocks, it looked like to Nick. He was glad, since his gun wasn't going to cut what he had to do later in the morning.

They both moved a bit closer. "We're not leaving here without you," the first one said.

Nick shrugged. "You're not leaving here at all," he said.

He figured the guy on the left was the leader. When two thugs worked for somebody, one is typically higher in the pecking order, and that person is the one who does the talking.

The guy on the left had done the talking. If Nick took him down first, the guy on the right, not used to making decisions, would probably hesitate for a fraction of a second, which would give Nick the opening he needed.

Nick lined himself up with the guy on the left. The only danger now was if Nick had guessed wrong, and the guy on the right made the first move. Then Nick would be out of position and at a distinct disadvantage.

He guessed correctly.

The man on the left took a step forward, non-dominant hand out to grab Nick's collar. The gun never wavered from his other hand.

Nick didn't waver, either. He had learned early on that you act, not react. As soon as the man moved, Nick launched himself at him from the wall, using his foot against the wall as leverage. He brought his right elbow up at the same time, fist sliding across his body, and slammed his elbow into the man's throat. As the man staggered back, Nick jabbed his elbow the other way, straight into the bridge of the second man's nose.

The first man staggered back and fell to his knees, clutching his throat. Nick grabbed his gun, now forgotten as it clanged noisily to the floor. He reversed the grip in one fluid motion and smashed the butt against the man's temple. The Russian's head slammed into the floor and bounced. After that he didn't move.

The second man also staggered backwards, his movement sending him crashing into a shelf of CDs. Man, blood, and CDs cascaded to the floor with a loud crash.

Nick kicked several CDs away as he waded in. Right hand still firmly on the barrel of the Glock, Nick sent the butt end into the temple of the second enforcer. Like his partner, he went down hard and didn't move.

Anya ran in the store and saw the two men on the floor. "Is this how you ask nicely?" she said. Nick thought he saw a hint of a smile on her face.

"They were mean first," he replied.

"I don't think I'd want you mad at me," she said.

Nick checked the magazine on the first Glock, then reached for the second gun. "No, you wouldn't," he said.

He found Boris crouched down behind the counter, cowering with his arms over his head.

"Get up," Nick ordered, casually flicking one of the Glocks in Boris's direction.

Boris stood up hastily, eyes on the gun.

"I assume you'll need to call this in," Nick said.

Boris didn't move and didn't tear his eyes from the gun.

"Tell you what," Nick said. "Give me fifteen minutes, then call. In return, I'll move the bodies out the back door. You can tell

Maxsim that his goons chased me out the back door and you haven't seen us since."

Boris gulped and showed no comprehension to what Nick had just said.

Nick reached out with his other hand and lightly slapped the Russian's face. "Yo, you got that?"

The slap brought Boris around. "Wh-what?" he asked.

Nick sighed and tried again, in simple English. This time Boris seemed to grasp the concept. He nodded, but looked worried.

"What?" Nick asked.

"I still can't say where your friends are," he said.

"You don't have to," Nick answered. "I'll ask them." He motioned with his Glock towards the two goons on the ground.

Boris finally tore his gaze from the gun and looked at Nick. "I can't give you fifteen minutes."

"Why not?"

"They'll know. Then they'll kill me."

"In a few hours they'll be dead."

Boris shook his head. "I'd like to believe that. If you lose, I die."

Nick nodded. "OK, then what?"

"Hit me."

Nick stared at the man for a long moment, then sighed and nodded. "In the head?"

Boris pointed to his temple. "Yes, here."

Nick sighed. "Are you sure this is what you want?"

"Yes. Then do me favor."

"What?"

"Never come in my store again."

Chapter 15

Nick stepped up to the first would-be abductor, the man who had done the talking. A dribble of blood ran from the guy's temple, his face was ashen, but he was starting to come to.

Nick slapped his cheek to speed the process up. The man opened his eyes, saw Nick, closed them again, and opened. Unfortunately for him, Nick was still there.

"Where are the Americans?" Nick asked without preamble. Anya moved in behind him.

"Fuck you," the man said, and coughed.

Nick slapped him again. "Wrong answer, asshole. I'm done playing. Where are they?"

The man shook his head to clear it. Nick knew he had a horrendous headache, but then, surprisingly, the man grinned weakly and whispered something.

Nick leaned in, as did Anya. "What?" he asked.

The man whispered, "Your friend is dead. And his woman is Maxsim's whore now. So who's the asshole?"

It took a second for the words to process, a second that seemed much longer. When they finally got it, Anya stumbled back and fell hard on her butt. She put her hand to her mouth to stifle a scream.

The roaring started in Nick's left ear again. He knew it wouldn't go away this time. He let it take over. They crossed the line.

He swung the gun at the man's head with all his force.

Chapter 16

The entryway of the brothel took up the front half of the ground floor of the three-story building. Nick was surprised at how nice it looked, given the crumbling façade of the outside. He was expecting something more along the lines of a hotel that rented rooms by the hour.

Several couches ringed the sides of the room. Gaudy art ordained the walls, mostly watercolor nudes. Sunlight streamed in through outsized windows, highlighting dust floating through the air. Women lounged on the couches, not moving much, smoking.

A large desk occupied the space to Nick's right. A receptionist sat behind it. She was dark haired, cute, and wore a black business suit at an attempt at class. Nick had to admit it almost worked. At least it offset the art a bit.

Nick scanned for male faces first. They would be the threats. He only saw one, a large bulk sitting on the edge of the desk, chatting up the receptionist. Nick quickly thought back to the night at the club, and couldn't remember the face. Good. Hopefully the man was not aware of him. The man on the edge didn't register any emotion at Nick's appearance except annoyance that his conversation with the receptionist had been interrupted. He gave Nick a professional once over and then stood up with a sigh. His time to impress the woman would have to wait.

Nick stood in the entrance for several seconds, not moving, taking it all in. The roaring in his head had subsided somewhat, but it was replaced with an all-consuming desire to find Scott and Katie and get them the hell out of there.

Back at the CD shop, he and Anya had moved the bodies of the two Russians out the back of the store. The first man was dead but the second would be fine, eventually. They dumped both men in the alley behind the store, and Nick liberated their Glocks and spare ammo. He told Anya to stand guard across the street from the brothel. He knew Katie, at least, was in the brothel, and perhaps Scott was as well. But he didn't want to have to keep an eye out for Anya. And he needed her to alert him if the police showed up, anyway.

She wasn't happy about not going in after them with Nick, but the look on his face told her it would be futile to argue.

The look on *her* face said she felt sorry for whoever tried to stop him.

Nick was ready to leave if he sensed any danger, but it appeared safe. People were either curious or not interested in him. He didn't rush anything; silence unnerved most people, and caused them to say and do things they wouldn't normally say or do.

But it was quiet. The large man disappeared and the receptionist looked at him expectantly, a smile on her face. Nick started to walk towards her.

A movement to his left made him pause. A woman stood up abruptly, and he could tell she was watching him intently. He tensed, ready for trouble, and turned towards her.

It was Lauren's friend. He didn't know her, had never talked to her, but he remembered seeing her near Lauren at the club. He remembered her eyes, silver and flashing angrily at him even in the dark light of the Dolphin. Perhaps friend was too strong of a word, but she was at least Lauren's acquaintance.

She had dark hair, appeared worn out in a pink robe. Her feet were bare. She was smoking and looked as if she had been crying.

Her eyes never left Nick and he knew she recognized him as well. She bent over, quickly stubbed her cigarette out in an ashtray on a small table next to the sofa, and crossed over to Nick, forcing a smile.

"Come back to see me so soon, baby?" she asked in a husky Russian accent. She reached up and gave Nick a quick smoky kiss on his cheek, then pulled back, looking at him intently, warily, her hand on his arm.

Nick wasn't expecting a welcome and didn't move for a long moment. She kept looking at him expectantly, eyes on his.

His training took over. When in doubt, just go with it. He smiled at her, making sure the receptionist saw it, and said, "Of course, honey. I missed you."

She squeezed his arm slightly and turned to the receptionist. She said something to the woman behind the desk and both laughed. The receptionist replied and marked something in her book.

"Fifty dollars, please," the receptionist said to Nick. Nick was tempted to protest when he felt another squeeze on his arm. Sighing slightly, he pulled out his wallet and handed over fifty dollars American. He knew by now they didn't like rubles.

Transaction completed, the receptionist turned away and the prostitute led Nick back to her room by the hand. She didn't look at him and walked fast.

An opening out the back of the lobby led to a short hallway with three doors on either side. More, but smaller, paintings of nudes and couples engaged in all sorts of sexual activities adorned the walls. They were probably there to inspire the customers, Nick thought, so they popped their corks sooner and got out faster. Capitalism in action.

Stairs at the end of the hall led up to the next floor, but the woman stopped at the last door on the right. She opened it and led Nick in.

The room was small and sparsely decorated. A medium-sized bed dominated the room, with a dresser and mirror at the foot of the bed. A large window took up most of the far wall. It was open, which was good because the room had a distinctive odor of sex. Nick tried to take shallow breaths. If this woman expected action from him, she was going to be disappointed. He wasn't sure if he'd even be able to get it up at this point.

But sex wasn't on her mind. She closed the door and leaned against it. "You were at the club," she said. It was a statement, not a question.

Nick nodded, didn't say anything. She looked him up and down. "Galina is dead," she said, and tears welled up in her eyes again.

Nick was confused. "Who?" he asked.

"Galina. Your…friend."

"You mean Lauren?"

She smiled through her tears. "That's the name she used with you? She loved Lauren Bacall, from old movies we used to watch. She always said it was a pretty name, and it would be hers when she went to America."

Now tears formed in Nick's eyes. "I'm sorry," he said.

She sniffed and rubbed a sleeve across her nose. "Maxsim killed her," she said simply.

"How do you know it was Maxsim?"

"Because he's a bastard!" she shot back. "Anyone crosses him, he kills them."

Nick sighed. He wasn't surprised. "What's your name?"

"Alenka."

"Alenka, he's taken two of my friends," Nick said. "I'm afraid he's going to kill them as well."

"The Americans," she said. "I've heard them. They're here."

Nick's ears perked up. "Do you know where?"

"Is this why you're here?"

"Yes."

"OK," Alenka said. "I thought so. This is why I came to you. You want to help them."

Yes, Nick thought. For Galina.

"I heard them upstairs. I heard shouting and screaming."

Nick froze. "Male or female?"

Alenka shrugged. "Sometimes it is difficult to tell."

Nick shook his head and said, "Shit," under his breath. Time for Plan B, which didn't involve tip-toeing around.

"There's more," Alenka said. She took a step forward and placed her hand on his shoulder. He could smell the smoke and sweat on her. It reminded him of Galina. As did her red, dulled eyes.

"There is a story among the girls that we have new...how do you say it...new competition. American competition."

Nick stared at her. He shook his head. "No, no way. Maxsim's nuts, and maybe he kept her for himself, but I don't believe he'd kidnap an American and put her to work in his brothel. If the police found out about that, he'd end up in the gulag!"

Alenka smiled sadly. "They pay the police to look elsewhere. He can do what he wants."

"No, he can't," Nick replied. He checked his pockets. He had the Glocks and his knife, plenty of firepower. "Do you know where she is?" he asked.

Alenka pointed skyward. "Upstairs," she said. "He has a few, what do you call them, 'VIP rooms' on the top floor. She would be there."

"Have you heard anything about the American man with her?" Nick asked.

Alenka shook her head, black hair curling over her eyes. "Not much, but he must be there near her. He's not down here."

Nick nodded and crossed to the door. He opened it slightly and peeked out. Nobody around.

"Galina's room is there," Alenka said sadly as she pointed to the wall next to the head of her bed. "We used to knock on the wall when we were alone. It made me feel less alone."

Nick nodded and sighed.

"We were together since the orphanage," Alenka said. Her voice was low, miserable, her mind back to her childhood. "We had beds next to each other in the baby home."

"You studied English with her," Nick said.

She smiled at the memory. "Yes. Somebody gave us a book on English. We thought perhaps if we knew the language, somebody from America would take us home together. But nobody came for us except Maxsim."

She put her face in her hands and began to cry, hair falling over her fingers.

Nick put his arm around her shoulder and pulled her to him in a brief hug. "I'll make sure Maxsim doesn't do it to anybody else."

Alenka looked up at him with tear-stained eyes. "Thank you. But what will happen to us when he's dead?"

Nick didn't have an answer to that. He slipped out the door and was gone.

The hall was still deserted. Nick flicked open the knife and crept to the stairs. The stairs reversed direction halfway up, so he couldn't see what was above him, just that it was darker than the ground floor. The only sounds he heard came from the lobby, and he figured he was safe. He walked up the stairs as if he knew where he was going. His air of confidence might give him a precious few seconds on the attack if he ran into somebody.

The second floor was dark. Not pitch black, as sunlight came through a curtained window at the far end of the hall, but it had the look of a storage area, perhaps purposefully separating the commoners on the ground floor from the elite at the top. Gripping the knife harder, Nick went up to the third floor.

Vladimir had never felt so powerful. And that was saying something.

True, the woman underneath his great bulk was not responding as well as she might, but this was understandable given her situation. Vlad didn't know all of the details, nor did he want to. He just knew the woman was an American who had somehow crossed the freak Maxsim, and now she was Vlad's for the taking.

Of course it had cost Vlad a large sum to be the first to take the American, but what was the use of money if not to provide entertainment? Whoever came after him would have to deal with damaged goods. Vlad knew his sex was far from gentle and there would likely be blood on her before they were done. But again, he had paid a handsome dowry for her. If she didn't last long after he was done, that was of no consequence to him.

Vladimir Zhorovski was the head of a large oil and gas conglomerate near Rostov. He didn't get to his position by backing down and not taking risks. He knew if he showed weakness, the jackals positioning for control of resources in Mother Russia would come after him like a swarm of locusts. So he was as merciless as he had to be.

Plus, he had to admit he enjoyed taking down his rivals. Such as Anatoly Makarikhina. Anatoly had envisioned himself as the next leader of the company. Vladimir had no problems with the man giving himself those delusions, but Anatoly had the bad taste to try to act on them before Vladimir was ready to leave.

Anatoly had ended up at the bottom of a gravel pit. More specifically, Anatoly's torso had been tossed into the gravel pit. His head, hands, and feet were somewhere at the bottom of the Don, in a large metal barrel. Vlad had separated his rival personally, starting with the feet so Anatoly would spend several minutes screaming madly before Vlad took his head off.

Right now this woman was his rival. She didn't scream, didn't even open her eyes, but she knew who was in charge. That thought aroused Vlad even more, and he grunted loudly as he thrust.

Nick heard the grunting as soon as he hit the landing. It came from the first door on the right. The door looked identical to Alenka's, and Nick had to assume the room behind it was the same as well. Bed just inside, with the head of the bed to the right. His first move would be straight in and to the right, where their chests and heads would be. If he was wrong, and it was Katie, he'd make the adjustment on the fly, and the man might live for another second.

Nick listened for sounds down the hall. Faint voices came from somewhere along the far end. They were behind another door, but were most likely less than twenty feet away from this first room, so he would have to be as quiet as he could be.

He checked the knife in his hand. The blade glinted dully in the low light.

He put his other hand on the doorknob.

Vlad was getting close, he could feel it. He fed off the power of it all, using it to thrust harder into the American. His face and bare chest glistened with sweat, the sweat dripping on her breasts, the ample fat around his gut rising and falling like waves. His hands were on her shoulders, pinning her down. He knew he could just move his hands closer together around her throat, and she'd be dead in seconds. But Maxsim wouldn't be happy. Not that Vlad cared about Maxsim, but he did care about being first in line next time, so he knew he wouldn't be able to kill the wench under him. Pity.

Her eyes were closed and she had bit her lip so hard it bled. The blood gleamed up at Vlad invitingly. He bent down to lick it up.

At that moment he felt a slight draft of colder air to his right. The door was opening quickly. Vlad felt a surge of anger. For the price he paid, he was going to finish before he was interrupted, dammit!

Before he died, it dimly registered in Vlad's head that the new man was large, very angry, and carried a knife.

Chapter 17

Nick flew through the door, his angle sending him directly towards the heads of the couple having sex.

Nick took it all in immediately. The woman on the bed faced away from the door but he knew without a doubt it was Katie. The fat man on top of her turned his head to look at Nick, mouth open. Nick could tell the mouth was open due to exertion, and not a prelude to a warning. This huge man looked like he hadn't exercised in the last few years, and the sex was wearing him out. Nick was glad of that. The man would be less trouble.

Nick jumped on the bed, his right hand covering the man's mouth as his left plunged the blade into the man's neck. His momentum carried them across the bed and off the far side. The man hit the floor between the bed and the wall with a loud thud, Nick landing on top of him, knife deep in the man's neck. Blood poured out and covered his hand before it cascaded onto the floor, but he held the knife in silently, and kept pressing until the thrashing gradually ceased.

He straddled the fat man for several seconds after he stopped moving, then gradually pulled the knife out and wiped it on a sheet. Then he turned to Katie.

She was not the same person he had seen two days before. Even with the death struggle inches away from her, she showed no emotion. She simply turned on her side, away from the men, and curled up in a fetal position. Her eyes remained closed.

Nick crawled out of the back of the bed so as to not disturb her, then walked over to her side of the bed. She lay still, with her head on her hands. She didn't look up.

Shock, Nick knew. The body's defense against something terrible happening to it, and that fat Russian was all kinds of terrible. He didn't try to rouse her from it. Perhaps shock was the best thing for Katie right now.

He wrapped the bed sheet around her body and gently lifted her in his arms. He wasn't sure where he was going to put her while he searched for Scott, but he knew it would have to be someplace safe. As soon as Maxsim found out what had happened, he'd begin looking for Nick as well as Katie.

His first thought was Alenka's room. He peeked out the door, saw that the hallway was still empty, and carried her down the stairs. She was a solid woman but Nick was running on adrenaline, and he carried her without a problem. When he got to Alenka's door he stopped. There was really no need to get Alenka involved, since there was an empty room right next door. He pulled open the door to Galina's room with one hand and gently placed Katie on the bed.

He bent low over the still body. "I'll be right back, Katie. I'm going to get Scott. You stay here and rest."

He hated like hell to leave her, but he had one more person to find. Anyway, he was pretty sure she wasn't going anywhere on her own.

Katie's blank eyes stared nowhere as Nick softly closed the door behind him.

The hallway was clear, but the roaring in his ears had returned. Nick stopped for a moment and shook his head slightly to clear it. Now was not the time to throw open doors, guns blazing, although at that moment he wanted nothing more than to shoot every one of Maxsim's people in the head.

Gradually the noise subsided, and Nick stepped forward.

The third floor was still quiet, which was surprising since he had just killed a man there. Apparently others were in another area or preoccupied with various activities.

Nick crept past the door to the room containing the fat dead Russian. He cracked the door and looked in to make sure nobody was nosing around the body. The room was silent, the body out of sight on the floor on the other side of the bed. Nick could smell the metallic odor of blood, lots of it, but there wasn't anything he could do about that. He closed the door and moved on.

Maxsim and Scott were most likely on the top floor, Nick figured. Maxsim wouldn't want the American too close to the innocent, or at least relatively innocent, bystanders on the ground floor, and he would want to keep himself close to Katie, if for no other reason than to show everybody he was still in charge. So he was close.

In fact, he could possibly come checking on his charge any moment now, Nick realized. The thought made him stop in the middle of the hallway. The Russian would likely pass right by where Nick was standing, on his way to Katie's room. He could send an aide to check on her but odds were strong he would do it himself, to remind the fat dead Russian who was in charge.

There were two doors on the other side of the hall. Nick pressed his ear to the first one and thought he heard breathing. It was deep and rhythmic. Somebody sleeping, probably one of the girls. It was late in the morning but they obviously didn't keep regular hours. He moved on to the next door.

The second room sounded much quieter. If somebody slept, they slept very softly. He turned the knob silently and poked his head inside. The room was similar to the one he just left, except no dead body. He glanced around, head just inside the door, until he was satisfied it was empty.

Nick slipped through the doorway, then turned and closed the door until it was cracked. The door faced away from where the man or men would come from, so they wouldn't see him unless they happened to glance behind them after they passed. He pulled out one of the Glocks and made sure a round was chambered.

It took longer for them to check on Katie than he had hoped. They probably didn't want to disturb the fat Russian in the middle of his activities. He couldn't lean against the door without closing it, so he stood behind the door quietly, waiting, becoming increasingly nervous that someone would come in before his target passed.

Several minutes into his vigil he heard footsteps in the hallway. A shadow passed the room and Nick peered out from behind the door.

He was wrong. It wasn't Maxsim.

Nick cursed silently, but it wasn't the end of the world. He could corner the man in the room and get him to tell where Scott and Maxsim were. After all, he had a gun and the Russian probably didn't. No need to remain armed in your own headquarters.

He watched the man knock on the door, ten feet away. The Russian waited a few seconds, then knocked again. After a few more seconds he put his ear to the door. Finally, he opened it slowly, stuck his head in the door, and disappeared into the room.

Nick crossed over to the other room quickly and silently. He checked his gun to make sure a round was chambered. Taking a silent breath, he moved into the doorway, gun first.

At that moment his plan began to unravel. He had been correct about the gun, but something else never occurred to him. The man had a walkie talkie.

Chapter 18

Nick stepped into view in the doorway. The Russian was bent over the body, checking for a pulse and murmuring into the walkie talkie in his hand.

The man looked up and saw Nick. To his credit, he didn't panic. He simply continued to speak into the walkie talking, not moving. Nick caught the word "Americanskaya," which Nick took to mean himself, before he put a bullet in the man's left leg.

The man grunted in pain and sat down hard next to Vladimir's blood-soaked body as Nick stepped into the room. Nick kicked the walkie talkie across the room and rapidly frisked the man, who was too busy holding his leg to put up any resistance.

No guns. Nick checked the wound quickly. He had put the shot away from the femoral artery, as much as he could, so the guy wouldn't bleed out before help arrived.

Nick didn't bother to ask where Maxsim was. The man was obviously a professional and wouldn't give in quickly enough to Nick's pressure tactics. Nick briefly considered putting the gun against the man's head before asking any questions, but he didn't think it would do any good and besides, it would take too much time. Plus, he'd done that enough in his life and didn't want to go there again if he didn't have to,

Instead, he tore the top sheet off the bed, balled it up, and tossed it to the man. If he was as good as Nick suspected he was, he would turn it into a tourniquet for his leg. Without a gun and no mobility, the man was no longer of any consequence.

Without looking back, Nick ran out of the room. He took a right out the door and walked carefully down the hallway, gun in front of him. With any luck, Maxsim was on the other end of the walkie talkie and was now leaving his room to seek out Nick, making plenty of noise so Nick could find him.

But the hallway was silent. Nick slowed as he neared the end of it. He held his gun out, ready to shoot where he saw or heard movement.

It was quiet.

Damn, what to do? He had no idea where Maxsim was. He didn't even know if the guy was in the building, although he was pretty sure Maxsim wouldn't stray too far from Katie. The worst thing he could do now was bang around, looking for the bastard. That would be the quickest way to get Scott killed.

So he stopped. Dead in his tracks. Nick flattened himself against the wall, gun up in a neutral position, and again waited. The seconds seemed like hours.

Soon he heard a clattering at the other end of the hallway, behind him. Somebody was coming up the stairs in a rush.

Nick dropped to the floor and rested his pistol on his other arm to steady it. If the person coming up the stairs was not a friendly, any shots from the hostile would likely go high. Not only was he running up the stairs so his bullets would have a high trajectory anyway, but typically people on the move tended to place their first bullet high.

Plus, he blended in with the floor, especially if he didn't move.

Maxsim appeared on the stairs. He slowed down and bent over at the waist to make a smaller target. He was sneering and it looked like he had blood on his arm. Nick sincerely hoped it was Maxsim's own blood.

Maxsim paused at the top of the stairs, looked around, and headed for the door to the room containing the two Russians. Nick aimed at the man's head, then lowered his sights a bit. He still needed to know where Scott was and he was running out of people to ask.

He fired from his prone position and Maxsim screamed as the bullet went through his side. He fell back against the wall and slide down, leaving a thin trail of blood on the wall.

Nick jumped up and ran to Maxsim, who had dropped his gun and was weakly fluttering his hand towards it, trying to will it to him.

Ignoring the gun, Nick grabbed Maxsim by the collar of his expensive-looking, but now severely bloodstained, shirt and pulled him into the room. Maxsim grunted in pain as he as was manhandled through the doorway.

Nick looked around quickly and spotted the enforcer he had shot in the leg. The man was sitting against the far wall, a bloody rag around his leg. He looked at Nick dimly. He face was ashen and his mouth hung open. He would need medical attention soon. Apparently Nick hadn't missed the artery as much as he had hoped.

Nick let go of Maxsim's collar and Maxsim slumped to the floor, moaning loudly and clutching his side. Blood poured between his fingers and puddled on the wood floor.

Nick didn't care. His only goal was to get Scott and Katie out of there, the faster the better. He jammed his gun against Maxsim's forehead.

"Where's Scott?" he asked

Maxsim glared at him. "Fuck you," he said. It took him two breaths to get the words out.

"Why do you people always say that to me?" Nick said as he pulled the gun away from the man's forehead and jammed it into the bullet hole in his side. Maxsim screamed again, a sound cut short when Nick's hand clamped roughly over his mouth.

Nick waited a moment, then removed the hand. Maxsim's eyes rolled up in his head and Nick knew he was losing the man. "Where is he?" he yelled.

"He'll never tell you," said a voice behind him. Nick whirled around and stared at the large man standing behind him, gun in his hand. Oh, shit, was all Nick could think. In his single-mindedness he didn't think to keep an eye out for more bodyguards. He was in big trouble.

He recognized the man. It was the second bodyguard from the club. The man with the scar.

"Move," the man said, and motioned Nick to the side with his gun. He had the drop on Nick, who had no choice but to comply. Nick pulled his gun out of Maxsim's bloody shirt and reluctantly moved away from the man, expecting a bullet any second.

Despite his agony, Maxsim looked at Nick with triumph. "You die now, American," he said, and even managed a pained laugh. He glanced at the bodyguard. "Shoot him," he ordered.

The bodyguard looked at Maxsim, at his comrade sitting against the wall with the tourniquet on his leg, and finally at Nick. "Your friend is in the basement," he told Nick.

Nick just looked confused as Maxsim choked. A thin line of blood rolled down from the corner of Maxsim's mouth. He said something in Russian to the bodyguard, something accusatory, and the bodyguard smiled. This increased Maxsim's anger, and he began to cough violently.

"You don't have much time," he told Nick in English. "Your shot alerted people downstairs and the police will be here soon."

"Kill him!" Maxsim screamed with the rest of his breath, which wasn't much. The bodyguard looked at the man with a mixture of disgust and pity, and took a step forward. He bent down and placed his hand on Maxsim's chest, restraining him. He gently placed his gun against the struggling man's forehead, then bent over and whispered in his ear. Whispered for several seconds. As he talked, Maxsim's eyes widened and he began to thrash more, but he was too weak to make any headway against the bodyguard's hand.

Finally the man pulled back, and Nick knew he was going to kill Maxsim.

Nick scrambled back a few feet as the bodyguard pulled the trigger. Maxsim's head blew apart, bits of brain and bone flying through the room. The sheet on the bed behind Maxsim instantly turned crimson.

Nick struggled to his feet. "Shit!" he yelled.

The bodyguard looked at him calmly. "Maxsim was a madman," he said. "We're better off without him." He slid Nick's gun back to the stunned American. "You should leave now. Before the police arrive."

"What did you say to him?"

The man inclined his head towards the door. "Go," was all he said.

Nick didn't need further prompting. He grabbed the gun off the floor and headed for the door. He stopped in the doorway.

"Your friend will need help quickly," Nick said, motioning towards the Russian propped against the wall.

The man nodded. "Da," he said. "Thank you for not killing him."

Nick paused, started to reply, thought better of it. He ran out the door.

The stairs led straight to the basement. Nick heard commotion on the first floor as he took the stairs two at a time. He hoped he could get back to Katie, but with Maxsim gone he knew the danger to her was most likely past. Scott was the one he was worried about now.

The stairs ended three floors below, in the basement. In contrast to the main floors, the basement was one large, unfinished room. Nick found a light switch and flicked it on.

It didn't take long to find Scott.

He was at the far end of the basement, dumped unceremoniously on a mattress. In Nick's opinion, he had been dead for at least an hour.

In a rush, all of the adrenaline left Nick's body and he sat down hard on the mattress, staring at the hole in Scott's head. No blood trickled out of it. He was dead before the finishing shot.

Nick held his face and yelled into his hands, face shaking, mind numb, for a long moment.

Finally, hearing sirens, he composed himself, wiped his face, said goodbye to Scott, and left the brothel through a window in the back as the Rostov police came in through the front.

Nick looped around the block and approached the brothel from across the street. He wasn't too concerned with anybody recognizing him. At that point he didn't really give a damn.

He found Anya watching the brothel, sitting on cracked stone steps in front of an apartment building. She stood up when she saw him, relief on her face.

"Scott's dead," was all he told her.

She stepped forward and hugged him. "Oh, god, I'm so sorry."

"I couldn't save him," Nick said. A tear fell from one eye but his face was rigid, keeping the emotion in. "He was dead before I got there."

"What of Katie?"

Nick sighed. "She...went through something nobody should have to go through."

"Oh, god," Anya said again, and started crying.

"She's alive, though. I had to leave her there. She'll be OK with the police," he said, as much to convince himself as to inform her.

"I'm sure she will be."

110

"I need a place to stay. I can't stay at the hotel."

"Did you kill Maxsim?"

"He's dead, but he's not the man pulling the strings," Nick replied. He decided not to tell her that the bodyguard plugged the madman. He still wasn't sure what the hell happened and he wanted to process it before he talked to her.

"How can you be sure Maxsim isn't in charge?"

"Because the guy's a cokehead who couldn't run a lemonade stand, let alone a business like a brothel. No, there's somebody else."

"But Maxsim was the one who killed your friend, no?"

Nick turned the corner and paused while he surveyed the street. Nothing unusual. "Yeah, Maxsim killed Scott and had Katie raped. He probably killed Lauren—I mean, Galina—too, but I don't think that was his idea." He stopped and thought. "No, I don't think he would've gotten rid of one of his girls. I think he was ordered to take her out to find me."

"Why?"

"Because they're freaks, that's why!" Nick said loudly. He quickly looked around but there wasn't anybody close enough to hear him. God, he needed a drink. "I'm a thorn in their side, and they don't like thorns."

"So you think this other man will come after you."

"Yes, I do," Nick said. "At least, I can't take the chance. If I'm wrong, then nothing bad happens. If I'm right...well, I don't really want to think about that."

There was a pause, then Anya said, "Well, of course if you want to stay with me you can. I'd like to help."

"Thank you, Anya," Nick replied. "I appreciate it. I don't know what I'd do without you."

Anya laughed but it sounded strained. "You'd survive. I don't really know you but I know you'd be OK. Do you know where I live?"

"No."

He gave her his phone and she typed in the address. As she typed she gave him directions. Fortunately it wasn't far from the Olymp, so he wasn't too worried about finding it.

"You go there now," he told her. "I'll meet you there."

"When will you come?" she asked.

111

"Soon," Nick said. "I have a few things to do first."

Chapter 19

The key lady on the fourth floor of the Rostov hotel paused when she saw the American come up the stairs. She had just hung up with Dmitri, a man who scared her more than anybody else had in her long life, including Stalin. He had told her to call him if she saw the large American.

He said terrible things had just occurred at the brothel, and he didn't expect the American to show up at the hotel any time soon, if at all, but if he did she must notify him immediately.

She hung up and had just opened the newspaper again when the large American appeared at the top of the stairs. Her breathing increased and she sensed her face reddening, but she knew enough not to act suspicious. She smiled at the man as she handed him his room key. When he disappeared around the corner she quickly dialed Dmitri's number. This was sure to earn her a big bonus.

Nick turned the corner in the hallway and stopped. The key lady had obviously heard about the brothel because she smiled at him. If there was one thing the key ladies never did, it was smile. He gave her to the count of three to make the call.

Dmitri didn't answer directly. When you're that important, you never answer your own phone. A female voice answered.

"Yes?" she asked.

"I need to speak with Dmitri," the key lady said softly, a bit breathlessly.

"Regarding what?"

"Never you mind, just put him on!" The key lady was not about to share her bonus with any young tart who answered the phone.

She heard a sigh, then dead air as the woman walked the phone to Dmitri.

Before Dmitri could pick up, a large hand snaked in front of the key lady and grabbed the phone. She was too startled to react, then too afraid. She looked up into the American's face and saw an expression that told her to back off.

Nick put the phone to his ear and his finger over his lips, silencing the old woman. He said "Hello?" into the phone and was greeted with dead air. So he waited.

Within seconds he heard a click on the other end of the line and a man's voice said, "Da?"

"Who is this?" Nick asked.

A pause, then the voice, louder now, said in English, "Ahh, my American friend! So you are back at the Hotel Rostov." Nick could sense him waving to his subordinates to get their butts to the Rostov as soon as they could.

He looked at his watch and gave himself one minute to talk.

"For now," Nick answered. "But by the time your friends get here I'll be gone, so we'll make this quick."

Dmitri laughed. "   Good luck, my friend. So, what would you like to talk about?"

"A truce."

There was another pause and Nick knew he had surprised the man. "A truce? You put several of my men in the hospital and you expect a truce?"

"Don't bullshit me, Ivan," Nick answered. "Maxsim's dead, not in the hospital. He got lazy and lost his head. Well, most of it, anyway."

"Even more reason for no truce."

"Listen, buddy. Your men keep coming after me, and they keep getting hurt. Your man Maxsim had one of my friends raped, and killed the other one. Not to mention killing his own girl. So I took him out, like a rabid dog. Now we're even." Not even close, Nick thought to himself, but the madness needed to end now.

"One dead American is not equal to one dead Russian," Dmitri answered.

"Trust me, Ivan, in this case it is. I may have even done you a favor."

"Perhaps, but no truce. You'll die here without ever seeing your beloved America again."

Nick felt a chill, then anger. He fought it down. "I hope you change your mind. I want no more bloodshed."

"You will have it, my friend."

114

Nick looked at his watch. The minute was up. Before he turned off the phone he glanced at the name at the top of the screen. The name of the person she had speed-dialed.

Dmitri.

Two minutes was all it took to clear out his things. First he wrote a note to Tom and Michelle, explaining as little as possible about why he wouldn't be around for a while. He paused, and then wrote his cell phone number at the bottom of the paper, after his name.

He left his suitcase with the CDs in his room, and jammed his clothes into a large shopping bag he had folded up and stuffed in the suitcase for dirty laundry. He grabbed the blue backpack lying on his bed and slung it over his shoulder, then ran into the bathroom to get his ditty bag from the vanity. He tossed it on top of his clothes and left the room with the shopping bag in one hand, not looking back. He slid the note under Tom and Michelle's door as he passed.

Nick passed the key lady without stopping. She just looked at him blankly, not even asking for the key. He wasn't about to give it to her anyway. He planned to use it later, when his new friends were all dead.

He took the stairs down two at a time. At the bottom he moved to the side of the lobby so he could watch the door from a better angle as he left the hotel. He was fairly certain Maxsim's cohorts wouldn't be there just yet, but he took no chances. It seemed quiet, so he walked out of the hotel as casually but as quickly as he could.

Anya's apartment was behind a nondescript door in the middle of a grimy hallway on the third floor of one of several huge Stalin-era apartment blocks. The anonymity suited Nick perfectly.

"Thank you, Anya," he told his host as he set his bag and backpack down inside the doorway. "Nobody will look here."

To contrast the depressing exterior, Anya had decorated her apartment in bright colors and unique art, both in paintings on the walls and small sculptures on her tables. Nick had to admit it made a nice oasis in a dismal apartment complex.

"Do you sculpt?" he asked, pointing to what looked like two hands grasping each other on a coffee table.

Anya laughed. "Oh, no, that's not me. I'm not one for creativity. I buy things from an old woman down by the river. Her granddaughter makes them." She paused. "I think that's the only way they have to make money, and they seem very nice."

Nick nodded. "Well, I'm sure they appreciate your taste in fine art."

Anya smiled and pointed to the kitchen. "Would you like some tea? And I have cake if you're hungry."

"That'd be great, Anya, thank you," Nick said. What he really wanted was a stiff drink, but he knew that wasn't a good idea under the circumstances. "I'll cut the cake."

Nick wasn't much for tea, he was more of a coffee drinker, but he had to admit Anya made a good cup of tea. She served it in cups that were well used but looked like they had been fairly expensive originally. Perhaps handed down through the family.

She grew somber as they worked their way through the cake and had a chance to think and talk. "I'm so sorry to hear about Scott and Katie," she said.

"Thank you," Nick said. "I'm not really sure how this all escalated. I mean, I turned Galina down, but that has to happen at least some of the time. The girls shouldn't get beat up every time they come home empty-handed."

"I don't know much about prostitutes," Anya replied, "but I do know about Russian men, and they can be real bastards. They need to be in charge of their women, and many don't mind hitting them if the girls get out of line."

Nick sighed. "I just can't imagine hitting a woman."

Anya smiled sadly. "You're a bit naïve, Nick. And that's why you're here, with me. You thought Russian men were more like you. You're not ruthless enough."

I doubt that very much, Nick thought as he sipped his tea. I'm just a slow starter.

"So now what will you do?" Anya asked.

"Well, I have about a week left before I can leave with Nonna," Nick replied. "I figure I'll just lie low."

"You said you talked to Maxsim's boss?"

"Yes. I told him we were even and asked for a truce."

"What did he say?"

Nick sighed. "He said no."

116

Anya picked at her cake. She had eaten half and didn't appear to want to finish it. "I'm not surprised," she said. "You fought back, and need to be punished."

"As you say, that's why I'm here."

Anya got up and poured them both more tea. She sat down and gave him a hopeful smile. "Well, perhaps he will not find you, and in a week you can leave with your daughter and forget all about us."

"I'll forget about him," Nick said, "but I won't forget about you and your kindness."

Anya blushed and changed the subject. "So, will your wife stay home with Nonna?"

"No, actually I will."

Anya looked surprised. "You? You don't seem like a man to stay home with his daughter." She flushed slightly. "No offense."

Nick smiled. "None taken," he said. "I'm looking forward to it, actually. I just want to stay home and play with her for a while."

"You don't think you'll be bored?"

"I hope so. I need some boredom."

Anya took another sip of tea and stared at him over the top of the cup. "You don't look like a man who's been bored much."

Nick paused. She was obviously fishing. How much to tell her? He didn't like to talk about his past, and there were some aspects of it that would make a few government agencies nervous if they got out. On the other hand, she was a young Russian girl who he'd probably never see again.

"No," he finally said. "I haven't been bored."

"You were in the military, no?"

"Yes, many years ago."

"Were you in wars?"

He nodded. "I was in the middle east," he told her. He didn't want to go into too many details about where or when. "I was with a group of men who would go into towns to make sure the bad guys had left."

"And had the bad guys usually left?"

"Sometimes yes, sometimes no. If not, we persuaded them to leave."

117

She put the cup down carefully. "That sounds dangerous."

"It could be. Although, to be honest, we preferred to watch and take notes rather than fight."

"How long did you do that?"

"Several years," he said. Her eyes widened. "Yeah, it was a while. I had always wanted to be a Marine. My father had been a soldier and that was what I knew growing up."

"Was your father happy that you followed him?"

"I think he was, but he never said much about it. He's not one for talking."

Anya nodded. "Mine, neither."

Nick took the opening. "So, what does your father do? You said he has some...troubles in England."

Anya looked nervous, and Nick instantly regretted bringing it up. "You don't need to tell me, Anya. It's really none of my business."

"No, that's OK," she said hesitantly. She looked down, and he knew it was her turn to decide how much to tell him. "He, well, he's in the import-export business."

Nick had a good idea what he was importing and exporting, especially if he had to leave England on a moment's notice. But he didn't want to press it. Instead he said, "But you didn't want to do that, so you're working at the Olymp instead?"

"Yes," she said. "I worked with him a little, but didn't like it. I have more fun at the restaurant and get to meet interesting people." She winked at him and Nick smiled.

"But your cousin is working with your father," Nick said.

"He is. Andrei likes money. He likes power, too. I'm sure he'll take over for papa one day."

"Are you OK with that?"

Anya shrugged. "Sure. He's a good guy, really. Sometimes he doesn't think through things, but he's better than most men with power around here."

"But you don't want any part of it."

She looked at him strangely. "Nick, I'm not some little angel, you know. What they're doing, I don't really have a problem with it. I just don't want to do it myself. But I support my father and cousin and will help them when they need it."

118

Nick finished off his tea and sat back in his chair. The afternoon was turning into evening and he knew Anya had to get to work soon. "I know you're not a little angel, Anya. Most people aren't. We do what we need to do, even if we don't enjoy it."

Anya sighed and leaned back as well. "But sometimes papa and Andrei seem to enjoy it."

"Yeah, the old eighty-twenty rule," Nick said.

"What's that?"

"Kelli talks about it all the time. Generally eighty percent is the norm and twenty percent are outliers. So with her computer security, she concentrates on the twenty percent initially. Once they are taken care of, she goes after the twenty percent of the twenty percent, and so on."

She looked confused. "So what does that have to do with anything?"

"Well, the theory is that eighty percent of people are good, and twenty percent take advantage of the situation to do what they want. Look at Nazi Germany, for example. Hitler really had no problem finding people for the Gestapo and SS. Most of the Germans were good people, just misled. But a subset, probably twenty percent, really got into it and willingly did things they couldn't normally do in civilized society."

She looked doubtful. "I think more than twenty percent of the Nazis were murderers."

"Perhaps, or it may just seem that way because a few did so many horrible things. And of course you have to take into account the twenty percent of the twenty percent."

She raised her eyebrows. "Oh?"

"Yeah, those are the real badasses. The ones who are just waiting for an opportunity to chop somebody's head off. The Maxsims."

Anya nodded. "You may be right. I guess I've never thought about it much." She looked at him sideways. "So where do I fit?"

Nick laughed. "Not sure yet, but I'm pretty sure I'd put you in the eighty percent. You have a good heart."

She shook her head sadly. "You don't know me very well, then. I've done some dark things."

"Like what?"

"Nothing I'd care to share, honey, sorry." She saw his look and laughed. "I haven't chopped anybody's head off, if that's what you're thinking. "

"I'm glad. I'll sleep better tonight."

"And where do you fit?"

"Ugh, don't ask."

"No fair! I told you."

Nick thought about it for a long time. "I like to think I'm part of the eighty percent, but have spent most of my time with the twenty percent, or even the twenty of the twenty."

"The, what do you call them, the badasses?"

"Yep."

"How did you handle them?"

"Usually lethally," Nick said. He drummed his fingers on the table absently as he thought about his part. How did he really handle them? Probably not very well, in hindsight. Like the insurgents who ambushed his team in the northern Iraqi mountains. The Americans lost six men in an intense, moving firefight before the enemy melted away. The insurgents thought they were safe, until the Americans tracked them down in a narrow ravine. Nick's squad leader trekked to the top of the ravine while Nick and his men kept the enemy pinned down. It didn't take long for the helicopters to show up and blast the hell out of that ravine.

"Well," he finally said. "If we weren't shooting at each other, we tried to talk to them."

"How did that go?"

He shook his head. "Not well, generally. We were infidels on their land. They didn't want to talk, they wanted to fight."

"So then you fought them?"

Pause, then "Yes."

"And killed them?"

A longer pause. "Yes," Nick said quietly.

"That really bothers you, no?"

Nick nodded.

"Good."

He looked at her and she smiled back.

"If you've done dark things, and it bothers you, then there is hope."

Chapter 20

Nick groaned and sat back from the computer monitor. Kelli's e-mail glared at him from the screen.

"Where Are You?" blinked the subject line. Underneath it, the body read, "Made it back home safe. I tried calling you at the hotel but no answer. Please reply when you get this. Love you! Me."

Nick looked around the internet café. More like an internet classroom, really, since the computers were placed on long tables, roughly five feet between monitors. Nick sat in the back row so nobody could see his screen. Not that he had much to worry about, since there were only two others there at nine in the morning, and they weren't paying any attention to him.

He leaned back, crossed his arms, and thought about how best to proceed. He knew he'd have to talk to Kelli sooner or later but had hoped things would be resolved by then. Perhaps they were, but sleeping on Anya's couch last night made Nick realize they probably weren't.

It was a bad night. Once Anya left and Nick turned the lights down, his anger left and the guilt and sadness hit. He felt terrible about Katie, and Scott, and especially Galina. She deserved none of what had visited her in her last days.

But when he thought about Nonna, the tears and sadness left him, replaced by resolve. Galina's death wouldn't be in vain, he promised himself. He was going to get Nonna out of Russia no matter what.

The wave passed. He spent the next two hours thinking, planning.

Anya got home late, with a dinner for Nick from the restaurant. He dug into the steak gratefully, because he had only eaten some bread earlier in the evening and didn't want to venture out to hunt and gather dinner. He wasn't afraid of running into Maxsim's cohorts. He just didn't want them to follow him back to the apartment and place Anya in danger. So he waited and thought and listened to his stomach growl.

They talked while he ate, but this time about nothing in particular. Andrei had stopped by the café for a few drinks, as he usually did, and inquired about Nick. Anya just said that Nick had called and said he had some trouble at the brothel, but hadn't gone into details. She told Nick that she didn't want to lie to her cousin, but was OK withholding information. Nick could tell him later.

But he had to tell Kelli now. He wasn't about to start keeping secrets. Like Anya, he wasn't too concerned about withholding information, at least for the short term, but this was too important not to share with his wife.

But he didn't want to do it via email. So his reply was simply, "Are you home? I'll call." She replied within a few minutes. He sighed, got up, and went to the front of the room.

A geeky-looking kid with zits and spiky blond hair sat in front of a computer. Nick glanced at the screen as he walked up. The guy was playing some kind of war game. The kid saw him, grimaced, paused the game, and turned to Nick.

"Yes?" he asked. No smile, his brain was obviously still in the middle of his game. He spoke in English, though, so at least he remembered Nick.

"Telephone?" Nick asked.

"Da," the kid replied. "To America?"

"Yes."

The kid pulled out a pricing sheet and pointed to a section labeled Phone. "Two hundred rubles connection," he said. "One hundred rubles every minute."

Nick did the calculations in his head and whistled. Several dollars just to dial, and a few more each minute. But he didn't have much of a choice, not if he wanted to do it right.

"Da," he said as he nodded.

The kid held out his hand. "Now," he said.

Nick peeled off a thousand rubles and handed it to the man. Enough for eight minutes, which should be plenty of time to get chewed out by Kelli.

The kid grabbed a cell phone, dialed the number Nick gave him, and handed the phone over. He went back to his video game as Nick shuffled a few steps away, phone to one ear and finger in the other.

Nick heard a series of clicks, then a tone as the phone rang half a world away. It only rang twice before Kelli answered.

"Hi, honey!" Nick smiled broadly as he heard his wife's voice. It was tinny, but no matter how stressed he got, Kelli had a way to calm him down.

"Hey, babe," he said. "How was your flight back?"

"Ugh, long," she replied. "But before I get to that, there's someone who wants to talk to you."

He heard her say, "Danny, daddy's on the phone!" There was a pause, then she said to Nick, "Here he is." Nick could hear her hand the phone to their son, replaced by the sound of quiet breathing. Nick could barely hear it through the connection.

"Hi, Danny!" Nick said with excitement in his voice. Danny got more out of the tone of the voice than the actual words.

"Hi, daddy," Danny replied, calmly.

"How are you?"

"Happy!" Nick knew this was just a stock answer. Danny tended to respond that way when asked how he was. It wasn't ideal, but better than a blank look.

"Good!" Nick replied. "I'm happy, too!"

There was a pause, then Nick heard softly, "Bike ride McDonalds?"

Nick laughed. Danny's favorite activity was riding his three-wheeled bicycle two miles to McDonalds with Nick to split a small fry and drink. "Bike ride McDonalds?" was typically the first thing out of Danny's mouth if Nick was home when he got off the bus on school days.

"Sorry, buddy, but daddy's on an airplane ride. I'll be home soon, though, and we can bike ride to McDonalds then, I promise."

There was a pause, then Danny said, "Bye bye, daddy." He could hear Kelli take the phone.

"Hi," she said. "He misses you."

"I miss him, too. How was your flight?"

"Long," Kelli said. "Rostov to Moscow, Moscow to Frankfurt, Frankfurt to Chicago, Chicago to Portland, then the drive here. I felt like I've been traveling forever! After you get home I want to stay home and nest for a while."

Nick forced a laugh and said, "Deal."

"How are things with you? I tried to get you at the hotel yesterday."

Nick closed his eyes; here it comes. "Yeah, I haven't been there much."

"No?"

"No. There've been...complications."

He heard an intake of breath, silence over the connection, then, "Talk to me."

"Nonna is fine and the adoption is still on," he said quickly.

"But..."

"Well, we've had some trouble with a few locals," he said. He didn't want to bring up the obvious mob connection just yet.

"What kind of trouble?"

"Well, Scott got involved with a few local troublemakers. There was an...altercation at a club a few nights ago. A few of their guys got hurt."

"I assume you were involved."

"Yes. Scott needed help."

He heard her sigh, then silence.

"It gets worse."

More silence.

"Scott's dead," Nick said.

Still more silence, then she said softly, "Oh, my God. What happened? Was it the fight? How did he die? Oh, my God!" Her voice ended up much louder than it had started.

"We knew the other guys worked at the brothel down the block from the hotel. You know how hot-headed Scott can be. Well, he went to the brothel after the fight. He was looking for trouble, and he found it."

"Oh, my God," she said again. "That's horrible. How's Katic taking it?"

Nick paused, then said, "Well, that's the other part of it. Katie went after Scott. They caught her and raped her in the brothel."

Kelli suddenly started crying. "I feel sick, Nick. Hold on, I'm going to sit down." He heard some rusting, and Danny said in some consternation, "It's not OK!"

"It's OK, honey," Kelli told him. "It's all good."

No, it wasn't.

She came back on the line. "OK, Nick, you need to tell me everything."

So Nick did. He decided not to leave anything out, what was the point? Kelli didn't interrupt. She just listened, although he did hear her swear softly when he told her about Katie's rescue.

About halfway through his story, the kid tapped Nick on the shoulder and pointed to his watch. Nick pulled out another thousand ruble note and handed it over without stopping the story. The kid held up five fingers, made a fist, and help up five fingers again to signify Nick had ten minutes left. Nick nodded and went back to talking

"So," he said as he started to wrap up, several minutes later. "I talked to whoever works with Maxsim. I told him I want this to be over with."

He paused. When Kelli spoke, her voice was a bit hoarse. "Do you think he'll listen?"

"I don't know, which is why I'm not staying at the Rostov. I don't want to take any chances."

"And who's this chick you're staying with?"

"Anya. I met her and her cousin a few nights ago. They're good people."

"I'd feel better if you stayed with her cousin. Actually, I'd feel better if you stayed in another hotel."

"I don't want to risk writing my name down and producing papers. Who knows if those damn key ladies are all working for Dmitri. And as for the cousin, Andrei is a nice guy but he's into stuff, too. Anya is a safer option."

Kelli sighed.

"You trust me, right?" Nick asked.

"With Anya? You fooling around is the least of my worries right now, Nick. You just killed a man, for Christ's sakes! And who-knows-what might be after you. I just want you to get Nonna and get the hell out of there."

"So do I, Kelli, and this is the best way I know how."

"You should've called the police when you had the chance."

"I know that now," Nick said and sighed. "I honestly thought I could walk into the brothel, reason with Maxsim, and get Scott and Katie out without the cops complicating things. I was afraid they might jeopardize the adoption."

"I love you, but you're way too optimistic."

125

Nick thought about Anya, who had said he was naïve. Once is a fluke, twice is a trend. He sighed again.

"I just can't believe you got yourself into this, Nick," Kelli said. He could tell she struggled to keep her voice even so Danny didn't get upset. "You aren't in Russia to fix the world's problems, you're there to get our baby girl!"

"I know, honey."

The kid ambled over and held up two fingers. Nick nodded.

Kelli continued. "I know you want to protect people, and I love you for that, I really do. But there's only one person I want you to protect, and that's Nonna. Got that? Just bring her home!"

"I will honey, I promise."

Kelli paused, then said, "I'm serious, honey. An orphanage is no place for our daughter."

"I know, Kelli. She'll be home in a week or so, and we'll never have to deal with these people again."

"Just do what you have to do. And Nick?"

"Yes, dear?"

"Keep in contact. I need to know that you and Nonna are safe."

"I will."

"But don't tell me what you have to do to get her out of there. Especially if it's messy. I don't want to know. But you have to get her out of there."

"I know, honey. I will. Nonna is worth any risk I have to take."

Kelli paused, and Nick was pretty sure she was crying. "I love you very much, and I know you'll do the right thing," she said.

"I have to go, babe," Nick said. "My time's up. I'm going to go see Nonna now."

Kelli sniffed. "Give her a big kiss from me," she said.

Nick smiled. "I will, babe. And in a week you can kiss her yourself."

"I really miss you. Be safe," she said, and was gone.

Nick handed the phone back to the kid, who saw the tears in his eyes but didn't say anything.

Chapter 21

Nick's cell phone buzzed as he neared Anya's flat. The original song had been some disconcerting Russian jingle. It didn't take Nick long to change it to a basic ring.

It was an unknown caller. He was tempted to ignore the call, but after a moment clicked the Talk button.

"Da?" he said. It would be tough to identify a voice from one word.

"Nick?" The voice was American. Nick relaxed slightly.

"Hey, Tom."

"Thank God I got you," Tom said. "Listen, I'll be quick. There was a cop here this morning, asking about what happened at the brothel."

"What happened at the brothel?"

"Don't be coy, you bastard. You know damn well what happened at the brothel. I read your note. Trouble is, the cops seemed to find more bodies there than you mentioned. Any idea what happened to them?"

"No."

There was a pause. "OK, then, but this cop is interested in talking to you. He wants to interview everybody who knew Katie and Scott."

Nick saw an empty bench ahead of him. He sat down on one end and said, "How's Katie, anyway?"

"She's fine, considering. Pyotr, the cop, said she's in the hospital but is out of danger. She's going back to the states in a few days."

Nick shook his head. "I assume the adoption is off."

"Of course the adoption is fucking off! Who are these animals, anyway?"

"Tom, you're on an unsecured line."

"I don't care! I know Scott shouldn't have messed with them, but they went way too far. And now you can't even stay at the hotel."

"I'll be fine. What did you tell this guy?"

"Pyotr? Just that you were out, and that I'd tell you to call him when I saw you next."

Nick sighed. "Thanks for covering for me, Tom. I owe you one."

"I don't think so, if you took out a few of the bad guys yesterday."

"Unsecured line, dude. I don't know what you're talking about."

Tom sighed. "OK, whatever. Anyway, Pyotr wants to talk to you."

"What's his number?"

Tom read it out. Nick typed it into his phone, thanked his friend, and hung up. He sat on the bench, thinking, for a long time. Finally he sighed heavily, put the phone in his pocket, and got up.

Anya was washing dishes. She turned to him with a smile when he opened the door, plate in one hand and wash cloth in the other. She looked the picture of domesticity.

Her smile faded when she saw his face. "What is it?" she asked.

"Cops are sniffing around the hotel," Nick answered as he took his wallet and phone out and tossed them on the table. He grabbed a water bottle from the fridge and cracked it open.

She frowned. "About yesterday."

"Yes."

Anya finished wiping the plate and put it away. "Do they know about you?"

"Yep. They want to talk to me."

She pursed her lips. "You need to see them, you know."

"I'm not sure that's wise."

She moved closer to him and motioned to a chair at the table. "Sit down." When he hesitated she said, stronger, "Sit."

He did, and she took a spot across the table from him. "You need to know something about Russian police. They only ask for so long, then they tell. And if they can't find you, they'll keep looking. And you don't want them to find you. So, you find them."

Nick sighed and nodded. "Tom gave me the guy's number."

She smiled. "Perfect. Call him, now. Show him you don't have anything to hide."

"But I do have something to hide. I have lots to hide, including a dead fat Russian."

She shook her head. "They have nothing. If they had even a little bit of evidence, you'd be in handcuffs right now. Talk to them." She flipped the towel over her shoulder. "I think you can lie to them without problem."

Nick wasn't so sure, but he couldn't think of another option so he dialed the number. Anya watched with interest.

The connection completed and a man answered in Russian. All Nick caught was the word "Peter" but it was enough.

"Zdrastvoytye, this is Nick Wallace," he said. "I understand you wanted to talk to me?"

There was a moment of silence on the other end, then the voice said in halting English. "Yes, Nick. Thank you for calling. My name Pyotr Archipenko. I'm with Rostov police. I need to talk you about…" there was another pause as the man apparently consulted notes or a computer screen. "…Scott and Katie Pearson. Do you know them?"

"Yes."

"Do you know what happened?"

Nick paused for a beat. "I've heard things from my friend Tom, yes."

"Scott is dead and Katie is in hospital. Can we meet to discuss why this may have occurred?"

"Yes, of course," Nick replied.

"May I come to hotel to talk?"

Nick thought quickly, then mentally shrugged. The guy probably knew anyway. "I'm not there. I've changed locations."

"Oh? And why is that?" The man was not surprised; he had obviously known. Nick was glad he didn't try to lie. Yet.

Nick pressed the phone against his leg and whispered to Anya, "Where can I meet him?"

"Gorodskoy Park," she whispered back.

He lifted the phone back to his ear and said, "Can we meet at Gorodskoy Park?"

There was a long moment of silence before the man said, "Da, we meet at Gorodskoy Park. Today?"

"Yes. In about an hour?"

"Da, that is good."

"How will I know you?" Nick asked.

"You won't. But I'll know you."

129

Nick hung up the phone and rubbed his eyes.

The park was a tree-filled square nestled between four busy streets a few miles from the river. Benches with peeling red paint lined dirt paths. Kids ran among the trees, followed by tired parents. The sun was hot but the trees provided good cover.

Nick walked the paths, watching the people and waiting for Pyotr Archipenko to show up. He was tense. He did not like the thought of talking to the police, and he did not like the thought of not knowing who the hell he was about to meet with. Information was power, and right now he felt powerless.

He passed a couple kissing on a bench. Their faces were partially hidden, but the man appeared to be at least twenty years older than the woman and he was the only one wearing a wedding ring. They were lost in their own world and didn't notice him. The man had his hand on the woman's naked thigh, sliding it up and down, fingers roughly gliding under the hem of her skirt, pushing it up towards her waist. His breathing was labored. Nick could hear it from several feet away.

He thought of the fat man on top of Katie and sneered. He slowed and took a step towards the couple. Shook his head to clear it and sped up, past them. He didn't look at them. He was afraid at what he might do if he did. Especially with an unseen cop around. Soon they were behind him and he breathed easier.

He thought briefly about turning around and going back to the apartment. This meeting had the chance of getting real ugly real fast. And even if they didn't have anything concrete against him, as Anya said, Nick had no doubt they could and would keep him in the city until their investigation was complete. Perhaps he wouldn't be in jail, but he wouldn't be free, either, and Nonna would probably go someplace else. Why would the orphanage want to place one of their children with a man under investigation by the police? The short answer was they wouldn't.

And that's why Nick had a huge, sour knot in the pit of his stomach.

But he also knew he couldn't ignore them. Despite what Anya said, Nick was certain he could avoid the police for a week. But if they didn't know about Nonna yet, they would soon. He could possibly leave Russia without talking to the police, but the seat next to him would be unoccupied.

He spied a man at the far end of the path, probably thirty yards away. Light blue shirt, dark blue pants. Hands in his pockets. He was watching Nick, not making any moves to disguise himself. Nick squared his shoulders and walked over.

Pyotr was younger than Nick was expecting, perhaps thirty, but his light brown hair was already receding over the top of his head. He had blue eyes and angular features. His shirt was rumpled, as if he had been sitting for a long period of time, and one side was pulled out of his pants, bulging over his belt. The rest of his waist was narrow, although from working out or simply not eating, Nick didn't know. He didn't smile, he just watched Nick with his head cocked.

Nick stopped three feet in front of the man and nodded. Only then did Pyotr pull his hands from his pockets. In one hand was a pocket voice recorder.

"Hello, Nick," he said in heavily accented English. "Thank you for meeting me."

Nick nodded again. "Of course," he said. "I'd like to help in any way I can." The words sounded false as he said them.

Pyotr raised the hand that grasped the recorder and made a show of pressing the play button. "Do you mind if I record? My English is not so good. I can listen to this later and translate better."

And use it in court, too, Nick thought. He replied, "Yes, you may record." He spoke in a loud voice, to make sure it registered on the recorder. Pyotr smiled slightly. Both knew they weren't fooling the other

They sat down at a nearby bench, Pyotr placing the recorder on the scarred wood between them.

"I wish to speak to you about Scott Pearson and Katie Pearson," Pyotr began somewhat formally. "Did you know them?"

Nick thought for a moment. He knew he had to be careful. "Yes, I knew them somewhat. We were here to adopt children. However, I had never met them before last week."

Pyotr nodded. "I understand Scott had…what is the word? Difficulties with somebody?"

"Yes," Nick replied.

"What do you know of them?"

131

"The difficulties?"

"Da. Er, yes."

Nick's phone vibrated silently in his pants pocket. Ignoring it, he leaned back, away from the other man, and thought for a moment. "I know he got mixed up with some men who wanted money from him."

"Why did they want money?"

Nick shrugged. "I don't know. I heard rumors about a girl."

Pyotr sighed. Nick could see any hopes of easy information evaporate from the man's mind. Nick almost smiled.

"What rumors?"

"I heard he slept with a call girl," Nick said. "The men in charge knew he was married and decided to blackmail him." Nick knew this was common knowledge and figured giving the man information he already had wouldn't hurt.

Pyotr nodded, didn't write anything down. "Do you know who these men were?"

"No."

Pyotr looked surprised. "No? More than one person said you bloodied one and threatened another in a club."

Nick shrugged. "I don't need to know who I hit."

His phone vibrated again. Nick placed his hand on his pants, over the phone in his pocket.

"And why did you hit them?"

Nick exhaled slowly. "You know why I hit them," he said. "I hit them because they were threatening Scott and Katie. Now why are you asking me all of these questions, when you already know the answers?"

Pyotr smiled thinly. It gave him a predator look, one that Nick hadn't seen before. "And what questions should I be asking? Perhaps why my colleagues found the body of Vladimir Zhorovski in a brothel with large hole in his neck?"

Nick didn't miss a beat. "Who is Vladimir…?"

"Zhorovski. Vladimir Zhorovski is a very rich man, a personal friend of several powerful leaders. His death will be investigated."

"As it should. But that has nothing to do with me." Nick looked into Pyotr's eyes as he said it.

"Perhaps," the Russian said slowly. "Or perhaps you're not telling me everything you know."

Nick's phone vibrated a third time.

Without taking his eyes off Nick's face, Pyotr said, "Will you please answer that? They've called three times." He smiled at Nick's surprised look. "I've talked to many people, and know when their phones go off."

Nick sighed, stood up, and reached into his pocket. He interrupted the phone in mid-vibrate. "Hello?" he said, crossly as he took a few steps away from the bench.

"Nick, this is Andrei."

"I'm a bit busy now," Nick said. He almost said his friend's name and then thought better of it. "Can I call you back?"

"Are you with a detective?"

Nick knew better than to glance at Pyotr. "Yes," he replied.

"Then get out of there quickly."

"Why?"

"Because he works for Dmitri."

Chapter 22

Nick was glad he was turned away from Pyotr. His stomach clenched tight and he was sure his face betrayed everything. He took a deep breath to steady himself, then said, "Oh?" casually.

"Yes. He's on Dmitri's payroll. He's there to find out how much you know. If you give him anything, he'll bring you in."

Nick felt his face heat up. "Ahh, OK," he said. He hoped his voice didn't sound as strained as it felt.

"Have you said anything yet?"

"No."

"Good. Get out of there."

"OK, thank you."

"Call me after you leave."

Nick cut the connection, turned off the phone, jammed it back in his pocket, and sat down.

Pyotr looked at him closely. "Are you well?" he asked.

Nick shook his head. From what he knew about the detective, he wasn't going to fool him. "I just received some news about the adoption. I'll be OK in a moment."

"I hope it wasn't bad," Pyotr said.

"I hope so, too," Nick replied. "Guess I'll find out soon enough."

"Do you wish to end our discussion?"

Nick thought for a moment. If he left now, he was sure he'd just have to finish the conversation later. Best to get it over with now. He was already starting to calm down, to regulate himself. Just do it, he told himself.

"What do you want to know?"

Pyotr pursed his lips, nodded. "I want to know why two Americans, one dead, were found in the brothel."

"I'm not the one you should be asking."

Pyotr raised his eyebrows. "Oh? And who should I ask?"

Nick realized he was getting into dangerous territory, but he was getting annoyed. If Pyotr was in bed with Dmitri and his goons, it was about time they were served notice. "I'd check with Sergei first. He's the one who started this."

"Who's Sergei?"

Don't play dumb, Nick thought. You know damn well who Sergei is. "He works at the Chicken Shack—uh, at that restaurant outside the Rostov Hotel. He's one of the ones blackmailing Scott."

Pyotr made a "hmm" sound and didn't write the name down. "From what I know, I believe Scott started it."

"Scott made a mistake and slept with a hooker," Nick replied, voice rising. He fought to calm himself as he noticed a small smile cross Pyotr's face. It was fleeting, but it was there. "There was no reason for him to die."

"I agree. However, it seems he, how do you say it, went looking for trouble."

"What do you mean?" Nick asked, his surprise only partially faked.

Pyotr shrugged and picked at something on his coat. "It is ongoing investigation, I cannot say too much."

Nick grunted.

"However," Pyotr went on, "From eyewitnesses, Scott went to a music store, with a gun, looking for those who blackmailed him. Do you know why he would do this?"

"Because he had a bad temper, and was sick of being threatened by a bunch of thugs."

Pyotr nodded. "Of course. And his wife went there—"

"Looking for him," Nick finished. Pyotr nodded again.

"Unfortunately, she found the wrong people," he said.

Nick looked hard at the detective. The man seemed genuinely concerned about what had happened, and wanted to get at the truth. If he really was a stooge for Dmitri, why all this dance?

Unless it was to get Nick to admit to something that could get him tossed in jail. Dmitri had said the war was just beginning. If Nick was arrested, the war would be over before it really started.

He swallowed his next statement and stared straight ahead. Pyotr seemed to notice his change in attitude.

"They did terrible things to her."

Nick turned to look at the detective. He could feel a tingling of adrenaline in his chest, above his heart. He knew the roaring would start in his ear soon enough. He had to be away from the detective when that started.

"So what are you going to do about it?" he asked the Russian.

Pyotr put his hand on Nick's arm. "I'm going to find the people who did this. I must do it through lawful means, however."

"Just do it," Nick said through clenched teeth.

"There are...complications," Pyotr said. "For example, the body of Vladimir. Do you know why he was killed?"

"No."

"Do you know who he was with?"

"No."

Pyotr eyed him carefully. "He was with Katie."

Nick fought hard to keep his face composed. He thought of Nonna. He thought of his wife and his daughter playing in a sandbox in their back yard in Bend. He thought of cruising through the Oregon desert with Danny, yelling and laughing.

He thought of the fat Russian on top of Katie.

He swallowed.

"Then he deserved to die," Nick said.

"Why did you leave the hotel?" Pyotr asked.

Nick blinked hard, caught naked by the change of questioning. "What?"

"You've moved out of the hotel."

Nick reached out and brushed dirt off his pant leg. "My things are still in room 402," he replied.

"Perhaps, but not all of them, and you haven't been seen in the hotel for at least one day."

"I've been busy," Nick said.

"Doing what?"

"Am I under investigation?"

Pyotr smiled and waved a hand. "Of course not. I must look at everything. It seems odd that you would leave the hotel they put you in."

Nick didn't reply. He watched as a figure approached and bided his time. Anya walked up to them demurely and put her hand on Nick's shoulder.

"Hi, honey," she said. "I'm getting bored. Are you done talking yet?"

Nick snaked his arm around her waist. "Soon, dear, soon." He turned back to Pyotr. "What did you want to know again?"

Pyotr eyed Anya and said slowly, "I wondered why you were no longer at the hotel."

Anya laughed, a pretty, lilting sound in the park. "He found nicer accommodations."

Nick gave her a squeeze. "She cooks better than I do."

Pyotr stared at the two of them, for once at a loss for words.

"Is there anything else I can help you with?" Nick asked.

Pyotr slowly shook his head. "No, not for now."

Nick got up. "OK, thank you."

"I do have one more question," Pyotr said. "When do you leave Rostov?"

"I pick up my daughter in three days," Nick replied.

"Good. Please make yourself available if I have more questions," Pyotr said.

Nick nodded slightly. "Good day, detective."

He walked away with Anya, arm in arm. His back tingled and he knew Pyotr was watching him.

When they turned the corner he took his arm out from around Anya and wiped his forehead. He had been doing a lot of that lately. "Thanks for rescuing me," he said.

"I wasn't sure if you were giving me the signal or just wiping your pant leg," Anya replied.

"Oh, that was definitely the signal," Nick said. "He was getting too close. The man is good. He doesn't stop."

"He's a detective, he's had training."

"His English isn't nearly as bad as he'd like me to think, either."

She raised her eyebrows. "Oh?"

"Yeah. He started by whipping out a voice recorder, spewing something about how he wanted to record me because his English stunk. But as he got into it, suddenly he was speaking pretty damn well."

Anya nodded. "Not surprising. Most of them have good language skills."

Nick stopped and turned to Anya, taking her hands in his. He glanced back but didn't see Pyotr. It didn't mean he wasn't there, watching them, though.

"I had a call from Andrei," he said quietly.

Anya raised her eyebrows and looked guilty. "When you were meeting?"

137

"Yes. Did you tell him that I was going to talk to a detective?"

She looked down. "Yes,"

"Why?"

"Because he already knew. He has connections."

"He told me that Pyotr is on Dmitri's payroll."

Anya looked surprised. "Really? I wouldn't have thought that. Then why would he want to talk to you?"

"According to Andrei, so I'd incriminate myself."

Anya gnawed at her lower lip and thought for a moment. "Perhaps, if they knew they couldn't get at you another way. I'd think they'd try something more...direct first, though."

"Like just shoot me?"

"Yes. A bullet in your head as you walked the streets."

"That would raise questions, and get the American embassy involved."

"Throwing you in jail would also get your embassy involved," Anya replied. "You must be very careful. I think you have stirred up a, how do you say it, a bee's nest?"

"A hornet's nest, yeah," Nick replied. He released her hands and they started walking again. "I need to talk to Andrei."

She stopped and looked at him. "No, you don't, Nick. Andrei is one of the hornets! Please just stay away from him."

Nick shook his head. "I wish I could, Anya, but I need to know what he knows about that guy." He hooked a thumb behind him, in the direction of Archipenko. "Pyotr is one smart man. If he wants to arrest me, it's gonna happen no matter what I say or do. I need to know what his plans are."

She put a hand on his arm. "Just be careful."

Nick smiled and nodded. "Always. And do you want to know something interesting?"

"What?"

"Pyotr never mentioned Maxsim's body."

Chapter 23

The chime rang as Nick pushed through the door to the candy store. Andrei was standing on a step stool against a wall, stocking chocolate bars. A man with brown hair, larger than Andrei and with a dour expression on his face, glanced up as Nick entered the candy store. He didn't look happy at the intrusion.

Andrei looked over his shoulder, candy in both hands, and grinned when he saw Nick. "Ahh, Nick!" he boomed. "I'm glad to see you're not in jail. One moment, please."

He stepped off the stool, put the bars in a small cardboard box on the glass counter, wiped his hands on his apron, and motioned Nick to sit down. "Would you like some chocolate?" he asked. "I have some new stuff come in from Hershey's. Caramel in the middle."

"No, thanks," Nick replied. He remained standing, staring uneasily at the third man. Andrei followed his gaze. "Nick, this is Ilia, a comrade of mine. Anything you say to me you can say in front of him."

Nick wasn't so sure of that, but he didn't have time to argue. "I want to know about this cop, Archipenko."

Andrei grabbed two bottles of water out of a small glass case and handed one to Nick. Nick ran the cold bottle across his hot forehead before opening it, and both men sat down at one of the small round tables. Ilia remained standing, looking annoyed. Nick wondered if he had any other expressions.

"Ahh, Archipenko," Andrei said. "He's a bad one. Very smart, sees everything. He and Dmitri are tight, like this." He clasped his hands together and squeezed hard.

"So if Dmitri wants revenge for Maxsim, then Archipenko is probably a good way to do it."

Andrei nodded and drained half the bottle. He wiped his mouth. "Da. They find something on you and you end up in Lubyanka."

Nick groaned. "Lubyanka prison is not a place I'd care to visit," he said.

"So, what will you do about it?"

Nick absently picked at the label on the plastic bottle. For some reason the company put a picture of the Kremlin on the label. Authentic Russian water, maybe. Nick worked it until a spire was missing before he spoke.

"I plan to stay quiet. Don't do anything to provoke them for three days, then I take Nonna and get the hell out of this madhouse." He looked up at Andrei. "No offense."

Andrei smiled thinly. "Of course. I'm sure it seems like a madhouse to you. It's life to me."

"I just want to get Nonna out of here."

"You know it might not be that easy," Andrei said. He was uncharacteristically grim. "Think of it from Dmitri's point of view. You killed one of his men—"

"Where did you hear that?" Nick cut in. He glanced quickly at Ilia but the man looked like he wasn't paying much attention to their conversation.

Andrei smiled. "Word gets around quickly here. An American walks into the brothel and disappears with a girl. Minutes later two Russians, including your friend Maxsim, are dead. The American is not seen leaving."

"I didn't kill Maxsim, his bodyguard killed him," Nick broke in.

"Oh? That's quite interesting. I doubt Dmitri has that information," Andrei said. He glanced at Ilia. "What do you think, my friend?"

Ilia stirred. "I think no matter what you say, Dmitri will want you dead," he said to Nick, his voice a low rumble. Nick glared at the man while Andrei nodded.

"He thinks you killed Maxsim, one of his men," Andrei said. "And he knows that everybody else knows it. What would you do if you were Dmitri?"

"Make an example out of me," Nick said grimly.

"Exactly. Do you really think hiding will deter him?"

"Probably not. But I'm not going to parade around the streets of Rostov, waiting for him to knock me off."

Andrei got a curious look on his face. "I agree. So maybe you take the offensive."

Nick sighed and continued to pick at the sticker. "Andrei, we've been through this before. I didn't come to Russia to kill people, I just came to adopt my daughter." He leaned forward and raised his voice. "I have no interest in getting caught up in a gang war. Tomorrow I'm going to see my daughter. I'm going to play with her and bring her a nice stuffed toy. I'm going to bring my Glock. If anybody hassles her or me, I will shoot them. But I'm not going to go out looking for trouble. Three days, Andrei. Three days and then I'm out of everybody's hair. Then Dmitri can say he scared me so much I left the country, I don't care."

He sat back, breathing hard. Andrei just looked sad.

"Nick," he said, "Do what you need to do, but be careful. I think in three days either you or Dmitri will be alive, but not both."

Nick caught a slight smirk on Ilia's face out of the corner of his eye. He grabbed the edge of the label and pulled hard. The label came off and water sloshed out of the bottle and onto the table.

The next morning Nick took the long way to the orphanage again, and double-backed several times to make sure he wasn't followed. He planned to do the same thing on the way home, since they'd stake out the orphanage if they were serious about going after him.

It had briefly occurred to Nick to skip seeing Nonna today, but he immediately rejected the idea. He didn't see her yesterday and he wasn't about to make it two in a row. He'd just deal with the mob later.

He walked through the gate casually, staring straight ahead. He saw a few parents in the courtyard, sitting or walking around with their babies. Everything seemed normal and his spirit began to pick up. This is the important part, he told himself. All the rest is temporary.

He opened the door and was greeted with the orphanage odor he had come to know and like. Food, baby powder, probably some other unsavory smells but together they made a nice mix that reminded him of Nonna. He looked forward to seeing her and forgetting about everything else for ninety minutes.

The door to the nurse's station was open so he let himself him. The head nurse, Olga, was the only one there. She was bent over a table, writing something in a ledger. Probably feeding or changing times.

She looked up and smiled, but her smile faded as she recognized him. She suddenly looked afraid. The brown hair under her cap was matted with sweat, and her uniform was dirty.

But she was scared. Nick began to get a bad feeling.

"You want see Nonna?" she asked. Her English was not good, but they got by with pantomimes so it didn't seem to matter. Typically laughter accompanied the communication, but not today.

Nick nodded.

She straightened up and brushed down her uniform. "Moment, please," she said, and quickly walked out.

Nick stood in the room, alone, confused. He could hear a few babies crying in the crib room. He wondered if one of them was Nonna. There were four buildings in the orphanage, with the main one holding the babies. He had never been in the other three but hoped they were as well kept as this one.

The nurse quickly returned with the director of the orphanage. Nick tried to remember her name. Marina, he thought. He had met her on the first day when they were introduced to Nonna. She was tall, blonde, maybe fifty years old. Right now she wore a worried expression.

"Follow me, please, Mr. Wallace," she said, which didn't make Nick feel one damn bit better. They walked down the short hallway to her office, not talking. Nick began to sweat. Was Nonna OK?

"Please sit," Marina said, and motioned to a wooden chair in front of her desk. He sat down obediently and waited as she crossed over to her side of the desk.

She sat down, clasped her hands in front of her, and looked at Nick. He could tell it was bad news. Please let Nonna be OK, he thought.

"Mr. Wallace, your adoption has been revoked," Marina said.

"*What?*" Nick exclaimed. He leaned forward. "Why?"

She looked uncomfortable. "There have been...complications. I do not know the exact nature, but your request has been turned down."

Nick sprang to his feet. Marina shrank back, obviously afraid. "No way," he said. "We did our paperwork, the court approved us. The only problem we could have now is if her parents came forward, and we know damn well that her parents didn't come

142

forward." He leaned forward, knuckles on the desk, and glared at Marina. "So what really happened?"

She hesitated.

He leaned forward, his face inches from her, and she could obviously read his anger. "Tell me," he said, more softly.

She sighed and closed her eyes. "We had a request from…higher up. You're not to be allowed to adopt Nonna."

"Why?"

"They didn't say."

"And how do you feel about that?"

"It's not my decision to make," Marina replied.

"Are you aware of what's happened to me these past few days?" Nick asked. He felt like a prosecutor.

"No."

"But you do know a woman was found dead outside the orphanage."

She looked at him, eyes suddenly flashing with fear. "Yes," she said.

Nick leaned back. "No, I didn't kill her. But I think whoever did was the person who wants to stop this adoption."

Marina looked away and chewed her lip. "I know nothing about such things," she said softly. "But I know you cannot see Nonna. I'm truly sorry."

Nick felt the frustration well up inside of him. He fought it down. She was not the person keeping him from Nonna, not really. And scaring the hell out of her was not going to solve anything. He closed his eyes and willed calm. Deep breaths. You're not defeated yet, he told himself.

"May I at least see Nonna?" he asked Marina. He gave her his best sad look.

"No, I'm sorry. You must leave."

"Please?" he asked. "One minute, then I promise I'll leave peacefully."

She shook her head, but he knew she'd give in even before she said, "OK, one minute only. Then you must go and not return."

Nick smiled. "Thank you, Marina."

With another huge sigh, she stood up and led him into the crib room. He had never been there before; they had always brought Nonna out to him. Now he could see where she lived.

143

It wasn't pretty. At least fifteen cribs were stored in the room, most of them around the outside of the room but several in the center, side-to-side. Babies slept or sat in all of them, hardly making a sound. Nick had read about that: babies in orphanages were generally very quiet, since they had learned at an early age that crying doesn't bring help. After a few weeks, they'd quit crying. Kelli had actually cried herself when she showed him the clipping.

Nonna was in one of the cribs against a wall. She sat in the middle of the crib in a white shirt that snapped closed between her legs. She looked at Nick with interest as they walked up, but held out her arms to Marina.

Marina smiled, reached into the crib, and tussled Nonna's short black hair while she deftly avoided the baby's hands. She cooed something in Russian to the baby.

"I'm really very sorry," she said to Nick without looking at him. "I can tell how much you love her. Please know she will find a good home and be happy."

Damn right she will, Nick thought. Out loud he said, "Thank you. I'm sure she will."

"I'll leave you alone to say goodbye," Marina said. "I'll be just outside." Nick wasn't sure if that was a statement or a warning. He nodded and she walked out.

Nick reached in the crib and picked Nonna up. She weighed practically nothing. He gave her a big kiss on the cheek and she wiggled a bit. He thought she smiled, but at eight months he wasn't sure that was possible. Maybe it was gas. At any rate, he could tell she was happy to see him. At least a little. Perhaps.

"Hi, honey," he said to her and held her up in front of him so he could look her in the eyes. She gazed back at him impassively.

"I'll be gone for a few days," he said quietly. Marina had left the room but he didn't put them above bugging the place. "But I'll come back for you, I promise."

She looked at him, and he blew a bronx cheer on her cheek. She wiggled again, he was sure in happiness.

"I have to fix some things before I can take you home. But soon you'll be home with your brother and your mother." He hugged her tight. "I promise," he said again.

"Go kick some ass, daddy," he could almost hear her say. "Then come back and get me and we'll blow this place."

Nick smiled, gently placed her back in the crib, and kissed the top of her head. "I'll be back soon, honey." She reached out for him as he drew back, and he felt a surge go through his body.

No way in hell was he leaving her here.

Chapter 24

Nick left the orphanage quietly. His first thought was, keep Kelli out of the loop for now. As much as he wanted to tell her, as much as he needed to keep her informed, as much as he needed her advice, this was not the time to get a mother, five thousand miles away from her cub, involved.

His second thought was to call Nadia, his adoption coordinator. Perhaps she could do something to get the adoption moving again. But as quickly as the thought came up, he discarded it. She had to work through official channels, which would involve the courts and potentially the police. Everything would become very public, very quickly. Nick wasn't exactly an innocent in all of this, and he saw very few scenarios where he went home with Nonna as if nothing had happened. No, this was his mess to fix.

He was not upset. He was beyond upset. The Calm had returned.

Somebody would die.

He walked and walked, not caring where he went, but knowing where he was at all times. He wasn't concerned about tails. In fact, he kind of hoped one of Dmitri's men was following him, as he needed an outlet for his aggression.

Nick thought about what he needed to do next. The end result was that he was going to leave the country with Nonna in his arms. He didn't care if he left a trail of dead bodies behind him, although he'd try to avoid that situation if for no other reason than to keep the cops off him. However, at this point the fate of anybody who stepped in front of his adoption was irrelevant to him.

As of this moment they were dead men walking, even if they didn't know it yet. Nobody took his daughter away from him and lived.

After a few hours, with a plan formed in his mind, he found a familiar landmark, turned left, and a short time later ended up in front of Andrei's candy shop.

"Dmitri?" Andrei's eyes widened. "You changed your mind, then."

"I had it changed for me," Nick replied. He explained what had happened at the orphanage. Andrei frowned, his mouth forming a thin line, and Nick saw his left hand was clenched tightly.

They sat at the same table as before. Andrei jumped up and brought out two bottles of beer. Nick accepted one gratefully, even though it was only shortly after noon.

"That bastard," Andrei muttered between gulps. "You need to be careful with him. He's one bad mother."

"Doesn't matter," Nick said. "He stopped the adoption. It had to be him. I don't see too many other options."

"He won't talk to you, you know."

"I know," Nick replied.

"So you're going to do…what?"

Nick clenched his teeth as he thought about it. "I'm going to have to reason with him."

"What does that mean?"

"It means, dammit, that he's going to undo whatever the hell he did to stop the adoption. I'm going to hit him where it hurts, so he has no choice."

Andrei looked worried. "You're a brave man, Nick."

"Are you kidding me?" Nick said. He took a deep pull from the brown bottle. "No, I'm not. I'm desperate. If I could snatch Nonna and leave the country, I'd do that in a heartbeat."

Andrei nodded and tapped his fingernails on his beer bottle. "So, what do you need from me?" He still looked concerned.

"Just information, Andrei," Nick said. "I don't want you to get involved. You live here."

"Thank you," the Russian said, relief on his face. "We're a small operation, one that Dmitri could gobble up without blinking. I can't afford to confront him."

"And you won't," Nick replied. "I just need information. Where can I find him? What kinds of operations does he run?"

Andrei smiled. "That I can give you," he said. He got up and grabbed a map of Rostov from behind the counter. He sat down again and spread the map out on the little round table. "Dmitri mainly works the western part of the city," he said. "Where you are—were—staying. He has several brothels and liquor stores, and provides protection for many small businesses."

147

He circled several blocks on the map. "I don't know where he lives or where his offices are, but if you want to disrupt his business, concentrate in here." Most of what he circled was within walking distance of the Hotel Rostov, and included the orphanage and Crazy Boris's.

Nick studied the map. He began to get an idea of where he would start. "OK, thanks. I can take it from here." He paused. "But you know, a photo of Dmitri would be nice. Do you happen to have one?"

"I'm sure I can find one," he said. "We like to know who the competition is."

"Thanks."

But Andrei wasn't finished. "You need to be very careful, Nick. Dmitri has many men working for him, some as crazy as Maxsim was. You can't go charging in there like a Cossack."

"I don't plan to go charging in anywhere, not when Nonna is at risk," Nick replied.

He stood up. Andrei stood with him. He folded up the map and handed it to Nick. "Good luck, my friend." He snapped his fingers. "I just thought of something. That gun I gave you won't help you much."

Nick pulled out his new Glock. "No worries. I upgraded."

Andrei looked impressed. "OK, then, I guess you don't need help from me."

"No, I'm good," Nick replied. "Actually, you can help. Can you please call Anya and tell her what happened? I don't want to talk to her, she'd probably try to talk me out of my plan."

"Are going to start shooting them?"

"Nope," Nick said. "I have a better idea."

Five hours later, Nick finished his third cup of coffee at the café. He sat outside on the sidewalk, chair tilted so the front legs were in the air, back against the brick wall. The café was on the west side of a relatively busy street in Rostov, across from several shops. It occupied the ground floor of a dingy three-story building in the middle of the block. Most of the tables were inside, but a single line of dented metal tables lined the sidewalk outside the large windows, under a faded blue awning. Nick had chosen an end table and was currently several feet away from any other paying customers, which was exactly how he wanted it.

The weather was warm, which made coffee an odd choice. But Nick wasn't in the mood for soda and the café didn't serve beer. So coffee it was. The brew was decent. It was reasonably strong and the caffeine kick kept him alert.

The same waitress had filled Nick's large ceramic mug all three times. She was short, thin, with close-cropped blonde hair and a tattoo of a butterfly on her shoulder, which Nick caught a glimpse of every time she bent over. Her smile widened as Nick tipped her generously after each fill. He knew she wasn't about to say anything to the owner about the man sitting outside for hours, drinking coffee and watching people.

He watched as pedestrians rushed by, in a hurry to get somewhere or at least attempting to give the impression they had to be somewhere. He watched as couples meandered slowly up the street, standing in front of the windows at the electronics shop or furniture store across the street. Later in the afternoon he watched as kids with backpacks ran along the street, done with school and anxious to get home. He watched as two men in suits walked into the furniture store.

Eyes narrowing, Nick lowered the front of his chair to the ground and leaned forward, elbows on the table. He could see through the glass as the men went to the back of the store. They moved deliberately. They were not shopping.

The waitress stopped by with a refill but Nick stood up and waved her off. "Spasiva," he told her. She looked disappointed. He dropped a final tip on the table, pushed in his chair, and walked across the street and into the store.

A chime rang softly in the back room but nobody came out to greet him. The men had disappeared, apparently with the owner of the store, into the back. Nick moved around the showroom, casing the business and keeping an eye on the back. He was the only shopper.

After a few minutes three men emerged from the back room. The two men in suits flanked another man, who looked angry and afraid at the same time and who was obviously in charge of the store, but not in charge of the visitors. He was saying something softly to the men. Softly, but urgently. They had the look of people who didn't give a damn what he had to say.

Nick studied their suits. Slight bulges off to the side where one would store a gun. One of the men had a bulge on the other side of his suit. A bulge that Nick assumed to be a payoff. A man in a place like this, with very few customers throughout the day, wouldn't have many large bills on hand. Therefore his protection money was made up of small bills. Bills that would cause a nice bulge in a suit.

Nick stayed off to the side as the three men walked towards the door. The two suits barely gave him a glance, and the third man was too preoccupied to look at him. He talked fast in Russian and Nick had no hope of catching anything he had to say.

As they neared the door one of the men turned towards the shopkeeper and said a few words in a deep voice. Whatever he said seemed to stop the man in his tracks. He stared at them as they adjusted their suit coats and walked out.

Nick headed towards the door. The shopkeeper turned to him with a tentative, fake smile and asked if he could help Nick. At least, that's what Nick figured he asked.

Eyeing the suits, Nick brusquely replied "Nyah zhnyoo" to the man without looking at him. He left the shopkeeper alone in his store, arms hanging limp at his side, a surprised look on his face.

The two men stopped in the electronics shop. Nick walked past them, not looking, and turned right a few steps beyond, into an alley. He knew from his reconnoitering earlier in the afternoon that there were three shops with small storefronts in the alley. Tiny one-person businesses that couldn't afford a spot on the street. One looked to be a tarot card reader. Heavy orange curtains hung over the window, and a picture of a hand holding several cards was painted on the door. Further down the alley hung two more signs, but Nick wasn't interested in them. The two men would never make it that far. He looked towards the end of the alley and saw it was stopped prematurely by a high chain link fence with barbed wire across the top. Good. Nobody was getting out that way.

The door was recessed, with about two feet of protection from the street. Nick pressed himself in the doorway and waited.

He hoped nobody was planning to leave the shop in the next few minutes or there would be two surprised people in that doorway.

He waited, breathing shallow, ready for the two intruders. He supposed he should feel guilty for planning to attack them without provocation, but he was too keyed up. Besides, they had been provoking him for days now. Anyway, he wasn't planning on doing any killing. Not them. Not yet.

He heard footsteps and low voices in the street, and tensed. The two men came into view not more than three feet from Nick. One was talking and gesturing to the other with his right hand. The other had turned his head to look back at the street. Nick went for the talker first.

Neither one saw him until it was too late. Nick's right fist came out of the doorway hard and fast, impacting squarely with the first man's jaw. It cut him off in mid-sentence and he grunted hard as he fell. Nick wondered briefly if the man had bitten his tongue. He hoped it was not bitten all the way through, as it might hinder things if Nick needed information from the guy.

The other man jerked his head towards Nick instinctively as his partner went down. Nick stepped left and brought his hand up in a quick jab to the man's throat. Nothing hard enough to kill him, just incapacitate briefly. The man forgot about his partner as his hands went to his throat. He gagged and bent forward. Nick stepped forward and dropped him with a right to the temple.

Nick looked around quickly, but nobody had witnessed the attack. He grabbed one man by the back of his shirt collar and dragged him across the alley. He propped him up against the brick wall and went back for the second man. When both were leaning against each other, backs to the wall, Nick stuck his hand inside the suit coat of one of the men. He pulled out a thick envelope. Opening the flap, Nick smiled slightly as he saw a stack of rubles.

One protection payment that was never going to make it to its destination.

Nick stuck the envelope in his own pocket and went back to work on the men. Only one had a cell phone. Nick opened the back, took out the battery, threw it into a drain, and placed the phone back in the man's pocket. He then stood up, brushed his pants off, and casually walked out of the alley. He went back to his café, sat in the same chair, waved to the delighted waitress, and waited.

He figured the men had two options. First they'd try the cell phone. When that didn't work they'd have a choice: either go straight to the boss's office to fess up, or go the other way and find a dark bar to discuss next moves. Their decision would tell Nick a lot about how much fear they had of the big guy. Dmitri obviously fancied himself a tough guy, but did his minions think the same way?

The only potential snafu was if they had a car. Nick could easily follow them on foot, especially if they were still wobbly, but if they got into a car he was lost. It was a chance he knew he had to take. If they shook him he'd just come back the next day with Anya or Andrei, and a car.

He waited nearly an hour and began to wonder if he had hit the men harder than he had intended to. The sun sunk lower in the sky behind him and the shadow of his building stretched across the street. Nick could see the entrance of the alley and was fairly confident the men wouldn't be looking for him. The last thing they'd suspect was that the mugger would hang around to watch them stumble away.

He watched as a few people came and went. No alarms were raised, which Nick had counted on. The two men looked like drunks huddled together. Nobody was going to get involved with them.

He sipped a coke slowly. No more coffee for him today. Three large cups was enough, but he still wanted the caffeine. He took one of the bills out of the envelope and handed it to the waitress. When she reached into her apron for change he just waved his hand. Dmitri was feeling quite generous that day. The waitress said "Spasiva" with a smile and touched his shoulder before leaving.

Finally he saw the two men emerge from the alley. They moved slowly and one, the talker, rubbed his jaw. The other had his phone out and angrily punched buttons. He held the phone up, probably trying to get a signal, then gave up and thrust the phone back in his jacket pocket in disgust.

The two men stood there talking as Nick finished his drink in several large gulps. More gesturing and obvious disagreement. Finally one threw up his hands in surrender and they began to walk back the way they had come, past the stores they had already entered. They walked unsteadily, weaving on the sidewalk. Nick gave them a block before he slowly stood up, stretched, and headed after them.

To Nick's relief, they continued on foot for several blocks and he was able to follow at a discreet distance, stopping several times to allow them to get further ahead.

They left the main thoroughfare and headed into a residential area of large houses. Nick had never been to this part of town before, and was impressed with the size of the houses and the yards. The men turned into a gated enclosure and walked up the steps to the house. Nick walked quickly by on the other side of the street, focusing in front of him. The yard was ringed by a wrought-iron fence, and hedges completed the secrecy. He glanced at the house and saw an imposing three-story structure. High eaves, steep roof line. It kind of reminded him of the old Addams Family house. He half expected to see bats flying around the upper stories.

Sunlight reflected off glass nestled behind iron bars. All three stories were barred. The inhabitants liked her privacy.

He kept moving, trying not to appear too curious. The houses turned into shops two blocks away. He stopped at a grocery store and bought a package of granola bars. Munching them one at a time, he walked back to the house. The men had been in there for perhaps fifteen minutes. He figured it would take at least that long for them to explain what had happened and for Dmitri to mobilize.

Nick walked up the steps of a duplex across from the house. There weren't any lights in the windows of the duplex, so if his luck held he'd be able to squat there for a while. Peeking through the door, he saw steps up to the second floor, with hallways to the main floor rooms on either side.

He went in and sat on the stairs. He could see the house across the street through the glass in the front door of the duplex. Leaning back, elbows on the wooden steps, granola bars by his side, he waited and watched.

And nothing happened. Fifteen minutes went by, then thirty. An hour after he sat down, Nick knew his attack wouldn't provoke a response.

Time to poke the hornet's nest a little harder.

His phone rang a few minutes later, unnaturally loud and shrill in the silent duplex. He stood up and walked out the door, hitting the talk button on the phone before it could ring again.

It was Anya. "Hi, Nick," she said. "I just got home from work. I brought home some leftovers if you'd like dinner."

He glanced up at the house as he walked past. It will still annoyingly quiet, and he had the feeling nothing more would happen that evening. "Sure, that sounds great. I can be there in about..." he did some rapid calculations in his head. "In about twenty minutes."

"OK. Where are you?"

"Outside Dmitri's house."

"*What?*"

"Well, technically it's probably his office, and I haven't actually seen him yet, but I'm pretty sure it's where he does his dirty work."

She whistled. "I'm impressed. How did you find it so quickly?"

"I beat up two of his men, stole their money, and then followed them here."

There was a long silence, then a sigh. "You really don't care about Russian laws, do you?"

"Today the only law I care about," he replied, "is the one that says I get to take my daughter home soon."

"Unless you end up in a Russian jail."

"I have no intention of doing that."

She paused, then said, "So, what *do* you intend to do?"

By this time Nick was twenty yards past the house and walking away. He stopped, turned, and looked back. "I'm going to borrow a few of Dmitri's things, and then trade them back for Nonna's freedom."

"Nick, he'll never go for that."

The door to the house opened and two men came out. They walked down the steps and, without a backward glance, turned right and headed away from Nick.

"He will, Anya," Nick said. "He just needs the proper motivation." He checked his watch, then his free hand went to one of the guns in his pocket. "You know, I might be a little delayed. Make it about an hour, around eight o'clock. And then tomorrow we'll go to the orphanage and I'll introduce you to Nonna."

Anya hung up and sat in silence for several long moments, staring down at her hands in her lap, breathing heavily. Finally she wiped her eyes, turned her cell phone back on, and dialed a number.

Chapter 25

The bodyguard moved slightly to the left as the water bottle flew past his head and slammed against the wall behind him. Water flew everywhere, soaking his shoulder and the side of his neck. He ignored the wetness and returned to his original position quietly. He waited, hands clasped in front of him.

Dmitri's guest wasn't as composed, probably because the water bottle had been aimed at his head. Pavel gulped loudly and sweat had formed on his upper lip. He didn't say a word – the enforcer had been around long enough to know at least that much

As quickly as he lost control, Dmitri regained it. He sat down behind his desk, bad leg stretched out in front of him. It was late and the damn thing ached like a sonofabitch. He looked at his watch. A little past seven. He was now late for dinner with two executives from a cement conglomerate who were interested in a loan. They could wait; they needed him more than he needed them. But Dmitri knew their patience would only last so long, so best not to make them wait forever.

He glared at the hapless messenger. "So what the hell happened? How can one American keep putting my *enforcers* in the hospital?" The insinuation was obvious.

Pavel licked his lips before replying, an act which did not go unnoticed by Dmitri.

"He came out of nowhere when we were in an alley," Pavel replied. "We weren't expecting him. He hit Nicolai—"

"You weren't *expecting* him?" Dmitri exploded. Only his leg kept him from rising and towering over the young, scared enforcer. "You were carrying my fucking take from the day, and you weren't *expecting* him?" Damn newbies. This kid was next to worthless but Nicolai had been good, which was why he put the two together and entrusted them with thousands of rubles. He had lied to Pavel, of course. It was only a small portion of his daily take, but Dmitri was careful not to let on exactly how much he made.

The object of Dmitri's rage squirmed uncomfortably in his chair. "We haven't had any trouble lately, so—"

"Shut up!" Dmitri roared. Pavel flinched and quieted, looking at the ground in front of him. Dmitri hadn't warned them about the attack on two of his other enforcers earlier in the day. In hindsight, he had to admit to himself, that was probably a mistake. One that had now cost him several thousand rubles and was making him late for dinner.

Damn Americans.

"Where's Nicolai now?" he asked.

Pavel looked relieved to be on to a different line of questioning, and the words rushed out. "They took him to the hospital. He couldn't walk. I think his knee was broken. I got hit in the head, but otherwise I'm OK." He turned his head so Dmitri could see the oozing bandage over his temple.

Dmitri waved his hand dismissively. The man's relative good health was only temporary. "But the money's gone," he said, getting back to important matters.

Pavel gulped again, and nodded.

Dmitri sighed. "Leave us," he said. "Go change your bandage and wait for Mikhail."

Pavel stood up abruptly. He winced slightly, nodded to Dmitri, and walked out. He limped, Dmitri saw. So he wasn't as healthy as he said.

The door closed behind him and Dmitri turned to Mikhail. "This American is annoying me," he said.

Mikhail nodded.

"Tomorrow I want you to follow Boris and Sasha on their rounds. Keep back so the American doesn't see you. Tell Oleg to do the same with Vitaly and Leonid." Damn, those were the only enforcers he had left. They'd have to work hard to get the money, but he paid them well to work hard. He briefly considered sending Mikhail and Oleg out on their own to visit his shopkeepers, but quickly dismissed the idea. Getting the American was now his top priority.

Mikhail nodded again. Dmitri knew that if the American attacked either of his remaining teams, Mikhail or Oleg would easily take care of him. Surprise worked both ways.

"What of Pavel?" Anton asked.

"He's no longer of use to me."

"He's young," was all Mikhail said in protest.

"He's stupid," Dmitri countered. "He doesn't have balls. I can only teach so much."

157

Mikhail nodded again, impassive. Only his eyes showed his feelings.

Shortly before eight o'clock, Nick rapped lightly on Anya's door. He heard a rustle inside her apartment, a pause as she scoped him out through the keyhole, and the scrape of the chain being released.

The door opened and he caught a blur of color before Anya was on him. She flung her arms around him and buried her head in his chest. When she raised her head a moment later he felt wetness through his shirt.

She wiped her eyes and then looked at him sternly. "Don't *do* that! You could've been killed attacking Dmitri in his own office. Then your baby wouldn't have a papa." She hit him on the shoulder, hard. It stung. He winced slightly.

"Who are you and what have you done with Anya?" he said.

"What do you mean?"

"The Anya I know would tell me to go in there after Dmitri and take no prisoners."

"Well, maybe the new Anya thinks there's a time for not taking prisoners and a time for being careful so you don't get shot, idiot." She grabbed his collar and pulled him into the room. "Now get out of the hall so the babushkas next door don't see you."

She closed the door behind them. A fantastic smell permeated her apartment. "Wow, what are you cooking?" Nick asked.

"Kotleti," Anya replied. "Kind of like meat balls. I thought you might want something heavy after attacking bad guys."

"Oh, stop it," Nick said. "I didn't get in. He left with some other guys. I have it under control."

"The hell you do!" Anya shot back. "Dmitri's bad. You need to watch out what you do to him. He's crazy."

"Bullshit," Nick said. "He's a bully. He's used to people wetting their pants in front of him. I know his type."

"Just be careful. You push him too hard and bad things will happen."

"Bad things have already happened. Now he's going to make it right."

"God, you men," Anya said with a heavy sigh. "Come in and have some kotleti and tell me what happened."

They walked into the kitchen. The meat simmered in a pan, sizzling lightly and making Nick's mouth water. Noodles boiled on the next burner.

"You really are an awesome cook," he said.

Anya blushed. "Thanks," she said. "It's nice to have someone to cook for. Now set the table, please."

Later, their stomachs comfortably full, Anya leaned back in her chair. "You and Dmitri keep escalating this," she said. "You seem to think he's going to reach a point where he says, 'Just get this crazy American out of my sight!' But he's more likely to say, 'Kill the bastard.' He's not sane, Nick."

"I know that, Anya," Nick said. "But my options are kind of limited, now, you know? I can't reason with him and I need his help to get my baby back." He winced as he said those words, knowing full well how unlikely he was to see Nonna again. His chest hurt just thinking about it.

"He's going to try to kill you," Anya said. "You know that, right? Nobody stands up to Dmitri."

"You seem to know him pretty well."

She shrugged. "Stories. The guy's ruthless."

"I've run into ruthless people before, Anya," Nick said. He absent-mindedly ran his fork through leftover gravy on his plate, making little furrows where the white porcelain showed through for a moment before the liquid seeped back. "More people that I care to admit have wanted me dead."

"From the war?"

He nodded. "That, and after."

Her eyes widened slightly. "Oh?"

He continued to look at his plate. "Well, you may have noticed that I have a habit of sticking my nose where it doesn't belong."

Anya giggled. "Really? I never would've thought that."

Nick didn't smile. "Yeah, I have a habit of pissing people off. Usually bad people," he said as he continued to make designs in the gravy. He finally looked up at her. "But you know what? They haven't gotten me yet. And some of them were pretty nasty."

"I'd like to hear about them," she said.

Nick shook his head and put the fork down. "No, you wouldn't. Some things got pretty bad."

She reached across the table and put her hand on his. "Yes, I would, Nick. I want to know more about you." She gave his hand a squeeze.

Now he did smile. "Well, maybe later, when this is done and I'm holding Maria in my arms, I can tell you some stories."

"Maria?" Anya pulled her hand back, a confused look on her face.

"Oops," Nick said. "That slipped out, sorry. Yeah, we plan to name her Maria Christine when we get home."

"That's a nice name," Anya said. "Does it have significance in your family?"

"No, it was one of the few names we could agree on," Nick said. "It took a long time to come up with that one. We ended up yelling it out the back door several times. You know, like calling her to come home for dinner after playing outside with friends all day. That was the one that rolled off my tongue the best."

They laughed together, then he looked down again. Quiet, thinking.

"You'll get Maria back again," Anya said.

Nick nodded and wiped at his eyes. "Damn right I will. But can you do me a favor, please?"

"Of course."

"Call her Nonna. She's not Maria Christine until I get her home."

Nick stretched out on his back on Anya's sofa and pulled the blanket up to his chin. His feet hung out over the other side and his shins pressed painfully into the high arm of the sofa. He knew he'd eventually end up sleeping on his side with his knees drawn up into his chest, but he wanted to at least start the long night stretched out so he wouldn't be so stiff in the morning.

He reached up and turned off the lamp next to the sofa. The room darkened slightly. They had closed the curtains but light snuck in around the edges. Living in a large complex with hundreds, if not thousands, of other families made darkness a luxury. Silence, too, he thought as he listened to people moving around and talking, voices muffled but audible, in the adjoining apartments.

Kind of like the Marines, he thought. Never a quiet moment. He raised his legs to ease the pressure, then put them back down again in a slightly different spot. It didn't help a whole hell of a lot. His left knee started to throb.

He heard a rustle in the room. He looked up as Anya sat down on the edge of the couch. Her hip pressed up against his.

"You don't have to sleep on the couch again, Nick," she said softly.

Nick's heart sped up. He said, "I think I'd better."

"You need your sleep. You won't get it here. Come to my bed."

"I'm not so sure I'll get it there, either."

"We won't do anything. You know that. I know that."

Nick thought about it. He trusted Anya enough to know she wouldn't push herself on him. It was the height of passion thing that had him worried. On the other hand, he was so keyed up about Nonna that he wasn't sure he'd be able to get it up anyway.

"OK, thanks, that'd be good," he said. She stood up and gave him room to swing his legs off the couch. He got up and followed her into her room. He had glanced in one day but had never really studied her bedroom. Now it was too dark too see much. He smelled vanilla and noticed a candle burning in her dresser.

She followed his gaze. "I love candles," she said unapologetically. "I'll blow it out before we fall asleep so we don't burn the place down."

They awkwardly climbed into her bed, she on the side by the window and he by the door. The bed wasn't large, somewhere between a twin and a queen, and he knew they wouldn't be far apart from each other for the next eight hours.

And he realized he was fine with that. A little physical support was what he needed right now. And if Kelli wasn't there, he just had to do what he had to do to make sure he was ready for what came the next day. He felt better.

Anya grabbed a small stuffed animal off of her pillow and hugged it in front of her as she turned on her side and faced him, one arm crooked under her ear. She was in a light t-shirt that rode up her neck, but not much else. Nick wondered if her heart was thundering as loud as his.

"This is my pal, Cheburashka," she said, wiggling its ear. It looked like a brown bear with large round ears. Or maybe a monkey.

Nick shook its paw. "Nice to meet you, um…"

"Cheburashka," she said, pronouncing it slowly. "He was my favorite cartoon as a little girl. In the show, he tumbles around a lot and is best friends with a crocodile."

"Well, how can you not like that?"

She pushed the animal at Nick's face playfully. "Be careful what you say about Cheburashka," she said. "You don't want him biting you in the middle of the night."

Nick smiled as she hugged the animal to her chest again. They lay next to each other silently for several moments. Nick's eyes began to droop as his body relaxed in the warm bed. His heart slowed.

"So what's your plan for tomorrow?" she asked. Her voice was low, sleepy, her breath warm on his face.

"I'm going to visit the orphanage," he said. "If Dmitri doesn't totally have his head up his ass, I'll be able to play with Nonna." He decided not to tell her he was going to pay another visit to Dmitri first.

Anya giggled. "That's a funny saying," she said. "I'm hoping his head is not in his ass as well, for your sake and for Nonna."

Nick kissed Anya on her forehead. "Thank you, Anya," he said. "Believe it or not, that's one of the nicer things anybody has ever said to me."

He woke up several hours later. Early morning sun was streaming through the bedroom window and the candle was still lit. They were spooning, facing towards the window, and his arm was over Anya's stomach. His hand rested on hers.

Anya's hair was in his face. He breathed it in for several minutes, savoring the warmth of her scalp and feeling the rhythmic rise and fall of her chest. He smiled. He was ready for anything.

Chapter 26

Nick was back on his perch in the duplex an hour later. At that point he didn't care if somebody came down the stairs and saw him. He'd just deal with it when it happened.

Within thirty minutes a car pulled up to the house. It was long and black. Nick couldn't see the make but knew it was high-end, one of those cars that the owner doesn't drive himself.

The rear door opened, and after a few seconds a thick, dark-haired man stepped out. He moved slowly, and Nick's pulse quickened as he realized it was Dmitri. He pulled out the photo Andrei had given him. Yep, it was definitely the sonofabitch. Dmitri limped into the house, with one bodyguard following a few steps behind him. A house guard opened the door for the two men and they stepped inside. Nick looked at his watch. Eight o'clock exactly. Punctual bastard.

There were at least three men inside, Nick knew, and probably more. As he watched, two men arrived on foot. This time nobody opened the door for them. Rank and file, Nick thought.

Several minutes later two more men showed up, then two more. They all looked the same: hulking, with dark suits. Now was definitely not the time.

Nick sat on the side of the stairs for another hour, not moving. At one point a heavy, older woman clomped down the stairs, carrying a large bag. Nick heard her coming and moved out of the way. She walked past without looking at him, rheumy eyes on the dirty wood in front of her. Nick opened the door for her and stood aside as she passed through silently.

He thought about Kelli and Danny. He'd been thinking about them a lot lately, trying to figure out what they were doing at that exact moment. Oregon was ten or eleven hours ahead. Maybe they were having a late dinner now. Chicken nuggets, or perhaps mac and cheese, which were two of Danny's favorites. Perhaps they were thinking of him, wondering what he was doing. He grimaced. Good thing they had no clue what he was up to. He suddenly felt very lonely. God, what he'd give to be eating mac and cheese with them right now.

After nine o'clock the men started leaving. First two, then one, then two more, then one. The first three went one way, the last three the other. There was about a minute lag between each team of two and the one behind them.

Nick smiled in the deserted foyer of the duplex. They took the bait. They were all out looking for him, protecting their money.

Now it was time.

The guard sat on a bench on the porch of the house, relaxing. He obviously wasn't expecting anybody. Nick walked past the gate, looked in, stopped, looked closer at the guard, looked down at the map in his left hand, appeared to make up his mind, and opened the gate.

The distance from the gate to the porch was about twenty yards. Nick used all of it looking confused, consulting his map, looking left and right as he walked up to the house. He knew the guard was watching him, so he was careful to appear hapless, innocent, a muddled tourist.

He gave the guard his most disarming smile as he got close. The man was standing now, machine gun at his side but not yet ready to use it. He gazed at Nick, more curious than anything else.

"Excuse me," Nick called out in English. "I'm looking for the GUM department store." He was nowhere near the store, and the guard started to laugh.

The guard walked down the three stairs, adjusting his gun so the barrel pointed to the ground. He had a look on his face that said, "Stupid Americans."

Nick had chosen a destination to his left, which made it towards the guards' right. The guard made a comment that sounded derogatory, and pointed to his right.

With his gun hand.

His eyes shifted right to follow his hand, and at that precise moment Nick's right hand, which had slipped into his pocket, came out with the Glock.

The guard didn't see the gun as it smashed into the side of his head. Nick caught him as he fell, and quickly dragged him into the bushes. He pocketed the Glock and unslung the man's machine gun. It was a Czech SA.26. Nick looked at it appreciatively. Old, but reliable. Another upgrade.

He checked the magazine, slung the gun, and walked in.

Dmitri looked up sharply as the door swung open. He had left explicit instructions not to be disturbed. He didn't like disruptions when he was angry, and he was angry now. He started to speak, to release some of his anger on the hapless bastard who dared walk in on him.

His words died in his throat when he saw the stranger. The man was dressed in drab clothing but Dmitri immediately knew he was a westerner. Almost as immediately, he realized it was the American. The one named Wallace.

And he had a submachine gun. His guard's submachine gun.

Dmitri was instantly livid. How dare the American barge in to his private quarters with a gun! He stood up, pressed a button under his desk. The man didn't notice.

The American had a second gun, a pistol, which he brandished as he stepped forward. "Sit down," he commanded softly. Those two words were enough to ensure that Dmitri remained standing.

Dmitri studied Wallace. He wasn't what the Russian expected. He was larger, for one thing, and harder. Most Americans, especially ones adopting Russian children, were soft. This one wasn't. And he appeared calmer than most men Dmitri encountered. His eyes, while angry, were calculating.

Dmitri wasn't concerned. The man would soon learn to fear him.

"What do mean, barging into my office like this?" Dmitri asked, in a conciliatory tone. He had to stall the man for several minutes. Mikhail had been paged when the alarm went off and would be on his way back now.

"You have something I want. And I have something you want," the man replied. "Let's trade."

Dmitri laughed. "You steal my money, attack my men, walk into my office with a gun, and propose to trade my money back to me?" He laughed again. "I must admit, you have balls the size of watermelons."

The man shrugged. "Perhaps. But I want my daughter, and then I'll leave you in peace."

Arrogant prick. Like it was his decision to make. Dmitri felt his anger rising. "You don't know who you're dealing with, friend. I can easily have you killed."

The man shook his head. "No, you can't. You've tried, and the only thing that's happened is that I've sent a lot of your men to the hospital. Let's just call it even and go our own way."

Dmitri's face turned red and he fought the rage building inside him. This man needed to learn respect, dammit! He knew the rage would win soon enough. He just hoped Mikhail would arrive quickly.

"I don't make deals with Americans," Dmitri seethed. "You have no honor, you break your word."

"You don't know me," Nick replied. "I'll keep mine."

"You peasant!" Dmitri exploded. He leaned across the table and glared into his intruder's eyes. "You won't make a deal with me! The only deal you get is that I'll buy you a nice grave here in Rostov, and in that grave your bones will turn to dust!"

The American smiled, which infuriated Dmitri even more. "This is your last chance, asshole. After this, the price for my cooperation goes up."

"You bastard!" Dmitri yelled, face purple. Veins bulged in his forehead and he saw stars around the periphery of his vision. "You'll never leave Rostov alive! And when I'm finished with you, after you're cut up into pieces and thrown into the Don, I'll take your daughter and bash her head open! She'll—"

But then the American was on him.

Nick lunged over the desk, knocking papers and a laptop onto the floor, and grabbed Dmitri by the collar. He threw the Russian against the wall and held him there, a foot off the ground. Nick pressed his face inches from Dmitri's and spoke in a savage whisper, spittle landing on the stunned Russian's face.

"Listen, you little pissant," Nick said. "The only reason you're still alive right now is that I need you to get my little girl." Dmitri struggled, eyes wild, but he made no headway against Nick's strength. "Don't you *ever* get between me and my family, you cocksucker. I'll give you until noon to get the adoption going again. If you do, you'll get your money back and get to keep this nice fucking office. If you don't, I'll be back and shoot you in your fucking head! Do you understand?"

Dmitri spit in Nick's face.

Nick hesitated a moment, shocked, then slammed his forehead into Dmitri's nose. The man sagged in Nick's hands as blood poured down his face. Nick hadn't hit him hard enough to put him out, because he needed action from the man, but Dmitri wouldn't be going anywhere for a while.

Five minutes later, Dmitri began to get focus back. He saw as the door swung open again and, to his relief, Mikhail run in. What the hell had taken him so long, Dmitri thought dimly. Mikhail's gun was out, but when he saw Dmitri awake and looking at him, the guard put it away.

Something was different about the room. In his haze, it took Dmitri a moment to realize what it was.

His treasures, the items on his wall, his *heritage*, dammit, were gone.

Chapter 27

Anya slapped Nick lightly on the cheek, mock anger on her face. "Stop worrying, you old babushka. I'll be fine. They've never seen me before."

Nick looked doubtfully at the car parked across the street from the only entrance to the orphanage. Dmitri's men had been easy to spot. Nick was vaguely disappointed Dmitri hadn't told his men to be more careful, after all they'd been through.

"I don't know," he said. "I should be the one to go in..."

"That's stupid and you know it," Anya said. "They'd spot you in a minute. Now let me help you." She reached in a pocket. "Besides, I brought a hat." She slipped a black beret over her hair and adjusted it. Nick saw it went well with her eyes, now flashing impatiently.

She noticed his expression and smiled. "Thank you," she said as she adjusted her skirt. "Now stay off your cell phone and I'll call you in five minutes with good news."

She stepped out from behind the edge of the building and walked confidently up the street. Nick watched her stroll past the black car without stopping or looking. She disappeared through the gate without a backward glance.

Nick settled back, out of sight of Dmitri's thugs, and waited for Anya to get back to him with news on Nonna. He had called her after leaving Dmitri's office, and she immediately suggested that she go to the orphanage at noon to see if Nick's daughter was cleared for adoption. Neither one really expected that she would be, but both thought it would be more correct for Anya to make the queries, since Nick has basically been barred from the orphanage. He didn't expect that she'd be able to see Nonna, but Anya should at least get a feel for if Nonna was safe.

Nick felt guilty about putting her in harm's way, but Anya insisted, and her arguments had validity. She pretty much stayed away from her father's business, so she should be an unknown quantity to Dmitri's men. But there was always a chance that somebody would recognize her as somebody's daughter or cousin.

He felt better now that she made it in without incident.

The minutes crept by. He kept checking his watch, willing it to move faster. As the ten minute mark passed, he began to be more hopeful. Perhaps she was visiting with Nonna. Or perhaps she was arguing with the orphanage doctor about getting information on the baby.

Finally, after nearly fifteen minute, the phone buzzed. He saw her name flash, clicked the talk button immediately, and put the phone up to his head.

"Yes?" he asked.

There was silence, punctuated by his heart beating in his ear, then she said slowly, "I have bad news."

Nick felt his body deflate. "The adoption is still off? Perhaps they haven't had time to make the change yet. Maybe if you ask the doctor—"

She cut him off. "It's worse than that."

"Oh, god. What?"

"Nonna's gone."

"*What?* What happened?" He abruptly felt dizzy, and sat down hard on the grass.

"They took her."

"*Who* took her?"

Anya started to cry. "Oh, I'm so sorry, Nick. She won't tell me! She said she can't say."

"Put her on."

"I had to leave her office to make the phone call."

"Put her on."

Nick heard the sound of footsteps, and the muffled voice of Anya talking. Another voice answered, even more muffled, but definitely a man's voice. The went back and forth for a moment before Anya pulled the phone away from her clothes.

"She had to go check on the babies, Nick. They won't let me see her."

Nick stood up. "OK, I'm coming in."

"That's not a good idea."

"Tough shit," he said. "I'll try the back, see if I can get in that way. Sounds like breaking and entering is the least of my worries now. Can you stay there for now?"

"I think I can. I'll sit in the waiting room."

"Good. Hold tight. Call me if you see her."

She sighed. "OK. I'm so sorry, Nick," she said again.
"Don't be. It's not your fault. And I'm not done yet."

Nick knew the tall wrought-iron fence ringed the orphanage,
except where the buildings stood. The fence was about eight feet
high, but was probably designed more to keep short kids in than tall
adults out.

At least, that was Nick's hope.

He crossed the street, ducking his head in case one of the
enforcers checked their rear-view mirror, and disappeared behind the
back of the orphanage. With the large building blocking him from
his adversaries, he stood up and moved fast. Around the back side
of the orphanage, in the courtyard between buildings, he saw several
large trees near the fence. He picked one near a building, relatively
out of sight from casual observers.

He sped up as he neared the tree, then jumped and jammed
his foot in the tight space where the trunk split in two. He reached
up, grabbed a large branch, and swung himself up into the tree. He
quickly slithered out on a branch hanging over the fence. Once over
the fence, he swung his legs over the side and slid off the branch
until he hung by his hands. The branch cracked ominously as Nick
hung there for a second. He dropped into the orphanage courtyard.

There were a few parents playing with kids near Nonna's
building, but nobody looked his way. Nick straightened up, brushed
leaves and a few sticks off his shirt, and walked to the building.

He saw Anya in the waiting room outside the doctor's office.
She looked surprised to see him so quickly, and began to stand up.
He made a motion with his hands to keep her in her seat as he
walked through the waiting room and out the door on the other side,
to the hallway that led to the crib rooms.

He heard the cries of the babies and smelled the orphanage
smell. This time, however, the familiar smell didn't make him feel
happy. It seemed to mock him. These aren't your babies, it said.
Your daughter is gone and you'll never see her again.

Instinctively his hand felt for the gun in his pocket. He left
the gun hidden there, reassuring, unused but ready.

The doctor was in Nonna's room, shaking a rattle in front of a little boy sitting up in his crib. The boy's eyes tracked the rattle but he didn't reach for it, and there was no smile on his face.

There was no smile on the doctor's face when she noticed Nick next to her, either. A flash of fear, then her composure returned.

"You shouldn't be here," she said.

Nick ignored her. "Where's Nonna?"

"She's gone," the doctor replied simply.

"Where?"

"You needn't concern yourself."

Nick stepped closer, causing her to flinch slightly. "I'm her father. Tell me."

She looked at him with eyes that were not unkind, and pursed her lips. "Please don't," she said softly. "There are...powerful people who don't want this adoption to proceed. I cannot fight them."

"I'm not asking you to fight them," Nick replied. His voice choked with emotion. "I just need a little help, *please*. Nonna needs me. And I need her." *We* need her, he thought.

A trail of tears wove their way down from each of her eyes as she spoke. "I'm sorry, I cannot say anything. If I do, they'll hurt me or, even worse, take my children. You must leave!"

Something in her voice, or in the tears she made no effort to wipe away, convinced Nick that she would be no help. But he had to try one more time.

"Is it Dmitri?" he asked.

She looked down for a long moment, until he was sure she wouldn't reply. She shook her head. "I can tell you'll be a wonderful father. But Nonna isn't in your future. Just leave her be, for everybody's sake, including hers."

Air hissed out through Nick's teeth. His mind began to work, to plan, to leave the orphanage. The image of the doctor began to fade from his sight, bit by bit, until a dismembered face looked at him with concern. He brought her back long enough to say, "No, that won't happen."

Then he left her, an unreadable expression on her face.

Anya sat in the same position she had been in three minutes earlier. Nick doubted she had moved a muscle. He noticed her beret was off, probably stuffed in her pocket because of the hot air in the waiting room.

"Let's go," he said. His throat felt hoarse.

She stood up. "Any luck?"

Nick shook his head. "She clammed up. They have her scared to death. But I'm sure Dmitri knows, even if he didn't grab her himself."

She nodded. "So you visit Dmitri again?"

"Yes. But this time he's not getting off so easy."

She nodded as she slipped her beret back on. "And if he doesn't tell you what you need to know, what will you do?"

"I'd rather not think about that."

She turned to face him, her expression earnest. "Nick, it's time to, how you say, man up."

He stared at her for a long moment. "Man up."

"Yes. You want your daughter, let's go get her." She held out a hand. "You told me you have two Glocks."

"Damn right I do," Nick said. He pulled the second one out from behind his back. It had been sticking into his skin for the past hour, but the pain was security. He handed it to Anya.

She checked it expertly, making sure a round was chambered, and slipped in into her purse.

"You seemed familiar with guns."

"I'm my papa's little girl. You ready?" Her eyes glinted. He had never seen her like this. He was glad she was on his side. He wondered if she had stayed out of daddy's business as much as she said she had. At that moment he hoped not.

"What's the plan?" Nick asked.

"You know those two guys out front?"

"Yep."

"It's time for them to be useful."

"How so?"

"They can give us a ride to Dmitri's place."

It turned out to be easy. Anya sauntered around to the passenger side of the car, knocked on the window, played the demure female, toyed with the man in the passenger seat, then shot him in the leg as Nick hopped in the back seat.

"Sorry," she said to Nick with a shrug as the man screamed and held his leg. Nick, busy holding a gun to the driver's head, said, "No worries. Take off his belt so he doesn't bleed out. I don't want any attention."

She tied the makeshift tourniquet quickly and the passenger settled down to a whimper as she cinched up his leg and relieved him of his sidearm. She slid into the back seat next to Nick.

Nick focused his attention on the stunned driver, who had both hands on the wheel. "We want to talk to Dmitri," he said, and pressed the barrel of the gun into the man's head. "I assume you have orders to take us to Dmitri. So we're all happy."

The man looked confused.

Anya said something to him, and the man nodded quickly "Go," Nick said.

The man started the car and screeched out of the parking spot.

"Slowly, for Christ's sake," Nick said. "None of us wants the cops."

They pulled up to a gate in the alley behind the house. The driver, with no prodding, produced a card. He pressed it against the reader and the gates slowly swung open. He drove into a small parking lot and stopped in a spot, engine idling.

Nick didn't relax his grip on the Glock in the back of the driver's head. "Do you have a family?" he asked.

The man looked at him in the rear-view mirror, confusion on his face.

Anya sighed and translated. He nodded quickly and rambled out a few sentences in rapid fire Russian.

Anya turned to Nick and said, "He says yes, he has a wife and two children."

"Good," Nick replied. "Tell him to take his friend to the hospital and then find a new job."

Anya relayed the message to the driver, who paled as she continued to speak. When she was done, he nodded.

"What exactly did you say?" Nick asked.

"I told him what you said," Anya replied, averting her eyes.

"Did you use the word 'dog?'" Nick asked. "I thought I recognized 'dog.'"

She blushed. "I may have told him I'd hunt him down like a dog if he talked to the police."

Nick nodded. "Fair enough."

They relieved both men of their guns and cell phones and got out of the car. They ducked next to the wall of the building and waited, guns at the ready, as the car sped out of the lot. The driver believed Anya, apparently, or at least her gun, and didn't try anything.

Nick turned his attention to the wall they leaned against. Two windows on one side, door on the other. They were in a blind spot from inside the house but would easily be spotted by a camera in the parking lot or on the wall separating the lot from the street. Therefore, time to move.

Anya stood next to him, arms touching. He motioned to the door and she nodded. They slid along the wall until they came to the door. It was a standard door, not reinforced, with a small window at head height. Nick jiggled the doorknob and felt it give, unlocked. He breathed a sigh of relief, glad that he wouldn't have to pick it or, even worse, shoot it off and alert Dmitri and his minions.

He eased the door open and the two intruders entered Dmitri's headquarters.

Chapter 28

Once inside the door, Anya shouldered her way past Nick. "I'll take point," she whispered as she moved ahead.

"Why?" Nick asked.

Anya turned her head, dimpled, and batted her eyes at him. "Why do you think, dummy?"

Nick shrugged and followed. She had a point.

They were in a kitchen. White-paneled cupboards over granite countertops, a coffee maker in a corner, surrounded by several bags of beans. A cutting board with a knife lying across it, breadcrumbs everywhere. Nick was briefly tempted to grab the knife, but Anya made her way across the kitchen quickly and slid up to the door at the far end. Nick glanced at the knife, then followed her.

She cracked the door open and peered out. After a moment she closed the door again. "Where was Dmitri's office?" she whispered, glancing at him.

"Third floor," Nick replied.

"Did you notice any bedrooms?" she asked.

Nick shook his head. "Didn't see any. I assume she'd be on the second or third floor, though."

"Yes," Anya agreed. "If Nonna's here she's probably on the second, if Dmitri does business on the third. We can start there anyway."

The hallway was short, running from the kitchen in the back of the house to the entryway in the front. At the far end were the front doors, with double doors on the left and a stairway on the right. Nick put his ear to one of the double doors and listened. No sounds. He nodded to Anya and they quickly went up the stairs to the second floor.

The second floor was darker due to no front window. The hallway ran to the back of the house, like its twin one floor below. There were two doors on each side on this floor, all open. Nick and Anya quickly looked in all of them. All were bedrooms, all empty. The house was silent.

Nick swore softly. "Where is everybody?" he asked.

"Out looking for you," Anya replied.

"Not everybody," Nick grumbled. "Somebody has my daughter."

Anya turned to say something, but they were interrupted by noise from downstairs. The door slammed open and at least two people walked in. There was arguing, somebody yelling. Somebody cursing.

Nick looked at Anya and without a word they crept into one of the bedrooms. They huddled together, guns drawn, as the voices snaked up the stairs. They passed the second floor and headed to the third. Somebody was obviously being propelled along against their will, based on the shouts and bangs as something hit the wall.

Nick looked at Anya, concern on his face. Anya shrugged. Both kept their guns at the ready, even as the sounds began to recede.

There was a moment of silence, then Nick clearly heard a crunch of something hitting flesh. There was a muffled scream, followed closely by another crunch. The second scream was softer than the first.

"I'm going to check that out," he told Anya.

She shook her head. "No. That doesn't concern us. Focus on Nonna."

Nick thought for a moment, but another scream from the third floor made up his mind. "No. You stay here. I'm going up."

"I'm coming with you," she said.

"Give me five minutes," Nick replied. "Then you come up. If I get in trouble I'll need your help."

Anya thought it over. "Two minutes. I'll stay here. But be careful."

Nick checked his Glock. "Always," he said.

The door was closed but Nick knew exactly where they were. The third floor of the house was smaller than the first two due to the roof line. There were only two rooms, and Nick knew whoever was in the house was not in Dmitri's office.

He stationed himself in front of the other door and waited. The roaring had started in his left ear but he controlled it. He built up the tension in his arms.

When he heard the now-familiar thwack of something hard against skin, and a muffled scream, he kicked the door in.

It all happened in slow motion after that. He took in the sight of Sergei, absurdly dressed in the uniform of the Chicken Shack but with a truncheon in his hand. Against the wall, tied to a metal bed frame turned on its end, was a man. It took Nick a moment to realize it was the furniture store owner. Anton, if he remembered correctly. The man was trussed up by his hands and had blood running down his face. He didn't look up as Nick burst into the room, but Sergei did.

Sergei's face was contorted in rage as he turned. Nick could only imagine what Anton had done. Sergei gripped the truncheon in his right hand tightly. He saw Nick and his face transformed into something even uglier, as if Nick was a rodent that Sergei found in a trap, a rodent that Sergei could do with what he wanted.

Sergei advanced on Nick, truncheon held high.

Nick shot him in the left knee.

Sergei went down hard, screaming in pain, blood gushing from his knee through his pants. He dropped the truncheon and grabbed at his knee with both hands, swearing incoherently.

Nick advanced, almost casually, on the man writhing on the floor. He took one look at Sergei's shattered knee, then stomped on it with all his strength. Sergei howled again, even louder than the first time.

"Shut up, Sergei," Nick said. He bent down and picked up the truncheon, now lying harmless on the carpet. He looked it over carefully and glanced at Anton as Anya ran through the door.

"I heard the shot, are you OK?" she asked Nick, then stopped abruptly when she saw Sergei on the floor. "Did you shoot him?" she asked.

"Yes," Nick replied.

"Why?"

"He pissed me off."

She sighed and glanced at the man on the ground, then over at Anton. She nodded. "What now?" she asked.

"He answers some questions."

She looked doubtfully down at Sergei. Blood had stained a few square feet of carpet under his leg, and his screams were trailing off into whimpers as he started to go into shock. "You'd better hurry, then," she said. "He won't be able to talk much longer."

Nick knelt down by the bleeding Russian. He held the truncheon in front of him like a microphone and prodded Sergei in the face with the end of it. Sergei looked up, eyes bleary and unfocused.

"Where's Nonna?" Nick asked.

Sergei just stared at him, a blank look in his eyes. The eyelids started to close. Nick prodded him harder with the baton and Sergei's eyelids fluttered a bit.

Nick tried again. "Where's Dmitri?" he asked.

But it soon became evident that Sergei wasn't going to answer anything. Nick stood up and the Russian slowly toppled over on his side, both hands covering his knee. Blood continued to seep through his fingers.

"We should get him to a hospital," Anya said.

"We're not taking him anywhere," Nick replied. "We can call the police from one of Dmitri's phones when we get the hell out of here."

"He could die here."

Nick shook his head. "He won't. I missed the important bits. He'll even be able to walk again, eventually. He's getting off better than he should."

"Who's this guy?" Anya asked, gesturing towards Anton. Anton was in sad condition but much better than Sergei. His head was bleeding where he had been battered and blood oozed down his arms where they had been fastened, none too gently, to the bed frame.

"He's the guy who owns the furniture store," Nick replied. He started to untie Anton's wrists. "Looks like he pissed off Dmitri."

"Maybe he can tell us something," Anya said.

"That was my thought," Nick replied. He finished with the straps and Anton stepped away from the frame, rubbing his wrists. Blood smeared his hands. Nick led him over to where a mattress was lying, apparently pulled into a corner by Sergei before he trussed Anton to the frame. Anton sat down shakily and Anya grabbed a blanket for the blood. She dabbed at his head while Anton pressed the other end against the cuts on one wrist.

"Spasiva," he said, weakly.

"Do you speak English?" Nick asked him. There was no time to waste.

Anton shook his head. "Nyet," he replied.

Anya said, "What do you want to know?" She kept pressure on the head wound as she glanced at Nick.

"Where Dmitri is," Nick said.

Anya spoke softly to the man, trying to calm him as she questioned him. He replied, voice muffled by the blanket on his head. They went back and forth for a few minutes before Anya spoke in English again.

"He said he had trouble paying Dmitri what he owed him. I assume it was protection money. They've been taking more and now they are…using…his wife. Anton resisted and…" she shook her head. "Here he is."

Nick glared back at Sergei, who wasn't moving. "I should put a bullet in his groin."

"Yes," Anya said. She was furious, but trying not to show it for Anton's benefit. "You should, but we need to leave and call the police. They'll take care of him."

"Where's Dmitri?"

"He doesn't know."

Nick groaned.

"But he knows where he lives."

Two minutes later the police had been alerted. Nick and Anya stopped just inside the back door, Anton supported between them.

"Hold on a moment," Nick said.

"Why?" Anya said. "We have to leave."

"This'll just take a second," Nick said. He helped Anton lean against a side wall, then ran downstairs. Anya waited an impatient thirty seconds, supporting Anton, before Nick popped up again. He had a large sack over his shoulder and Anya was reminded of Grandfather Frost, even though she knew Grandfather Frost never looked that good.

Nick dumped the contents in the side of the entryway. They made a metallic clang.

"What're those?" Anya asked.

"Dmitri's things," Nick said. "I took them as leverage, then hid them in the basement. I don't need them anymore. He won't either. His kids can divvy them up."

They helped Anton out the door as they heard sirens in the distance.

Ten minutes later they were a few blocks away from the house, passing through a residential neighborhood of large houses. Nick thought of the New Russians. This was probably where they lived.

Nick and Anya were alone. Anton had come around slightly and insisted on walking himself home. He was embarrassed and angry and Nick didn't want to ask him any more questions. He had been through enough. They had Dmitri's home address. That would be plenty.

"I wonder how he knew where Dmitri lived?" Nick asked.

Anya looked disgusted. "He had to drive his wife there," she said.

"Bastards," Nick mumbled.

"I wish you had shot Sergei in the head instead," Anya said.

"I needed information from him."

"And how did that work out?"

Nick grimaced. "Yeah, guess I should've popped him in the head. Well, the cops will take care of him,"

"Not if they're on Dmitri's payroll," Anya replied.

That stopped Nick. "Damn, I never thought of that."

He could sense Anya smile next to him. "No worries. If he's dumb enough to show his head again, we'll take care of him."

"We?"

She shrugged and didn't answer. They walked a few steps and she said, "So, what's your plan?"

"Pay Dmitri a visit at his house tonight."

"I doubt Nonna will be there," Anya said, quietly.

"I know," Nick said. "But she's near and he knows where. At this point my only way to her is through him."

She nodded. "I don't have to work tonight," she said. "Want some company?"

Nick looked at her. "Thank you, Anya. Yes, that'd be great."

She smiled. "Good. I want to see you and Nonna together one time. Then you can leave and be happy in America."

Nick put his arm around Anya and gave her a squeeze.

Nick sat down at Anya's table and pulled out his cell phone.

"Who are you calling?" she asked.

"I'm going to beat the bushes," he replied.

"What? I don't understand."

"I'm going to see if I can flush any game," Nick said.

Anya sighed. "You Americans and your slang. You're much more difficult to understand than the English, you know."

"Yeah, and I'm not even a woman."

"What?"

"Nothing."

The call was answered quickly. "Archipenko," said the now-familiar voice.

"Detective, this is Nick Wallace," Nick said. Anya's eyes widened and she quickly sat down next to him. She made a "what the hell are you doing?" gesture with her hands, and Nick shushed her.

"Mr. Wallace," Pyotr answered. "I must to say, I wasn't expecting you to call."

"To be honest, I wasn't expecting to call you, either, detective, but something has come up."

"Oh? And what has come up?"

"My daughter is gone."

There was a long pause on the line. Long enough for the hisses and pops to get very loud in Nick's ear.

"Excuse?" Pyotr finally said.

Nick spoke slowly. "My daughter is missing. She's no longer at the orphanage."

"Where is she?"

Nick took a breath. "I was hoping you could tell me that, detective."

Archipenko sounded confused as he spoke. "I don't know anything. But I could ask here…" his voice trailed off.

"Dmitri has her," Nick said.

"Dmitri? How do you know?"

"In retaliation for what I've done to him."

"What, exactly, have you done to Dmitri?"

"That's not important right now," Nick said. "What's important is what I plan to do to him later today."

"Nick…" Anya whispered. "What are you doing?"

He ignored her. "I'm going to his house tonight. He's going to tell me where Nonna is, or I'll kill him."

Anya put her head in her hands. Archipenko said, "Why are you telling me this?" He sounded out of breath.

"Because I need to know whose side you're on, detective," Nick replied. "If you're with Dmitri, then I want you to tell him I'm coming for him and I want answers."

"Do you think I work for Dmitri?" Archipenko said. He sounded angry.

"That's what I want to find out," Nick said.

"I could arrest you," the detective said.

"Not yet."

"I could arrest you tonight."

Nick shrugged. "You could. But I don't think you will. If you're not one of Dmitri's stooges, then I think you want him off the street as much as I do."

"I don't want more killing in my city," Archipenko said. "There are…other ways to, how you say, get him off the street."

Nick laughed, a hoarse bark. "And what might those be, detective? A trial? You want me to press charges?"

"Yes. Let Russian law help you."

"Of course not. For one thing, I doubt I'd live long enough to testify. For another, my daughter will be killed if they even think I'd testify."

"We can protect you, Nick."

"But you can't protect Nonna, detective, and that's who needs our help."

"You have to stay within the law."

Nick rubbed his forehead with his free hand. "You don't work for Dmitri."

"Of course not!" Archipenko said.

Nick looked over at Anya. She was hearing it all, a shocked look still on her face.

"Will you help me get my daughter back, detective?" Nick asked softly.

"Yes, I will, but we must do it within the law," Archipenko repeated.

"I'm sorry, but that won't happen. If you want to arrest me, be at Dmitri's home tonight."

"But—"

Nick clicked off.

Chapter 29

Sergei rested in the hospital bed, heavily sedated, a large bulge around his left knee under the blanket. An IV was plugged into his left hand. His cheeks were pale and his eyes bloodshot. He looked dimly at the figure standing over him.

Mikhail held the cell phone to his ear, vaguely listening to the ramblings of a madman over the speaker. His attention was more on the figure in front of him and what he knew he was about to be asked to do.

Dmitri stopped ranting long enough to take a breath. He said, "Has Sergei said anything to the police?"

"No," Mikhail replied. "Nobody's been here since I brought him in."

"Good. Who worked on him?"

"Friends," was all Mikhail said. The police weren't the only ones on Dmitri's payroll.

"Good," Dmitri said again, somewhat calmer now. "Is he asleep?"

"No," Mikhail said. "But he's not awake, either."

"No matter. I assume you know what you have to do."

"Yes." Mikhail knew better than to hesitate. Not that it would do any good.

"Call me when it's done."

"Will do." Mikhail clicked off and looked at Sergei with something close to pity. He didn't care for the man but didn't like taking lives to satisfy the whims of a madman. Unless the life was of the madman himself.

"Sorry, comrade," he said quietly to Sergei. He turned to the nurse standing silently next to him and nodded. With a sigh, she prepped the syringe.

Anya parked her car two blocks from Dmitri's house. It was a red Lada Kalina, polished to a brightness that stood out on the street, even in the dim late-evening light.

She locked it from her key fob with a beep, walked a few steps away, turned back to look at the car, then walked back and checked all the doors. She returned to Nick with an embarrassed smile.

"Sorry, I'm somewhat, what's the word, obsessive about security," she said.

Nick, preoccupied, barely nodded.

Dmitri lived, not surprisingly, in one of the fanciest neighborhoods in Rostov. Gates stood in front of many homes, and they heard the crunch of leaves as guards patrolled inside the perimeters.

"It's up here on the right," Anya whispered as they approached the middle of a block. "I think it's the dark one."

Nick peered across the street. Lights burned brightly in the house directly across from them, then again at the house on the corner. The large hulk in the middle was completely dark.

"What time is it?" he asked.

She checked her phone. "Half past nine," she said. "He's probably out to dinner."

"So we wait," Nick said.

"So we wait."

They found a spot between two houses across and down the street from Dmitri's. They sat down behind a row of hedges, after making sure there were no guards patrolling at either house. Anya pulled a blanket out of her backpack and spread it on the grass. Nick looked at her.

"I thought we might be here for a while," she said, slightly embarrassed.

They settled back and waited. The heat of the day dissipated quickly and the air became more comfortable. They huddled together to make a smaller target, and so they could talk.

"What will you do if Dmitri won't tell you where Nonna is?" Anya asked.

"I'd rather not think about that," Nick replied. His face was grim. "I'm hoping I've become a big enough pain-in-the-ass that he just decides to call it a draw."

Anya's voice sounded doubtful when she said, "That doesn't sound like Dmitri."

"No, it doesn't. So I guess Plan B is that I beat on him until he tells me."

She was silent. He sat and thought for a few minutes, vaguely listening to the crickets. "You know, I need to get her tonight."

"Nonna? Why tonight?"

"Because tomorrow is the last day of the grace period. My contact will be back from Kiev tomorrow."

"She went to Kiev? Why?"

"Her mother lives there, and I guess whenever Nadia gets paid she drives a care package over to Kiev."

"Kiev's a long way from here, in Ukraine."

"I know," Nick replied. "Nadia's been gone for four days, and hadn't really been around before then, anyway. With everything else going on, it's probably for the best."

"She might know somebody who could help," Anya said.

Nick shook his head. "Nah. More likely, she'd run. She has our money now anyway. All I was supposed to do was visit Nonna every day while she was gone." He sighed. "Guess I didn't handle that one too well."

Anya paused, then said, "You know, there are other babies out there."

Nick closed his eyes. "Don't go there, Anya."

"I'm serious, Nick. There are other orphanages in Rostov. Surely Nadia has connections in other orphanages, and in other cities. A different baby would be much…less complicated."

"No!" Nick said loudly. They both looked around nervously, but after several seconds it became apparent that nobody had heard them. "No," he said again, softly this time. "Nonna is our daughter. If this falls through because I messed with the Russian mob, nobody here is going to have anything to do with us."

"There are other countries," Anya tried, picking at a tuft of grass and avoiding his eyes.

Nick shook his head. "We're getting older," he said. "We're already too old for many countries, like most in Central America. If we have to start over, it'll be another year before we can adopt again, and who knows who'd accept us then."

She nodded.

"Besides," Nick said. "The important one is Nonna. I can't leave her here with Dmitri. She's a hostage, leverage. Do you think they'll just put her back in the orphanage? I doubt it. More likely they'll sell her themselves, or maybe even keep her, to grow up in the mob."

"I grew up in the mob," Anya said, defensively.

"True," Nick replied, "but that was different. You were blood. Nonna isn't. She'd be more likely to end up like Galina than you." He pursed his lips as he thought about the prostitute on the ground in front of the orphanage. "No way that's gonna happen. She goes home with me tomorrow."

She looked across the street. The house was still dark. "I'm not sure he's coming home tonight."

"I wonder if Pyotr said something to him?"

"You thought he wasn't working with Dmitri?"

"I didn't think he was," Nick admitted. "But I don't know for sure. He could easily have told Dmitri not to show up tonight."

"He could easily have had ten gunmen waiting for us, too," Anya pointed out. "Perhaps Dmitri is just out late."

A truck went by and they fell silent, watching it. Lights were going out in houses up and down the streets, and the few pedestrians they had seen walking the street were long gone. The only sounds they heard were the crickets.

They waited.

Anya dozed off around midnight, her head resting on Nick's shoulder. He put his arm around her to keep her from falling over. They sat like that for another hour before she stirred.

She said something sleepily in Russian, then caught herself as she awoke further. "Oh, god, I fell asleep, didn't I? I'm sorry!"

Nick laughed softly, "No worries. You didn't miss anything. It's still dark. I don't think he's coming home tonight."

She laid her head on his shoulder again. "I'm sorry, Nick."

"Let's give it a few more minutes," he said. "Then we'll go."

"OK," she replied. "Tell me something."

"Tell you what?"

"I don't care," she murmured. "A story. Something about you."

"Hmmmm, a story," he said. "Well, I was just thinking about the kids in Iraq. They're not so different from kids here."

"No?"

"No. My unit was an advanced guard. We were the first Americans to enter new towns. The parents would hide but the kids would rush out to see us. They didn't care about politics or infidels, they thought we were cool. We'd have soccer balls and candy with us, and the kids just glowed. They laughed and ran around and for a while forgot there was a war on. It was dangerous, but part of me loved going into a new town. I didn't trust the adults, but the kids were awesome."

"How long did you stay in the towns?"

"Not all that long. Sometimes only a day or even a few hours, just long enough to find out if there were insurgents in the town. Then the regular army would come in."

She nestled her head deeper into Nick's shoulder.

"The kids were so innocent, you know?" Nick continued. "They just wanted to have fun. If we were around long enough and they got to know us well enough, they'd play jokes on us or show us around the town."

Anya smiled against Nick's shoulder.

"Although," Nick said, "we didn't like them to be too public about it. The insurgents weren't above shooting parents of friendly kids, or even the kids themselves. That happened twice to me, and I swore never again to let a kid give me a tour."

"I'm sorry, Nick. Iraq sounded bad."

"Not all of it, but so many people hated us and hated each other. It was like they didn't want peace, or the only peace they wanted was the peace when the other side was dead. It got old real quick, and I was happy to leave."

He stared across at Dmitri's house, but his thoughts weren't on the Russian.

"I just wish I could've brought some of those kids home with me," he said. "Kids deserve to be happy, not screwed up by the enemies of their parents."

She caressed his hand. "You're a good man," she said.

"Not really, but thank you," Nick said.

"What about your family?"

"What about them?"

"Do you see them?"

"Not very often. I live near my half-brother, and my parents live near my sister in Minnesota."

She looked blank.

"Have you ever heard of Minnesota?"

He could feel her shake her head. He grinned in the dark.

"It's a state in the north, near Canada. Very cold in the winter. It's a long way from Oregon."

"Kind of like our Siberia," Anya replied.

Nick grinned again. "Yeah, probably."

"Do you get up there much?"

"Sure, I've been there a few times, in the summer. Dad and I don't talk a whole lot, but he's a good guy. He's an old soldier, set in his ways. He's kind of mellowed with age, though, I guess. I get along well with my mom and sister, too. They're good people. I hear Vicki and her husband might come to Oregon to welcome Nonna home."

"So you have a brother and a sister. That's nice."

"You don't, do you?"

Anya sighed against Nick. "No. I wish I did, at least a sister. There are too many men in my family. Too much...manliness. Momma and I need more women. It'd be nice to have a sister to talk to."

"Do you have many female friends?"

She shrugged. "Some, but many of them are getting married, and they don't have time to spend with me."

Before Nick could say anything she reached up and put her finger to his lips. "No, I don't plan on getting married anytime soon. I have enough drama in my life without a husband."

"You'll meet the right guy and change your mind real quick," Nick said.

"Perhaps, although I've yet to find a man who can keep up with me," she said.

Nick laughed quietly and hugged Anya. He believed her.

They left an hour later, defeated. The house was still dark. All the houses around it were dark. The streets were dark. Nick's mood was darker.

"So that's it, then," Anya said. She clicked her fob and the car doors unlocked loudly. "If Dmitri has the power to take Nonna, he knows he only has to wait you out one more day."

Nick slid into his seat silently. Anya got in and looked across at the American. "I'm out of options," she said.

"There's one more," he replied.

Eight hours later the black SUV pulled up in front of Nick. It had tinted windows and the spinning "look at me" hubcaps that annoyed him for some reason. Back doors opened on both sides of the vehicle opened and two thick men with guns advanced on him.

Nick knew it would be only a matter of time, but was still impressed at how fast they had found him. He started at the Rostov hotel and walked slowly towards the orphanage, lingering slightly outside the brothel. They caught up with him a block from Nonna's home. He feared he'd be walking all day before they finally figured it out.

"Come with us, please," one of them said. His accent was slight and Nick could tell he was higher up the pecking order than the goons Dmitri had sent after him before. At least he was polite.

"Make you a deal," Nick replied evenly. "You keep your guns out and I break your arms. You put them away and I'll come peacefully."

The second man looked shocked but the first one, the one who had spoken, only smiled slightly. It was as if he had expected Nick's response. He nodded to the other man and both put their guns away.

Nick stepped into the back seat, between the two men. The SUV pulled away from the curb.

Several seconds later, long enough for two cars to pass, a red Lada Kalina crept out from a side street and followed them.

Chapter 30

Nick glanced at the large bulk sitting on one side of him, then glanced at the large bulk sitting on the other side of him. They were squeezed into the back seat of the SUV, arms pressed together. Each guard held a gun in his outside hand, and in the cramped quarters Nick doubted he could grab one, even if he had been inclined to.

The driver sat alone in the front seat, separated from the three men by a sheet of glass. No doubt bulletproof glass. Nick wondered how many people in the back seat would have wanted to shoot the driver.

But it gave them some privacy. Time to go to work.

He turned to the guy on his left, the leader, the one who had talked and almost smiled at Nick's crack before they got in. He stared straight ahead, keeping Nick in his periphery.

"Your boss is a nutcase, you know," Nick said. The man's lips twitched, a virtual grin. He wasn't going to give Nick the satisfaction of smiling, but he didn't have to.

Nick knew he spoke English quite well, even to the extent that he knew what "nutcase" meant.

"And he's going to go down today," Nick continued. "I don't know how much he pays you, but you should plan on collecting unemployment tomorrow."

"Shut up," the guy on the other side said.

Nick turned to him. "I wasn't talking to you, Ivan," he said. "I doubt you're even smart enough to find the unemployment line. I'm guessing you'll just be out on the street, or maybe in jail. Maybe you'll go down on guys to make some money."

"Shut up," he said again, a bit louder, a bit slower, emphasizing both words.

Nick turned back to the first bodyguard. "Nice command of the language. Is that the only English he knows?"

"Fuck you," the second bodyguard said.

Nick laughed. He knew laughter would piss the guy off. "Yeah, I knew you'd know that one. You can put it to good use in Lubyanka tomorrow, with your new friends."

The first bodyguard shook his head. "I think you should not talk until we see Dmitri," he said.

"Oh, I don't plan on talking much to that ass," Nick said. "I'm going to find out where my daughter is, then I'm going to shoot him in his ugly face."

"That might be difficult," the first man said.

"Shut up," the second man said.

Nick looked from one to the other. "He told *you* to shut up? Wow, the little pissant has delusions of grandeur."

He felt the second bodyguard tense up against him and wondered if he had pushed it too far. Maybe, but at this point he didn't have many cards to play. Aggravating the bodyguards would make what came next easier to handle.

"No more talk," the first man said, and raised his gun slightly to show what would happen if the directive wasn't followed. Nick knew the man wouldn't shoot him; that prize would be saved for Dmitri. But a gun could do a lot of damage to a face or a groin without being fired.

Nick stopped talking, and they rode the rest of the way in silence.

They pulled up in front of another ornate house. Nick realized that Dmitri had probably stayed here last night. As fanatical as he was, Nick thought, Dmitri was definitely successful. The car pulled up to the curb and the guy to his right got out first. He motioned Nick out of the car, and the second bodyguard followed out the same door. Two guns were on Nick the entire time. Perhaps three if the driver was packing. They needn't have bothered.

The two men escorted Nick up the sidewalk and into the house. Nick hoped they stayed with him to Dmitri's office, or else his prodding in the car would be wasted.

To his relief, they did. One on each elbow, through the ornate double doors, up the stairway, to a closed door on the second floor. With a grin towards Nick that lacked any semblance of humor, the second bodyguard knocked on the door with the butt of his gun.

A grunt came from inside. The first bodyguard opened the door and ushered Nick in.

The office was ornate, just like Dmitri's other office. A large desk, large window overlooking a garden, treasures on the wall.

Nick looked closer and saw some of the items he had pilfered after his previous run-in with the mob boss.

Dmitri saw his double-take and said, "Yes, my things are here with me."

"You're welcome," Nick said.

"Excuse me?"

"You wouldn't have them if I hadn't been nice enough to return them," Nick said.

Dmitri smiled. "That's not going to save you."

"Where's my daughter?"

Dmitri waved a hand, dismissing the question. "Sit down," he said.

Two hands on his shoulders forced Nick into a chair in front of the desk. The two bodyguards stood over him, one on each side.

"You've caused me a lot of trouble, American," Dmitri said. "You put one of my men in the hospital—"

"I put at least three of your men in the hospital, Russian. And one in the morgue."

Dmitri's calm demeanor slipped momentarily. "Perhaps. So, what do you think I should do with you?"

"Tell me where my daughter is," Nick said.

"You no longer need to concern yourself with the child," Dmitri said. "She's with an associate of mine, and quite out of your control. You should worry more about yourself."

Nick looked calmly across the desk. "You know, I didn't think you'd tell me where my baby is. At least, not voluntarily. Let's see how you do with a bullet in your leg. I think you might sing like a bird then."

Dmitri leaned forward and frowned. He seemed surprised. Maybe he was used to store owners who were too weak or afraid to fight back. And if they did, he'd send enforcers like Sergei after them instead of going after them himself.

"Of course," Nick continued. "I have to hit the correct leg first. We don't want anybody getting a splinter."

Dmitri stood up angrily, awkwardly, and pointed a finger at Nick. "Look around, American. You're in no position to talk that way to me."

Nick snorted. "Ha, these two? They're amateurs." He didn't look at the two men on either side of him, to underscore his opinion of them. "They can't protect you. You're going to end up as my bitch."

Dmitri snapped. He yelled something at the two bodyguards, and Nick felt himself being grasped and lifted by his arms. He sagged, but the strength of the two men was too much for him and he quickly found himself standing in front of a furious Dmitri.

Dmitri punched Nick in the mouth. "Now who's the bitch?" he yelled as he swung again.

The punch connected and Nick felt searing pain rip through his jaw. Dmitri reared back again, in slow motion, and Nick closed his eyes. He had time to think that maybe he didn't wait long enough to bait Dmitri into a frenzy.

But as the third punch landed, the door to the room burst open.

There was a brief pause, which seemed an eternity to Nick as another jolt of pain went through his jaw, then a shot rang out. The man to Nick's left, nearer the door, screamed and let go of Nick's arm. Immediately Nick jammed his elbow up and back and felt a grunt from the second bodyguard. He let go of Nick, either because of the elbow or of the gun facing him. Nick didn't really care which.

He turned on his heels and came face-to-face with the second bodyguard. The man's face showed confusion and fear. Nick head-butted him savagely and the man dropped.

Nick turned back in time to see Dmitri rush to the window. Whether he meant to jump through it to the relative safety of the ground below, Nick would never know. The gun barked again. Dmitri screamed and went down, clutching his side.

Anya stepped forward, into Nick's view. She was breathing heavily but had a smile on her face. Nick quickly looked behind her.

"I thought I said to bring backup?" he told her.

"No time," she panted. "I didn't need them, anyway." She crossed over to Dmitri as Nick ruffled through the clothes of the bodyguards. He quickly retrieved his Glocks from the first man's suit coat.

Dmitri sat on the ornate wood floor, holding his side and rocking back and forth. Nick saw that the bullet had only grazed the man's side. Enough to bring him down but not incapacitate him.

"Nice shot," he told Anya.

"Damn right," she replied. "And you're welcome."

"Yeah, thanks for saving my skin. Anybody else around here we need to worry about?"

She shook her head. "I don't think so. I took out two coming up, and didn't hear anything else except Dmitri yelling."

"I was afraid you wouldn't be ready," Nick said. "It didn't take long for Dmitri to go off."

"I'm glad he did," Anya said as she looked down at the man on the ground. "I see movies about the cabaret coming to the rescue—"

Nick looked at her. "The what?"

"The cabaret?"

Nick laughed. "You mean the cavalry. The cavalry comes to the rescue."

She made a face. "Oh. I like the cabaret better."

Nick smiled.

"Next time you can rescue yourself," she pouted, only half-joking.

"I'm sorry, Anya," Nick said. "I really am. I appreciate what you did for me."

She waved a hand. "Yeah, yeah. Let's pull what we need out of this bastard and get out of here."

Nick nodded and turned his attention to the man on the floor. He knelt down near him and said, "Hey, Dmitri."

Dmitri had been watching them talk, hands plastered to his side, blood oozing through his fingers. He glared at Nick but didn't say anything.

"Looks like another one for the hospital," Anya said, and clucked.

"Yep," Nick said. "They're going to get pissed that we send them so much business."

"Maybe they'll thank us."

"I'm not telling you a damn thing," Dmitri said.

"You already did, dumbass," Nick told him. "You have no clue where Nonna is. Your 'associate' has her, and you told him not to tell you, didn't you?"

Dmitri was uncharacteristically quiet.

"You knew I'd be coming for you."

Dmitri smiled.

Nick sat on the edge of the desk and looked over at Anya. "But he didn't know you'd be here," he said.

She nodded.

"So you were able to take care of the first line of defense,"

She nodded again, a little slower this time, concern creeping over her face, realizing what Nick was getting at.

"So where's the second?"

Dmitri stirred and reached into his shirt pocket. Nick hopped off the desk and pointed his gun at the man, but Dmitri didn't hesitate. He pulled a cell phone out of his shirt pocket. It was a small, silver device. Not an iPhone but not far off, probably a Russian version from the same blueprints.

A green light at the top glowed brightly. "They'll be coming in the front door any second now. They heard everything you said, 'dumbass.'"

Nick fired from his standing position and Dmitri's wrist exploded. The phone flew across the room, hit the wall, and fell to the ground. Dmitri yelled and clutched his ruined hand to his chest.

"Nice shot," Anya said.

"No it wasn't," Nick replied. "I missed." He fired again and Dmitri fell backwards, a round hole in his forehead.

"Oops," Nick said.

"I assume you were done talking to him."

Nick shrugged. "He wasn't saying anything I wanted to hear, anyway."

"Time to go," Anya said. She didn't seem fazed by the death of a madman.

"In a second," Nick said. "Before you came in, Dmitri said that Nonna was with an 'associate.' What does that make you think?"

Anya crossed to the window and looked out carefully. "That Dmitri's not working alone. So? Can we go now?"

"If he has an associate, then he's not the top."

"No, that fool wouldn't be the top," Anya said. "He's medium level. Does his own thing, but there's somebody higher up that keeps things going."

"Keeps the jackals in line, you mean," Nick said. "Makes sure they don't eat each other."

"Yeah, something like that."

"So who's the top?"

"Could be a couple of guys, not that many," Anya replied. "All senior, all well protected. You won't be walking in to see them unannounced. Oh, look at the time. Let's go," She said.

"Then I guess I'd better find out who he is and send him an invitation," Nick said as he went to the desk. His jaw felt on fire, and he wished he had some ibuprofen. Or Scotch. He started rifling through the papers on the desk.

"Can you do that someplace else?" Anya asked, words rushed. She kept an eye out the window. "If somebody's coming, they're not going to be far away."

"Yeah, yeah," Nick said. "If you saw the name of his boss, would you know it?"

"Perhaps," she said slowly.

"You look, I'll watch for friends," Nick said. They traded places quickly. Nick poked the drapes over the windows back and looked to his left. Dmitri's office overlooked the side yard, and he could see the street in front of the house if he pressed his head against the glass. So far it looked quiet.

Anya glanced through the papers on the top of the desk. Apparently she found nothing to her liking, as she swept them all to the floor and opened the top drawer.

"Need another gun?" she asked Nick, holding up a small pistol.

"No. Focus," Nick said as he glanced out the window. He watched in dismay as a black car screeched to a halt in front of the house. Four doors opened and four men jumped out. They all rushed out of sight towards the front of the house. Their excitement overrode their brains, Nick thought. They should have sent somebody around the side of the house.

"We've got company," he called out. He ran to the side of the room and scooped up the bloody phone. He held it by two fingers before wiping it on Dmitri's shirt. He stuck it in his pocket.

"I found something," she called back. She had the second drawer open and was leafing through a brown binder. Nick saw long rows of numbers, like a ledger.

The front door slammed.

"Now, Anya," Nick said.

"Hold on!" she said.

He opened the sash and jammed his hand into the window screen. It popped out and fell several feet to the ground.

"Got it," she said as he turned to her. She put the ledger back in the drawer and closed it. She ran to the window and swung a leg outside. Nick grabbed her arms and she swung the other leg out. She dangled against the side of the house, Nick supporting her weight, for a second before he let go and she fell the remaining few feet. Nick didn't wait. He swung out the window, grabbed the sill for support for a second, and dropped down. He landed in a small bush and kicked his way out quickly. Anya was already running towards the alley behind the house.

Nick followed as he heard shouts in the house. By the time the first man shoved his head out the window, they were gone.

Chapter 31

Anya laughed as they entered her apartment. "That was fun," she said. "My heart hasn't raced like that for a while."

Nick was not as amused. "Yeah, well, we aren't any closer to Nonna," he said as he sat down heavily on her couch. He felt his world start to close in on him. Less than a day before he was supposed to pick his daughter up and leave for their new life. *Her* new life, outside of the orphanage.

"Don't be an old woman," Anya said. "We now know who Dmitri reported up to. If his partner has Nonna, then Alexander will know who it is."

"Alexander?"

She nodded. She walked over and sat near him on the couch, legs folded demurely under her. Nick's knees always hurt when he saw somebody sit that way. "Alexander Bocharova," she said. "One of the oligarchs who run the city. He's in charge of this section of Rostov. Seems quite logical, really. We probably could've just gone straight to him instead of killing Dmitri."

"No, we couldn't," Nick said.

She shrugged. "Yeah, maybe not. Doesn't matter. We have his name now and I assume you have his number on Dmitri's phone."

Nick had forgotten about the cell phone he'd lifted from the mobster. He took it out of his pocket and pressed the large circle at the bottom. The phone sprang to life. It had been left on and had plenty of battery left. He noticed it didn't have a password. Nick flicked over to the contacts section, the one with the icon in a shape of a head.

The letters were Cyrillic. He sheepishly handed the phone over to Anya.

It only took her a moment to find him. "Here we go, Alexander. I'm surprised he didn't put in a fake name."

"Same reason he didn't password-protect his phone," Nick said. "He knew he was too smart to lose his phone or have somebody take it from him. If you're that smart, you don't need passwords or fake names." He shook his head.

Anya harrumphed and held out the phone to him. "Do you want to call Alexander?"

Nick was surprised. "Just like that?"

"Well, I figure you have two ways of doing this. Either sneak into his headquarters, kill the highly-trained bodyguards sprinkled throughout the building, and beat the information out of him."

"Or?"

"Or call him and ask for an appointment. If he says no, then you can attack him."

Nick thought about it for a moment, then shrugged and took the phone. "Guess it can't hurt to ask nicely. He might just want to get me out of his city."

"He probably does, since you've been killing his people."

"Or maybe he wants to make an example out of me," Nick said thoughtfully. "Like Dmitri tried to do."

"I hope not," Anya said. "It didn't end up well for Dmitri and it probably wouldn't end up well for Alexander, either."

The phone rang. Nick looked down at the one in his hand. It was silent, motionless. Nick felt a vibration in his pocket as his other phone rang again.

"You're a popular guy," Anya said.

Nick set Dmitri's phone down on the couch and reached into his pocket for the one Andrei gave him. "It's probably your cousin, asking what happened."

But it wasn't. Pyotr's voice came through the speaker and he wasn't happy.

"So you told me you were going to kill Dmitri, and then we find Dmitri dead in his house, a nice big hole in his head to match the one in his hand and the other in his side," the detective said. He was almost yelling and Nick held the phone away from his ear. Anya heard every word and gave Nick an evil grin. Pyotr continued, "So, by all accounts I should arrest you."

"So why are you talking to me instead of putting handcuffs on?" Nick said.

Pyotr said something in Russian that sounded like a swear word. "Is Anya with you?" he finally said, after several moments of sputtering.

"Yes."

"Give her the phone. I wish to speak with her."

Nick pressed the phone to his chest and whispered, "He wants to talk to you."

She held out her hand. "Good. I want to talk to him as well."

"Why?"

"To keep your ass out of jail, of course," she said without a smile. He handed the phone to her and she got up. She cleared her throat and spoke into the mouthpiece. As she did, she turned her back on Nick.

He watched her from the couch for several minutes as she talked to Protr. She was animated, gesturing with her hands as she paced her apartment. Twice she glanced at Nick, but she was speaking in Russian so she knew he couldn't understand her. He just sat there on the couch, feeling like a squirrel watching a bank robbery. He could see what was happening but had no idea what was really going on.

She crossed over to the window looking out over the courtyard between the large apartment blocks. She stood there, back to Nick, one arm crossed in front of her chest, the arm holding the phone resting on her wrist, and talked low, urgently, into the phone. Nick was tempted to get up and go to her but her posture was tense, so he stayed where he was.

Eventually she finished the conversation and clicked the phone off. She continued to stare out the window quietly, then turned to Nick.

"Well?" Nick asked.

She chewed her lip. "He wants to arrest you for the murder of Dmitri. I think I talked him out of it for now, but he knows you did it."

Nick stood up and walked to her. "Thank you for that," he said. "I'm sorry I put you in the middle of it."

She stepped back. "That was a stupid move," she said. "You shouldn't have told him what you were going to do."

"Anya," Nick said, "If Dmitri ended up with a bullet in his head, Pyotr was going to come to me no matter what I told him. I didn't have much to lose. I wanted to shake the tree a little and see what fell out."

Anya shook her head. "Perhaps," she said, "but it was like you were taunting him. 'I'm going to kill Dmitri. Come arrest me.'"

"I had to do that, to see if he was on Dmitri's payroll."

"And now you know he isn't."

"Yes, which means he's not on Alexander's payroll, either."

"Probably. But that doesn't mean you can just go and pop Alexander in the head."

"I don't plan on shooting Alexander," Nick replied. "But I do need information out of him and I don't want some cop watching my every move."

She smiled a bit, finally. "Well, you're welcome."

"What did you say to him? You spent a lot of time talking to him."

She shrugged and wouldn't look him in the eye. "Just talking him down. He was quite angry."

"Did you make any promises?"

She laughed. "Not about you, no. But you'd better behave yourself. You're on his list now."

Nick looked at her sideways. "Not about me? What did you promise him?"

"I didn't promise him anything," she said, and laughed. It sounded strained. "You're a worrier. He's off your back for now. Just go with that and do what you need to do."

"I'd better call Alexander," Nick said. "I need to meet with him today."

"Do you want me to do it?" she asked.

Nick shook his head. "Thanks, but this is something I need to do myself. I assume he speaks English."

She nodded. "I'm sure he does," she said. "If I remember correctly, he has several legitimate businesses. He'd need English for them."

Nick grabbed Dmitri's phone, scrolled to Alexander's name in the contacts list, and pressed the Call button.

It was answered on the second ring by a woman. A middle-aged woman, by the sound of her voice. She sounded pleasant enough, if not overtly friendly.

"Zdrastvoytya," Nick said. "Do you speak English?"

She switched effortlessly to English. "Yes, of course. May I help you?"

"I'd like to speak with Mr. Bocharova, please," Nick said. He gritted his teeth at the submissive tone in his voice, but he knew he wasn't going to get past Alexander's filter without it.

"He's in a meeting right now," the woman replied automatically. "But I'd be happy to give him a message."

Nick took a deep breath. "My name is Nick Wallace. I'm an American in Rostov to adopt a baby girl. I've had problems with some people in one of his, um, businesses that I would like to talk to him about."

There was a pause. "What kind of problems?" the receptionist asked. He could hear light clicks of keys being pressed on her end.

"My daughter has been taken and I need to get her back. I'm hoping Mr. Bocharova can help me."

"His associate couldn't help you?" she asked politely.

"No. He wouldn't tell me, and now he can't."

"Oh?"

"Unfortunately, he's dead."

The clicking stopped. "And what did you say your name was?"

"Nick Wallace."

"Mr. Wallace," she said, "I believe Mr. Bocharova's meeting just concluded."

Chapter 32

Anya turned the car off and they sat in silence, listening to the clicks as the engine cooled. Once the air conditioner shut off, heat coursed through the windshield and sweat quickly beaded on Nick's forehead.

They were in a small, tree-lined parking lot in front of a three-story glass office building. It was an ornate building, with a curving passenger drop-off in the front that circled around an area of colorful flowers. The windows were glazed, effectively hiding all activity inside.

They sat in the back row of the lot, where Nick thought they'd be out of sight of curious eyes. He and Anya glared at each other.

"I trust we won't have an incident," Nick said.

"I just think I should come in with you," Anya replied. "You don't know what you're getting into. Alexander could take you out as soon as you walk through the door."

"Which is why I don't want you coming in," Nick said. "No sense in both of us getting killed."

"But—"

"Quiet," Nick said. "When I'm in there I want you someplace safe. Find a spot and wait for me to call. Got it?"

"Yes, sir," she replied, sticking her lower lip out.

"And no cavalry. Or even cabaret," he said.

She didn't smile. "Be careful. Don't make him angry. He's more powerful than you know."

Nick sighed and opened his car door. "Will do. I'll be courteous and respectful. I just hope he doesn't make me blow his head off."

He turned to get out of the car.

"Hey!" Anya said.

Nick turned back. "What?"

"You armed?"

He pursed his lips. "Hmm, yes. That probably wouldn't go over very well with them, would it?"

"No. Leave them here."

Slowly, sadly, Nick put the two Glocks in the glove box of Anya's car. He felt naked without them. Then he thought of Dmitri's cell phone in his pocket. That would probably go over even worse than the guns. He popped it into the glove box next to the guns.

"Your cell phone is on, right?" he asked her.

Anya checked quickly. "Yes," she said.

Nick sighed. "Good. OK, wish me luck."

Anya flashed a smile. "Good luck," she said. "See you soon."

He mounted the steps with a feeling of dread. He wasn't afraid of Alexander as much as concerned about what the man would tell him about his daughter. If this boss wasn't interested in playing ball, there wasn't much Nick could do about it, especially in the few remaining hours he had left. He prayed Alexander would cooperate. The thought "take pity" flashed through his mind, but Nick chased it away quickly. He wasn't here for pity. He was here to get his daughter back.

And, dammit, he would. His back straightened as he pushed his way through the glass doors.

There was a metal detector in front of him. Alongside it stood a man in a black suit, hands clasped in front of him. Behind a console next to the detector sat another man, ready to look into anything Nick brought with him.

Nick thanked Anya for remembering the guns.

The standing guard motioned Nick forward with a terse wave of his hand. Nick stepped up to the man who, without smiling, spoke in Russian. Nick flashed his ID. The man glanced at it, then down at a sheet of paper in front of him. He said something in Russian. Nick assumed he was asking about who Nick was there to see.

"Alexander Bocharova," Nick said simply.

The man looked up at Nick, studied his face, looked down again at the paper, and made a check mark about halfway down the sheet. He pointed to the metal detector.

Nick stepped through the detector, then waited on the other side as the second man scanned the image. He must have passed because the man waved him through. The first guard fell into place beside Nick and said, "I show you."

They walked down a short hallway to a bank of elevators. Everything seemed bright and airy, and Nick had a hard time believing anybody in the building was connected to anything nefarious. He had to remind himself that Alexander was at the top rung of a very nasty ladder of people in Rostov.

They stepped into an elevator and rode to the top floor in silence. The man stood still, facing forward, hands once again clasped in front of him. Nick couldn't tell for sure but assumed there was a gun inside the man's suit pocket. Once again he wished he had at least one of his Glocks with him.

With a ding, the elevator stopped at the third floor. The man showed Nick out and pointed to a door in front of them. "There," was all he said. He waited for Nick to step through the door, then disappeared back into the elevator.

Nick found himself in a large lobby, potted plants on either side, a woman at a desk in front of him. She was middle-aged, with streaks of unapologetic gray in her black hair. She wore a nice business suit with a scarf around her neck. Nick found the scarf surprising, given the heat outside. Fashion has its price, he thought.

She glanced up and smiled slightly when she saw him. She said something in Russian, and the voice confirmed that she was the person on the other end of the phone.

"Mr. Bocharova," Nick said. He knew she'd know who he was as soon as she opened her mouth.

Her mechanical smile still in place, the receptionist nodded. "One moment," she said in English. She picked up her phone, dialed a number, and spoke softly. She didn't look at Nick as she talked.

She listened for a moment, nodded again, and hung up. She turned back to Nick and said, "Mr. Bocharova will be with you in a moment. Please have a seat." She motioned to two chairs flanking a table across from the desk. The chairs were upholstered and cushy. Nick sank deep into one. It made him uneasy, knowing he'd have trouble getting out of his seat if somebody came through the door with a weapon drawn. He didn't want to get back on his feet, though. He would appear nervous. Probably not as nervous as he was, he thought wryly, but no sense advertising.

So he picked up a magazine on the coffee table and leafed through it idly. It was in Cyrillic but he recognized the Men's Health masthead. He made it through the section on Building Bigger Biceps and was just getting to How To Have Fantastic Sex when the door opened. He quickly closed the magazine and placed it on the table.

A man walked through the door. He was short, thin, with dark hair. Nick was surprised to see he only wore an open-collar shirt with his suit pants. Apparently they were informal here in the Bocharova empire.

Nick stood up and discreetly wiped his palms on his pants.

If the man noticed the gesture, he didn't comment on it. His eyes never left Nick's face as he offered his right hand. Nick shook it and was surprised at the strength of the grip. The man was stronger than he looked.

"Good morning, Mr. Wallace," the man said. "My name is Vitali Popravko. I'm Mr. Bocharova's assistant."

"Nice to meet you," Nick replied. It wasn't nice to meet him, of course. Not even close. He didn't really want to talk to Bocharova, but he had to. And now he got an *assistant* while his daughter was out there somewhere. Nick wanted to scream. He gritted his teeth instead.

Popravko led Nick to a small office. It was empty except for a desk, a few chairs, and some filing cabinets. Blinds were open on the window behind the desk but the window faced an inner courtyard. All Nick saw was another building, and no sunlight.

The Russian motioned Nick to sit down in a chair in front of the desk.

"Due to the, ahhhh, sensitive nature of our relationship," Popravko said as he took a seat behind the desk. "Mr. Bocharova has asked me to begin the discussions with you. We will join him momentarily."

Nick nodded cautiously. He kept his mouth shut.

Popravko glanced at a sheet of paper lying on his desk. It was next to a laptop, and Nick would have bet ten to one that Popravko had been doing some internet searches prior to the meeting. "So in your phone call to us this morning, you said that you are in Russia to adopt a little girl, and she has gone missing."

"That is correct," Nick said.

"We're very sorry to hear that," Popravko said. He said it in a way that made Nick almost believe he was sincere. "Please know we had nothing to do with her disappearance. It was apparently handled at a lower level, and we were not kept informed."

"Are you not aware of what your people are doing?" Nick asked.

If Popravko was offended at Nick's words and tone, he didn't show it. "It's difficult to follow everybody's movements," he said. "I'm sure you can understand that, having been in a leadership position in the United States Marines."

Damn internet, Nick thought. Sometimes it just got in the way. "Yes, I can understand that," he said. "And I'm sure you know that when my people did something incorrect, I was held responsible for their actions."

"Of course," Popravko said smoothly. "Which is why you're here with me. Now, before you see Mr. Bocharova, I have some questions for you."

Nick settled back in the chair and nodded.

"Thank you. First of all, we'd like to understand what happened with Dmitri Kopolov. As you may know, he was found dead in his house just a few hours ago."

Nick nodded again. With their resources, he knew any lies would be uncovered quickly, perhaps instantaneously, and then his one remaining link to his daughter would be severed.

"I killed him," he said simply.

Popravko seemed surprised at Nick's honesty. The Russian was silent for a moment, as if trying to figure out what to say next. "Surely you understand how serious a situation you are in," he said.

Nick leaned forward. "Yes, I do," he replied. "And surely you understand how desperate I am. My daughter is missing and right now you are the only people who might know where she is. And now you tell me that you are unaware what Dmitri was up to?"

Popravko held up a hand. "I said we *were* unaware. We're aware now, and it's my hope that we can help you."

Nick settled back, not mollified. "How?"

"All in due time, please. So, why did you believe Dmitri took your daughter?"

"We've been having some issues with Dmitri and his people for several days," Nick said. "It escalated to the point where Dmitri took Nonna."

"And why would he do that?"

"I was pissing him off."

Popravko smiled thinly, quickly. "I can't imagine. So, you confronted Dmitri at his home. How did you know where to find him?"

"I didn't," Nick replied. "He found me. I made myself visible and he picked me up."

Popravko pursed his lips for a moment, looked hard at Nick, then made a note on the paper. He shook his head faintly as he wrote. Nick could almost hear the Russian curse Dmitri in his head.

"He wasn't the sharpest tool in the shed," Nick said. Popravko didn't glance up, but he smiled slightly.

He finished what he was writing and tapped his pen on the paper several times as he thought. Finally he looked up and spoke. "So, you are taken to Dmitri's house, you ask him where your daughter is, and he says…"

"He said to go screw myself. Just not as nicely."

"And you were able to kill him and injure two bodyguards by yourself?"

He was obviously fishing, and just as obviously knew the answer. Nick would have been surprised if Dmitri's house didn't have multiple security cameras in it. "No," Nick said. "I had help."

Popravko showed no surprise. "Russian help?"

"Yes."

"And why would this person help you?"

"She's a friend."

"Does this friend have a name?"

"Yes, most definitely," Nick said. Popravko put pen to paper, then raised the point off the sheet with a sigh a few seconds later when it became evident Nick wasn't about to divulge the name. He didn't pursue it, for which Nick was glad. He didn't want to bring Anya in on this, not unless he had to. And even then he'd think hard about it.

"What else?" Nick asked.

"Pardon?"

"I'm on a schedule. Ask your questions or get out of my way."

Popravko nodded, letting the comment pass. "Did Dmitri say anything else to you or anybody else before he…ahhh…expired?"

Nick thought back to the frantic few minutes in the house. "No. He pretty much freaked out when I got there. He said Nonna was with an associate, and—"

Vitali Popravko suddenly leaned forward, interest on his face. "An associate? He used those words? No names?"

"No name, just 'an associate.'" Popravko looked disappointed. Nick stared at the Russian for a long moment before it came to him.

"Oh, my God," Nick said. "He's been double-crossing you. You have no idea who he's working with, do you?"

Chapter 33

Popravko was gone for several minutes. When he returned he ushered Nick into Bocharova's office without a word.

The office was classy. Plenty of light, abstract paintings on the wall, a desk that was beautiful without being gaudy. A television was perched in the corner, tickers running across the bottom of the screen while a blonde anchor mouthed silent words.

Nick took it all in within seconds, before turning his attention to the man behind the desk.

Alexander Bocharova looked the part of a high-end entrepreneur. Dark hair slicked back with just a bit of gray at the temples, white shirt immaculately starched. Gold cufflinks. Nick had never seen cufflinks in person before. He really couldn't think of a good reason to wear them.

Alexander motioned for Nick to sit. Nick took a seat across from the Russian and looked at him expectantly. Alexander gazed back at Nick for a moment, then said, "Can we get straight to the point?" His voice was deep, refined, reminding Nick of a politician on TV. Nick had to remind himself that, for all of his trappings, Alexander was a mobster. A high-end mobster, but a man who dealt in drugs and prostitutes.

Nick nodded slowly. "Yes, we don't have a lot of time."

Alexander leaned forward and clasped his hands together on the top of the desk. "You need something from us, something quite important to you," he said,

"Yes," Nick replied.

"We also require something from you, something important. Information."

"You need to know who Dmitri was working with."

"Yes," Alexander replied. He looked slightly embarrassed. "We wish to know who Dmitri was working with." He stressed the second word, making it clear that they didn't need the information. But Nick knew better, or Alexander wouldn't be playing nice.

Nick started to open his mouth, but Alexander cut him off with a wave of his hand. "The 'why' is not important. Yes, he's dead, but we need to know what he told his, how did he say it, his 'associate'. And we need to know what his associate plans to do with the information."

Nick shook his head. "I'd like to tell you, Mr. Bocharova—"

Bocharova cut him off. "Please, call me Alexander. We're on the same side here, I believe."

"Thank you. I'd like to tell you, but I really don't know."

Alex frowned. "Surely you heard something. It sounds as if you had several altercations with Dmitri."

"I did. Well, mainly with his people. But I never saw him with anybody else."

Alexander steepled his fingers. "That's a shame. And he didn't mention anything about the person who took your daughter?"

"No, he didn't."

Alexander sighed. "It will be difficult to get her back, then."

"If you don't know any more about this person than I do, then you're right. Maybe we can talk to his people."

"The few you left conscious, yes. We're talking to them."

"But since you were willing to meet with me, I assume they don't know much."

"True," Alexander said. "Dmitri never did trust people."

"If he was double-crossing you, I can understand why he kept his mouth shut."

"Yes. Unfortunately for you." He paused and looked closely at Nick. "I understand there is a policeman asking questions about you."

Nick stiffened. "You seem to be well-informed, Mr. Bocharova."

"I make it a point to know what's going on in my town."

"Then you'll know that he has nothing to go on," Nick said. His ears began to feel hot.

"Let's hope it stays that way," Alexander said. He sat back in his chair. "You know, there are ways for the police in Rostov to find out things."

"I'm sure. But if I can tell you who was working with Dmitri…"

"Then the police will never know what happened to Dmitri."

"You're a real bastard," Nick said.

"I'm a realist, Nick," Alexander replied smoothly. "You've been dealing with Dmitri's people quite successfully so far. Now you just have to point your talents at his associates."

Nick froze. His face suddenly tingled. "What did you say?"

For the first time, Alexander looked uncertain. "I said, you've handled Dmitri's empire quite successfully. Normally I'd be upset that you've taken down my men, but as it turns out, you did me a favor. Now you just have to finish the job."

Nick barely heard Alexander's last words. His mind raced, breath coming out of his mouth in short gasps. Alexander looked at him with interest.

"You thought of something," he said.

Nick shook his head quickly to clear it. It didn't work. "No, not really," he said automatically. He had to get out of there. He felt like he was going to throw up all over Bocharova's fancy desk. "No," he said again. "But I may know where to look."

"Tell me, Nick," Alexander said in earnest. "I have the resources to help you."

"No," Nick said. He softened his tone. "I need to do this. Alone."

Bocharova leaned forward, all friendliness gone. "If you know something, Nick, I suggest you tell me now. It'll be easier on all of us. "

Nick stood up.

"And you'll get your daughter back in time," the Russian said. "I don't make war on babies. I want her to go home with you."

"I'll get my daughter back," Nick said. "And I'll solve your problem."

"No. Tell me what you know," Bocharova spat as he stood up as well. Nick now saw the mobster within the man, the part of him who propelled him to the top of the food chain. Nick knew Bocharova was not a man to be underestimated. But he had no plan to underestimate him.

"No," Nick said. He was about to tell Bocharova to trust him, but he know how that would go over. "Give me some time to check out an idea. I'll call you in two hours."

The Russian took out a business card and wrote on the back. "Here's my personal cell number. Use it. Don't give it to anybody else."

Nick took it and shoved it in his pocket. "Two hours. And don't follow me."

Bocharova nodded. "But if I don't hear from you in two hours, I'll find you. I don't make war on babies, but I have no trouble with men who cross me."

"You'll hear from me," Nick said. He left without another word

When the door closed behind Nick, Alexander took out his phone and dialed quickly. He paused, then said, "The American is leaving. Follow him. Stay well back so he doesn't see you. Tell me where he goes."

Nick pulled out his cell phone at the same time. Anya answered on the first ring. "Are you OK?" she asked.

"Yes," Nick replied tightly. He didn't want to say too much. "Where are you?"

"At the KFC down the street from you," she said.

"OK, good," Nick said. "Stay there. I need to lose a few goons on my tail."

"Bocharova's having you tailed?" she said. She sounded concerned. "Did you see them?"

"No," Nick said. "They'll be good. But they'll be there."

"Why?"

"Because it's something that bastard Bocharova would do. I'd do it if I were him. Give me about twenty minutes."

"OK," Anya said. She sounded doubtful. "Call me if you get in trouble. I can drive over and get you."

"Bad idea. They'll know your car then. Stay still and stay quiet," Nick said. "I'll be there as soon as I can."

He cut the call before she could protest any further, and headed west, towards the river. He knew how he'd lose them.

The two men followed at a discreet distance, one on each side of the road. They walked casually, not looking concerned, glancing in store windows, but the American never looked back. He walked purposefully towards the river.

He definitely was on to something.

Nick spied the market ahead of him. He had been there before, a lifetime ago when he was looking for souvenirs of her homeland for Nonna to have as she grew up. He had bought a blue and red Moscow Football Club scarf at a kiosk in the market several days before. It was in a bag in his hotel room now. He hoped he would see it again.

The street he was on began to slope downwards as he approached a busy intersection. Nick saw the first kiosks of the market ahead, in the sunlight. These were the newer sellers, the ones who had to hawk their wares in the hot sun of the Rostov summer. The more prosperous sellers were the ones under the road.

It was a large marketplace, almost entirely under the intersection. The tunnels branched out in multiple directions, with at least four exits, maybe more. Nick had found four the last time he was there. At the time it was damn annoying. Now it may be a lifesaver. He doubted there were four people following him.

He disappeared underground.

The two men behind him cursed. As Nick disappeared from view, one ran across the street to the other. "What do we do?" the junior one asked breathlessly.

The older one pointed over the cross street. "He's probably going straight towards Shkolnaya Ulitsa," he said. "If he was going to turn he would have done it by now. Stay on the left and I'll stay on the right."

"Should I follow him?"

The older man shook his head. "Too risky. You don't want to be seen. We'll catch him on the other side."

The younger man nodded and raced back across the street, dodging the light traffic.

The older man clicked the Call button on his cellphone. It wouldn't hurt to send a few men north and south, just in case.

He gave his orders, disconnected the call, cursed again, and ran up the ramp to the cross street.

Nick stopped at the kiosk where he had purchased the scarf. There was a large rack of scarves, gloves, shirts, bags, and anything else they could make for the Moscow football club. Nick walked around it, discreetly looking back at the entrance to the tunnel. A few women, a few kids. Nobody who looked related to Alexander.

The kiosk owner glanced at him silently as Nick fingered a hat. He gave her a smile, then headed toward the light, back where he had come from.

Anya was in her red Lada on the side of the small KFC parking lot. She saw Nick as he approached from the front. Her relief was plainly visible through the tinted windshield.

She unlocked the passenger side door and he slid in. She locked it behind him.

"How'd it go?" she asked.

Nick didn't answer. Instead, he reached into the glove box and pulled out Dmitri's cell phone. He opened the contacts and quickly scrolled down. He didn't have to go far before he found the name he hoped he wouldn't see.

Lips pursed, he showed the screen to Anya. She looked confused as she scanned the names. Then her eyes widened.

"Oh, my God," she whispered. She sat back in her seat, stunned. Then she abruptly smashed a closed fist against the steering wheel. She yelled something in Russian. Nick assumed it was an expletive.

She turned back to him quickly. "I had no idea," she said. The tears began to flow freely down her face.

Nick put his hand on her leg. "I know, Anya. I never thought you did."

"That fucking Andrei," she said bitterly. "He's a dead man."

"Not until he gives me back my daughter," Nick said.

216

Chapter 34

Bocharova wasn't surprised, and he wasn't angry. Setbacks happened all the time. He already had Plan B in motion. He always started working on Plan B as soon as Plan A was in action. He didn't become concerned until he had to work on Plan C, and fortunately that was rare since Plan B typically took care of the problems of Plan A.

"Where are you now?" he said into his phone. It was a land-line, which he favored over cell phones. His technical people kept telling him that his cell phone was secure, but there was always that nagging doubt. Plus, he preferred the solid stability of his Binatone. He always felt as if he was going to crush a cell phone, especially when confronted with Plan C.

"I'm on the bridge, watching the west exits," the voice said. "I sent Makar to watch north. That's all we can cover." The tone was unapologetic. Alexander had drilled into his men that you don't worry about setbacks, you just move on. Plan B.

"Good," Alexander replied. "Stay there another five minutes. If he doesn't show, come back here. With a head start, you'll never find him." He ended the call and motioned to Popravko.

"They lost Wallace. Tell Alexei to hurry with the parking lot video. I want to know how Wallace got here."

"We should kill him," Anya said again as she fought traffic on prospekt Siversa, heading towards the Don. They hadn't talked about where to go or what to do yet, but both knew they had to get away from Alexander's offices. So she drove.

Nick watched the cars around him without replying for a moment. Most seemed to be large trucks, their cargo hidden by dirty canvas, smoke spewing from their tailpipes. The dirt and the sound of engines racing through gears made for a lively but unhealthy atmosphere. The rancid smell of exhaust filled the car, even though they had the air conditioner on high.

"Once I'm holding Nonna again, you can do with him what you want," he said.

"We'd be doing him a favor, you know," Anya replied without taking her eyes from the road. "When papa finds out about this, he'll tear Andrei apart."

Nick didn't reply.

She glanced at him quickly, then back to the road. "My father has done some things that are...morally flexible, I know. In fact, a lot of them, for most of his life. But a person's word is very important to him."

"Papa doesn't like liars?"

"No, papa doesn't like liars. Especially people who lie to family." She glanced at him again. "Or friends. Or even colleagues."

She whipped into the left lane and passed a particularly noxious truck, then slid smoothly back into the middle lane.

"How did you realize it was Andrei?" Anya asked.

"It was something Bocharova said. He told me I did a good job taking down Dmitri's empire. He said normally he'd be pissed off, but I was doing him a favor. The thought popped in my head, who else would benefit from this? And boom, it came to me." He sighed. "I should have seen it a long time ago."

Anya shook her head. "That bastard," she mumbled again. They drove in silence for a few minutes until Anya looked at him again.

"Andrei's father is dead," she said.

"I didn't know that."

"He died when Andrei was young. He was never any good. Drank a lot, hit Andrei's mom." She shook her head. "I think if the old drunk hadn't froze to death one night, Andrei would have killed him eventually."

Nick nodded.

"So papa took him in, gave him a job."

"As an enforcer?"

She shook her head. "Not at first. Andrei was still pretty young so he worked in papa's warehouse for a while."

"Papa has a warehouse?"

Anya smiled. "Papa has lots of things. He has a big warehouse down by the river. Barges bring in the stuff and he turns around and transports it to...wherever."

"Papa has his fingers in a lot of pies."

"Yep. But anyway, papa wasn't sure if Nadezhda—that's his sister, Andrei's mom—wanted Andrei to learn the, uh, family business. But Andrei wanted in, and after a few years he became an enforcer. He did well, and it wasn't because he was papa's nephew. He had a good way about him. He was strong but was willing to work with people."

"You know, you're talking about him in the past tense."

She thought about it for a moment. "Yeah, I guess I am. I suppose we'll have to get used to that now."

"Would you really kill him?"

"Not without papa's blessing, which I don't think will be a problem. But we need to talk to Andrei first."

"I know. I need to get Nonna back. Nadia's coming back from Kiev today. She's going to want to meet with me."

"You know, Nick," Anya said slowly. "This is getting bigger than just Nonna. We'll do what we can to get her back, of course, but if Andrei was planning to screw Bocharova, things could get bad."

"If Andrei doesn't tell me where my daughter is, I'll guarantee things will get bad," Nick replied. He stared hard at Anya's ear but she didn't turn to meet his gaze.

She shut the car off. Nick could see the Andrei's candy store down the block. "Wonka's" glared brightly out at him.

"I'll never be able to watch that damn movie again," Nick muttered.

"What?"

"Nothing, never mind." He looked across at her. "Please don't shoot anybody."

She smiled grimly. "No guarantees."

"I'm serious, Anya," Nick said. "If you can't calm your ass down, we'll sit in this car all day."

She looked at him. Her eyes were bright, from anger or reflected tears he wasn't sure. Probably both. Her knuckles were white where she gripped the steering wheel. Nick knew it would take a big effort to talk her down enough to see Andrei.

"I notice you're not upset," she said, almost accusatory.

"Oh, I'm pissed as hell," Nick said. "But if I thought losing my temper and putting holes in Andrei would help, I'd be through

219

his door by now, Glock-first. But we need to reason with him, make him realize what a mess he's in and help him get out of it."

She frowned. "I think it's too late for that now."

"Let's try."

She looked away.

"Please?"

She looked back. "Fine," she said. "We'll talk to him first, try to help him. But if it doesn't work…" She left the threat unspoken.

"Deal. You ready?"

"No," she said. "But the more I sit in this car listening to you, the angrier I'm going to get. So let's just do it."

Nick felt relief with the victory. But as soon as it came, it left again when he realized what they were about to do: confront the man who had stolen his daughter.

He sighed heavily, felt for his Glocks, and got out of the car. He was afraid Andrei's candy store would soon hear its first gunshots.

The chime rang as they walked through the door of the candy store. It sounded merry and ominous at the same time.

Andrei sat at a table in front of them. Legs crossed, hands clasped in front of him. Two chairs were pulled up to the table, one on either side of him. Three drinks were on the table. Clear liquid. Vodka.

He didn't smile at them, he just watched carefully as they crossed over the threshold. They stopped, stared back. Nobody moved for a long time.

Finally Andrei stirred, managed a weak smile, and motioned to the chairs. "We have things to talk about," he said.

"Damn right we do," Anya shot back. She and Nick took their seats, Anya to the left of Andrei and Nick to the right. Nick pushed his chair back from the table so he could be face-to-face with Andrei. Anya saw that, got up, moved her chair so it was opposite her cousin, and sat down again. She crossed her legs like Andrei and glared at him.

Nick sighed. He knew it would be up to him to play peacemaker if he wanted to get Nonna back.

"We know you and Dmitri were working together," he said. It sounded strange to speak those words.

Andrei nodded. "I know. When I heard Dimitri was killed by an American and a 'crazy young woman,' as they said, I knew who it was. And I knew you'd figure it out quickly. You didn't disappoint me."

"Don't patronize us, Andrei," Anya said. Nick grew more nervous as he watched her body language. She was tense, right hand gripping her right knee. Left hand under the table. He tried to remember if she had a gun. She had given him his Glock back, so he didn't think she was carrying, but he couldn't be sure. He pulled one of the Glocks out under the table but kept his finger away from the trigger. Glocks had no external safety and the last thing he wanted to do was shoot Anya, even it was just in a spot that kept her from shooting Andrei, but Nonna came first. Not even close.

Andrei raised both hands. He said something in Russian, gesturing with his left hand. She replied, loudly. Soon they were going at it across the table, yelling in Russian, leaving Nick way behind.

"Hey!" Nick yelled, loud enough to get their attention. "I hate to interrupt a family discussion, but I have a problem." He turned to Andrei. "Where's Nonna? Give her to me, and our business is done. And speak in English, dammit!"

"Our business isn't done, Nick," Andrei replied, effortlessly switching to English. "You need to do one thing for me, one small thing, and then you get your precious little girl."

Nick gripped the Glock hard under the table. "I've told you before, Andrei, I don't do jobs for you. Find somebody else."

Andrei shook his head. "Nyet. You have a reason to get close to Alexander. You've already been close to him. You can easily kill him."

Nick was stunned. "Kill Bocharovo?"

Anya snorted loudly from across the table. "Are you crazy? You kill Alexander and you'll start a war."

"Not to mention the fact that I'll be gunned down as soon as I pull the trigger," Nick said.

Andrei pointed a finger at him. "I've seen you work, Nick. I know you can do it." He swiveled on his cousin. "As for your war, Anya, isn't it time to shake things up around here? The oligarchs have too much power! They're lazy and they're allowing foreigners in to get a piece of our action. We need new blood in Rostov."

"You can't do it alone, cousin," Anya said, softer now, trying to calm Andrei. "You aren't in that position. Come with me back to the restaurant. We'll talk with papa, see what we can accomplish together."

"No!" Andrei shouted. He slapped the table hard, causing the three glasses to tremble. Nick jumped and almost shot Andrei in the leg. He kept the gun out, pointed away from the cousins.

"No," Andrei said again. "They will talk, drink vodka together, and in the end nothing will be done. Your father is too scared of Alexander to do anything."

"Then perhaps you should be scared of Alexander as well," Nick interjected. This bickering was getting him no closer to Nonna. He was getting frustrated. "The man knows you screwed him."

"Which is why you're going to kill him," Andrei said.

Nick shook his head. "Not gonna happen," he said. "I'm done killing."

The front door of the candy store opened, the bell rang, and two large men stepped through. Nick saw the immaculate suits, the close-shaved hair, the scar on the side of the mouth of the one in back. His heart dropped when he realized who it was.

Andrei grinned at his comrades, then turned to Nick. "No, your killing is just beginning, Nick."

He wouldn't have smiled if he realized how right he was.

Chapter 35

Popravko wasn't gone long. He knocked lightly on the open door and walked in when Alexander glanced up. He couldn't hide a smug look. Alexander knew he had good news.

"A red Kalina with a woman inside. We don't have a detailed picture of her because she stayed in the car, but we did get the license number." He handed a slip of paper to his boss. "We're tracing it now."

"Good," Alexander said. "Get people out looking for it, too. With luck, they headed directly to this damned 'associate.'"

Popravko nodded. "The word's already gone out. I'll let you know when we find them. Shouldn't be long."

Alexander nodded and smiled. He loved when Plan B worked.

Anya swiveled in her chair and groaned when she saw Ilia and Mikhail in the doorway. "You dumb Cossacks," she said, and stood up. She walked over to Ilia's bulk and jabbed a finger in his chest. It was at eye height for her, but she didn't back down. "If you've been working with Andrei on this stupid plan, you're in the shit just as bad as he is."

Ilia smiled. He appeared more amused than anything else. "Little girl," he said, his voice a low rumble, "I've been in the shit for a long time now. It's where I'm happy. Now sit down."

His reaction, or lack of it, deflated Anya, and she plopped heavily back into her seat with a sigh.

"And I see we're speaking English in honor of our new friend," Mikhail said. He walked over to Nick, who stood up to meet him. Unlike Anya, Nick matched Mikhail's height and width. The two men stared at each other for a long moment before Mikhail stuck out his right hand.

Nick ignored it.

Not embarrassed, he brought it back and said, "I've been watching you for several days. You do good work. We could use a man like you on the team."

"I was just saying the same thing," Andrei commented with a chuckle.

"And like I told your handler," Nick said, "It's not gonna happen." He glared at the bodyguard.

"I'm afraid it already has," Andrei said from the table. "You've helped us more than you think."

Nick grunted. He started to get a bad feeling in his stomach again.

"We didn't know about you until that run-in at the Dolphin Club," Andrei said. "Mikhail saw you. Saw how you handled Sergei and Vlad after Maxsim beat up that hooker."

"Zatknis," Anya hissed.

"I will not shut up, little sparrow," Andrei said. He picked up one of the untouched glasses on the table and drained it. He was feeling confident, Nick realized. The thought made him feel some hope. Confidence is dangerous with so many unknowns.

Andrei went on. "Mikhail got your name and called me. We did a little research on you and realized that all you needed was a little push. After that, well, you could take care of the rest."

Nick stared at Andrei as he processed the words. Then he turned to Anya with a look of fury.

"You bitch!" he yelled. "Our meeting was no accident, was it?"

Andrei and Ilia burst out laughing, while Anya just looked miserable. Mikhail took it all in from the sidelines, watching.

"Of course it wasn't, Nick," Andrei said, wiping tears from his eyes. "My God, you're so naïve."

Nick pulled his gun and pointed it at Andrei's head. The man didn't move, but immediately the muzzle of Ilia's gun was inches from Nick's temple.

"Now just calm down, everybody," Andrei said. "What's done is done. We have to work together to get out of this."

"Fuck you," Nick said through clenched teeth. But he lowered his gun.

"Nick…" Anya said, and he looked at her. "I'm sorry. Andrei said to get to know you, then introduce you to him. I had no idea what he was up to." There were tears in her eyes.

Nick stared at her, then turned back to Andrei. "I'm in this mess because you needed help to take down your enemies."

"Wrong," Andrei replied. "You're in this mess because your friend slept with the wrong woman, and you were foolish enough to help him. Now sit down! You're out of options."

Nick sat.

"Maxsim helped us, you know," Ilia said. "He made a big mistake in killing the hooker. He was always a, how would you say it, a hothead? She helped you and embarrassed him. He never could deal with that, so he killed her."

"Thank God for that," Andrei cut in. "We thought we had you after the attack on the street, but you didn't follow it up."

Nick glared at him.

"We were impressed with how you dealt with the two enforcers," Andrei said. He was completely in control now. Anya sat in her chair, not moving, and Nick stared at him impassively. Nick only vaguely heard the words. He was busy judging angles, openings. It didn't take much to conclude that Andrei was right, he didn't have many options. Mikhail was off to the side, but Andrei and Ilia had him flanked, and both were armed. If he rushed one, the other would take him out before he got halfway, and the way they were situated meant that one wouldn't have to worry about hitting the other. To make it worse, if he went after Ilia and Andrei retaliated, Anya would be in the middle. He was livid at her betrayal, but he didn't want to see her shot after what she had done to help him. Nick doubted Andrei would shoot at his own cousin, if for no other reason than not to risk the wrath of his uncle, but he couldn't be sure of that. So he waited.

Andrei continued. "After you took out Dmitri's men, we knew you were capable of doing more damage. We just had to…lead you."

"Why couldn't you do it?" Nick asked. Keep them talking.

"Why should we? An unstable American comes to town and shoots up Bocharova's network? Everybody'd believe it, since we hear so much about unstable Americans."

"And you don't have to get your feet dirty," Anya said. She sounded as angry as Nick felt.

"Exactly," Andrei said. "He does the work, we get the benefits."

"Did you take Nonna?" Nick asked.

"No," Andrei said. "That was Dmitri's idea. Well, with a little prodding by us. After you attacked him at his house and took his things, he was looking for a way to get back at you. We…suggested he go after the thing most dear to you."

"It was quite easy, actually," Ilia said, nodding. "Dmitri has a relationship with the head of the baby home, so he was able to intervene with the adoption."

"He was a fool," Andrei said. "Dmitri approached me for an alliance, saying he wanted to take down Alexander. I knew right away he was too glupyy, too stupid, to make it work. But with my brains, we could get it done. And as long as he was the visible partner, he would take the fall if things went wrong."

"How did that go for you, Andrei?" Nick shot back. "Dmitri is dead and Alexander knows he was working with somebody. He's coming after you, asshole."

Andrei shook his head. "If he was, he'd be here already. I have men around the building, ready to call in if they see anything. So far no calls. So I suspect you protected me, Nick. And why would that be?"

Nick said nothing.

"Is it because I have your daughter? And if I die, we both lose?"

Nick said nothing.

"But I only lose my life. You lose so much more."

Nick pursed his lips, sat still.

"So, like it or not, we're on the same side," Andrei said.

"That's exactly how Bocharova put it, "Nick said. "And he was wrong, too. I'm not on your side. I'm not on his side. I'm on Nonna's side, on my family's side. That's it. And you can both kill each other as far as I'm concerned."

"But we know that won't happen, American," Ilia said. "We know you'll protect Andrei until you're dead."

Nick gazed at Andrei. "Or until I beat the information out of him."

Ilia grunted. "Maybe we should just kill him now, Andrei. We can take out Alexander and blame it on him."

Nick glared at Ilia. The roaring in his ears was there, just beneath the surface. "You know, Ilia, I think you're going to be the next one I send to the hospital. You're too dumb to be allowed to roam free. I'll be doing everybody a favor by shooting you."

Ilia turned red. Nick glanced at Mikhail, who gave Nick a look that told him to shut up.

They stayed that way for a long moment, ready to pounce on each other.

And then Alexander arrived.

Andrei rose as a noise came from outside the candy store. He drew his gun. Ilia whirled and pulled a gun from his suit coat. Nick raised his Glock above the table. Mikhail pulled his own weapon and released the safety.

The door burst open and two men ran in. They were out of breath, wild-eyed. Both had guns in their hand.

Nick was relieved to see Andrei lower his gun. Andrei said something in Russian and one of the men replied, words rushed, not pausing for the breath he needed. Andrei and Ilia looked at each other and Anya jumped up.

Nick knew it had to be bad.

Andrei quietly gave what Nick assumed to be orders to the new men. They nodded and disappeared through the back door of the store, into the warehouse area.

Anya spoke to Andrei frantically. He looked undecided, then nodded. He obviously didn't like what he was agreeing to. He turned to Nick, livid.

"Alexander's men are at the corner. At least four. They know where we are. You led them right to us!"

"No way," Nick replied. "I shook them."

"Doesn't matter," Anya replied. "We need to go right now."

Andrei raised his gun and pointed it at Nick's forehead. "Not him. Nick, you stay here and give us at least five minutes."

"Andrei!" Anya protested.

"Nonna will thank me later," Andrei said.

"Where will you be?" Nick asked.

Andrei shook his head. "If you don't know, you can't tell Alexander."

"We'll find you," Ilia said with an evil grin.

227

Anya stepped up to Nick and put a hand on his arm. "I'm sorry, but Andrei's right," she said. "You can't tell what you don't know."

"Unless they don't believe me," Nick replied.

Ilia shrugged. "Convince them," he said.

"We'll find you," Anya whispered, looking in his eyes. He could see she didn't believe it herself.

"No," he whispered back, glaring at her. "I'll find you."

She looked uncertain for a moment, hand still on his arm, then she turned and followed the two men out the back, Mikhail close on her heels.

Nick was back sitting at the table when the two men burst through the door. He had moved around just inside the door a few times, hoping they'd think there were multiple men in the candy shop, hoping they'd delay their attack, and hoping like hell they didn't come in with guns blazing.

They didn't, whether because they wanted to be discreet or because they had eyes on Nick, he didn't know. He didn't really care, either, as long as he didn't have any extra holes in his body ten seconds after they forced their way in.

Both men screamed at Nick and motioned to the floor with their guns. He didn't move, just stared back at them impassively, hands in his lap, palms up, as they swept the room.

His failure to comply threw the men for a moment, until one motioned Nick to stand up. He did, holding his arms high. They frisked him quickly, professionally, and found nothing. His Glocks were hidden in two large bowls of hard candy. He still had plans for them.

One spoke into a walkie talkie and almost immediately four more men rushed into the store. Behind them were Bocharova and Popravko.

Alexander immediately walked up to Nick. He clucked his tongue. "I was waiting for my phone call."

"It's not two hours yet."

Bocharova glanced around the store. "And yet you obviously found what you were looking for. Where are they?"

Nick glanced at his watch. The five minutes were up. Well, close enough, if he rounded up. "To tell you the truth," he said, "they wouldn't say. They mumbled something about how I couldn't tell you what I didn't know."

Alexander looked closely at Nick, who met his gaze full-on. After a moment he nodded. "At least you can tell me how they got out of here."

Nick pointed over his shoulder with his thumb, towards the back of the room. "Five minutes ago. They saw your men. You should've been more subtle."

Alexander made a growling sound. "No need. We'll find them. We know about Andrei now. He's not going anywhere." He motioned for the remaining men in the candy store to search the rear.

"Did you follow me?" Nick asked.

Alexander hesitated, then shrugged. "Doesn't matter now. No, we found your girlfriend's car in the surveillance video. Somebody spotted it across the street."

Nick nodded. "Fast work, nice."

"We have more good news," Alexander said.

"Yeah?"

Alexander motioned to Popravo. "Tell him, Vitali."

Popravko stepped up to the men, looked at Nick, and said, "We found your daughter."

Chapter 36

Nick felt light-headed. "You found Nonna? Excellent! Where is she?"

"She's with Andrei's girlfriend, in their apartment," Popravko said. "We have two men watching it now."

Nick shook Alexander's hand. "Thank you, Alexander. How'd you find her so quickly?"

The Russian shrugged in a self-deprecating way that was very unlike him. "Andrei is known to us. Not well, but we know where he lives. We sent a man there. Andrei wasn't home, but he saw the woman with a baby through the window."

"I want to go there now."

Alexander smiled. "Of course, I understand. Vitali will take you there."

Nick nodded, and the two men shook hands again. "Good luck with Andrei. There's a young woman with him, his cousin Anya. She had no idea of his plan. I hope you can keep her out of this."

"She's not a complete innocent," Alexander said. Seeing Nick's face, he added, "However, I also don't make war on women unless I have to. If she was unaware of what her cousin was up to, I'm sure we can find a satisfactory solution for her."

Nick wasn't sure he liked the sound of that, but Popravko was already pulling at his sleeve. "We need to go now. Alexander has things to do."

As they walked to the door, they passed the two large glass bowls holding his Glocks. Realizing that pulling two guns out of candy bowls would raise more questions than he wanted to answer, Nick passed them with just a quick glance. He was very happy to not have to use them after all.

They emerged into the bright sunlight and turned right. Nick squinted and held his hand over his eyes for a moment, until he was used to the glare. He didn't realize how dim the candy store was, even with the glass storefront.

They passed two men standing guard a few feet from the entrance. They nodded at Popravko and stared at Nick, expressionless. He ignored them. Now that he had a bead on his daughter, he had no intention of dealing with them any longer than he had to.

"It didn't take long to find me," Nick said.

Popravko smiled slightly. He took the comment as a compliment and seemed embarrassed by it. "It wasn't difficult. After we lost you in the market—"

"Ahhh, so you were following me," Nick broke in. He laughed, a short bark. "I figured you would."

The Russian shrugged. "It didn't matter. We checked the tapes and saw you get out of the Kalina. Fortunately one of our men was in this area and noticed the car. It was good luck that we found it so quickly, but it would have happened soon enough anyway."

They crossed the street. Nick frowned.

"Did Andrei say anything to you in the store?" Popravko asked. "Anything that could help us find him?"

"No, he didn't," Nick replied slowly. "I don't think they had any plans. When your men swooped in, they just bolted. They told me to hold you for a few minutes, until they got away, or else my daughter would be in danger."

"Ahhh, yes," Popravko said. "Well, at least you won't have to worry about them and your daughter any longer."

"You said she's with Andrei's girlfriend?"

"Yes, they're in their apartment. Hold on, I'm going to call our man there."

He pulled out his cell phone and dialed a number. Spoke a few words quietly. Listened. Nodded. Talked again. Hung up. Nick listened intently but was unable to make out any specific words. He felt in his pocket for the Glock, then remembered the candy bowls. He cursed his stupidity.

"Good news," Popravko said as he put the phone back in his breast pocket. "They're still there, and have no idea that we're on to them. Once you get there, we'll rush in and surprise her. You'll have your daughter in just a few minutes."

Nick forced a smile. "That's wonderful news, Vitali. I can't thank you enough."

"Of course," Popravko said. "You helped us, we'll help you. As Alexander said, we're all on the same side here."

Nick nodded absently. "So what happens to Andrei?"

231

"He'll be dead within the hour," Popravko said. "As I'm sure you can understand, we can't let him live now, not after he plotted against us. He needs to…" He paused.

"Be made an example of," Nick finished.

The Russian looked at Nick sharply, but Nick simply stared straight ahead as they walked.

"Yes, he must be made an example of. Our authority must not be challenged."

"And those with him?" Nick asked, meaning Anya.

"I'll be honest, Nick. Everybody with Andrei will likely have the same fate."

Nick nodded. Unwittingly, Popravko just gave away the game. "I understand. Others know, or will soon know, that Dmitri and Andrei plotted to overthrow Alexander. They must be punished. Publicly punished."

"Exactly!" Poprakvo said with enthusiasm. "I'm glad you understand. It's the way it has to be."

"Oh, I get it, all right," Nick said. They crossed another street. Cars crossed in front and behind them, diesel cascading around them. There wasn't a light at the intersection, and the two men stopped in the middle, between lanes of traffic, and waited for a break in the flow. It came and they sprinted across the street.

Once they had slowed down and moved away from the road, Nick said, "From what I've heard, Andrei works with his uncle. Will his uncle be made an example of as well?"

"Of course," the Russian said.

The answer sent a shiver through Nick. "Even if he had no idea about Andrei's actions?"

"Oh, I'm sure he knew something," Popravko said. "And even if he didn't, this is a perfect time to take him down."

"Take him down," Nick repeated slowly.

"Of course," Popravko said again. "Nick, you're not Russian. After Gorbachev, things are always changing. It is difficult to make a good living here without being…aggressive."

"You seem to be doing a good job."

"And we are, because we're aggressive. When we see a chance to move in, we take it."

"Ahhh, I get it!" Nick said, feigning enthusiasm to match Popravko's. "You're going to use this little incident to kill everybody associated with Andrei, and take over his business. Brilliant!"

The sarcasm flew over Popravko's head. He made a fist with his left hand and held it up in a sort of a victory salute. "Exactly! Whether he is guilty or not is irrelevant. Nobody will question us because everybody will agree it should be done."

"I must say, Vitali, we could learn a lot from you."

Popravko smiled. "It's a pity you're going to be with us for such a short time." He laughed as though at an inside joke. Nick laughed with him.

"Here we are," Popravko said. He pointed to a brownstone on their right. A short flight of concrete stairs led into the building, which looked to house six or eight apartments. "This is where your daughter is." They walked up the steps and into the dim lobby.

Popravko grabbed Nick's arm. "Please wait here," he said. "I'm going to go up and check the situation. I'll be back in a moment."

"OK, Vitali," Nick said agreeably. When the Russian disappeared up the stairs, Nick searched the lobby. There wasn't much to search. A bank of mail slots perched on one wall. Otherwise, the space was empty except for the stairs.

Nick turned around. They had entered through a simple doorway. One heavy wooden door, no screen. Two small windows on either side. Nick went to one window and felt along the sash. Dirt and dead bugs clung to his fingers. He wiped them off quickly and felt up along the side. The window was a crank out and Nick found the metal rod that supported the window. He grabbed it and pulled. Nothing. He cranked the window in a few turns and tried again. This time, with reduced tension, the rod wiggled in his hand. He cranked the window in more and tried the rod again. This time he was able to bend it back and forth until it slipped out of its track.

He quickly pocketed the metal rod and stepped back to his original position.

He heard the clatter of shoes on the stairs and soon Popravko appeared on the landing above Nick. He gestured down at him. "Everything is ready, come with me," he whispered.

Nick climbed the stairs behind Popravko. They went up two flights, to the top floor. At the top of the stairs was a man with an assault rifle. Nick's heart sped up when he realized it was a Nikonov

233

AN-94. Designed to replace the AK-47, the Nikonov had a two-round burst mode. A person could do some serious damage with a two-round burst mode.

The man stared silently at Nick as they mounted the landing. He held the AN-94 in both hands, barrel pointing down and towards a door, buttstock open.

"She's in there?" Nick asked.

The guard didn't move, but Popravko said, "Yes, they're inside."

"I thought you said there were two men here?"

"Excuse me?"

Nick spoke slower. "I thought you said there were two men here. I only see one."

"Ahhh," Popravko said. "Yes, one is outside, keeping an eye on the window so they cannot escape."

"I would think that a woman with a baby wouldn't be able to escape very easily," Nick replied.

Popravko shrugged. "We take no chances."

Nor do I, Nick thought.

Popravko said something to the guard in Russian, and the man nodded. He released the safety on the AN-94.

Nick moved his right hand behind him. His fingers touched the metal rod he had stashed in his back pocket, and he slowly pulled it free. He rolled it between his fingers so he had it in a reverse grip, pointing down and away.

"Are you ready?" Popravko asked him. The Russian's breathing had become faster. The man was nervous, ready for the action to start. Nick forced his breath to slow. He concentrated on what would happen next, visualizing it, concentrating on it. His pulse rate slowed.

"Anatoli will go in first," Popravko said. "We'll give him a moment to find the woman, then come in after him."

Nick nodded.

Popravko waited a long second, then gave a signal to the guard. The man squared himself to the door, hesitated, then kicked out with his right leg. His heel connected with the door just below the lock, and the door splintered inwards.

At the same time, Nick pivoted to his left, brought his right arm up, and buried the rod in the side of the guard's neck as deep as he could.

Immediately the man screamed, a liquid gurgle, and released his grip on the assault rifle. He clutched at his throat, fingers frantically searching for the source of the agony. It was all involuntary. The man's brain had no time to process the threat coming from the side, rather than the front.

Popravko had no time to process the threat, either. Nick continued his pivot until he faced the man head-on. He reached up with his right arm, snaked it around the man's head, twisted, and broke his neck. Popravko's dead body was falling as Nick turned back to the guard.

The guard managed to pull the rod from his neck but was slowly sinking to the ground as blood poured through his fingers. Nick grabbed at the straps of the AN-94. The man was in no shape to resist, but the straps were. They hung up around his neck. Nick frantically pulled but couldn't free the gun.

A voice came from within the room. A man's voice.

Nick cursed, maneuvered around behind the guard, lifted him up under his arms, and propelled him into the room. As the man staggered to his feet, Nick moved his hands to the gun.

"Help me!" He yelled in English. "This man's been shot!"

The second guard was several feet inside the door, on the right side of the room. He had his gun aimed towards the door, but no idea that the person crashing through the door would want to shoot him. The person crashing through the door was supposed to get the hell out of the way so the guard in the room could shoot the unsuspecting American in his pain-in-the-ass head.

Nick saw the guard with the upraised AN-94 at the same instant the man spied Nick. There was a flicker of confusion on his face as he saw his comrade, covered in blood, gasping as his life poured out his neck, thrown into the room.

The second guard hesitated for a fraction of a second. There was no hesitation on Nick's part. His index finger found the trigger of the AN-94 and he pulled. The fire selector was set to a two-round burst. It worked to perfection. The first two rounds hit the second guard in the chest, while the second pair took off the top of his head. He flew back into a wall, turning it crimson.

Nick dropped the guard with a grunt of disgust and checked his shirt. A large splotch of blood had splattered onto the right side, over his chest. It looked purple on his blue shirt. Nick shrugged. He didn't have anything to change into, so it was what it was.

He poked his head out the door and looked around. To his surprise, nobody came out to investigate the shots. He quickly grabbed Popravko and pulled him into the apartment. He shut the door behind him and took a deep breath. He closed his eyes, paused, and opened them again.

Nick looked at the three bodies around him. All three were very dead. Popravko's head was at an unnatural, grotesque angle. He had a look of surprise on his face. The first guard also had a surprised look on the part of his face not covered in blood. The other guard had no face left, but Nick assumed there would have been surprise there. He rummaged through the second guard's suit coat, being careful to sidestep the blood on the chest. But outside of the gun, the man had nothing that would help Nick.

Slower now, all sense of urgency gone, Nick pulled the strap over the first guard's head and lifted the AN-94 free. He did the same with the other guard. Both guns had four-stack box magazines, sixty rounds per gun. After a few minutes of searching, Nick found additional magazines in a backpack tossed in a corner. It looked like they were ready for a war.

He glanced around the room. It was empty except for a few chairs. Obviously nobody lived here.

He knew that would be the case, since Andrei had told him he and Svetlana lived above the candy store.

This place was probably owned, but not used, by Alexander. A perfect place to kill an American without too many inquiring eyes. In fact, the entire building might be empty, which would explain the lack of curiosity by other tenants.

Which would suit him just fine, as he preferred the three bodies stay hidden for a few days. Eventually the smell would attract attention, but by then he'd hopefully be on his way home over the Atlantic.

The guard's blood soaked through the shirt and felt warm and wet on Nick's skin. He pulled the shirt over his head, taking care not to get the blood in his hair, and took it into the bathroom. The shirt reeked of blood, but the smell in the room masked it. A combination of copper and gunpowder that brought back unwanted memories. Nick was glad to close the bathroom door behind him.

The bathroom was bare except for a single green towel on a rod by the toilet. He opened his shirt to expose the stain, and rubbed it under warm water in the sink. The water swirled red in the drain, then pink. It took a few minutes to get to a light pink. Eventually Nick was satisfied and turned off the water. He dried the shirt by wrapping it in the towel and squeezing hard several times.

He pressed the shirt to his nose and inhaled. A faint smell of copper, but manageable. He had the feeling he was not done with the copper smell yet.

He left the bathroom and wandered around the room slowly. Eventually he found what he had been hoping for: a green duffel bag, empty, lying on a chair. Nick assumed it had been used to bring in supplies. He quickly stashed both weapons and the extra ammunition in the duffel. He lifted it carefully and slung it over his back, adjusting it as the weapons and ammo settled into their new position. He shook the bag slightly to make sure they were stable.

He took one last look at the men who were ready to kill him. Blood soaked into the old, brown carpet around the two guards. It was going to be a bitch to get out, he thought with grim satisfaction. He hoped that bastard Alexander had to pay overtime to the carpet cleaners.

With a shake of his head, Nick closed the door behind him and walked down the stairs.

Anya's phone answered on the first ring.

Then silence. Nick heard breathing.

"Anya?" he asked quietly. He looked around the street. Nobody paid any attention to the man walking briskly, carting a duffel bag over his shoulder.

"Oh, thank God!" Anya replied. "I was afraid you were dead."

"Not yet," Nick replied. "But I just killed three of Alexander's men so I guess I'm in it now. Where are you?"

There was more silence. "Are you alone?" she finally asked.

"Yes."

"Remember that place we talked about, where Andrei started to work?"

"Yes." Papa's warehouse.

"We're visiting."

"I thought Andrei said he'd never…um, talk to anybody there."

"That was before our plans were changed for us," she replied. Her voice was low, hurried. "I can't talk now. We're going to meet with him."

Her father, Nick thought. Andrei's hold-out didn't last long.

"I'm coming there," he said.

"I'm not sure that's wise," she replied. "It could get messy. We'll have visitors soon."

"That's why I'm coming. You need help."

"Nonna's not here."

"I know. But Andrei is. I'm going to check one more spot. If she's not there, I'm coming to you."

"Where?"

"Svetlana, Andrei's girlfriend."

After a beat, Anya said, "I'm sorry, Nick. Nonna's not with Svetlana."

Nick cursed. "How do you know?"

"Because Svetlana was here with us. She picked us up. Papa just made her leave. But she didn't have Nonna with her."

Nick groaned. He suddenly felt like hitting somebody. He thought of the guns in his bag, and felt sorry for whoever got between him and Nonna.

"Damn. Then I'm coming to you."

There was a long pause. "OK…thank you," Anya said, and hung up. It was a danger sign that she didn't try to talk him out of it more. She may have been blowing him off, but more likely they were outgunned enough to accept help from a rogue American.

And he hadn't even told her about the two assault guns.

Chapter 37

The voice answered on the second ring. It was an American voice, but not the one Nick was expecting.

"Hey, Michelle," Nick said. "Sorry, I thought I was calling Tom's phone."

"Nick! You are, but he's in the shower," she replied. "I'm glad you called, we've been worried to death about you. What's going on? How are things with Nonna?"

"Not so good, actually," he said. He paused, then it all came out in a rush. He didn't leave anything out. There was no reason to. Anya's deception. Andrei's plot. Alexander's plan to kill him, followed by the three deaths in the apartment. He left out the details but she could put the pieces together.

To her credit, Michelle didn't gasp or cry. He knew she wouldn't. She was a cop, and a tough woman. Therefore he wasn't surprised when her first words were, "What can we do to help?"

"Nothing," he said. "I don't want you involved."

"Tough," she said. "We're friends, even if you make it hard to back you up."

"No, Michelle, I'm serious," Nick said. "It'd kill me if I took Alexei's mom or dad away from him. But there is something you can do for me. Something that's less...lethal."

Michelle sounded doubtful. "Yeahhh...what?"

"If something happens to me, tell Kelli everything. Tell her that I tried and that it, well, that it didn't work out. Tell her that I love her and Danny more than anything and that I went down fighting. She'll understand."

Now Michelle did start to cry. "No, dammit!" she said. "You can tell her that yourself, right now."

"No, I can't," Nick said. "I don't have a world phone, or whatever the hell they call them, so I can't call her now. And I don't have time to get to the internet café."

"So you're just going to run off and get yourself killed without saying anything to her?"

"I have no intention of getting myself killed, Michelle," Nick said. "Kelli's last words to me were to do what I have to do to get

Nonna. I'm going to do that. I just need you to cover my back in case…things don't go as planned."

Michelle sighed heavily. "OK, Nick, I have your back. But I wish there was something we could do. Can't you call the Rostov police?"

"That's exactly what I plan to do next," Nick said.

"Archipenko."

"Zdrastvoytye, detective, it's Nick."

There was a long pause. "What do you want?" Protr asked. His voice was gruff.

"I know you're angry with me," Nick said, "and you have a good reason to be. But Gennady and his family are in trouble." Nick had decided quickly not to make it about Nonna. He figured Pyotr had more allegiance to fellow Russians than to a current and future American.

"I've heard," Pyotr said. "Rumor is that Alexander is planning to move on Gorev's operation."

"Gorev?"

"Your girlfriend's father." Pyotr sounded impatient.

"She's not my girlfriend," Nick said. "We said that so you wouldn't ask why I left the hotel."

"I know, Nick. Anya told me. At least you're no longer lying to me."

Nick grunted. "I'm done lying to you. And it's not a rumor about Alexander. The two plan to talk at Gennady's warehouse."

"So how does this impact me? Unless you still think I work for Dmitri."

"No, of course not," Nick said. "But there could be a battle there. I was hoping you'd want to prevent it."

"I assume your daughter is there. I can see no other reason why you'd care."

Nick sighed. "No, she's not there. But she's missing and the people who know where she is are going to be in the middle of a shit storm in a few minutes."

"Nick," Archipenko said, "I'm not your personal enforcer. You can't just call and ask me to help you out. Put Anya on the line."

"I can't."

"And why is that?"

"Because she's with her father."

Nick heard Archipenko swear under his breath, a series of Russian words that didn't sound optimistic at all.

"Who's with Gorev?"

Nick rattled off the names. There was silence on the other end. Nick could practically hear the gears going in Pyotr's head.

"You know, detective, if you were to help them, they would certainly show their appreciation," Nick said.

Now it was the detective's turn to grunt. "If they live through it, yes," he said. "But we've heard that Bocharova is calling in his men. They'll overwhelm your friends."

"Don't count them out just yet," Nick said. His words were more optimistic than he felt. "And if they come out on top, you could come out on top as well."

There was a long moment of silence. When Archipenko finally spoke, his voice was soft. "The police aren't coming, Nick. We'll let them fight it out."

Nick shook his head and gripped the cell phone hard. "And then you'll work with whoever wins," he said bitterly.

"Yes," Archipenko said. "It's too late to save your friends, Nick. It's time you accepted that."

He hung up the phone before Nick could reply.

Chapter 38

Nick squeezed through the rusted door onto the roof. He was in a long, narrow building across the Beregovaya Ulitsa from Gennady's warehouses. The street, fairly busy in the south part of Rostov, narrowed as it went north, and in this area it was no more than a lightly-traveled two-lane road with cracked asphalt and no stop lights.

To Nick's right were two empty concrete frames, formerly known as houses. Four walls, no roofs, pitted concrete, a few holes where windows once were. They were only one story high and Nick could see down into their centers from the four story building he was in. Not that there was anything to see. Green and brown scrub covered the interiors where the concrete floor had broken away. The sun, still high in the sky but starting to sink, created a line across both interiors, separating light from shadow.

The roof was flat and topped off with asphalt. The asphalt was hot in the sun and grainy bits stuck to Nick's shoes. He made his way to the eastern side of the building, towards the warehouse and the Don, holding the duffel bag in his left hand. Pigeon carcasses littered the roof, and several vodka bottles, most broken, were heaped on one side. Nick stepped closer and saw dozens of cigarette butts littered among the bottles. Apparently he was not the first to spend extended time on the roof.

He had no intention of drinking or smoking. He got down on his belly as he neared the ledge overlooking the road and, beyond that, Gennady's complex. He crawled slowly up to the ledge, dragging his bag alongside, and peered over the side.

Across the road, perhaps fifty yards away, were four low buildings arranged in a square. Beyond that he could make out train tracks, then a gray warehouse with a rounded roof. The warehouse was huge but Nick couldn't make out details from his distance. He wished the AN-94 had a sniper scope.

Beyond Gennady's warehouse flowed the brown water of the Don. Nick could see a few barges on the river, but the warehouse roof obscured the near bank. Nick couldn't tell whether there were any boats docked in front of Gennady's complex.

He saw a high fence between the road in front of him and the four buildings. It opened at a driveway near Nick's building. A solitary figure sat in a chair on the side of the driveway, front legs of the chair up, leaning back into the fence. He didn't move and Nick wasn't sure the guy was even awake. Nick didn't see a gun but assumed the man was armed.

He watched as the cab that had dropped him off several blocks away drove north on Beregovaya, looking for a fare. The cab slowed as it reached a curve in the road. It stopped, turned around, and headed south, out of sight. The man in front of Gennady's complex still didn't move.

It looked quiet. Nick was pretty sure Alexander's men were not there yet. He wasn't sure what to do, and knew from experience that if you don't know what to do, the best thing to do is sit on your hands.

So he settled in behind the wall, keeping as little exposed as possible, and watched.

Anya stared at her father with wide eyes. "You invited Alexander *here*?" she asked, which was about as close to contradicting Gennady as she was willing to get.

Gennady Gorev looked across the table at his daughter. He stood, while she sat next to Andrei. He wore a blue suit, which looked crisp in comparison to his haggard features. Anya realized he had probably recently put it on, in anticipation of his meeting with Alexander. Gennady's gray hair shot off in several directions, and his eyes blazed with anger. To Anya, he looked exhausted and wired at the same time.

Anya and Andrei's phones were on the table in front of them, which Gennady had ordered as soon as they walked in.

He was angry at his nephew, but addressed Anya.

"You've put me in a bad position with Alexander," he said. "We're competitors but we must respect each other." He looked at Andrei, who stared sullenly back at him. "We don't do this to our colleagues. And now that you have, I must make it right."

"But you know he won't make any deals," Anya said.

Andrei nodded. "He'll use this as an excuse to take advantage of you."

Gennady shook his head. "No, he won't. He respects me. Yes, there will be…reparations. But nothing too drastic. However, Andrei, you'll lose your position in my organization."

"Bah," Andrei snorted. "*You'll* lose your position in your organization if you try to bargain with Alexander. You don't know him like I do. When he senses weakness he'll move in for the kill."

"I don't plan to approach him with weakness!" Gennady said, eyes flashing. He waved his right arm as he talked. "We're not as strong as he, but we're not to be trifled with, either. If he tries to take more than we've agreed to, he'll find he's bitten off more than he can chew."

"I mean this with respect, Gennady," Andrei said, even though his expression betrayed his words. "You've risen high in Rostov because you've been ruthless. Alexander is like you once were, you must believe me."

"I've risen to my position because I've been honest with my friends and with my enemies," Gennady replied. "I don't expect you to understand this, although perhaps you will when you get older. If you're honest with them, they'll respect you and trust your word."

Andrei sat back, disgusted. Anya just had a sad look on her face.

"You're trusting the wrong person here," she said.

Nick watched the large black SUV approach the entrance to Gennady's complex. Immediately he knew it contained Alexander, the epitome of the 'new Russian.' Nick looked up the street, but the SUV was alone. It slowed in front of the gate, turned right, and rolled up to the guard.

The guard stood up quickly. He reached into his coat and pulled out what Nick assumed to be a handgun. He approached the driver's side of the SUV, gun held at the ready but muzzle down. He leaned in and Nick lost sight of his head. After a moment he backed away from the SUV, made a motion for it to stay where it was, and put a cell phone up to his ear.

A few seconds later he apparently received the confirmation he was looking for. He pointed to the right and waved the car through. Once it had passed beyond the gate he put his gun away and settled back in his chair.

Nick shook his head. If they allowed Alexander in without a fight, they were in big trouble. He took out his cell phone and called Anya.

Gennady had just finished his conversation with the gate guard when one of the confiscated phones on the table buzzed. It was Anya's. She looked at him expectantly.

"No calls," he said as he shook his head. He leaned forward and looked at the screen

"Nick Wallace," he read. He looked at her with irritation. "He's the one who got us into the middle of this. You don't need to talk to him."

"He didn't get us into anything," Anya said, but Gennady cut her off.

"He's a liability," Gennady said. "We'll take care of him after we meet with Alexander." He took the phone, muted it, and jammed it in his pocket.

They waited in silence for Alexander. They sat in a small conference room in one Gennady's office buildings. It would only take Alexander a minute or two to park and come in. Gennady had already sent Ilia outside to watch for the man and guide him in.

Anya glanced over at Andrei. He sat back in his chair with a look of disdain on his face, but she could see he was perspiring heavily. Rivulets of sweat ran down the side of his face and into his collar, and his fingers tapped repeatedly on his knee.

She didn't blame him. Things were going to be bad for him now, without Dmitri around to deflect any of the blame. He'd likely lose his position in Gennady's organization, and maybe become a simple candy salesman. And that was the best case scenario.

Gennady stood up abruptly. He glared at his daughter and nephew. "You two stay here. I'll be back in a moment." He stalked into his office.

"I wonder if he's gonna piss, or suck down some vodka," Andrei said. He shook his head.

Anya ignored him and reached out for Andrei's phone, still on the table. She dialed a number and fidgeted while it rang. When a man's voice answered she said, "Viktor. No, it's Anya. We need your help at the warehouse. Alexander's on his way over." Pause. "Long story. I don't have time to get into it now. Get as many men and guns as you can and get over here." Another pause. "That's bullshit, Viktor, and you know it. Gennady needs you. Figure out a way—" she paused and listened to the protests over the phone. Finally she growled. "You worthless sack of shit. After what papa's done for you." She hung up and dialed another number. No answer. Same with a third number. She didn't look at Andrei. "Like rats running from a storm," she muttered.

"You can't really blame them," Andrei said. He sighed. "Nobody wants to go down with us."

Anya swore again as she tossed the phone back on the table. "They'd better pray I die here, because if I survive this I'm going to kick some chickenshit asses." She dropped in her seat and slumped back, arms crossed in front of her, eyes narrowed and lips pursed.

A moment later Gennady returned and silently took a seat at the head of the table. He glanced at Anya, opened his mouth, thought better of it when he saw her expression, and turned away. Anya's phone in his pocket vibrated. He ignored it.

They waited.

Nick put his phone away with a curse. Where the hell was Anya? Not that he really cared about her personal well-being at the moment, but with Anya and Andrei out of reach, his odds of getting Nonna were slim.

He assumed she was in the compound somewhere, since that was where they were headed the last time he talked to her. But he hadn't seen much movement there since he hit the rooftop, and now she wasn't answering her phone. He thought about calling Andrei but quickly dismissed it. The only thing he wanted to hear from that bastard was where Nonna was, and Andrei wasn't going to spill that over a phone.

His uneasiness didn't abate as he watched Alexander's car drive slowly along the road inside the compound and stop next to one of the four buildings. Brake lights flashed as the car stopped. A moment later four doors opened and four men got out. Even at the distance, Nick recognized Alexander as he stepped out from the back seat. He didn't recognize the other three.

The men congregated in front of the car and huddled together for a moment. A fifth person, the moody one from the candy store who Nick had taken an instant dislike to, walked out to meet them.

Ilia, Nick thought the guy's name was. If he was the welcoming committee, things wouldn't go well.

Without shaking hands, he led them into the building.

Gennady rose as the door opened. Ilia entered first, a carefully neutral look on his face. Behind him came Alexander and three others.

The tension in the room immediately soared. Anya felt rather than saw Andrei gulp. She didn't look at him, but kept her eyes on Alexander. She didn't trust the man, especially with the feeling of power she knew he felt.

Alexander's eyes quickly swept the room before ending at Gennady. He offered his hand.

"Gennady, my friend," he said, as the two men shook hands. "It's nice to see you." He paused for effect. "Although I would have preferred it be under more agreeable circumstances."

Gennady nodded. "I wish so, too, Alexander, and I want to thank you for coming out here on short notice."

"Of course," Alexander said smoothly. "And I trust Lena is well?"

Gennady smiled and nodded again. "Yes, she is, thank you. Although of course she has decided that the house must have new furnishings again."

Alexander's hearty laugh boomed through the room, causing Anya to flinch. "Isn't it always the case? Olga is the same. We personally keep half the furniture shops in Rostov open."

He abruptly became serious. "I think we must now discuss our present predicament."

"Yes, of course," Gennady said. He motioned for Alexander to take a seat in the middle of the table. Without a word, Alexander walked around Gennady. One of his men closely followed him and pulled out the chair Gennady had been sitting in. Alexander sat down and spread his hands out on the fine wood, as if feeling his new possession.

Gennady looked surprised for a moment, then quietly took his place in the chair he had motioned Alexander to sit in. Anya sighed.

"I'll get straight to the point," Alexander said. He glanced at Ilia. Gennady hesitated, then nodded to the bodyguard. Ilia hesitated much longer, to the point where Alexander turned towards him, then walked out of the room. He slowly closed the door behind him. One of Alexander's bodyguards moved over to stand in front of it.

Alexander's demeanor immediately turned grim, pleasantries about spousal spending habits long gone. He pointed a finger at Andrei. "This man tried to destroy me, to take away my power!" His finger curled back into his hand, which he smashed on the table. "Reparations must be made."

Gennady raised his hand. "But of course, Alexander. I have thought about this and—"

"I have thought about it as well, you little toad," Alexander broke in. "And here are my demands."

Gennady slowly lowered his hand. Anya and Andrei instinctively leaned forward.

"First of all, you will pay me twenty-five percent of your gross proceeds on a monthly basis," Alexander said.

Gennady's eyes widened. "Twenty-five percent of my gross? That'll put me out of business!"

Alexander shrugged as if the matter was of no consequence to him. "If you're clever, you should be able to make it up elsewhere. In addition, I want control of all of your brothels west of Penskaya prefect. You've obviously shown that you don't have the personnel to control them."

Gennady closed his eyes and sunk back in his chair, seething. Anya looked on in horror, seeing her father's life come crashing down.

"Finally," Alexander said, his voice booming in the small room. He looked straight at Andrei with naked hatred. "This man, this brute who would have my kingdom, forfeits his life."

Gennady's eyes flew open. "No!" he shouted. He started to stand up, but one of Alexander's thugs had positioned himself behind the old man. He put his hands on Gennady's shoulders and forced him back down in his seat, none too gently.

There were tears in Gennady's eyes now. "You can have my money, but please don't take my nephew. He made a mistake, I know, but…"

His voice trailed off as Alexander glared at him with disdain. "Don't you understand, my friend," he said, the last word now

248

mocking, "I cannot trust this one at all. As long as he's alive I'll always need to look over my shoulder, waiting for him to approach one of my men and turn them against me."

There was silence in the room.

"No, this point is not negotiable," Alexander said. "He must go."

Andrei made a noise deep in his throat and rose from his seat. "You fucking animal—"

His words ended in a shriek as Alexander's bodyguard made a quick move around the table. In one motion he pulled a truncheon from his coat and swung it at Andrei's head. It connected with Andrei's temple and the man went down hard.

Anya screamed and jumped out of her seat, chair flying back to crash into the wall. She moved towards her cousin as Gennady also stood. The bodyguard raised his truncheon again, preparing to smash it into her skull. Before he could finish his swing she changed course. She lashed out with her foot and connected solidly with his groin. He gasped loudly and fell to his knees, hands wrapped around his testicles, eyes squeezed shut in agony.

Anya knelt by Andrei, feeling for a pulse. She sighed with relief when she felt a strong one, and allowed herself to be pulled to her feet by the other two bodyguards. She knew putting up a fight would do more harm than good at this point.

Alexander was furious. He turned on Gennady fiercely. "This is how you propose to work with me?" he yelled, and hit the old man across the side of his head. Gennedy fell back in his chair, blood welling up on his cheek.

Alexander turned to Anya. "You are the only one with guts here," he told her. "I can't have that. You will come with me until I determine what to do with you." He licked his lips. "But first, we will have some fun." He motioned to his bodyguards. "Take her to my car. I'll be with you in a moment."

"What of Lev?" one of the men asked, pointing to the man on the ground. Alexander looked with disdain at Lev. His bodyguard was on all fours. A thin line of spittle ran from Lev's mouth to the mound of bile on the floor.

"Put him in Gorev's office, then take the girl out," Alexander said.

The men complied silently. They tried to boost Lev to his feet but he groaned pitifully and sagged against them. They pulled him by his arms into the office, came out, grabbed Anya, and hustled the struggling woman out of the room.

When they were gone Alexander pulled his gun. He looked at Gennady. "Plan B will no longer include Lev," he said. His voice was calm, his face composed. Gennady looked on in mute confusion as Alexander turned and carefully walked into the office. He closed the door.

Gennady heard Alexander's voice through the door. It was soft enough that he couldn't make out the words. He started to rise from his chair, curiosity getting the better of him.

Three quick shots from the office. Gennady sat down again.

Alexander opened the door quietly and gently closed it behind him. He turned to Gennady, who stared at the door in shock. "You'll need to clean your office," he said, almost apologetically.

Alexander pulled out his cell phone and hit a button. Almost immediately a voice came out of the phone. Alexander said one word in Russian and clicked off. The fear in Gennady's eyes intensified.

Chapter 39

The doors to Gennady's building opened and Nick saw Anya emerge from the shadows. She was flanked by two men and struggled furiously. Apparently things had not gone well with Alexander. He didn't see Andrei with them. Not good.

Nick quickly scooted back from the ledge, on his elbows and knees, gun cradled in the crook of his elbows, the strap of the duffel clenched tightly in one hand. The bag scraped noisily on the asphalt as it trailed behind him.

Once he had gone back several feet, Nick jumped to his feet and ran to the access door. He quickly checked the safety on his AN-94. It was off. He took the other assault gun out of the duffel, checked the magazine, and slung it over his shoulder. He jammed the other magazines in his pockets and left the duffel bag in the stairway.

He flew down the stairs, two at a time, not caring how much noise he made.

Anya screamed and kicked out at the man on her left. He had seen what she did to Lev and easily avoided her blows. Each man grasped her arms harder and moved her with difficulty towards the car.

Ivan Petrovich, the guard at the gate to Gennady's compound, was confused. This was nothing new to Ivan, who spent much of his life trying to catch up with what seemed to come naturally to others, but now he was scared, which was a new feeling for him.

He heard the shouts from behind him and turned to see Anya being forced into the car he had, no more than ten minutes ago, been told to let in without question. Even worse, neither Gennady nor Andrei were around to tell him what to do.

Ivan took several steps towards the car, intending to ask Anya what was going on. He had been instructed not to talk to any of the new men, and until Gennady told him different, he would leave them alone.

He didn't notice two black Volvo XC-90 SUVs pull up behind him. The front passenger side door opened in the lead car as it rolled slowly towards Ivan. A man leaned out. Left hand grasping the top of the door, he brought his right hand up and rested his forearm across the top of the door. The Glock in his hand shook slightly as the SUV bounced on the uneven pavement, but at the small distance between the Glock and the back of Ivan's head, the man didn't expect to miss.

He didn't. Ivan's head blew apart as the slug shattered his skull and flew out his eye socket, and the guard fell away from the path of the two XC-90s. The door closed quickly. Both cars took a hard left and sped towards the warehouse.

Nick burst out of the building and ran fast across a deserted Beregovaya Ulitsa, one AN-94 in his hands and the other clanking painfully into his back with each step. He swung the assault gun ahead of him, looking for the guard. He expected to be challenged at the entrance, but the man was nowhere to be found. Nick had a brief hope that perhaps the man had gone to Anya's aid.

That hope was shattered when he saw the broken body of the guard lying on the side of the road. There was a mass of blood and brains where he head had been. Nick didn't slow down. There was no need to check for a pulse.

The access road he was on made a dogleg left, around a small wooden building with a tin roof and dirty windows. From his vantage point on the roof across the street, Nick knew Alexander's car was parked on the other side of this first structure, in front of the office on the other side. He slowed and pressed himself up against the wall, out of sight of the car.

He stayed there for a moment, panting from the run, then got down on his stomach and crawled up to the edge of the building. He looked around the corner and saw Alexander's SUV. It looked empty at first, but then he saw a head move dimly behind tinted glass in the back seat. Another head moved next to it. Two people in the car. Anya and somebody else, definitely not a friendly.

Nick sat up, put the guns against the wall, and pulled out his knife. He didn't know how many men he was going up against, but he wanted to handle the first one quietly.

He heard gunfire on the other side of the complex, over by the warehouse. Automatic fire in bursts of two. Somebody with an AN-94, which likely meant Alexander's men. It was answered almost immediately by several single shots. Pistol fire. Nick assumed at least one of Gennady's guys. Two double burps replied.

Good. A distraction.

He checked the safeties on both guns one more time. He might be coming back in a hurry and didn't want to deal with anything on either gun that would hinder bullets coming out at a rapid rate.

Both were still off. Nick set them against the wall again, grabbed the knife, and looked around the corner again.

Still quiet.

Nick stood up, took a deep breath, and ran, crouching, towards the car.

Anya pressed herself up against the side of the vehicle, as far from her captor as possible. Only one man had stayed with her. The other tossed her in her seat, slammed the door hard against her side as the first man climbed in through the other rear door, and disappeared. Back to the office with Alexander and her father. The thought made her wince.

She took several deep breaths and forced herself to think. The guard next to her had a gun, but she was not concerned about him firing it in the confines of the SUV. The noise and concussion would hurt him as much as her. Well, she thought ruefully, maybe not quite as much. But she was more concerned about the butt end of the pistol. It could do some damage against her skull.

She looked across the seat at the man. The gun was in his right hand, nearest her. He had a good grip on it, but with surprise and an element of luck she might be able to get her hands on it. She knew one thing for sure: she was not going back to Alexander's house without a grab at that gun. Once behind his doors she was in big trouble, but she wouldn't go without a fight.

A motion out the back window caught her eye. A figure ran towards the car. Instinctively she knew it was a man, but not one of Alexander's. She kept her face composed and watched his progress out of the corner of her eye. It only took him a few seconds to travel the open ground to the car. A moment before he hit the car she screamed.

Her scream, ear-shattering in the car, had the desired effect of scaring the hell out of the guard. Immediately, and probably without thinking, he raised his right arm and started to swing it at her head. In that split-second she realized she was wrong: he wouldn't use the butt of the pistol to hit her, but the barrel.

Then the door flew open and an arm swung in. Attached to the arm was a blade. It looked long and lethal for the brief moment it was visible. It caught a ray of light from outside, then the reflection disappeared as the intruder slammed the knife into the chest of the guard. It made a sickening crunch as it pierced the breastbone. A second arm came in and grasped the handle of the knife, giving it more leverage and jamming it up to the hilt in gore.

The guard's hands flew up to grasp at the hands on the knife that now caused him excruciating pain. His mouth opened in a scream, a noise that was quickly muffled by Anya's hand. She pressed her hand down hard, shoving his head back into the seat.

The guard struggled for several seconds as his life ran out over the blade and down his shirt. Then he was still.

Anya removed her hand slowly, wary of a resurgence in the man that seemed to happen so often in the movies. But his eyes were still, unblinking, and his hands fell down to his sides, limp.

"Took you long enough," she told Nick.

Nick panted from the exertion. "Yeah, well, you're lucky I tracked you down. You need to answer your phone more," he said as he wiped the blade on the man's pants. He was getting fond of his ceramic knife.

"Papa took it."

Nick nodded. "Where are they?" He assumed Alexander, Gennady, and Andrei were all together.

Anya pointed out her window towards the building. "Back in there. Andrei's down but seemed OK. Alexander wants blood."

Nick snorted. "I plan to give him blood."

"There's more," she said quickly. "I saw another two more cars. Big. Must be reinforcements."

"Damn," Nick said. "Which way?"

"Past us."

"OK. I heard shots from the warehouse. Not these guys. So assume two carloads of bad guys. Probably eight men."

"At the warehouse?" Anya said. She chewed her lip. "I sent Mikhail over to the warehouse to warn the guys there."

"Good idea. That's who's putting up a fight then."

"But there are probably only a few men in the warehouse. And they're up against eight guys."

"They're gonna need help."

Anya nodded. "I need a gun," she said.

Nick stared at her, saw she was composed and likely wouldn't shoot the first thing she saw, which would probably be him, and nodded. "I have guns. Come out this side so they don't see you."

Alexander slapped Andrei on the cheek again. Andrei had come to and was sitting against a wall, groggy. Blood obscured his left temple where the truncheon had hit, and his skin was a sickly grey. His glazed eyes dimly tracked Alexander as he squatted in front of him. Ilia had come back in and now stood behind Alexander silently, but Andrei ignored him.

"Time to go, Andrei," Alexander said. He was still planning to kill the young bastard, but he wanted to get some information out of him first. It'd be easy enough to dispose of Andrei's body when the time came.

Andrei coughed, then winced. He didn't reply.

Alexander stood up, glanced at his last bodyguard, and motioned towards Andrei. "Pavel, take this piece of garbage out to my car. Put him next to the girl. They can have a last few moments together. Then come back here."

Pavel walked over to Andrei and tried to lift him, but Andrei was too far gone to be of much help. Pavel faced Andrei and put his hands under Andrei's armpits. He heaved but the body hardly budged. He moved around to the side and tried from a different angle, and got the same result.

He looked up at Alexander and shrugged, an embarrassed look on his face.

Alexander cursed again and turned to Ilia. "Are you going to be trouble for me?" he asked.

"No."

"Want a job?"

"Yes."

"Good. Help Pavel," he said. Andrei's former bodyguard, now ready to show his loyalty to the winning team, nodded and went to help Pavel.

With the issue of Andrei resolved, at least for the time being, Alexander turned on Gennady. Andrei's uncle appeared to be in worse shape than his nephew, and for a brief moment Alexander felt sorry for him. It will be tough on the old man to lose a daughter and a nephew in one day. On the other hand, they had brought it all on themselves. And Rostov would be better off without these idiots in charge of anything.

Alexander eased his body down into the chair next to Gennady, who barely acknowledged his presence. "I know you don't feel like it, friend, but it's time to come to an understanding of our future relationship."

"What future relationship?" Gennady mumbled. "You're killing my family."

"Not all of it, Gennady. You'll still be able to stay in business. You'll just work for me. I think eventually you'll enjoy it."

Gennady shook his head slightly. "I doubt it," he said, voice a little stronger. He looked over at his nemesis. "I doubt that very much."

"Safety here," Nick said, showing Anya the switch.

"Won't need it," she said.

Nick nodded and moved on. "OK, here's where you set single shot, double shot, or full automatic."

She nodded. "How many rounds in the magazine?"

"Forty-five. I have two extra mags."

"So probably not full auto."

"Right, at least not for now. I'm on double. And there's no recoil after the first shot so you'll do some damage. A double tap oughta do it."

She looked at the gun with admiration. "Nice."

Several shots rang out from the direction of the warehouse. Nick and Anya looked at each other, each one thinking the same thought.

"They have to wait," Nick said.

Anya nodded. "I know. I don't like it, though."

More shots. Mikhail and his men may have been outnumbered, but they weren't going down without a fight. Nick felt frustrated but he knew what they had to do.

He handed her the AN-94 but kept his hand on the barrel until she looked at him. "Now remember, we're not here to kill everybody. Let's get Gennady and Andrei."

She pulled at the gun until he let go. "Papa and Andrei are the priority, but Alexander's a bad man, Nick." She looked around the corner of the building, towards the car and, beyond that, where her relatives and enemy were together. "You should've seen him. He really enjoyed beating my men up. He's a monster." She said the last bit through clenched teeth.

"Fine, he's a monster," Nick replied. "He'll get his. We just have to be smart about it."

"Shut up," she replied.

"Hey," Nick said. "No need to—"

"No, *shut up*," she hissed. "Somebody's coming."

He fell silent. Sure enough, he heard footsteps on the gravel from the other side of the truck. Somebody coming to check on Anya, or the dead guy.

No good. He took a deep breath and flattened himself against the wall. Anya stood next to him and they waited.

The footsteps stopped. He heard a mumbled question, and a reply. He heard the car door open. A second later there was a curse and heavy steps on the gravel, coming closer, around the car. The other door swung open.

Nick and Anya looked at each other and nodded. She swung out and he crouched down, both pointing their guns at the car.

There was a man in the open doorway, checking on the guy Nick had killed. He was bent over at the waist, digging around in the back seat. It wouldn't take him long to realize his buddy wasn't coming back to life.

"Hold your fire," he whispered. "Let's see what he—"

His words were interrupted by a quick burp from her gun. Immediately the car's rear quarter panel, a foot to the man's right, smoked and a large hole appeared in the metal. The man jumped out of the car and turned towards Nick and Anya. His action was understandable but probably the dumbest thing he could have done. Both guns barked and he went down with four bullets in his body. Anya shot again and the body twitched on the ground.

Nick heard a curse from the other side of the car, but the second man was smarter and didn't show his head. Nick heard the crunch of gravel as he hustled back to wherever he had come from.

He swung on Anya. "You need to control yourself," he said through clenched teeth. "We can't just go barging around, shooting everybody we see."

"That's exactly what we should do!" she retorted, eyes blazing. They stared at each other for a long moment. The other man had disappeared, and they were safe for the time being. She took a deep breath and continued. "I saw a chance to kill one of the men threatening my family, and I took it."

"And now whoever is with the guy by the car knows we're here!" Nick yelled.

"So why are we standing here arguing?" Anya yelled back.

"Because you're being a bull in a china shop and you need to keep it together. Plus you lied to me and I'm still pissed off about that!" He swung the gun towards her, so she got the idea, but stopped short of pointing it at her. "I can't have you running around like a crazy woman. I'd rather shoot you in the leg and leave you here, out of the way, and I'll go get my daughter myself. I'm half-tempted to do that anyway!" He stood there, panting, red in the face, glaring at her. "The daughter I should be playing with at the orphanage right now, not tracking down at some goddamn warehouse because your fucking family wants to rule Rostov!"

She went still and stared in his eyes. She put her hand on the muzzle of the AN-94 and pulled it towards her. He resisted, hands clear of the trigger. She pressed the muzzle against her breast.

"You won't shoot me," Anya said softly. "You'd take a bullet for me. That's who you are."

Nick's anger drained away. She saw his face and let go of the muzzle. He swung the gun away from her.

"I'm so sorry, Nick," she said. She touched his arm. "I didn't realize what Andrei was planning, what he was capable of. I just wanted to help him out—"

"I know," Nick said. "It just got out of control."

"And when I got to know and like you, I tried to distance you from him, you know. I told you to stay away."

Nick forced a smile. "I wish I had listened to you then, Anya. You were right."

"Am I forgiven?"

He chewed his lip briefly, then sighed. "Of course. It's done, and we need each other. We need to get out of here and come up with a new plan," he said. "They're probably ready to come after us."

She squeezed his arm, then nodded and moved out. Nick followed, and they sprinted towards the other side of the building, away from the car, Nick expecting a bullet in the back the entire way.

Chapter 40

Alexander looked up as the door flew open and two figures stumbled in. Ilia still supported the groggy Andrei, but this time he did it alone.

"Where's Pavel?" Alexander asked.

"Dead," Ilia said. "So's Vadim."

Alexander swore and slammed his fist on the table. "What about the girl?"

"She's gone. Escaped." Ilia dumped Andrei unceremoniously into a chair next to Gennady. Andrei was starting to come around, but gripped the chair with both hands to keep from sliding off. Gennady looked at him without expression.

"She overpowered Vadim? I don't think so," Alexander replied. Vadim was one of his biggest bodyguards and wasn't the type to get taken down by a woman. Alexander thought for a moment, then slapped his hand on his forehead. He swore again. "She had help." With mounting dread, he pulled out his cell phone and dialed Vitali's number. He willed his assistant to answer the phone, but it rang. And rang. And rang. And finally went to voicemail.

Alexander closed his eyes and clicked off the phone. "That damn American is here," he said, voice strained.

Ilia looked surprised. "Wallace? I thought you'd kill him at the candy store."

"That was the plan, dammit. Vitali was supposed to take care of it. Something must've happened."

"So what do we do now?" Ilia asked.

"You find him and kill him. Kill them both."

Ilia looked concerned. "He's good. I'm not sure I should leave you. Especially with these two."

Alexander thrust a finger in his face. "It's your fault he's here! You and this idiot Andrei. So if you want to get on my good side, you take care of it, now."

Ilia nodded and reluctantly started towards the door.

"Wait," Alexander said.

Ilia stopped and turned around, eyebrows up.

"You're right, this guy seems to have a knack for not dying," Alexander said as he pulled out his cell phone. He hit a speed dial number and waited as it connected. "Constantin, what's your status?" A pause as the man on the other side responded. "Good. Can you spare two men to help round up the American?" Another pause, shorter this time. "Good. Ilia will meet you by my car."

He hung up and turned to Ilia. "I want the three of you to find this guy. Nothing fancy. Just shoot him and dump his body in the river. Try to take Anya alive if you can, but don't risk anything. Got it?"

"Yes, sir," Ilia said. He looked uncertain. "Nick and the girl will be by your car."

"I doubt it," Alexander said. "They probably got the hell away from there as soon as you left. But in case they didn't, keep your ass low to the ground."

"Yes, sir," Ilia said again, the uncertain look still on his face as he disappeared out the door.

After he left, Alexander turned to Andrei, who watched him nervously. "Now, in case they fail, you're going to tell me where this guy's kid is."

Rounding the corner of the building, Nick saw a line of rusted cars along a green chain-link fence that marked the northern boundary of the complex. They took cover behind one of the bigger ones, where they sat with their backs against a grimy trunk and breathed heavily.

"Two men down," Nick whispered. The shots had ended and an eerie silence pervaded the area. "That would leave nine or ten of Alexander's guys left, unless Mikhail took any out."

"Plus Ilia," Anya said softly. "I caught a glimpse of him after we shot the guy in the car."

"Where?"

"On the other side of the car. He was carrying somebody."

"He's working with Alexander's men?"

"Of course," Anya said. "That snake will jump into bed with whoever is winning."

"I'm surprised Alexander didn't just shoot him."

Anya smiled grimly. "Well, we've been taking out his men. He's probably running out of bodyguards."

Nick rolled to his side and peered out between two cars. He didn't see any movement, but his range was limited. "Speaking of that, it won't be long before they come looking for us."

"Yeah, and we're not in a good spot."

Nick looked back at the fence. It was at least eight feet high, with strands of barbed wire on the top. Beyond the fence was a wall of trees. No escape that way. They'd be trapped between the cars and the fence if anybody found them.

"Agreed," he said. "Let's take it to them instead."

"What're you thinking?"

"They won't be expecting us to go after them. They think they have us on the run. OK, maybe they do. Let's go on the offensive."

She looked doubtful. "By now he knows you're here, and he'll have everybody looking for you, with orders to shoot to kill."

"People have been ordered to kill me before. I'm still here. They're not."

She chewed on her lip, still looking doubtful.

"Anya, I'm out of time. My contact from the adoption agency is probably looking for me right now. She's not going to find me, and the adoption is off. I can deal with that. But Nonna's *not* going to be a victim of my mistakes. I'm getting her out of here."

"And then what?"

He looked at her.

"And then what?" Anya said again. "You can't take her home. She can't stay here. What will you do with her?"

Nick's eyes blazed as he got to his feet. "I don't know," he said, "But it's going to be better than she has now. Maybe the agency gives her to a new couple." He looked down at her. "She's out there somewhere. Are you coming, or am I doing this myself?"

She stood up. "Of course I'm coming with you. My papa and cousin are out there, too."

"We need to go after Alexander's men first."

"I thought you wanted to get Andrei away from Alexander?"

"I do, but what's the first thing Alexander's going to do when we attack?"

She nodded. "Call for help."

"Yep. And they'll already be on their way, because they'll have heard the shots. So we need to take out the cavalry first."

She almost smiled. "OK, so we go to the warehouse."

The warehouse was off to their left, near the river. They stayed behind the line of cars until they were close to the water, then ran across an open space to the corner of the huge building. Once pressed up against the metal wall, they heard a voice inside. One voice, shouting orders. It sounded as if it was just on the other side of the wall.

They backtracked and ran around the side of the structure. They found a cracked door facing the river and eased themselves in. The voice had ceased shouting but they could hear sounds of men moving in the front of the warehouse. It was quiet where they were, but they hid behind a pillar, pressed against each other, weapons pointing towards the catwalks crawling across the ceiling.

They were surrounded by tall shelves, probably ten or twelve feet high. Tall, but less than halfway up to the catwalks. Items perched on the shelves in haphazard fashion. Boxes here, open lights or pipes or flanges there, unidentified bulges under gray or blue tarps. It looked like Gorev handled a lot of industrial components coming down the river. But he didn't handle them very efficiently.

"What now?" Anya whispered.

Nick motioned towards the front of the warehouse. "Alexander's guys probably outnumber Gennady's by two-to-one, right?"

Anya nodded.

"And nobody's firing."

Another nod.

"So your papa's guys are probably down. But the winners are moving around like they're not done yet. So they're either looking for someone or something." He glanced around at the items on the shelves. "But they won't want any of this stuff. So, unless papa's hiding money in here, they're looking for somebody."

"Fair enough," Anya said. "Either they know somebody got away or they're mopping up."

"So let's make sure they find somebody."

263

Anya nodded. She slid around to the other side of the pillar and looked out. "We can stay hidden here until they walk into us," she said as she pointed to a cluttered area. Boxes, a tarp. Ideal for an ambush, Nick thought. Anya continued to circle the pillar until she faced Nick.

Her eyes slipped down to his chest. She froze.

"Don't. Move." Her face remained still as she whispered the words, her lips barely moving.

Nick instinctively glanced down, moving his eyes as much as he could without moving his head. "What? Spider?"

"Worse."

"Not to me. I hate spiders."

"No, this is worse. Left breast."

He tilted his head down as little as he had to, and moved his eyes to the left. He felt a chill go through his body.

In the middle of his left breast, five or six inches down from his collar bone, his shirt was lit up with a red dot.

He knew those dots well. He had used them many times when aiming on a sniper scope outfitted with a laser sight. Typically whoever wore one of his red dots had seconds to live.

"Shit," he mumbled.

"Don't move," Anya said again.

She was right, he knew. There was no chance he could duck out of the way fast enough. He'd be dead before he moved an inch.

He breathed in. He breathed out. He felt sweat roll down his side.

And then his phone rang.

Chapter 41

The phone buzzed in his pocket. He didn't move, except for an initial jump. It rang three times and stopped.

"What?" Anya whispered.

"My phone rang."

"You're busy."

"No shit," Nick said. If they were going to shoot, why didn't they do it? Unless they wanted to kill him by heart attack, which was a distinct possibility.

The phone buzzed again. It was in his right pants pocket. He slowly moved his hand down to the pocket. He didn't reach in. He didn't want whoever was on the other end of the scope to think he was reaching for anything lethal. He placed his palm over the phone and felt it buzz twice more before it stopped again.

The rod dot began to move. It slowly drifted down and to the right, before coming to rest on top of his hand.

The phone buzzed again.

"I think they want me to answer it," Nick said. He slipped his hand into his pocket and pulled the phone out slowly. It was on the third buzz before he hit the talk button.

He just as slowly lifted the phone to his ear. "Who is this?" he asked.

"Bang," said a voice.

Nick paused. He knew the voice.

"Pyotr?"

"Da. I thought you could use some help."

"Are you at the other end of this dot?"

"Da."

"You ain't helping."

Nick heard a quiet chuckle. "But I got your attention," Pyotr said.

Nick exhaled into the phone loudly. "You sure did," he said. He looked down at the light again and then up, towards the center of the warehouse.

"Further up, towards the ceiling," Pyotr said.

Nick looked at the catwalks. The light was low near the ceiling, but he could make out a vague shape about halfway across one of the structures. It moved slightly and when Nick looked down again the red dot was gone.

"Thank you," he told Pyotr. "And thank you for coming. I didn't think you would."

"I wasn't going to, and I'm not doing it for you, but I'll help you," Pyotr replied. His voice was a whisper in Nick's ear. Nick assumed he had a headset. "Tom called me as well, so I thought it must be important."

Nick smiled. Good old Tom.

Pyotr continued. "I won't shoot because they'll trace the bullet back to me, but I'll spot for you."

Nick nodded. He knew Pyotr would see movement through his scope. "Fair enough. What do you have?"

"Six men," the detective said. "I have eyes on three of them working their way towards you. The other three are off to my right."

"I thought there'd be eight."

"Possible, I haven't been here long. I think I saw them all."

"Any of them together?"

"No. They split up. Oh, and there are two bodies near the door."

Damn. "Noted," Nick said. He put the phone down but kept the connection open. He placed his gun on the floor gently, took out his knife, and extended the blade. Anya glanced from the blade to his face. He said, "Three guys coming our way. I want to take them out without noise."

"OK."

"Three more on the other side of the warehouse."

"OK."

"And two of your papa's men are down."

She pursed her lips and nodded.

Nick picked up the phone again. "OK, where are they?"

The first was on the other side of a bank of shelves, working his way to the end where Nick and Anya stood. Nick motioned Anya back behind a large stack of boxes, turned his phone off, and put it in his pocket. He crept along the side of the shelves until he came to the end, hidden from the target by the shelves. Unless the man was psychic he wouldn't know what hit him.

Nick glanced at the shelves he was pressed up against, trying to see through them to his target. The shelves were stacked with metal rods. No use trying to see through them.

He looked closer at the rods. They were two feet long and easily gripped in one hand. They looked to be iron. Nick figured they were plumbing supplies, and the Russians hadn't made it to PVC piping yet.

He grabbed one of the pipes, careful not to make any sounds, and hoisted it in his hands. He swung it around at his side, getting a feel for it.

He liked it. Alexander's men didn't deserve to die. Not yet. He put the knife away.

Nick held the pipe in his left hand, the hand nearest the edge of the shelving unit, and waited. He slowed his breath, calmed his nerves, and visualized what was to come.

The phone in his pocket buzzed. Instantly Nick swung out into the aisle, pipe headed right for the unsuspecting face of the enforcer. The man was looking off to the side, and his brain didn't have time to recognize the threat before Nick was on him.

The iron pipe hit the side of the guy's skull with a sickening thud. Nick finished his swing and clamped his other hand over the man's mouth as they both dropped to the floor.

Nick gently placed the guy's head on the concrete floor. His eyes were rolled up in his head, but he had a pulse. Faint and fluttery, but a pulse.

Nick stood up and pulled the phone from his pocket just as it vibrated again.

"Spasiva," he told Pyotr. "Good timing."

"There's another one, two rows over, towards me. Heading in the same direction."

"Got it," Nick said. He pocketed the phone again and crept quickly across the two aisles. He pressed up against the edge of the shelves again, pipe ready, and waited for the phone to buzz.

"Two down," he whispered to Anya a moment later as he returned to their hiding spot. She looked at him with something close to anger in her eyes.

"What?" he asked.

"You just knifed two people to death," she whispered.

"No," Nick said. He held up the pipe. "I didn't kill anybody. Not this time, anyway. They're going to have a hell of a headache when they wake up, but they'll survive."

Anya smiled. "I'm glad. They aren't the enemy."

"Well, they kind of are, Anya. But they don't deserve to die because they were unlucky enough to sign on with Alexander."

"Agreed. And they might be on our side tomorrow."

Nick looked at her sideways. "So you aren't really concerned about me killing two bad guys. You're more concerned about me killing two potential good guys."

She shrugged. "I'm a realist. I only like to kill bad guys."

Nick shook his head, then jumped slightly as the phone buzzed in his pocket. He popped it open quickly and put it to his ear. "Third man?" he said.

"No," Pyotr said in a rush. "Fourth. He just popped up and is moving towards you. Fast."

"Does he know we're here?"

"How the hell would I know?"

Nick put the phone down and said to Anya, "New guy, heading our way."

"Damn," Anya said. "One of Alexander's?"

"We have to assume so," Nick said as he eyed the pipe in his hand. "I hope I find out for sure before I brain him."

This guy was noisier than the others had been. And faster. Nick hit the edge of the shelving units just as a shape appeared around the corner. Nick swung the pipe but the other man had sharp reflexes. He raised his left arm and blocked the thrust. Nick felt a thud as the pipe connected with the man's forearm. The man cursed.

Nick pulled the pipe back and was ready to swing again when he caught a glimpse of his opponent's face. The scar was visible even in the low light.

Mikhail swung on Nick and raised his gun. He didn't fire, though, when he recognized the American. His eyes narrowed and the Glock was steady in his hand. It looked like a cannon pointed at Nick's forehead.

They stood that way for a long moment, Nick looking like a knight, with his pipe held in front of him. Mikhail calmly pointing his gun at his opponent. Nick knew he wasn't going to win that duel.

Anya ran up and stopped to the side of them. Neither man moved, neither man looked at her.

"Stop!" she whispered fiercely. "We're good. Put your toys down. Now!"

Nick was the first to blink. He sighed and lowered his pipe. Like it would do any good anyway. Mikhail nodded and brought the gun down to his side. They backed around the corner, out of sight of anybody down the aisle.

"What happened?" Anya asked Mikhail.

"When I got here," Mikhail replied, "there were three men. One coward ran away. We tried to ambush the attackers but there were too many. The other two were shot and I ran away."

"Retreated," Nick said.

Mikhail flashed a smile. "Retreated. I hid until they passed me, then I thought I could shoot them from behind." He glanced at Nick and nodded. "But you took care of them first."

"Only two," Nick said. "Which reminds me, I need to check in." He called Pyotr, hoping the man's cell was muted. Pyotr picked up on the first ring.

"One of yours, I assume," the detective said by way of greeting.

"Yes," Nick replied. "Where are the rest?"

"One working your way, two aisles over. The other three made it to the far side and are now coming back. I hope your reunion is over because it's going to get busy soon."

"OK, thanks. Hold on," Nick said. He pressed the phone against his chest and whispered to the other two, "One target two aisles that way." He pointed with his pipe. "Three more coming from the other side."

"Can you take the first one quietly?" Mikhail asked. "I can go behind the others and hit them from behind."

Nick nodded. "Good idea."

Anya said, "Can you take them down without killing them?"

Both men looked at her. "Perhaps," Mikhail said. "We can aim low."

Nick said, "Sure, if I can't hit them I can shoot them in their knees. That oughta keep them out of commission."

"Why?" Mikhail asked.

Anya chewed her lip. "Well, I doubt they're married to Alexander. If we spare them…"

"They might be papa's enforcers tomorrow," Nick finished.

"Yes," Anya said. "We need all the help we can get. Just so they're, as you say, 'out of commission' today."

Nick's phone buzzed. "Company," he said. He looked at Mikhail. "I got this one. We'll box the others." Without another word he ran across the aisle.

The third man went down much like the first two. Nick didn't feel good about the unfair fight, but he didn't feel good about getting shot, either, and at least the men would survive. He hoped Anya was right about the enforcers being essentially mercenaries, fighting for whoever would pay them. It made sense, he thought, as he stared down at the bruise forming over the third man's temple. Plus, he hoped they'd feel appreciative at being spared.

He pulled out the phone and was dialing Pyotr's number when a shot rang out. It was immediately answered by another. Nick swore and put the phone up to his ear. It rang three times and went to voicemail. Nick swore again and pocketed the phone.

More fire came from ahead of him and Nick heard shouts as he ran back to Anya. She was in the process of picking up her AN-94 when he rounded the corner, and jumped when she saw him. She recognized him a second later and glared.

"Sorry," he said as he grabbed for his gun. "I guess Mikhail missed."

"Mikhail doesn't miss," She said.

More shots.

"I hope the others do," Nick said.

They ran towards the fire.

They crept along a wall of shelves, keeping as low as they could, listening for either Mikhail or one of the enemy. Nick heard scrambling on the other side of the wall, and a whispered order. Putting his finger to his lips, he motioned for Anya to stay at one end of the bank of shelves while he snuck back to the other side, behind the targets.

270

He had almost made it to the far end when a figure popped out in front of him. The man was moving fast and apparently didn't realize Nick and Anya were there. He rounded the corner and bumped into Nick. Both men fell back and frantically struggled to bring their guns around.

Nick had just enough time to register the look of surprise on the other man's face when the guy's head blew apart, splattering blood and brains against the cardboard boxes next to him. A split-second later he heard the whine of the bullet as it passed by him. He instinctively dropped to his knees and whirled around.

Anya came up fast behind him. Nick glanced down at his unfired gun, then turned to look at Anya. She shook her head and pointed up to the catwalk.

"Thanks, Pyotr," Nick said quietly to himself as he glanced at the bloody mess on the floor. The body had flown several feet after the high-powered shot hit. In his shock, Nick hadn't registered any sounds but he assumed there had to have been a hell of a clatter as the body hit the opposite shelves.

"They'll know we're here now," Anya said.

"Yep," Nick replied. He shook his head to clear it. That was damn close and he was still foggy. "Sorry, but these guys won't be on your team tomorrow."

Anya nodded. They checked their guns and headed towards where Mikhail should be, moving slow, weapons swinging from side to side. Nick wanted to call Pyotr but didn't want to take his hands off the gun. He felt the shakes coming on but willed them back. The close call had unnerved him, but he knew he didn't have time to be distracted.

Then, banging at the front of the warehouse as somebody barged through the main door.

Whoever it was shouted in Russian. There was an answering shout close to Nick and Anya. Anya groaned. "Reinforcements. At least one."

There was another shout from the doorway, a different voice.

"At least two," Nick mumbled.

Anya craned her neck as she listened to the voices. She smiled. "They think Mikhail's alone. They're pointing out where he is." Then her smile faded. "Oops, no. Now they're asking about you. One of the new guys says you're probably in here."

Nick gritted his teeth. "Then it's showtime," he said. No more pussyfooting around. They had to hit the enemy before they could organize. He looked at Anya. "You ready?"

She nodded slowly. "Mikhail will join us when he hears the shots."

"Good."

He took a breath, calmed his nerves, checked his gun one last time, and turned to her. "Let's do it," he said.

The loading bay of the warehouse was a large, flat area. It was raised four feet off the ground so trucks could back up to it and receive goods without needing ramps. Two forklifts were parked parallel to each other on one side, and several dollies were stored haphazardly on the other. Two men stood near the forklifts, waiting for the two near the door to walk over to them. Nick didn't know whether it was hubris or inexperience, but they weren't expecting an assault.

Nick and Anya hit them with careful, measured bursts, two bullets at a time, jackets clattering around them noisily. The two men near the door went down immediately. The other two skittered behind the forklifts like cockroaches in the glare of sudden light. Nick ran after them, not wanting them to get set up. He peppered the forklifts with bullets until he heard a shout. One gun went flying over the side of the forklift and clattered noisily on the ground, not far from Nick's feet. Seconds later the other gun came flying out.

Anya, right behind Nick, yelled forcefully to the two men in Russian. Nick assumed it had to do with putting their hands up, because immediately four shaking hands appeared over the engines of the forklifts, followed by two stunned faces. Inexperience, Nick decided. They hadn't even attempted to return fire.

Nick motioned for the two survivors to step out from behind the machines. "Check the others," he told Anya, pointing with his gun to the two prone bodies by the closed truck entrance. She pointed the barrel of her gun at the ground and walked quickly over to them. The amount of blood on the ground gave him no reason to think they were still alive, but they had to be looked at. She knelt by one and checked a pulse. She didn't spend much time by the mangled body. She spent less time by the second. She looked up at Nick and shook her head.

Mikhail appeared. He had a smile on his face. "You have no fear," he said.

"I have fear, I just don't have time," Nick replied. "I need to get over to Alexander…"

His words trailed off as he glanced at Anya. She had stood up and was peering out the small access door near the open main loading dock door. He didn't like her showing her face to the street beyond. He opened his mouth to shout a warning, but before he could get the words out, the door exploded inwards and she disappeared in a cloud of smoke

Ilia watched in shock as his two men—he considered them "his" men now, even though he started the day attempting to bring down Alexander—bled out on the cement of the loading dock. He had been one street over, checking windows, heading south, looking for that damn American, when he heard the gunfire. He quickly reversed direction, ran to the edge of the building he was checking out, then cut across between buildings to meet up with the other two. He saw them inside the warehouse, in front of the half-open loading dock door, but before he could react they both stumbled and fell. A moment later he heard the shots.

He took cover across the street and surveyed the situation. His men weren't moving. A figure knelt by them, but he couldn't see much in the darkness of the warehouse so he didn't fire; it could have been Alexander's man. The figure moved away.

A moment later a small door opened slightly and he saw a head appear in the crack. He immediately recognized the bitch Anya, the one who was helping the American.

With a snarl he swung his assault rifle towards the warehouse and fired. He was on full automatic. He wasn't the kind to skimp on bullets.

The dust cleared to show an open doorway where Anya had just been. Nick ran to the doorway as his hand found the selection button on his AN-94. He flipped it to full as he neared the opening, and sprayed bullets across a wide arc across the street. Too late, he saw a figure running away from him, it was to the right of where he had shot, and no bullets hit near the man.

Nick roared as Ilia disappeared from sight. He was tempted to go after the bastard, but Anya was probably hurt, or worse, and he had to check on her. He swapped out a magazine as he ran to the entrance.

The wooden door was still hanging on its hinges, but had several chunks torn out of it from the bullets. Nick stepped over shreds of wood and was relieved to see that Anya had pulled herself up against the wall next to the door. She looked at him, eyes glazed over from shock. There was blood on her jeans, down low on her leg near her ankle. More cuts on her arms and her face. Blood trickled down her neck.

"What happened?" she asked thickly as Nick bent over and rolled her pant leg up. Her lower leg was a mess, but it appeared to be mainly surface wounds. He pulled a few smaller pieces of wood out of her skin, causing her to wince and increasing the amount of blood on her calf. Nick glanced around, but the warehouse was too dirty for any kind of makeshift bandage. He pulled his shirt off, then his t-shirt, and put his shirt back on again. He tore the t-shirt so it was longer and wrapped it around the wound.

"Ilia saw you," he finally said as he finished tying up the bandage. It wouldn't last long but would do until she got home and dressed it properly. He wiped the blood off on his pants and looked in her eyes. They were dilated, and she looked woozy. He suspected she had a concussion to go along with the banged-up leg.

"How do you feel?" he asked her.

Anya winced. "Like I got hit by a truck," she said as he dabbed at her face and neck.

"You're lucky Ilia was across the street," Nick said as he helped her sit up a bit more. All of the bullets had hit the door instead of Anya.

She tried to stand. Nick put a hand on her shoulder and held her down. She resisted for a moment but then gave up and sagged back against the wall. She put her hands up to her head and massaged her temples.

Nick's phone buzzed. He grabbed it and said, "Yeah."

"I'm coming down," Pyotr said. "Hostiles are neutralized."

"Thanks," Nick said and clicked off. Not all of them were neutralized, but they were safe for the moment.

274

"How is she?" Mikhail called from across the room. The large Russian glanced over at Nick and Anya but the muzzle of his gun never strayed from the two prisoners.

"She's hurt, but she'll survive," Nick called back. "You good?"

Mikhail nodded and gestured with the gun towards the two men by the forklifts. "Help me tie these guys up."

They found some rope and quickly trussed the two prisoners to the chairs on the forklifts. The men didn't put up a fight as Nick tightened the knots. Mikhail silently covered them with his gun. The entire process took less than two minutes, Nick seething the entire time, wanting to get after Ilia. He knew where Ilia was headed, and didn't want the man to have any time to organize before he hit him.

"I'm going with you," Mikhail said as Nick worked.

Nick looked up. "I'd prefer you stay here and protect Anya," he said.

"She'll be safe here. You're going to be in more danger."

"You want to protect me?"

Mikhail shrugged and gave a small smile. "Not so much you as Andrei. I think everybody wants him dead."

Nick nodded. "And for good reason."

"Maybe, but he doesn't need to die. He can still be valuable," Mikhail said as he looked over Nick's shoulder. Nick heard a noise and turned to see Pyotr walking towards them. Nick cinched the last knot and stood up to face the detective. He stuck out his hand, which Pyotr clasped in some surprise.

"Thank you for saving my life back there, Pyotr," Nick said. "I'm very sorry I ever doubted you."

He swore Pyotr blushed.

"You're welcome, Nick, and of course I understand why you must be careful." He glanced over at Anya and the ruined door. "Although I may not have saved your life, just postponed the end."

Nick nodded as he looked over at the girl. She was still, against the wall, watching them. "I guess that's all we can ever do, I suppose," he said.

"Will you stay with Anya?" Mikhail asked Pyotr.

The detective shook his head. "I must sanitize the area and leave before anybody sees me. I've been lucky so far."

Nick knew what Pyotr meant. The detective was planning to dig the bullet out of the skull of the man he shot and get the hell out of the warehouse before anybody arrived who could identify him. He didn't blame the guy.

Neither did Mikhail. He nodded. "Yeah, OK." He looked at Nick. "I'm still coming with you."

Once the prisoners were secured, Nick and Mikhail returned to Anya. Her face was pale and she was breathing heavily, but she didn't look to be in shock. Nick was impressed with her strength and resilience, but he knew she wasn't going anywhere.

He fished the last magazine out of his clothes and knelt by Anya. "We need to leave you here, but we're not going to leave you defenseless. We're going after the jackals, and don't plan to leave any to harass you. You should be safe here," Nick said. "I'll be back for you later."

"And if you're not?"

He looked her in the eye. He wanted her to feel as confident as he did. He didn't want her to sit in a dim warehouse, mind racing, wondering where the hell he was, feeling hurt, scared, and alone.

"I'm coming back," he said. "I've already taken care of most of the gang. Ilia and Alexander won't be anything. Then I come back for you, and then we go get Nonna. Piece of cake. So no worries."

He got up, brushed his hands off on his pants, and looked down at her. She looked small, leaning against the wall, bandaged leg seeping blood. He would've loved to use her, but he knew that wasn't going to happen. Not in her state.

"Oh, and one thing," he said.

"What?"

"Please don't shoot our heads off when we come back."

Anya smiled as she caressed the stock of the AN-94. "No promises," she said, voice soft, strained. "Just be ready to duck."

Chapter 42

Ilia burst into the office. He stopped when he saw Alexander against the far wall, huddled with Andrei. Alexander had his hand on his prisoner's arm and a gun to his head.

"What the hell are you doing?" he asked.

Alexander snarled as he stood up, dragging Andrei with him. "Protecting myself in case you failed. Which it appears you did."

Ilia nodded hesitantly. "Wallace killed the other two. Plus the men in the warehouse."

"Dammit," Alexander yelled. "Why can't you just kill this guy? He's taking down my entire network! Nobody is that good."

He stopped and glared at Ilia, a glint growing in his eye. Ilia knew immediately what he was thinking. "No way, boss. I'm not going in with the American over you. That'd be crazy."

"Maybe you're crazy," Alexander growled. "You already tried it once."

"We need to leave," Ilia said, anxious to change subjects. "He'll be coming here next. I'm pretty sure I killed Anya, and he's going to be mad as hell."

Andrei's head snapped up. Ignoring the gun jammed into his side, he leapt forward towards Ilia. Taken by surprise, Ilia barely had time to move before Andrei was on him. Andrei tackled the bigger man, slamming him painfully into the wooden floor. He began to pummel Ilia with his fists, rage in his eyes, spittle coming out of his mouth.

Alexander moved in quickly and flung his arm around Andrei's throat. He grunted and pulled the man off Ilia, being careful to keep his gun pressed up against Andrei's neck. Andrei's hands went to his throat as he tried to pry the strong arm from his neck. His legs kicked out as Alexander pulled him a few feet back.

Ilia jumped to his feet, blood running into his left eye from a gash on his forehead. Now the rage was transferred to his eyes. He took a step towards Andrei, getting ready for revenge.

"No!" Alexander yelled. "I need him alive."

"We should kill him," Ilia seethed. He wiped at his eye with his sleeve. "He's out of control."

"You can kill him soon, once the American is dead," Alexander said. Andrei thrashed harder when he heard the words, but Alexander's arm was cutting off oxygen and he was beginning to weaken. "If he's coming here—"

His words were cut off by a loud staccato of shots from just outside the building. There were loud pings of bullets hitting metal, and a small explosion, mostly concealed by the sound of the shots.

"The hell?" Alexander asked.

Ilia looked around wildly. He ran to the window and peered out of the corner. "He's here," he said, voice rising. "He took out your car." He ran over to the table, tipped it on its side, and took cover behind the new shelter.

Bullets shattered the large window facing the street, the crash of the glass competing with Alexander's scream.

Andrei whirled, right fist connecting solidly with Alexander's temple, cutting the scream off suddenly. It was not a disabling blow, Andrei was too weak for that, but it knocked Alexander off his feet, momentarily stunned. Andrei crashed through the matching window in the back of the room, putting his arms up to protect his head. By the time Alexander got to his feet, Andrei was gone.

Alexander swore. He was running out of options. "Get Gennady," he yelled to Ilia over the booming sound of more shells hitting, now inside the room.

"No time!" Ilia shouted back. "We need to get out! Come on," he said. He pointed to the back window. Cursing, Alexander jumped through the window, the glass now lying scattered in the dirt outside. Ilia followed close behind.

Nick looked at the shattered grill and flat front tires of Alexander's SUV with satisfaction. One escape avenue closed.

After spraying another volley of bullets into the room, Nick raced back to the passenger side of the car. He hacked at the rear view mirror with the butt of his gun until cracked and fell to the dirt. He picked it up, ran over to the wall and knelt by the window he had just fired through. He held the mirror up and angled it through the opening. It wasn't the best clarity, but he was pretty sure the room was empty.

Mikhail slammed against the wall next to Nick, ready to move in. He waited for Nick's signal.

Nick heard a pounding and muffled yelling from inside. He turned to Mikhail. "I think they're gone. They might have headed out the back." Mikhail nodded and moved out around the corner of the building to track them.

Nick dropped the mirror and crashed through the door, gun at the ready. Swung right, then left. The pounding and yelling continued, now slightly louder.

Nick spotted a door to the side of the room. He ran over to it and put his ear to the wood. At the same time the person on the other side pounded on it. Nick swore and jerked his head back. He shook it to try to get rid of the ringing.

He figured the door was locked but tried it anyway. No luck. He yelled "Step back!" Counted to three, and shot the lock to pieces. The door held so he kicked it in.

He had hoped Andrei was inside, but Gennady stepped into the light that seeped into the storage closet. He didn't waste time thanking Nick. Instead, he pointed to the broken window in the back. "They went out through the window," he said. "I heard the crash."

"How long ago?" Nick asked.

"Less than a minute."

Nick turned to chase after them, but Gennady grabbed his arm. "I heard Ilia say he killed my daughter. Is that true?"

Nick knew precious seconds would be lost, but he also knew how important the truth was to the father. "No, Gennady," he said. "Anya is fine. Hurt, but she'll live. She's in the warehouse."

Now Gennady did thank him. He leaned forward and embraced Nick, kissed him on both cheeks. His eyes were wet.

Nick untangled himself as quick as he could. "I have to get Andrei now," he said.

Gennady nodded quickly and said, "They probably went to the river."

Nick nodded and headed after them.

It was getting dark. Shadows stretched out from the buildings and made tracking the men dangerous. Nick went slow and tried to see out of the back of his head. There were many places

279

a man could hide and drop him as he walked past. His neck and spine prickled with anticipation. He wished Mikhail was with him but he hadn't seen the man since he ran out the door. Nick decided tracking his enemies was more important than finding his ally.

The warehouse fronted the river. He slowly walked along the north side of the warehouse, hugging the wall, until he saw the Don ahead of him. In the dim light the water looked almost black. Three small boats were moored to the wooden pier. They rocked gently in the current. None of them were big enough to carry a large amount of cargo. Perhaps they were used to motor out to ships anchored in the middle of the river and bring in smaller containers. Perhaps they were just used for recreation, although they were a bit beat-up for that. Perhaps they were about to be used as escape vehicles.

Nick crouched next to the wall and tried to peer into the boats. They were low against the pier; the water level must have been a few feet below the pier. They appeared empty, and as a hiding place they were lousy because there was no way to escape if seen. The men were likely elsewhere. He turned his attention to the buildings along the waterfront. The warehouse to his left. A long, narrow building to his right, at ninety degrees to the warehouse. A beached boat was jammed between the building and the river. There was a hole in the front, near the water. It reminded Nick of the capsized boat on Gilligan's Island. He wished The Professor was around to build something out of bamboo to help him out.

He stared hard at the boat. It was dark against the backdrop of the river. Nick concentrated on the center of the boat, the darkest portion, to acclimate his eyes. The edges faded out. Nick concentrated harder. That hulk was the perfect place to hide, to ambush.

He saw nothing, but he wasn't convinced. He ran to the back of the boat, away from the Don. Slowed as he got to the rotted wood. He held his gun up, ready to turn the corner to the back side of the boat. He took a deep breath and moved.

A large arm swung down in front of him. Attached to the end of the arm was a hammer, some kind of club hammer with a thick head that smashed into the barrel of his gun. The gun was rammed downwards, instantly breaking the strap painfully against

Nick's shoulder. Before he could react, the hammer swung back and slammed into Nick's chest.

Immense pain flooded Nick's senses and he knew at least a few ribs were broken. His legs flew out from under him and he landed in agony on his back. Strap broken, Nick's gun clattered to the ground several feet away, broken, its barrel bent.

Nick glanced up in time to see the hammer coming straight for his head. He frantically moved it to the side and felt the head of the hammer graze his ear before it slammed into the dirt. He reached up and grasped the handle, but stronger hands ripped it from his grip and tossed it in the bushes.

Ilia fell on him immediately, hands at his throat.

Nick grasped at the fingers but they were too strong and leveraged to move. Ilia was straddling him now, and Nick knew it would be only seconds before he blacked out.

His right arm left Ilia's wrist and jammed into his pocket. He found the ceramic knife immediately, and pulled it out. It was closed. He tried to find the release but couldn't. His mind was dimming and he began to see stars around the edges. He gave up on the release.

Nick grasped the knife in his fist and jammed the handle into the side of Ilia's head. Surprised, Ilia turned to look at the source. Nick jabbed again and the handle hit Ilia in the eye. It wasn't a hard hit but distracted Ilia enough that he took one hand off of Nick's throat to swat the knife away. He moved his other hand to the center of Nick's throat.

But one hand wouldn't be nearly enough to defend against a man fighting for his life. Nick immediately dropped the knife and grabbed Ilia's left hand. Instead of pulling the hand off his throat, Nick grabbed Ilia's pinky finger and wrenched it savagely. He felt it break.

Ilia roared, but didn't let up. His right hand went back to Nick's throat, but it was now blocked by Nick's hand.

Nick grabbed Ilia's fourth finger and broke it. This time Ilia was able to slide his hand under Nick's hand, and made the fatal mistake of leaning in to finish off the job.

Nick jerked his hands free and slammed them up into Ilia's face. His thumbs found Ilia's eyes and he fiercely jammed them into the sockets, popping both of Ilia's eyeballs out.

Ilia screamed this time, a scream of agony, terrifyingly shrill, and immediately let go of Nick's throat. Without hesitation, Nick kicked up with his legs, wrapped them around the front of Ilia's head, and flung him backwards. In no shape to resist, Ilia fell back off of Nick's body.

Nick was up immediately. He found his knife on the ground, flicked it open, found an open spot on Ilia's neck, and thrust the blade into it.

By that time Ilia was deep in agony, screaming, writhing, trying to jam his eyes back in his head. Nick doubted he even felt the final cut that ended his life.

Nick held on silently, pressing in, as Ilia gurgled and fell to his side. Ilia's hands, which had been clawing madly at his eyes, gradually lost their focus. They flapped uselessly a few times, then joined the rest of his body in stillness.

Nick stayed on Ilia for another several seconds, then with a grunt pulled out the knife and rolled off. Subconsciously he wiped the blade on his victim's shirt. He tried to fold the blade back in, but his hands weren't working just right. Nick mumbled "Screw it," and tossed the knife to the ground near his feet.

He sat down hard next to the body. His ribs were shrieking. He stretched out his upper body to ease the pressure and felt around. Yeah, at least two were broken. It hurt like hell, but he'd had worse.

"Bravo," a voice said. Nick looked up to see Alexander standing over him. At least he was pretty sure it was Alexander. For some reason the man was blurry. Nick's ribs shrieked again as he twisted to get a better view.

"You really are a talent," Alexander said. "You know, if you're willing to join my organization, I'm sure we could find a place for you here in Rostov. Your wife could return, and your son. We could find a comfortable place for the four of you to live."

It took a second for Nick's abused mind to comprehend what Alexander was saying. "The four of us? In Rostov?" he said thickly. Oxygen had returned to his brain but it still wasn't functioning property. Did this guy say four people?

"Yes, I said four people," Alexander said, and Nick realized he had spoken aloud in his fog. "Andrei told me where Nonna is." Alexander motioned to the side of him and Nick realized Andrei stood just feet away. He focused on Andrei's face. The man looked

282

terrified. Panic-stricken. The only thing keeping him in place was the Glock in Alexander's hand.

"Of course," Alexander continued. "This just means we don't need Andrei any longer." Before Nick or Andrei could react, Alexander turned to Andrei and calmly shot him in the stomach. Andrei grunted, folded over, hands going to the wound, and lurched backwards.

"No!" Nick yelled as Andrei took another step back. The back of his shins hit the small retaining wall on the pier, and he fell backwards into the water.

Nick was up before his mind processed what had just happened. Ignoring the pain in his chest as best he could, he stumbled over to the water and looked down. He could vaguely make out Andrei's body, on its side, already a few feet downriver. As he watched, Andrei rolled to a face-down position.

Nick jumped in. As he hit the water he dimly heard a shout from Alexander. He sank a few feet until his feet touched bottom, then thrust himself to the surface. The dirty water, which was likely warm but a good deal colder than the summer air, brought him to his senses. He broke the surface and took a big breath, causing more pain in his ribs.

Nick dog-paddled over to Andrei. He slid his right arm under the man, got his face out of the water, and pulled Andrei to him. Using his other arm, he slowly and painfully paddled back to shore. He landed thirty feet downstream, past the pier. Here it was just a concrete walkway along the river. Nick pulled Andrei as far as he could out of the water, but his strength was going. He had to perform CPR if there was any chance of saving Anya's cousin, but he knew it would be very difficult, if not impossible in his condition. Maybe if he just rested for a moment. Nick gently laid Andrei on his side, face clear of the water, and collapsed next to him.

He heard laughter and looked up to see Alexander standing over him once again. The Russian had followed them downriver, and now walked up to the two men on the concrete. He held Nick's knife in his hand.

"You're driven, Nick. I can see that, but I don't understand your motives," Alexander said. "I just told you Andrei said where Nonna was, and yet you dive into the water to save him. This vermin who has caused us both so much trouble. Why not just let him die?"

Nick grunted and rolled over on to his side. He slowly raised himself up on an elbow, then to his knees. The pain in his chest had lessened. Even a moment on his back seemed to help.

"I don't just let people die, Alexander," Nick said. It took him two breaths to get the words out. "Although I might make an exception in your case."

Alexander recoiled in mock pain. "You speak that way to me, the man who is going to reunite you with your daughter?"

"Where is she?" Nick asked.

"Will you work for me?"

"Hell, no. But give me my daughter and I won't kill you."

Alexander started to laugh again, then stopped. "You know, Wallace, coming from you, that's a deal I think I should make."

Next to him, Andrei suddenly coughed. He convulsed and threw up dirty river water. Nick looked over at him, but his attention was firmly on Alexander.

"Where is she?" Nick asked again.

"She's with Andrei's girlfriend, in their apartment. Nonna's been with her since Dmitri and Andrei took her."

Nick hung his head, feeling the roar build in his left ear. It quickly traversed to his right. It gave him strength. It didn't give him courage, but he didn't need that. Not any longer. He knew he had lost. But he wasn't going down alone.

He motioned to the knife in Alexander's hand. "That's great news," he said, feigning enthusiasm he didn't feel. "Can I have my knife, please?"

Alexander looked at the blood on Nick's knife in distaste. He glanced back at Nick and said, with a neutral expression on his face. "I don't think that's a very good idea." He raised his arm abruptly and threw the knife in the Don. It landed with a small splash behind Nick. Alexander's Glock was pointed at the concrete, but Nick could sense the pressure in the man's arm and knew he planned to use it.

Nick felt The Calm come over him, almost like a warm blanket. He smiled thinly, giving it a few more seconds to store up in his body. When the adrenaline had completely enveloped him, he held out his left hand. "Can you at least give me a hand up, anyway?" he said.

Alexander looked at him suspiciously for a second. He smiled. "I don't think so, Nick." He started to bring his Glock up. Nick could see the tendons in his arm tense.

Nick was still on his knees on the concrete. He jammed his right hand in his pocket as he put his left hand on the ground. The left hand gave him leverage to propel him forward.

The right hand gave him a weapon. An ancient, large, serrated, copper Russian hotel room key.

Nick's right hand flashed in a large arc, the edge of the key scraping across Alexander's neck. It immediately drew blood, but was not deep enough to be debilitating.

But it shocked Alexander. His left hand came up involuntarily to touch his neck as he gasped. He glanced down at the blood on his left hand, completely forgetting about his right.

Nick grabbed Alexander's Glock with his free hand, easily turned it around in Alexander's grip, and thrust it in the man's gut. He put his finger over Alexander's finger and pulled the trigger.

The shot was muffled by Alexander's flesh. The Russian's body shuddered with the force of the blast as Nick's right hand recoiled and plunged the key into the gash in his neck.

Alexander gasped again and sagged in Nick's arms. Nick lowered him to the concrete, both on their knees.

"Wrong answer, Alex," Nick said in the man's ear. "Nonna's not with Svetlana. Andrei lied to you. So we all lose."

He twisted the key. Alexander stiffened against him, then started to topple over. Nick jerked his hand out of the man's neck and let him fall to the wet concrete.

Andrei was on his left side, in a fetal position. His face was pale and glistening, hair plastered to his head from the river. His eyes were closed. Nick leaned in close to try to hear breath. He didn't have much hope.

He opened Andrei's shirt. It was heavy with blood and river water. The wound was not bleeding much, but it didn't give Nick comfort. Much of Andrei's blood was floating downstream in the Don, and based on his color there couldn't be much left. Water had seeped into the wound, cleaning it. Infection would set in, but it wouldn't be what killed him.

Andrei eyes fluttered open. He looked towards Nick. It took several seconds for his brain to process that somebody knelt in front of him. When he finally realized who it was, he licked his lips and struggled to find breath.

"I'm sorry," he whispered. "I'm s..." His voice trailed off.

"Andrei," Nick said urgently. He put his lips to the man's ear. "You have a chance to make it right. Tell me where Nonna is."

Andrei didn't move, and Nick was afraid the man had already died. He put his palm on Andrei's forehead and gently raised his head. Andrei coughed slightly.

"Please, Andrei," Nick pleaded. "I need to know. She's my daughter. Please!"

The urgency in Nick's voice brought Andrei around briefly. He struggled to form a word. Nick leaned in close, ear next to Andrei's mouth.

Faintly, the sound almost washed away by the swirl of the river a few feet away, Andrei formed one final word.

"Alenka."

Minutes later, Anya, Gennady, and Mikhail rushed up to the three men, Anya moving as fast as her injured leg would allow. She recognized Andrei on the concrete and wailed as she dropped to her knees, cradling his head to her chest. She cried over her cousin, her tears mingling with the river water on his face. Mikhail stood near her, far enough back to give them a little privacy. He looked resigned and not at all surprised to see the end of his friend. He reached up and rubbed his face in his hands silently.

Gennady looked furious. He glanced at Nick, nodded. He turned his attention to Alexander. He prodded the body with his toe, then looked back at Nick, eyes questioning. Nick held up the bloody key.

The beginnings of a smile on his face, Gennady pulled out his gun. Holding it a foot from Alexander's head, he sent a round into the man's temple. The body shuddered but the low-caliber gun didn't do a lot of damage. Circulation had already stopped in the body, and very little blood seeped from the wound.

Gennady sighed, took out a handkerchief, jammed it in the neck wound until it was soaked solid red, and squeezed it over Alexander's temple. Rivulets of blood ran down the Russian's face.

Gennady took out his cell phone and snapped three quick pictures of the ruined head of his competitor.

Then he turned away and began making phone calls.

Chapter 43

The same dark-haired receptionist was behind the desk at the brothel. She looked up as Nick entered. To his surprise, she smiled. She held up a finger and dialed a number. Whispered into the phone briefly, eyes on Nick. Hung up and pointed to a chair.

Nick was too keyed up to sit. He shook his head and moved to one side, out of the way. The brothel was quiet. The murmur of a male voice flowed softly out of a small black radio on her desk, mixing with the ticking of a grandfather clock against a wall. Dim evening sun filtered through blinds on the western-facing windows, but the light didn't illuminate any women in the room. The couches were empty. The brothel seemed closed.

Nick wrung his hands subconsciously as he waited, more nervous now than he had ever been at Gennady's complex. He didn't have to wait long. He heard a door open upstairs, then feet creaking across the second floor hallway. They started down the stairway.

Alenka came into view. Nick's breath stopped in his throat when he saw who she was carrying.

It had only been a few days since he'd last seen Nonna, but his baby seemed much bigger. Gone were the multiple layers of wool designed to keep her warm on a hot day. Instead, she wore dark blue overalls covering a lighter blue shirt, an outfit they had brought from America. Little pink booties peeked out from under the overalls.

Alenka smiled broadly, and Nick saw tears in her eyes that matched the ones in his. "I prayed you come back to Nonna," she said. She handed Nonna to Nick, who took her gently and gave his baby a huge hug. He felt a sharp pain in his ribs, but ignored it. He held on until Alenka put a hand on his shoulder.

"Thank you," was all he could say.

"You're welcome," Alenka replied. "She is good baby. You will love her."

"I already do," Nick said.

"I hope she takes bottle from you," Alenka said. She smiled. "Here, no. Only bottles from women."

Nick laughed. His body tingled with happiness. "I'm sure I'll figure something out."

"I was afraid you wouldn't come," she said.

"I didn't know where she was," Nick said. He shook his head. That was the understatement of the year. "As soon as I found out, I came right over." He didn't mention that Anya refused to drive them to the brothel until he changed out of his blood-soaked clothes, he was so anxious to see his little girl.

He shifted Nonna so she was nestled in his right arm, little legs dangling. She turned her head and looked at him impassively. He took it as a good sign that she had not broken down into tears yet.

"You have powerful friends," a voice said from behind him.

Nick turned to see Nadia, his contact from the adoption agency. He was so wrapped up in Nonna that he hadn't heard her walk in. He had called her only an hour ago, asking her to meet him at the brothel. He was relieved to see her arrive on time. She was short and heavyset, with thick black hair piled high on her head. As usual, she wore gaudy earrings and a flowery print dress. But she smiled, which made her look perfect to Nick.

"What do you mean?" he asked.

"Since we didn't know where you were," Nadia said, "We were going to cancel the adoption. However," she added quickly, seeing a quick spasm of panic cross Nick's face. "We received a call just before yours, requesting that we continue with the proceedings. It came from the judge who oversaw your case, so of course we were happy to oblige."

Nick smiled. Gennady had come through, as he promised he would. "Thank you," he said to Nadia. He was sure part of their happiness was due to the fact that they wouldn't need to return any money to the American adoption agency they had worked with. Plus, several embarrassing questions would now never be asked.

Everybody was a winner.

"Perhaps on the way to the airport," Nadia said, "You would be kind enough to tell me where you've been. Several people were quite concerned."

Nick shook his head. "I'm afraid you'd just be bored, Nadia. It wasn't very exciting."

The door chimed and the three of them turned to see Anya come in. She limped, and her face and arms were starting to scab, but otherwise she seemed in pretty good shape. Her eyes were swollen, and Nick immediately knew she had had a good cry in her Kalina after dropping him off.

She brightened up considerably when she saw Nick holding Nonna. She walked over and put a hand on Nonna's arm. "I'm very happy to see you with your daddy," she said in a cooing voice. "He went through a lot to get you." Nonna looked at her, squirming just a little in Nick's arm.

"A lot of boring things," Nick said for Nadia's benefit. Anya looked embarrassed but Nadia simply laughed. Nick knew she wouldn't cause any issues. She wanted the adoption to succeed as much as he did.

"We must go to the passport office to get Nonna's passport," Nadia said. "It's late and they are holding it open for you."

"OK," Nick said. "Do you have enough to show our, um, gratitude?"

Nadia shrugged. "I think not. They are staying there very late tonight."

"No problem," Nick replied. "I have more gratitude." At this point, he didn't care about the money. It was time to go home.

"I'll get the car," Nadia said. "Meet me outside in five minutes."

After she left, Nick turned to Alenka. "I can't thank you enough for taking care of Nonna. If you don't mind me asking, how did she end up with you?"

"One of Dmitri's men brought her here," Alenka said. "Gave her to Ludmilla. I know who Nonna must be, though, because they talk about a bad American, an American who hurts many of them. I felt happy when I heard that. Very happy." She made a face. "Ludmilla no kind of mother. I, how you say, convinced her to let me take Nonna."

"That was very kind of you," Nick said. "I wish there was some way to say thank you."

"No, no," Alenka waved her hand. "I do it for Galina. You were a good man to her. I'm happy to help you."

Nonna giggled at the hand wave, a soft and excited sound. Alenka did it again and was rewarded with another giggle.

"Wow, that's great!" Nick said. "I don't think I've heard her laugh before."

"She just started," Alenka said. "Many girls playing with her. She loved it."

Nick smiled. "I'm sorry I have to take her away from you all."

Alenka waved again, eliciting another giggle from Nonna. "Of course that's OK," she said, then abruptly turned serious. "I do worry about us now, though. We don't have somebody to watch out for us."

"Yes, you do," Anya said. "Now that Alexander and so many of his men are gone, my father will take over his activities. In fact, he has spent the last hour talking to the people who report up to Alexander, and they are all pledging their support for him."

"That's good," Alenka said, although she looked doubtful. "I hope he will find somebody good who can help us. Maybe better, maybe not. But even a little better is better."

"He already has found somebody, actually," Anya said. She started to blush. "I talked to him on the way over here. I told him I'd be interested in taking on more responsibility in his organization—"

"Good timing," Nick broke in, "Bringing that up after you saved his ass."

She smiled. "That's what I thought. I'd like to work with you here, Alenka. I hope I can make things nicer for the girls."

Now Alenka did smile, faintly. "That would be good, Anya. Spasiva."

Nick hoisted Nonna higher on his shoulder. The little squirt was getting heavy. "I think you'd be great here, Anya. But I thought you said you didn't want to get into papa's business?"

She made a face. "That was before I saw how bad my men can screw things up."

There was a loud honk from outside.

Nick groaned. "Guess that's my ride." He gave Alenka a hug and whispered "thank you" in her ear. Alenka wiped tears from her eyes and waved goodbye to Nick and Nonna as they left the brothel.

Nadia was in a car at the curb, looking impatient. But Nick turned to Anya. "I'll be leaving tomorrow, assuming everything goes OK with the passport."

Anya smiled as tears brimmed in her eyes. "It'd better go OK. If not, you send them to me. I'll take care of it."

She quickly reached up and snaked her hand behind Nick's neck. Getting up on her toes, she pulled his head towards her and kissed him deeply, firmly. Nick felt himself responding to the kiss, even though he knew it was a goodbye kiss. Perhaps because it was a goodbye kiss.

After several seconds she pulled back and looked at him with shining eyes. "That was nice," she said. "We would've made an awesome couple."

Nick smiled. "You're feeling pretty good about yourself, aren't you?"

She nodded. "I'm hurting, but I'm kind of feeling the power. I like it."

"Just don't let it go to your head, young lady," Nick said.

"No way. I've seen what that can do. It cost me my cousin."

Nick sobered, thinking about Andrei. "Anya," he said. "I'm so sorry about Andrei. He was a good man, just a little...misguided."

"He was a fool," Anya countered. A single tear coursed down her cheek. "But he was my cousin. I only hope some good comes out of this."

"It already has," Nick said. "Maxsim is gone. Sergei is gone. And Dmitri, and Alexander. Lots of bad people are dead."

"Thanks to you," Anya said. "I just wish I hadn't tried to deceive you."

"Anya, it's OK," Nick said. "It's over. Time to move on. I'm going to. I plan to consider this our version of labor."

She smiled at that. Nick looked at her closely. "You know, though, sometimes I wondered if you were helping me...or maybe helping yourself."

He wasn't sure how she'd take the comment, but she just shrugged. "What can I say, I'm a...how do you say it, an opportunist." She bit her lip. "You know I care for you, and I'm so happy that you and Nonna are together." She reached over and tussled Nonna's hair. "But I can't deny that I saw an opening. Things were going to change. I wanted them to change in my favor."

"You're a smart woman," Nick said. He paused. "I think Pyotr thinks so, too."

She laughed. "You're trying to ask me something."

"Well...yeah. When you were talking to Pyotr in your apartment, were you planning a...partnership?"

"Hmmm," she said, "At first I was just trying to stop him from arresting you. But I guess you could say I brought it up somewhere in there. And he seemed interested."

"So when he went to the warehouse, it wasn't just to save my ass."

Anya smiled. "That was part of it, of course, but I think Mikhail and I were on his list of asses to save, too."

Nick nodded. And they were probably higher up the list than he. The three of them would make a good team. The last he saw of Mikhail, the man was off with Gennady to personally talk to several key players. They certainly weren't wasting any time. Nick had shaken hands with the two men quickly, then they were gone.

It was all good.

Maybe not all good. Anya wiped away tears. "Thank you for trying to help Andrei. I know you risked yourself to save him. My father and I appreciate that. He didn't deserve to die in the Don."

Nick nodded. "He didn't deserve to die in the Don."

They stood, silent, alone together. He felt elated and miserable at the same time. He didn't want to leave Anya, but he knew he had to. His life would continue thousands of miles away, and hers would continue here.

She put a hand on his arm, stood on her toes, and gave him a kiss on his cheek. "You aren't nearly as tough and ruthless as you pretend to be."

Nick smiled. "Not any more, I'm not."

"But you must be smart, Nick. You'll die trying to save somebody if you aren't careful."

Nick shook his head. "I'm done with the People Saving business. Now my rescues are going to be on the playground or in the back yard."

She smiled. "Good." Her hand was still on his arm. She removed it reluctantly, tears brimming in her eyes again. She gave an embarrassed laugh. "And you have my email, so I want updates!"

Nick smiled. "Of course. You're Nonna's special Russian aunt, so you'll get lots of updates. Maybe she'll even want to come see you some day. You'll probably be running the town by then."

Anya nodded in mock seriousness. "Yeah, I probably will. So she'll eat the finest steaks and stay in the nicest hotels."

Nadia honked again and gave Nick a "hurry up" gesture when he glanced at her. He turned back to Anya. "You take care of yourself," he said. "You do have power now. I know you'll use it wisely."

"Sheesh, you sound like papa," she said, and they hugged again, squishing Nonna happily between them.

Nick hopped in the car and placed the seat belt around Nonna, who cuddled in his lap. Nadia glared at him in the rearview mirror and said, "I think the price of your gratitude just went up."

Nick turned his head as much as he could and watched Anya grow smaller as they drove away. She kept waving until they turned a corner and was lost from sight.

He settled back into his seat, arm around his daughter, feeling good. He knew Anya would take good care of Alenka and the others, and he, Kelli, Danny, and Nonna were about to start their new life together. The roaring in his ears was gone. Life was good.

"Whatever it is, it's worth it," he told Nadia.

Chapter 44

Room 402 of the Rostov hotel hadn't changed, but it had never looked so good, either. Nick placed Nonna gently on the old, threadbare couch. He thought about how Scott had spent one of his last nights on that couch. Tears started to well in Nick's eyes. He quickly brushed him away.

He made his way around the hotel room, picking up several items he had left behind when he last rushed out. He checked and double-checked the drawers and under the bed. Whatever stayed behind was staying behind forever. He had no plans to return to Rostov any time soon.

Nonna watched him as he moved around, a stoic expression on her face.

He piled everything by the door, and triple-checked Nonna's passport. It was Russian, with a little photo of her in the corner. Nick's large hand covered her chest where he had held her for the photograph. Her black hair was matted on top of her head and she didn't look happy. It had been hot in the passport office.

He scooped her up. "Come on, honey, I have somebody I want you to meet."

He knocked on Tom and Michelle's door and was relieved to hear movement in the wood. A chain was pulled back and the door opened to reveal Michelle's puzzled face.

When she saw who it was she immediately started crying. She turned and yelled, "Tom!" Nick heard a banging from somewhere inside, and a second later Tom appeared behind his wife. His face broke into a huge grin when he saw Nonna.

Michelle put her arm around Nick's side, the side that held Nonna, and squeezed hard. Nick gasped and said, "Not too much!" She immediately pulled back, just a bit.

"She's beautiful!" Michelle said, looking at Nonna with red eyes. "Can I hold her?"

Nick handed her over. "Of course," he said. Michelle took the baby and turned her back on the men, cooing at Nonna.

Nick and Tom stared at each for long seconds. Nick reached out his hand, but Tom knocked his hand away and embraced him.

"Thank you for everything," Nick said once Tom had pulled back.

"I didn't do all that much."

"Pyotr said you called him for me. Sounds like you may have tipped him over the edge. I don't think he was planning to come to the warehouse." Nick suddenly stopped and squinted. "You heard about the warehouse?"

Tom nodded. "Pyotr called me after he left. He's a good guy."

"Yeah, he is. Andrei told me that Pyotr and Dmitri were in bed together. Glad that wasn't true."

"Why would he say that?"

Nick shrugged. "To mess with my head, keep me from talking to him. And it worked for a while, too."

Tom shook his head.

"I'm guessing Pyotr and Anya will team up. I think that's what Anya had been planning. At least she was smarter about him."

Tom nodded. "She sounds like a smart one. He could do worse."

"What did he tell you?"

"Not a lot of details, but he knew you were safe because Alexander's men at the police station suddenly started talking nice about Gennedy. So he figured you must've gotten the bastard."

Nick nodded. "Someday I'll have to tell you about it."

"Later," Tom said. "Let's get home first."

"How are things with you and Alexei?"

"Good," Tom said. "We pick him up in two days. So far so good."

"He like you yet?"

Tom laughed. "No way. They hate guys, don't they?"

"Yep. I guess they know what trouble we can get them in."

Michelle wandered back with Nonna in her arms. Nonna looked completely comfortable, like she was going to fall asleep. Nick felt a bit jealous.

"Darn right you're trouble," she said. She kissed Nick on the cheek. "I'm so glad you're safe."

"Thanks," Nick said. He hesitated. "How's Katie?"

"Back in America now," Michelle said. She sighed. "It's gonna be tough for her. Her sister flew over to pick up her and Scott's body."

Nick nodded. Poor Katie, losing both her husband and her baby. It doesn't get much worse than that.

Tom's sigh matched his wife's. "Did the police follow up with you?" he asked.

"They're basically saying Scott and Katie were caught up in a mob war," Nick said. "They're sweeping it under the rug and leaving me out of it."

"Nice of them," Tom said.

Nick nodded. "Less work, too," he said.

They were silent for a moment, until Michelle perked up. "Hey, use my phone to call Kelli."

"That's too expensive," Nick protested.

"Nonsense," Michelle said, and Tom nodded. "Consider it a baby present."

She handed the phone to Nick. He dialed and stood, nervous, as the connection was made.

It was a good connection. Kelli's voice came through loud and clear.

"Hi, honey," Nick said. Tom and Michelle heard Kelli's excited voice through the tinny phone speaker. "Yeah, I'm great, no problem. Piece of cake. Hey, listen to this!"

He pushed the speakerphone button and held the phone up to Nonna. She looked at it calmly, not moving.

He gave it a few seconds and then spoke into the phone. "Did you hear that?"

"Hear what?"

"That was your daughter, staring at the phone!"

Kelli's laugh echoed out of the phone's speakers and around the room.

Nick handed his room key to the fourth floor key lady. Not surprisingly, it was Olga. She still had her typical stern look, but she also avoided Nick's eyes as he passed the key over.

The key was spotless. Nick had personally washed Alexander's blood off of it in the Don River. He spent so much time scrubbing at it that Anya finally told him it was good enough.

"It's never good enough for the key ladies," Nick had replied as he dried the key on his shirt. "Those women scare me."

The old lady put the key in the cubby marked 402 and started to write out a receipt. Nick stopped her. "Nyet, spasiva," he said. She stopped writing, gazed at him for a long moment, and slowly put the receipt back on her stack.

Nick started to walk away with Nonna. Nadia was waiting downstairs, ready to take him to the airport. He turned back to the key lady. "Oh, and thanks for the key. It was very helpful."

He could feel her glare on his back as he walked away.

Chapter 45

Nick saw Kelli standing in the gate area, a huge smile on her beautiful face. Next to her, looking taller than he remembered, was Danny. Kelli turned and said something to her son. Danny's eyes lit up and he started jumping and flapping his arms, looking for Nick.

Kelli's parents and sisters were there, next to Nick's sister and brother-in-law. They all began to wave as Nick neared the end of the jetway. He lifted his daughter's arm and waved back. Her new family cheered, and tears fell unashamed from Nick's eyes.

The woman next to him turned and said with a smile, "The reception is for your daughter?"

"Yes," he answered, and hugged his little girl tight.

"What a good little traveler she's been! What's her name?"

"Maria," he said. Maria rested her head on his shoulder and made a happy sound.

The End

Made in the USA
Lexington, KY
18 March 2015